CONTENT WARNING!

The Secrets & Scars Series is a dark MF contemporary MC age gap romance that contains subjects that may be triggering to some readers, including but <u>not limited to</u>:

- Emotionally dark and traumatic.

- Abuse from parents,

- Graphic violence,

- Drugging,

- Non-consensual acts including rape outside the relationship,

- Demeaning acts,

- Suicidal thoughts & self-harm,

- Kidnapping,

- PTSD Trauma,

- Trauma from Religious Extremism,

- Exposure to cultish situations,

- Emotional & physical blackmail,

- Explicitly detailed sex scenes,

- Killing, brutality and gore,

- Backstory includes stillbirth,

- Pregnancy trauma,

- Death of a child.

- Grief

- Sexual assault of a side character with an object

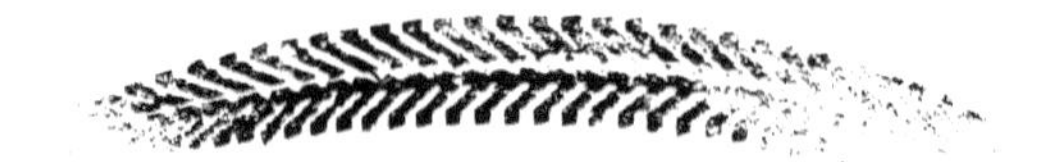

Beautifully SAVAGE

Secrets & Scars Series

— Book Four —

SARAH JD

Standard Paperback ISBN: 978-1-7642251-8-2

Cover design: DAZED Designs

Many thanks to my alpha, beta & proof readers: Jen, Gini, Heather, Melissa, Cheria, Anoesjka, Stevie, Tiffany, and Tamarra.

1

ABBEY

My palms are slick with sweat as I grip the steering wheel so tightly that my knuckles turn white. I barely see the paddocks and trees zip by as I drive erratically on the country roads towards Ringo's place.

I haven't driven in months, so getting used to the van with the gear shift up on the steering column took a bit. But I figured it out as I tore away from the airfield, ignoring Brody who dove into the passenger seat just as I slammed my foot down on the accelerator.

"We're approaching your property now," he mutters to Ringo over the phone, clutching the grab bar like he's holding on for his life.

Perhaps he is. I haven't exactly obeyed any road rules, driving this thing like it's a four-wheel drive tearing through the bush. Add in my rusty driving skills, and yeah, I can see why Brody is sweating right now.

I don't care, though. The van is replaceable. My sanity, though? It's hanging by a thread.

Daniel's words keep echoing through my mind, and I dissect them again and again, hoping to find even the slightest hint that I misheard him. But every time I go over it, I come up with the same truth.

"Your baby didn't die, Abbey. She's still alive."

Pain lashes my already broken heart every time I replay those words. Because what if he's right? What if he's telling the truth and Bobbi has been alive this whole time?

She'd be what? Seven weeks old now.

That thought alone nearly breaks me.

Seven weeks without me.

Is she even okay? Safe? Warm? Loved?

Has anyone held her the way I would?

And if she really is still alive, who has her?

The weight of not knowing crushes my chest, stealing my breath.

I *need* answers. I *need* to breathe.

Veering off the main road, the tyres screech as I speed up the gravel driveway towards Ringo's house.

I don't slow. I don't even blink as I fly past the gates, hitting a pothole hard enough to send us airborne for a beat, nearly launching us off the road.

In my irrational state, stealing one of the vans and going rogue makes perfect sense. I just need to know for sure if Bobbi is alive or dead before I get my hopes up. And the only way to do that right now is by coming back here, to where I thought I'd buried my little girl.

"Fuck! Abbey!" Brody hisses in a sharp breath as his side of the van nearly clips a protruding branch, before he snaps into his phone. "Dude, I'm *not* telling her how to fucking drive! I like my balls exactly where they are! She's your wife. You tell her!"

Under different circumstances, I'd laugh. Brody sounds comical, and I can just imagine Ringo barking orders at him through the phone.

But none of that matters. Not now, when Bobbi might be alive.

Black-clad Marx men scatter out of the way as I skid the van to a stop outside the barn, barely throwing it into park before I'm out the door and sprinting towards the orchard.

"Abbey?!" Alana yells from somewhere near the house, but I don't look back. I just run.

The moment the jacaranda tree comes into view, a sob lurches from my throat as tears blur my vision. Bile rises up as I keep pushing my legs to move faster, my eyes locking onto the two small gravestones beneath the tree.

One is a little more weathered. The other surrounded by colourful painted rocks, care of my little sister, Tahli.

"Bobbi!" I choke out, her name slicing through my heart as the strength I'd worked so hard to build over the last few weeks begins to crumble.

The moment I near her grave, I skid across the damp grass on my knees before diving my fingers into the soil.

I claw at the earth, determined to dig up the casket no matter how long it takes me, I blink past the tears as my gut churns with a combination of hope and fear.

If Daniel is lying, I won't kill him.

No.

I'll keep him alive and make him wish for death every day for the rest of my life.

"Abbey! What's going on?" Tahli's sweet voice reaches my ears as heavy steps rush my way, but I don't stop, my eyes trained on the weed-ridden soil and the small hole I've already clawed out.

"She's at Bobbi's grave," Brody pants, falling to his knees beside me, obviously still relaying details to Ringo over the phone. "She's digging it up... with her bare hands."

"Shovels!" Millie shouts from somewhere. "Get some damn shovels!"

I keep digging, covering myself in dirt.

Heavy feet run off as more knees fall to the ground around Bobbi's grave. Hands, some delicate and others strong, join me, clawing at the dirt without hesitation.

I barely spare anyone a glance, already knowing the delicate hands are Millie's and Alana's. I just sob and dig, knowing this could take hours, but not caring.

I'll do this all night if I have to. I need to dig up my little girl's casket. That's all there is to it.

"Abs... your fingers are bleeding."

Brody's voice is low next to me, his hand coming to rest on my shoulder, but I shake him off, not stopping, not caring if all the flesh peels away leaving only bone.

I won't stop until I have that casket out of the ground.

Sighing, Brody starts clawing at the ground next to me again before heavy feet pound our way.

"Shovels!" the deep voices bark, and as people shift away for the Marx guys to start digging, I remain in place, excavating the earth with my hands.

"Is she injured?" Millie asks from somewhere behind me. "Why is she covered in blood?"

Shit. I forgot about that.

What must I look like to Tahli? To Doreen?

A monster, most likely.

"It's not her blood." Brody answers for me, not going into any more detail than that, which I'm glad for. I don't really want Ringo's mum and my little sister hearing about how I pretty much shot Donny Allen's head off his shoulders and stabbed his uncle Ian in the ankle. Or how some of the fleshy chunks in my hair were once part of a Rebel's brain before Jols blew a hole in his head for attacking me.

"Why is she digging up Bobbi's grave?" Alana asks quietly, and another sob lurches from me as I answer this time.

"Daniel said she's still alive!"

My voice doesn't even sound like mine anymore. It's hoarse, unhinged and screechy, matching my mindset right now.

I feel like I'm all over the place, yet at the same time, extremely focused.

I need to know. To see for myself. To experience the truth of Daniel's words firsthand.

In the background as I claw at the earth, I hear faint voices talking, and cars skidding somewhere close by.

A few moments later, a barrage of heavy booted feet is getting closer, and then strong hands cling to my waist and start tugging me backwards.

"No!" I scream and thrash, but the strong arms wrap around me as warm breath fans my ear.

"Stop, Angel. You're hurting yourself."

Ringo.

I sob, collapsing in his arms even as I reach for the grave.

"I need to know!" I scream again, and he squeezes me tighter as JD comes into view, slamming his hands into the dirt to take over where I left off.

"Let me dig for you, Angel." Ringo's voice wraps around me like a warm hug. "Your fingernails are bleeding. If Daniel was telling the truth, you're gonna need those hands to hold your daughter. Please let me finish this for you."

He's right. *If* she's alive, I'll need my hands to hold her. To feed her. To care for her. I need my hands to be healthy and strong.

I nod through my tears, unable to speak, and Ringo's beard brushes my cheek as his lips press a kiss there, grounding me.

Then he gently passes me to Jols, who wraps me up in a tight, steadying hug as we watch our men, and the Marx guys, dig up my daughter's grave.

Some minutes later, the distinct sound of metal hitting wood echoes through the air, and my heart just about leaps from my chest as Jols tightens her hold on me.

"We got it," one of the Marx guys calls out.

"Dig around it so we can get it out," Ringo barks, and none of them stop. They just keep digging.

Each second stretches while I sit frozen in the damp grass, waiting to see if my world is about to shatter, or be made whole again.

I want to run in and help, tear at the earth with them, but I don't.

I do as Ringo suggested and leave them to it, knowing they are doing it faster than I ever could.

More Marx men move in, their boots pounding against the earth, and I can barely see what's happening through the wall of bodies.

Eventually, two men jump down into the grave, digging up more, dirt flying out of the hole as they work together for me.

It's not long after that when the shovels are tossed aside, and they start lifting out the tiny casket.

Everyone moves back, giving me space as my eyes fall to the grotty white box that is supposed to hold the remains of my baby girl.

Sobbing, I crawl over to it as Ringo is handed a crowbar and starts prying it open.

I hold my breath, my heart racing so fast I fear it might explode in my chest.

The crack of wood splintering pierces the air, and Ringo stills, his eyes locking with mine like he's silently asking me if I'm sure about this.

So, I just nod.

Then, he cracks the lid, lifting it open, his eyes falling to the contents as I hold my breath.

For a long moment, it's like the earth stops breathing.

There's not a single sound.

Not a single breath.

Not a single *anything*. Just muted stillness.

Shrugging Jols off me, I crawl closer, my whole body trembling as I close my eyes, working up the courage to see what's inside.

If I open my eyes and my baby *isn't* in there, then what?

What was all of this pain and suffering for?

How do I find my baby?

How do I get over being ripped away from her and made to think she's been dead all this time?

But, what if I open my eyes, and she *is* there? A tiny body decomposing, her resting place disturbed because I've been lied to.

It'd be like losing her all over again.

I don't know if I can do this.

"Angel," Ringo rasps, his voice laced with heartache and love, and knowing he's here with me, ready to catch me once again, is how I know I can do this.

I have to know, because not knowing will destroy me.

So, I slowly blink open my eyes and look down into my daughter's casket.

2

ABBEY

I t takes me a moment to figure out what I'm looking at. For my eyes and brain to work together and make sense of what's resting in the white satin interior.

And then, a barrage of emotions rip through me.

Confusion. Betrayal. Agony. Relief.

My eyes flick up, locking with Ringo's as tears streak down his cheeks, even as his lips quirk up a little.

"Angel."

I shake my head, another sob lurching from me as I force my gaze back to the casket.

There inside is a small hessian sack of sand. And nothing else.

"Where the fuck is my baby?!" I scream, my hands fisting into my hair as terror and grief slam into me.

Grief that nearly killed me.

Grief that consumed me.

Grief that fundamentally changed who I am.

Gasps echo around me as I lurch to my feet, rage twisting my face as I spin on the spot.

"Where is *he*?!" I scream, and Ringo rushes to my side, knowing exactly *who* I'm talking about.

"He's up in one of the vans."

Spinning, I storm towards the orchard, figures shifting out of my way, their faces not registering as my tunnel vision locks in.

Daniel Stone better give me answers, or I swear to fucking God, I will make him bleed in ways he never imagined.

Hurrying up the hill, I hear Ringo at my side, and others at my back as I go in search of answers.

"We interrogated him on the drive here," Ringo updates me as we storm forward. "But he said he'd only talk to you."

I barely acknowledge Ringo's words as we reach the top of the hill to find a few vans parked in front of the barn.

"Which one?" I snap, and Ringo's pointed finger comes into view, gesturing to the van flanked by four Marx security guards.

I head that way, and Ringo orders them to open the door as we near, and as it slides open, my eyes fall on a badly beaten Daniel Stone.

My ex-boyfriend.

And my cousin.

Vender steps up to the van without hesitation, fisting Daniel's hair and yanking him out as he screeches in pain, getting shoved to his knees in the gravel.

Without missing a beat, Vender presses a gun to the side of his head. "Give her the truth, and I *won't* kill you *today*."

"O-ok-kay," Daniel stutters, blood bubbling at the corner of his mouth, his puffy bruised eyes landing on me.

"Where is she?" I snap, swiping at the tears still streaming down my face, as Ringo steps closer.

"Let's move this into the barn," he suggests quietly. "There are innocent eyes that don't need to witness this."

Glancing over my shoulder, my heart splinters as I find Tahli crying, being led away by Alana, whose arm is around her as she tries to get my sister to look away from me.

She doesn't. Tahli may have innocent eyes, but she's worried about me right now.

Ringo is right. This needs to be taken into the barn.

So, I nod at Vender, and he yanks Daniel to his feet, dragging him into the barn while we follow.

I try to get control of myself, working at steadying my breath, but no matter how hard I try, I can't make my hands stop shaking.

Vender shoves Daniel down onto his knees in the middle of the barn, the sound of tables getting dragged out of the way loud as I start pacing.

My rage is building like a pressure cooker as I glare at the guy who destroyed my life.

Everyone shifts back, forming a loose ring around him, their dark gazes pinning Daniel in place as he squirms under their scrutiny.

Daniel dares to meet my eyes, and I bare my teeth like a savage as I fight for control.

I want to kill him. But it's not enough. That would be mercy, something he doesn't deserve.

He deserves pain, drip-fed over time, until he begs for an ending I'll never give.

But first, I need answers.

"Where's my baby?" I snap, pacing like a predator as Daniel's eyes track me.

"B-before I t-tell you," he stammers. "I w-want a-assurances..."

Is he fucking serious?

I see red!

I snatch up the cold bottle of beer on the nearby table, and lurch forward, smashing it across the side of his head.

He screams, tumbling sideways as glass and beer spray through the air, his eyes rolling to the back of his head as he whimpers.

"Where the fuck is she?!" I scream, grabbing a fistful of his hair and yanking his head back.

The jagged glass still clutched in my hand presses tight to his throat, and a drop of blood beads beneath it.

"I-I don't know e-exactly where s-she i-is. B-but I know s-she is s-safe," Daniel stutters, his Adam's apple bobbing against the glass pressed to his skin.

"If you don't know where she is, then why should I keep you alive?"

He blinks up at me, tears spilling from his eyes as his lip trembles. Our faces are mere inches apart, and I fight the urge to lurch forward and bite his nose right off his face.

"I h-have other information y-you need t-to know. A-about our f-families. About the c-church."

"The cult," I snap, and he nods frantically.

I glare into his eyes for a long beat, debating if I should let him talk, and while it's not directly about Bobbi, I know this *is* information I need.

Still, Bobbi takes top priority right now. Always.

"How do you know Bobbi is safe?"

He hesitates, a frown pinching his brow. "B-Bobbi?"

I roll my eyes.

"Her name is Bobbi. Stop fucking stalling, or the next thing you know you'll be drowning in your own blood."

"W-what's h-happened to y-you?" he stutters in disbelief, and my eyes go wide as I stare at the shitbag that started it all.

"*You* happened to me, Daniel." I dig the glass deeper into his skin, watching blood trickle down his neck. "What's wrong? You don't like what *you* created?"

His bottom lip quivers, and I see it now.

His fear.

He's scared of me. Not the men surrounding him. Not Ringo, or JD, or Vender. Not Riggs and the Marx security.

Me.

He knows what they will do to him. But me? That's a different level of crazy he doesn't know how to handle.

"I-I'm sorry," he whispers, and I scoff, shoving him back and pointing the blood-coated glass towards him.

"You're only sorry you got caught, you sick fuck!" I snap. "Tell me how you know Bobbi is safe, or I swear to God, I'll end you right now."

"Okay! Okay!" he sobs, his hands flying up in surrender.

"Y-your baby is w-with my m-mum."

My brows shoot up. "Your mum?" I ask and he nods. "How?"

"I don't know. My m-mum bailed the morning we were meant to be m-married at that c-chapel. After I told h-her everything I'd learned..." He shakes his head like he's trying to shake the memory of it away. "T-the next day, s-she sent me a picture of her holding your baby. Her m-message said, *That cult church will never get their hands on this baby.*"

I stumble back a few steps, Ringo's big gentle hands gripping each of my shoulders from behind before he runs his hand down to mine and subtly eases the bottleneck from my grip.

Elizabeth Stone has my baby?

I don't know how to feel about what Daniel just said.

On the one hand, it sounds like she's protecting Bobbi, which I suppose is a good thing.

But on the other hand, she fucking kidnapped my child!

"Tell me everything you know. Leave one detail out and I'll make sure you suffer for it," I snap, and Daniel nods quickly.

"The day Donny's uncle and his men brought you to the chapel grounds, my old man told me it was time I knew everything." Daniel swallows hard, his eyes flicking to Ringo like he's watching for the moment my husband will strike in my honour.

"I didn't know what he meant, but I knew something wasn't right. At first, I thought you were just being hunted so they could shut you up... you know... from telling the world about what me and the guys did to you."

A deep growl rumbles from behind me as Ringo's fingers dig into my hips. I can feel the tension radiating off him. How hard he's working to hold himself back.

God, I love him for how much he loves me.

I also love how Daniel's gaze drops to the floor, like he's too scared to see the rage emanating from my husband.

Maybe he *is* just as scared of Ringo as he is of me.

"Then I realised the church… I mean cult…" he corrects, "was in on it too. Banes was offering a shit-ton of money for your capture. Like serious cash. So, when Dad started spilling everything, it began to make sense as to why Banes was trying so hard."

Daniel coughs then, the sound a little too wet to be considered normal, like he suffered some real damage on the drive here.

Catching his breath, he swipes at the blood that bubbles at the corner of his mouth again, and continues, peering up at me.

"When I first started seeing you, it was because my dad told me you were considered a prime vessel in the church. As a mother and a wife."

My jaw tightens at his words, and my stomach twists.

Don't kill him yet, Abbey. You need to know everything.

"Securing you as mine would not only get my family to the top ranks in the church but would secure us some decent money." Daniel shrugs like that's totally a normal reason to start dating someone. "I didn't really care at first, and kind of liked you. You were a nice girl. A good friend. Pretty. I figured it wouldn't be so bad doing what my dad asked of me… even the part where he insisted I have sex with you."

I nearly retch, my mind going back to when he first showed an interest in me. How he seemed so nice. So normal. And so into me.

What a fool I'd been.

"I mean, what guy doesn't want to have sex, right?" Daniel keeps talking, his gaze dropping again, like it's easier to get it all out if he doesn't have to see my face. "I figured it was a win-win, even if my dad was going on about how claiming your virginity would secure our place in the church." Daniel's face contorts with pain then. It's not physical pain but the kind of pain that comes from the weight of traumatic memories.

"When my dad filled in the blanks after Allen kidnapped you, I realised not only had I been lied to and used, but that I had made things worse for everyone. Especially you."

"Get to the point, Daniel," I snap, not wanting to hear an ounce of his so-called sorrow about his actions.

"Apparently, the real reason my dad told me to claim your virginity was to keep you as ours, because Banes wanted you for himself. Something about your purity as a vessel and bloodlines or some shit like that." He shrugs again, like this is all so normal when it's anything but. "My dad thought if I fucked you first, you wouldn't be pure enough for Banes anymore, and my family would still benefit. We'd rise in the ranks, and Banes would back off. That was the plan."

His voice breaks as a sob escapes him, and he slaps a shaky hand over his mouth as he struggles to hold himself together.

Once upon a time, I would have felt sorry for him. Now I just want to find the bottleneck Ringo took from me before and put it to good use.

Luckily for him, he starts talking again.

"When your mum sprung us... you know... having sex, and all the craziness that followed, I felt trapped and wasn't strong enough to go against my old man or the church." He shrugs again, his bloodshot eyes locking with mine. "So I took it out on you. Treating you like shit. Hurting you." He gulps. "Raping you."

Ringo growls again, shifting to push me aside, his eyes trained on Daniel, ready to pounce, but I spin and put myself between them, pressing my hand to Ringo's chest.

"Cam. Not yet. I need to know *everything*."

Nostrils flaring, Ringo grits his teeth, finally dragging his murderous glare from Daniel to me, his gaze instantly softening.

"He needs to die."

"And he will." I nod slowly. "When I'm through with him, *I will kill him*. Don't forget he's mine to kill."

Ringo's jaw ticks, but he nods regardless, his hand coming up to cup my cheek.

"I'm sorry, Angel. I..." He trails off, not able to finish, and I step into him, weaving my arms around his waist.

"I know," I whisper, understanding this is hard for him to hear too.

We hold each other for a moment, and then I step back, linking my fingers with his as I turn to face Daniel.

"So you hurt me because you were angry? Been there, done that, Daniel. Now tell me something I don't know."

Daniel gulps and gives a shaky nod.

"At the chapel... before my old man told me the truth, I honestly thought I was being forced to marry you because I knocked you up. Fuck, I was so dumb," Daniel huffs, raking a hand down his face.

This side of him I haven't seen since we first started dating. The guy who actually has feelings. That seems to give a shit about someone other than himself.

What a pity I know who he really is.

"Then Dad told me everything. Told me what the church really worships. Their twisted beliefs. Why they are obsessed with bloodlines… that you were actually my… cousin."

Daniel shakes his head hard, like he's trying to fling that sick fact from his skull.

"I felt so sick. Still do." His eyes flick up to mine. "It's been eating me alive, Abbey. I've hated myself ever since." A sob lurches past his lips. "I swear to you, I really didn't know. I would never have gone along with any of it if I had known you were my cousin."

My stomach churns, and I can tell Daniel truly means what he's saying, but the damage is done. Apologies won't put me back together again.

Some things are irreparable.

"Is that why you were weird with me those days leading up to what was meant to be our wedding in that chapel?" My glare turns savage as I curl my lips in a sneer. "Is that why you wouldn't *rape* me, even though Donny and his uncle did?"

Daniel nods quickly. "I spent two days trying to figure a way out. My dad warned me not to tell Mum. Said she wouldn't understand. But I couldn't keep it from her." Anger twists his face as he stares at nothing in particular, his hands balling into fists at his sides. "She had no idea what was happening right under her nose. Who her husband really was. So I told her the morning of the ceremony, and she begged me to leave with her. To run away and never look back." Daniel shakes his head, his shoulders slumping as he speaks. "I stayed because…" He gulps, tears springing to his eyes. "Because… what if the baby *was* actually mine?"

My brows shoot up as my stomach rolls.

I hate this! I want to scream. I want to claw the guilt off his face and throw it back at him!

How dare he sound remorseful after everything he's put me through!

Ugh! But deep down, the old me lingers, crying at me to forgive this piece of shit.

What a pity she's too far gone to resurface.

What Daniel did to me… what all of those sick fucks did to me didn't just change me. They rewired me. Hardened me. And now, forgiveness is the last thing any of them will get.

"I couldn't leave you, Abbey. Not if the baby was mine." He shrugs. "So I stayed and my mum ran." He gulps, taking a moment as he struggles with emotions I don't care for. "I figured if the baby *was* mine, I'd have more power to protect it."

Daniel breaks then, tears bursting from his eyes as he shakes his head, pain-filled whimpers falling past his lips.

"I d-didn't want to h-hurt you." He cries, his voice pleading. "I chased you from that chapel thinking I could get you somewhere safe. Somewhere we could hide and figure out how to deal with Banes, my old man and your fucking psychotic mum."

He swipes at his tears, but they keep falling as his face morphs into horror.

"I d-don't know w-what came over m-me. Out in t-that forest… it was a split second of p-panic… y-you were right there within arm's r-reach and I thought…" He gulps, his whole body trembling. "I thought w-what if… what if y-you and the b-baby died?"

His anger falls away then, his face softening, almost child-like as he obviously remembers that day out in the forest when he and Craig were chasing me.

"At least then you'd be free. You wouldn't have to be wrapped up in this crazy bullshit. Your baby wouldn't have to be dragged into it…" His eyes meet mine, and even though I already know what's coming, it's not any easier to hear. "So I pushed you."

I have no control over the swing of my fist or the way it crashes into his cheek with a crack, or the way a lick of delight flashes through me at the way his head snaps to the side. But I do find the control to stop myself from doing it again, knowing I still need him alive.

For now.

He may not know where his mum is hiding with my daughter, but when we do find them, I'll need Daniel as leverage. A bargaining chip, or bait, or whatever I need to get my little girl back.

"How did your mum get my baby?" I snap, curling my lip as I fight to keep in control, and I start pacing again to keep myself busy.

Daniel shifts uncomfortably, his eyes darting to Ringo and the other men positioned around him before coming back to me.

"She's got a close friend who works in the maternity ward at the hospital. Somehow, she convinced her friend to help, and they dragged the doctor into it too. That's all I know. I swear. You can check my phone if you don't believe me."

He hasn't even finished talking when Vender rushes forward, patting down his pockets and locating his phone before holding it up to Daniel's face to unlock it.

Passing it to me, Vender gives me a nod, and I offer him a thankful smile as I take the phone and open the message app.

I spot the message thread between him and his mum and open it, scrolling up through the minimal messages, my breath catching as I stop on a photo sent seven weeks ago.

There she is, Elizabeth smiling, and in her arms is a little baby.

My baby.

Everything comes rushing back.

Flashes of details I must have suppressed.

When I first held Bobbi in the forest, she was covered in mucus and blood, and my vision was blurry from my unrelenting tears. I never let myself compare that version of Bobbi with the little baby in the morgue... but now... *oh my God!*

The baby in the morgue had a flatter nose, while the one in the picture looks more like the little button nose I first saw while Bobbi lay on my chest.

The baby in the morgue had a pointier head, too. Almost cone shaped, and the one in the picture looks more *in* shape, just as I'm now remembering little Bobbi.

There's no doubt in my mind that the baby Elizabeth is holding is my daughter.

But who did the baby in the morgue belong to?

Oh, God... is that why they insisted I not hold her? Did they know that holding her would feel wrong because that baby wasn't actually mine?

"Call your mum." I shove the phone towards Daniel, my hand trembling with the need to hold my daughter and let myself feel that this is real.

"I c-can't." He shakes his head. "She turned her phone off so she can't be tracked. She only switches it on once a week to call and check in. The next call isn't due for three more days."

Gritting my teeth, I fight the urge to slam my fist into his face just for admitting that.

How dare his mum be so hard to contact!

Glancing at his phone, I tap on Elizabeth's number, hitting call.

It goes straight to voicemail saying, *'the number you are calling is currently switched off.'*

Shit!

My shoulders sag as I hold out the phone to no one in particular, and Ringo's fingers close around it, taking it off my hands.

"Do you know the name of the nurse your mum reached out to for help?" Ringo asks, and Daniel shakes his head.

"I've told you everything I know."

"Do Banes or Allen know your mum has the baby?" Ringo asks, and Daniel shakes his head again.

"No. I promised Mum I wouldn't tell anyone. Everyone else thinks the baby died."

Sighing, Ringo looks at Vender. "Lock him up. Make sure he's comfortable."

Vender smirks. "Oh, I'll make sure he's real fucking comfortable."

Feeling depleted, I can't even muster a grin at how Vender will make sure Daniel is the complete opposite of comfortable.

"Abs." Ringo steps into my line of sight as Vender drags Daniel away. "We need to get you cleaned up."

I shake my head as my throat tightens, feeling like it might close up. "I have to find Bobbi."

"I know, Angel," Ringo sighs, "but unfortunately, it's not going to be today. We need to regroup." Ringo reaches up, cupping my face, and I can't help but lean into his touch.

God, he feels like home.

"Daniel's mum has her, and by the sound of it, she's safe. For now, let's take a couple of days to get our heads right, and I'll have our team investigate. Bobbi will need you alert and strong when we go to get her."

Staring up into Ringo's concerned gaze, I nod, even though my next words are a contradiction.

"We rest tonight. But tomorrow, we go back to that fucking hospital and find that doctor. She's going to give us answers." I place my hand over Ringo's and deadpan. "And then she dies."

3

RINGO

H er guttural cries are too much. The sound is ripping my heart straight from my fucking chest.

With my forehead pressed to the bathroom door, I ball my fists so tight my knuckles crack, fighting like hell not to walk in there.

When she stepped inside and slammed the door, it was a clear message. She wanted to be alone, and maybe she thinks that's what she needs, but fuck, this time, she's wrong.

Everything that's happened today... everything she's learned about Bobbi... fuck, it's too much to carry alone. And yet, all I can do is stand out here and absorb her pain.

Daniel better not be fucking with us. I hope more than anything, what he said is true. I hope more than anything that her little girl is alive and well so she gets to hold her again. To see her smiles. Soothe her tears. Teach her what love feels like.

I'll never get that chance again. My Hope will never rise from the dead, and as much as that rips me apart, I have to believe her time for life just wasn't meant to be yet. One day maybe, she'll come back. Reborn. Fuck, there's even a part of me that imagines she's been reborn in Bobbi.

That's gotta be why I love a little baby that isn't mine... right? Why I'd burn the world down for her, just to see her safe.

I struggled *not* to shoot Daniel on the spot at the airfield. The sick cunt deserves to bleed out for every fucking thing he's put my Angel through. But when Abbey bolted, too fast for me to catch, I had to remain fucking calm and rational.

We had Daniel. Donny Allen was dead. And Ian is still out there.

Thank fuck Brody was quick thinking, stepping up like a true Southern Sadist. He fucking launched himself through the passenger window of the van Abbey was stealing, his legs hanging out as she sped off. I thought the fucker was going to fall out. But he made it in. He answered my frantic fucking phone call. He relayed every turn they made so I at least knew where she was even if she was getting further and further away.

But at least she wasn't alone. Brody was there, and he could help me get back to her.

I knock my forehead gently against the door as Abbey's cries grow desperate, my own eyes burning, my throat tight as her pain drags me under with her.

Fuck. The moment I opened that casket to find nothing but a small sack of sand... for one insane heartbeat I thought it had to be a dream. Thought maybe I'd been shot at that airfield and was bleeding out, trapped in a hallucination.

On the other side of the door, Abbey's cries turn into chokes, and the moment she starts gagging, my hand is on the knob, and I shove the door open, ready to endure her wrath, because there's no fucking way I'm standing by while she breaks like this.

"Angel." I charge into the steam-filled room, yanking the shower door open, my eyes falling to the floor where she's curled on her side as she retches on nothing but air.

Not giving a fuck about my clothes getting wet, I drop to the floor, haul her into my lap, and wrap her tight against me as the scalding spray drenches us both.

"Fuck, Abs. I've got you." I choke out, holding on while she sobs like she just lost Bobbi all over again.

This is fucking cruel. If Daniel is lying, I'll make him wish he was never fucking born.

But surely the photo evidence is enough. The text messages between him and his mum have date stamps. It has to be real. It just fucking has to be.

Fuck.

I *need* it to be... for my Angel.

Abbey tries to speak, but it's incomprehensible, so I just hold her, my palms gliding over her wet skin, trying to soothe what can't be soothed, giving her the only thing I can... me.

Then, for a moment, I let myself break too.

I let myself remember the pain of losing Hope. The way it gutted me to live each day knowing I didn't get to her in time. That helplessness never fades. It chisels into your very being, leaving you hollow with scars that never stop burning. Wounds that never stop bleeding.

We stay there on the shower floor for a long while, Abbey trembling in my arms, her sobs slowly fading into softer cries, until finally, her tears run dry. And then, we just stay quiet, holding on to nothing but each other, taking the moment to just be silent and still and together.

My Angel feels peaceful in these quiet moments, and I start to think she's fallen asleep, but then, her quiet, husky voice breaks the silence.

"Part of me doesn't want to believe it, just in case it's not real," she whispers into my neck. "But there's a part of me that never felt like she was gone. Like I knew she still existed, but I thought it was just my mind desperately clinging to her."

Even though she can't see it, a faint smile tugs at my lips, and I press them to the top of her head before responding.

"Mothers have intuition about their kids," I rasp against her hair, pressing my lips to the soaked strands again before continuing. "Maybe you did always know, even if it felt impossible."

"It still feels impossible."

"It does," I admit, my voice rough with emotion. "It'll take some time to get used to after everything you've been through... but we *are* gonna get her back, Angel. If she's alive, I'll burn the fucking world down to bring her home to you. That, I vow."

Shifting in my lap, Abbey tilts her head back, her blotchy red face lifting until those puffy tear-filled eyes lock on mine.

"Everything but get yourself killed."

My lips kick up, and her hand lifts, her fingers grazing through the longer length of my beard, her touch so soft it damn near undoes me.

"I'll try my best to stay alive, Angel."

"I can't do this without you, Cam." Her voice shakes, but her gaze is fierce, like molten caramel searing straight into my fucking soul. "Promise me you won't get yourself killed."

I nip at her fingers as they brush my mouth and nod. "I *promise* I'll *try not* to get myself killed."

She rolls her eyes. "I guess that'll have to do."

Leaning in, I press a quick kiss to her lips, fighting the urge to linger, to taste more. Fighting the urge to claim, her bare skin warm against my lap, teasing my control.

Now's not the fucking time to be imagining my tongue tracing over every inch of her… right?

Fuck. Now I'm getting hard, my cock thickening in my soaked jeans.

Shifting, I somehow manage to stand with Abbey still in my arms. It takes every lick of control I have to not take her the way I've been dreaming of. Fuck, maybe I should. It would help her forget, but no. Fuck. Tonight isn't the right time.

Lowering her feet to the tiles, I reluctantly let my hands fall away from her, taking a step back, forcing space between us before she notices the bulge in my jeans.

"Finish up, Angel. I'll change into some dry clothes."

Her red-rimmed eyes lift to mine as a frown pinches her brow, and she opens her mouth to say something, but then stops. Her gaze drops, slowly roaming over me and the drenched fabric of my shirt plastered to my chest, to the cling of wet denim over my thighs, before her gaze stops, lingering on my crotch.

"What if I want what's under there?" She points towards my groin, and my fucking cock jerks in anticipation.

"You've been through a lot today, Angel." I take another step back, and her frown morphs into anger.

"So? What? That means I can't feel good?"

"No, that's not what I mean." I sigh, pushing the door open. "If you want me to fuck you, I'll fuck you. I just don't want you to *feel* like you have to because you know I'm hard. I can deal with it."

She shakes her head. "That is mine to deal with."

A low laugh rumbles out of me as I close the shower door. "Like I said, I'll fuck you if that's what *you* want."

Abbey huffs in the shower. "Then why are you walking away?"

"Because I'd rather throw you around my room than break our necks in the shower."

A small giggle falls from her, although it's a little strained. I know she'd love nothing more than to hunt down Dr Madden now and try to get answers about Bobbi. I know she's fighting against every instinct she has to just go on a rampage and tear the world apart until she finds her, but instead, she's trying like hell to use her head. To take the night to rest and regroup.

I'm tempted to step back inside that shower so I can wrap her in my arms and reassure her that everything's going to be okay. But since I don't actually know that, and since we most definitely will injure ourselves in the shower given how fucking exhausted we both are, I start peeling off my wet clothes and dry myself with a towel.

"I suppose you make a good point." She sighs, shutting off the water before opening the door. "I'll meet you in the bedroom then."

Smirking at my wife, I briefly wonder if I should shut this down.

It's not that I don't want her, because fuck, I do. I fucking ache for this woman every second of the day, but I worry she's using sex as a coping mechanism.

I guess it's better than turning to the bottle or drugs like some people do, though.

Leaving my soaked clothes in a heap on the bathroom floor, I decide that if my wife wants to feel good, then, fuck it, I'll give her so much pleasure she won't have a thought left in her head except me. I'll fuck her until she passes out and falls into a sleep coma where nothing can touch her.

Abbey is so different from the scared, curious girl that came into my life over four months ago. Now, she's comfortable with me. My body, and her own. And she's beginning to discover what she likes in the bedroom.

There are so many things I want to introduce her to. Teach her. Experience with her.

One thing I used to do a lot with Kylie, is tie her up. I started doing it because she was so erratic in bed, and binding her kept her under my control. I enjoyed that side of it, having her at my mercy, and I realise now that I'd been doing that to her for all the wrong reasons.

I haven't tried tying up Abbey yet, but the truth is, I don't need to do that to have my Angel at my mercy. What Kylie and I had was twisted and hollow, nothing compared to what I have with my wife.

Plus, Abbey was restrained by those fuckheads that assaulted her, and there's no way I'll risk dragging her back into that nightmare. There are so many other ways to explore each other's bodies and boundaries. Ways that build trust.

With that in mind, I snatch my phone off the bedside table, and I shoot Lans a message to keep Tahli occupied for a couple of hours. She replies with a smug little smirk emoji, and I shake my head, because fuck, I knew she'd get why I was messaging, but I don't wanna see her fucking encouragement.

My sister is getting more and more out of control. These fucking lockdowns are eating at her, winding her up tighter every fucking day. She's a social butterfly, and loves male attention too fucking much, so right now, she's like a caged tiger that needs to blow off some steam. Preferably far fucking away from where I can see or hear any of it.

When the bathroom door swings open, I drop my phone back onto the table and watch my wife step out completely naked, her head tipped to the side as she uses her towel to dry her hair.

Fuck. I want to devour her completely for hours on end until she forgets her own name.

Moving to the end of the bed, I sink down onto the floor, never breaking eye contact as I lean back against the mattress and crook my finger, gesturing for her to come to me.

Her brows lift in question.

"Get over here, Angel," I command. "*Now.*"

She stills at my demand, her lips parting as her breath quickens, and fuck, my cock turns to stone at the rush of power that surges through me from the simple act of bossing her around.

"Don't make me ask again," I snap, and she instantly drops the towel, moving towards me.

Ahhh, there's my little submissive.

Her cheeks are flushed, the pink deepening when her eyes flick down and lock on my cock, thick and hard, and already weeping for her.

I flex my arse, making my cock jerk in invitation, as my greedy little Angel bites her lip, her eyes drifting back up to mine.

Reaching out, I take her hand, guiding her until she straddles me with one foot planted on each side of my thighs, and I tip my head back to look up her naked body as she gazes down at me too.

"Bring those lips here." I tap my mouth, and the corner of hers kicks up as she leans down, her eyes on my mouth, ready to give me a kiss.

Ohhh, sometimes I forget how fucking innocent she is.

"Uh-uh. Not *those* lips," I say, and she stills, her brows furrowing in confusion.

I fucking love this side of her. A little inexperienced.

Tilting my head, I gesture lower, straight to the heat between her legs. "The wet ones between those pretty thighs, Angel."

She straightens, a small gasp escaping her, and I can tell by the way her eyes dart between us that she's going to need more coaxing.

I've devoured her sweet cunt before, but always with her flat on her back. This new position maybe feels more exposing or intimate to her, but fuck her vulnerability is beautiful.

"I wanna eat my wife for dinner, Angel. Stop making me wait and straddle my face."

Her brows hitch. "Straddle it?" she squeaks, and I nod, resting my head back on the mattress while dragging my tongue over my lips.

"Straddle it. Grind on it. Smother me with your pretty pink cunt."

Her chest rises and falls quickly, clearly affected by not only my demand, but the dirty words I use that I know she loves. Hell, she doesn't even flinch when I say the word *cunt* anymore.

"I can't. I'll like... suffocate you or something."

Gliding my hands up the backs of her thighs, I reach her arse and give it a sharp squeeze.

"I told you to smother me, Angel. Why are you making me wait?" I growl, tugging her closer, my fingers sinking into those perfect globes, and another squeak flies from her lips.

She stumbles forward, her hands darting out and slapping down on the mattress behind my head as she catches herself, and I lean in close, burying my face between the apex of her thighs, my nose pressing to her clit.

"Fuuuck, Angel. You smell so fucking good."

She moans, shifting her hands for balance on the mattress to either side of my head before she peers down at me, and when our eyes lock, I see the submissive in her eyes silently begging me to shove her over the line.

Releasing one of her perfect globes, I rear my hand back and bring it down hard across her arse, the crack bouncing off the walls of our room, and her gasping cry has the beast in me humming with approval.

"Fuck my face, Abbey. Now!"

She obeys instantly, her slick cunt pressing down against my lips, and I fucking groan as the taste of her hits my tongue.

It's like a drug to me. A euphoric hit that has me ravenous for more, and my cock jerks as the heat of her smothers me exactly the way I wanted.

My tongue glides through her folds, tracing every inch before moving back to her clit and flicking it. Then, I seal my lips around the swollen bud and suck hard.

"Oh!" she chokes, her body pitching forward, pressing her weight into me.

My fingers dig into the flesh of her arse, feeling the muscles tense and flex under my grip, and fuck yes! I fucking love turning her on.

There's nothing like it. Having her on the edge, bringing her to the brink, and knowing I have the power to shatter her with nothing but my mouth.

Small whimpers spill from her lips as I work her over, lapping, sucking, and every so often, driving my tongue into her pussy, fucking her with it until her thighs quake.

My cock is desperate for her, precum beading at the tip, the ache of it so brutal I know I could blow any moment. But fuck, who cares? It would be worth every drop of cum, because this right here, is fucking everything.

As my Angel surrenders to the pleasure building inside her, her thrusts grow sharper, harder, and more frantic. Breathing is no longer a fucking option for me, and fuck, you know what? If this is how I go, smothered under her, it's the only death I'd ever beg for.

The pads of my fingers dig into her arse, urging her on as she grinds against my face, and her cries fill the room as her sweet taste grows slicker on my tongue.

She's close.

This knowledge unravels me, and I fucking hold her to my face, making sure I can't take in a single slither of oxygen. I draw her clit into my mouth like I'm sucking on her nipple, and she cries out as her body locks tight before tremors ripple through her and her orgasm gushes across my tongue, lips and beard.

It's a long, body-jerking climax, her thighs shaking, the muscles taut before she finally goes slack, and because I can't help myself, I quickly grip her hips, moving her off me, and shoving her face first onto the bed.

I stand, my cock throbbing as I press it between her legs while I fist my hand into the hair at her nape.

She gasps when I give the strands a sharp tug, forcing her back to arch and that sweet fucking arse to point directly at me.

"Colour?!" I demand.

"O-orange."

I freeze, my grip in her hair loosening instantly.

Orange? Did she just say orange?

"Angel, I'm sorry," I rush out, shifting to release her hair completely so I can step back, but her dainty hand wraps around my wrist, stopping me.

"Don't go," she whimpers. "Just give me a sec."

Fuck.

FUCK!

"I'm sorry. I got carried away." I shake my head, wanting to fucking punch myself as self-disgust burns through me. "I didn't mean to be so rough."

Fuck! I'm such a fuckup!

A shuddering breath spills from her lips as her grip loosens on my wrist, her hand planting down on the mattress to steady herself.

"I know we've done it with my back to you before," she rushes out, her voice so small and panting, reminding me of when she first came to me, completely broken, terrified I was going to hurt her too. "It was just the combination of the position and the hair."

"We don't have to do it this way," I tell her, shifting to pull back, but before I can move, she presses her arse back, the tip of my cock caught against her heat like a magnet.

"I want to, Cam. So bad... I just need a second to prepare myself."

I blow out a breath and sigh, relief and guilt tangling in my chest. Leaning forward over her back, I press my lips to her shoulder as I murmur against her skin. "I'll never hurt you, Angel. I will always stop when you want me to."

"I know." She nods, turning her head until our lips meet over her shoulder, and fuck, her encouragement washes through me, even as we kiss in the awkward position.

Nothing about her, about us, feels fucking awkward, though. Us coming together feels like the most natural thing in the world.

"Ringo," she breathes as our lips part, "I'm green again."

To prove it, she shifts her legs wider apart on the mattress and presses back against me again, the swollen head of my cock sliding over her soaked folds, teasing us both.

"Fuck... you sure, Abs?"

"So sure." She rolls her hips, teasing me. "Please forget that just happened and fuck me the way you were going to."

Jesus fucking Christ. I don't know if I can do that now, and she must sense my hesitation because she shifts, her hand slipping between her legs to wrap around my cock, guiding it to her entrance.

"Fuck me, Cam," she begs. "Fuck me so hard it both hurts and feels good."

Fuuuuuuuck! Her words snap my control, flipping my fucking switch, and a growl rumbles from me as my fist tightens in her hair again, and finally, I surge in.

She cries out as I groan, her tight, slick walls clutching me, sucking me in like she's never going to let me go.

Fuck, I hope she never does.

My fingers dig into her hips, my gaze trailing down her arched spine to the valley of her arse where her pretty puckered hole is begging for attention.

Fuck. Would she let me?

Slowly easing out and back in, I watch how that tight little hole almost winks at me, torturing me. Teasing me.

"Angel," I rasp, thrusting a little faster as I tug her hair back, turning her head so she looks over her shoulder at me. "I wanna try something."

"Try what?" she pants, her rosy cheeks flaring hot.

Releasing her hip, I trail my fingers across the swell of her arse, running them gently through the valley, brushing over where I want her the most, and she tenses around my cock.

"Relax, Angel."

"No. Not there." She pleads, panic in her tone, but my thrusts don't falter, and I don't let her retreat.

Instead, I release her hair and graze my hand around to her front before finding her needy little bud and start circling it. She jolts, a strangled moan bursting free as her shock melts into raw need, and her body loosens around me again, surrendering in spite of her words.

"You can trust me, Angel," I rumble, my voice scratchy as the hunger inside me takes over every fucking cell in my body. "I won't hurt you."

She shakes her head. "I don't..." She trails off as I circle her rose with my finger. Teasing her. Coaxing her.

"Just a finger." I pant. "My pinkie. Nothing too much. Nothing you can't take."

I apply more pressure to her clit, and her breathing quickens, her body caught between resistance and surrender. I keep thrusting inside her slick cunt, my cock already aching to unload, but I fucking hold it back.

Not yet. I want her to feel this. My finger in her arse while my cock stretches her. I want her to understand how good it can be if she lets me.

"Will it... hurt?" she pants, her moans making it hard for her to speak as she becomes more pliable under my fingers and around my cock.

"No, Angel. I swear, it will feel fucking amazing."

She jostles forward a little as I pound into her, those caramel eyes flashing over her shoulder to meet mine. They are wide and uncertain, but brimming with heat, and fuck, it takes everything in me not to blow inside her.

Not yet, arsehole. Don't come yet. Hold it the fuck in.

"Promise?" she pants, her voice huskier by the second, matching mine, and fuck if that isn't the sexiest fucking sound I've ever heard.

"I fucking promise." My voice is raw as I press my finger to her puckered rose, teasing her there, while my other hand circles her clit faster, and her pussy gets slicker by the second. "All you have to do to make it stop is say orange or red. You know that."

She nods. "Okay."

That's it. That's all the invitation I fucking need.

Bringing my pinkie up to my mouth, I suck on it, coating it with my saliva before pressing it to her tight little hole.

"Here we go, Angel," I pant, stilling my hips to slowly, carefully ease my digit inside.

"Oh!" she cries out, tensing, so I roll her clit harder, hoping I don't fucking hurt her there, and finally, it's like she gives herself permission to feel good, relaxing enough for my digit to slip into her arse, nice and deep.

I groan as her body clamps around my finger and cock, and I start thrusting again, working her from every angle at once.

It's not the most glamorous position to be in, and fuck it's hard to hold myself up as I thrust my cock, curl my pinkie, and circle her clit at the same time. But I'm fucking dedicated to the cause, summoning every bit of multitasking skills I've learned over my thirty-three fucking years. This woman's pleasure is my fucking mission.

In a matter of seconds, my Angel cries out, tightening around me, her cunt slick as she explodes in a climax so hard and forceful that I have no control over my own, her body kneading my cock until I rupture with a guttural roar.

When the sound dies from my throat and I've spilled every last drop inside her, I slowly ease from her trembling body. First my pinkie and then my cock, holding myself over her so I don't crush her small frame.

Staring down at her closed eyes, she's panting, a slight grin kicking up one corner of her mouth, I wonder how the fuck someone like me got so lucky.

"Abs," I rasp. "Look at me."

Those big eyes blink open, staring up at me, and I bring my fingers to her cheeks, grazing them over her flushed skin.

"I love you more than life itself, Angel. I will move heaven and earth to get your baby back to you, and I'll make sure no one ever hurts you again."

Her eyes turn glassy, but she doesn't shed any tears. She simply looks up at me with adoration. It's right there. Without a single doubt.

She brings a hand up, pressing it to the side of my face, her fingers scratching through my beard, like she's combing the hair.

"I love you too. My big beautifully savage monster."

My lips kick up. "Angel, if there's anyone beautifully savage around here, it's you."

4

ABBEY

The rumble of approaching motorbikes draws my attention out the window, and I shift closer to see Smitty at the front of the pack as they ride in.

What are they doing here? They'd better not be here to drag Ringo away on club business. That's all I need right now.

I watch the leather-clad men park their bikes and tug off their helmets as my husband comes into view, walking across the yard to meet them.

God, just the sight of him has my cheeks heating, momentarily pushing past the churning anxiety nearly crippling me this morning.

Last night, he pushed my boundaries again. In the best way. It's such a thrill to give myself over to him. To trust him with my body and know he's going to make me feel things I never imagined existed.

Just remembering how I felt when I agreed to let him do that with his finger... it felt freeing. It was my choice, yet at the same time, he had control over how my body responded.

I'm not sure I'll ever truly understand the whole submissive nature I fall into, but I don't hate it like I used to, and I have my husband to thank for that.

Watching him from above now has my chest warming as he greets his club brothers and they all start chatting. Even though he's giving them his attention right now, I'm still the one on his mind, which I know because his eyes drift up to the window of his suite, landing on me like he knew I was watching.

Then he winks.

I don't know how well he can see me, but I smile for his benefit, just in case, and when his attention turns back to Smitty, my shoulders drop as my anxiety slams back into me.

Shit.

I should feel happy, right? My little girl is alive. Or at least I think she is. Unless Daniel was able to somehow create fake messages and images, which, let's be honest, in this day and age is highly possible... but something inside me is screaming that this is real.

So why am I filled with nothing but dread?

"Abs?"

I spin at hearing Tahli's voice to find her at the mouth of the hall that opens up into the small living area in Ringo's suite.

It hasn't been long since she's been here with us, but she's already putting on more weight and looks healthier.

"Hey, Chook. What's up?"

My little sister opens her mouth to speak, but then snaps it shut, and I hate that so much. I hate that she's struggling to speak to me.

"Are you angry with me?" I ask, and her brows shoot up before she shakes her head.

"No, never."

"You know you can tell me anything, right?" I ask, taking a step closer. "Even if it's something you think I won't like."

Her lower lip starts to wobble then, her eyes flooding with tears, and the moment I open my arms wide, she runs and crashes to my chest.

"Shhhh." I coo, stroking her hair as she falls apart, all while fighting back my own tears. "It's okay, Chook. I got you."

I realise I just said the words Ringo has said to me so often. Is this how he feels when he's consoling me?

Helpless?

"I'm scared." Tahli cries into my chest, and I squeeze her tighter, hoping it will make her feel safe somehow.

"You've been through a lot. It's only natural to be scared, but I promise, you're safe here." I try to reassure her, running my hand up and down her back. "I know that guy nearly got to you, but the fact is, he didn't. The men here protected you. Lans and Millie protected you. Everyone here only wants to keep you safe."

I still can't believe one of the thugs desperate to kidnap her for Banes dug a bloody underground tunnel onto the property. That is totally wild to me, and I know it scared the hell out of her.

She nods into my chest at my words, hiccupping on a sob as she pulls back, and her big eyes peer up at me.

"I know I'm safe, Abs. I'm not scared for myself. I'm scared for you. I don't want any more bad things to happen to you... you're different now."

My heart sinks.

She's not wrong. I'm so different now, and I realise in her young innocent eyes, the change in me isn't necessarily good.

"I know I am," I admit, gripping her shoulders as I hold her far enough away that she can see my whole face. "I've had to change to adapt to the situations I've been in. I know I'm not as... nice. But I am stronger. And right now, that's who I need to be. Someone strong. Who keeps fighting. Who won't give up until the bad people pay for what they did to me. To us."

Tahli bobs her head, her eyes dropping to my chest as her lip wobbles again.

"I know I shouldn't... but I miss Dad."

Jesus. My heart splinters open.

Does she know I was the one who gave him the gun?

"Tahli, it's perfectly normal to miss Dad. Despite his flaws, he was our father, and we will always love him in our own ways."

Those tear-filled eyes dart back up to mine. "He was weak. Why was he so weak? Why did he let Mum treat him like that?"

Sighing, I pull my little sister back to my chest in another hug. "I can't answer that. I really don't know other than that's just who he was. Mum probably picked him because she could control him. Bitches like that don't like to be told what to do."

"Except by our grandfather."

A chill ripples up my spine at Tahli's words. "Yeah. Except by him."

We hug each other for a few long beats before Tahli pulls back and swipes at her tears, her attention shifting to the window, and the men down below congregated outside the barn.

"Do you think I could have a motorbike one day?"

My brows shoot up at her words, and I dart my eyes to her as she stares in awe.

"Uhhh. No. Absolutely not," I snap, and she rolls her eyes at me.

"I don't think it's fair that you get to use knives and guns and ride on the back of Ringo's motorbike, yet I can't have one of my own."

"I'm older than you. And I didn't choose to use those things, Chook. I've had to learn how to use them to protect myself, and you."

She shrugs like that's not the point, her eyes shifting to a couple of the younger club brothers who are clearly flirting with Alana as she carries out a tray of muffins for them.

"If I can't have my own motorcycle, then I guess I'll just have to marry a biker so I can ride on the back like you do."

A strangled gasp falls from my open mouth as I balk at my little sister.

"Absolutely not, Tahli May Delany!"

She scoffs. "Don't be such a hypocrite."

I glare at my sister. "Who are you right now?"

"I'm the good sister, remember?"

A laugh bursts from my lips. "Good, but cheeky."

She shrugs. "My thirteenth birthday is in a few months. Guess what I want for it?"

"I think I'll regret this, but what?" I ask, and her smile tugs wide.

"When school opens back up..." Her eyes flick to me, bright and full of mischief. "I want Brody to take me to school on the back of his motorcycle so I can make Alice and Fiona jealous. And then also pick me up after school. For the whole term."

"You are... evil." I shake my head in disbelief.

"I'm the good kind of evil." She shrugs. "Just like you."

Well... she has me there, I guess.

"Whatever." I laugh. "But Brody isn't a patched member of the club yet."

"He's good looking and rides a motorbike. That's all I need."

I throw my head back laughing and chase Tahli, slapping her arse as she dashes for the door, and I hear her giggles all the way down the hall and on the landing as she rushes back downstairs.

I think I've somehow, without knowing it, created a monster.

Movement outside the barn snags my attention again, and I see Riggs step out, cleaning blood off his knuckles.

I guess he's been working Daniel over.

Shit.

My heart sinks again.

Not because I feel bad for Daniel. There's not a single part of me that does, but I do feel bad, and I realise it's every time I remember that Daniel said Bobbi is still alive.

My chest burns, and I clutch it as hot tears start to pool in my eyes.

Bobbi is alive, so why aren't I happy? Why do I feel more scared than ever?

Sucking in a few deep breaths, I force my tears away and give my face a little slap to help shake off this feeling.

Rolling my shoulders back, I head towards the door, forcing the thoughts away so I can focus on what needs to be done.

I have a doctor to visit and answers to get.

Downstairs, Alana's voice is high pitched with excitement as she comes back inside with an empty tray, and Tahli stands at the windows watching the men.

Jesus, I think I preferred when her obsession was with Care Bears.

"Great. Thugs in leather." Millie scoffs as she comes in from the back part of the house.

"I like the leather. I didn't know there were so many of them though," Tahli admits, and Alana giggles.

"Unfortunately," Millie mutters, and Doreen tuts at her daughter.

"Don't be so judgemental, Millie. Those men have had hard lives, and while they may not live the type of life that society considers as normal, they have done more good than bad as part of the club. Don't forget what they did for you."

My brows lift as I move further into the room, seeing Millie stiffen.

What did they do for her?

I want to ask but keep my mouth shut since it's none of my business.

"Hey Abs?" Tahli asks, glancing over her shoulder at me like she already knew I was there, which informs Ringo's sisters and mum of my presence. "Are they here to help you get Bobbi back?"

"They are."

Ringo's deep voice comes from behind me, answering my sister, and I swear just the sound of it has the tension leaving my body.

I turn to look at my husband, over six feet tall, muscles packed on top of muscles that strain underneath his black tee. His hair is tied back, but I already know that unless he's getting on his motorcycle in the next five minutes, he'll tug the band out and let his hair down.

I don't know why he doesn't just cut it. It annoys him to wear it down, but also annoys him to wear it tied back. It's not like it's a requirement to be part of the Southern Sadists. All the men have different hairstyles.

"Good morning, Angel."

My lips lift at the smirk peeking past his beard.

"Good morning, Cam."

"I'm confused…" Tahli's voice reminds me that she's here.

Jesus, Ringo has the power to make me feel like it's just me and him in a room sometimes. It's a dangerous thing.

"What are you confused about?" I ask my little sister as she glances between me and Ringo.

"Is your name Ringo or Cam?"

Ringo smirks, stepping closer and bending down to Tahli's height, bracing his hands on his knees.

"My real name is Cameron Musgrove, but most people call me Ringo."

"Why?"

"Well…" he sighs, his whisky eyes flicking to me briefly before returning to my little sister and giving her a one-shouldered shrug. "I used to be in a band back in high school. I was the drummer, and I also wrote some songs and sang lead vocals sometimes. Just like Ringo Starr from the Beatles. So, my mates started calling me Ringo."

"The Beatles?" Tahli screws up her face. "Aren't they all dead? Are you *that* old?"

A laugh bubbles from my lips while Ringo's sisters burst out laughing, along with his mum. Meanwhile, Ringo shoots me a glare, shaking his head.

"Actually, kid. A couple of them are still alive." He shoots her a wink. "But I guess to you they are old. I'm not that old though."

When Tahli's eyes narrow, I know her sass is about to come out.

"Old enough. I bet you were a teenager when Abbey was a baby."

I stiffen. "Tahli! Don't be rude!"

"What? It's true, isn't it? I wasn't trying to be rude."

Ringo chuckles. "She's not wrong." He straightens and ruffles her hair. "When Abbey was born, I would have been around fifteen years old."

I inwardly cringe.

That sounds so bad, right?

"Does that make you her sugar daddy?"

"Tahli!" I screech in mortification, slapping my hand over her mouth so she can't say anything else as Ringo's sisters laugh again, but the man himself just shrugs.

"If that's the easiest way for you to wrap your head around me and your sister, then sure." Ringo smirks, shooting me a wink this time. "I'm her sugar daddy."

I gasp, and Tahli shoves my hand away from her face.

"Next time you see my mum, can you tell her that and then take a photo of her face for me? I wanna see how crazy that makes her."

"Oh my God, Tahli." I giggle, gripping my little sister's shoulders and steering her to the couch. "What has gotten into you? And how do you even know what a sugar daddy is?"

"Sally's big sister is eighteen, and she has this app where she has three sugar daddy boyfriends who send her money and gifts. Sally was telling us at school that her sister only has to talk to them over video call for thirty minutes a week. She doesn't know what they talk about because her sister locks her bedroom door so Sally can't go in, but a few weeks ago she listened at the door, and she thinks one of them must have sent her a lollipop because she heard a man tell her to suck it and—"

"Okay, that's enough!" I slap my hand over her mouth again as the room fills with hysterical laughter.

Tahli shoves me off her again, glaring at me, and I sigh.

It's good that she feels comfortable enough to say what she thinks here, but I think we need to have a chat about a few things when I get back...

Shit... When I get back... from searching for my daughter.

My heart sinks as dread fills me again.

Is it because maybe I don't really believe she's alive? Or I don't want to get my hopes up just in case?

I ache to hold my little girl. I really do... so why am I so terrified?

It has to be my subconscious trying to protect me, telling me not to get my hopes up, because my heart... it won't survive being crushed again. There'd be no coming back from that a second time.

Doreen slowly shuffles her way over to the couch before sitting next to Tahli and showing her a basket of knitting needles and balls of knitting yarn. I step away, and Doreen smiles warmly up at me, like she's silently telling me it's okay, she'll look after Tahli for me while I'm gone.

These people... they are my saviours. I don't know how I'll ever repay them.

"Uhhh, Abs. Here's that paracetamol you wanted for your headache." Alana grins as she approaches me with a glass of water and something tucked in her palm.

Knowing exactly what she has, I move away from my little sister and Ringo's mum and take the glass and the small pill from her.

"Thank you," I mutter quietly before tossing the pill into my mouth and chugging back some water.

Ringo and I haven't exactly been careful when we have sex, and the last thing I need is to fall pregnant again. Maybe when I see the doctor today, I can arrange for something more routine rather than taking the emergency contraceptive that Alana seems to have a stash of.

I've considered asking her why, but I've learned that with Alana, sometimes you're best not knowing.

When I glance up, Ringo catches my eye, nodding his head towards the front door, so I follow him, stepping outside, where he weaves his fingers with mine.

It's such a simple act, yet means so much, and I focus on the way his thumb strokes over the back of my hand as he leads me off the porch, walking us over to the group of men gathered.

"Abbey," Smitty sings, holding his arms out. "So good to see you."

My brows lift.

"What are you doing here?" I don't mean for my words to sound so snappy, but unfortunately that's how they come out.

"Ringo told me about Bobbi." He grips my shoulders and leans in to press a kiss to my cheek. "I'm here to help."

What's happening?

"Oh..." I glance up at Ringo to see he doesn't look fazed by Smitty's weirdly friendly mood. "I didn't think the President would put himself in danger."

Smitty chuckles, releasing my shoulders. "If I'm not willing to die for my men, then why would they follow me?"

"So you'd die for Ringo?"

Shit... why does my tone sound so judgemental?

It's this man. He rubs me the wrong way, and I know he cares about his men and the club, but his tactics leave a lot to be desired. One minute we can be getting along, and the next minute he's doing something rash, shocking everyone around him.

I just feel so on edge around him.

"Yes, of course. Ringo has been a loyal member of the Southern Sadists for a long time, even if his more recent actions have been questionable."

"For fuck's sake," Ringo grumbles as I get my hackles up and take a step closer to his President.

Too close.

Ringo's arm slips between me and Smitty, and he tugs me back a few steps. "Angel. Smitty is here to help."

I huff, shooting him a glare. "But this is about me. My baby."

"Yes," Smitty says way too loudly, clapping his hands together. "Both of you are Southern Sadists family now. We protect our family."

My eyes narrow as I remember the dig he had at me the day we raided the Rebels' compound, reminding me that this is all my fault... but then, we kind of came to a truce the day I thought he'd killed JD.

Nate is a different kind of man. Irrational at times, but he does always seem to have his club's best interest at heart, even when I don't like it.

"You'd really die for me? For Bobbi?" I ask, zero snark in my tone now as I study this man before me, the aging lines at his eyes getting deeper as he smiles.

"That's right. I would. You are one of us now, so here I am." He holds his arms out again, doing a turn on the spot, making a spectacle of himself, as always. And then he beams at me with a slightly unhinged grin as he faces me again. "I'm fucking ready to burn this world to the ground so we can get your little girl back. So let's saddle the fuck up and start causing havoc."

Oh... tears burn my eyes as the other Sadists start cheering and thumping their chests, while Ringo presses a kiss to my temple.

Jesus... shit... these damn poetic monsters. I love them all.

My smile is wide, and Smitty steps forward, snatching me from Ringo as he sweeps me up in his arms and spins us around, forcing a laugh from my lips.

"Ahhh, put me down," I protest, and when my feet finally hit the gravel again, I spot Millie, Alana and Tahli standing on the porch wearing grins.

Ringo barks orders to his men as Riggs gets one of his SUVs ready, giving four of his men demands.

He's staying behind, just as I'd previously asked.

I want Riggs to protect Tahli at all times. We're not safe yet, and I'm not risking her life, and in some ways, Riggs reminds me a lot of Ringo.

Fierce. Brutal. Loyal.

Exactly the kind of man I trust to keep her safe.

I give my little sister a wave as I walk over to Ringo's motorbike, and she waves back, mouthing, love you, and shit, I fight the urge to cry for the hundredth time since waking up this morning.

"Let me help, Angel," Ringo rasps, taking my helmet out of my hands when I pick it up, and I smile up at him as he slips it on my head and secures it. "That tight enough?"

"Yep." I nod, smiling at him through the open visor, and he grips the mouth bar of my helmet, tugging me closer and leaning in awkwardly to press a kiss to the tip of my nose.

"Let's go cause some chaos, Angel."

"Hell yes." I grin, that idea finally kick-starting my heart, and he chuckles, slapping my arse before tapping the leather of the seat.

We all mount the motorcycles, and the roar of the engines starting up sends a thrill through me.

Never in a million years did I think this would be my life, riding behind a biker man. A sexy, much older biker man, going in search of trouble.

It's not only thrilling, but feels almost right. Like this is exactly where I've always belonged.

My fingers dig into Ringo's cut at his sides as we follow JD up the driveway, and just before we turn onto the road, I slide up close to Ringo, snaking my hands around to his front, knowing our speed is about to pick up.

My smile is wide as the bike rumbles louder, the steel demon between my legs a powerful reminder of the man steering it.

My man.

It takes over an hour to get to the Fox Pines Hospital. We don't bother with parking in the lot. We pull up right at the entrance, not hiding our presence.

We leave our helmets on as we dismount and head towards the doors, but as we approach, Ringo's steps falter.

"What is it?" I ask right as Vender draws his gun.

"Pandemic security guards aren't here," Ringo mutters, and my wide eyes dart back to the doors as they automatically slide open.

And that's when we see it.

All the blood.

5

RINGO

A s if anything would ever be that fucking simple. We are here to see Dr Madden, but instead we find carnage. Fresh fucking decimation.

"Gun out, Angel," I snap as my club brothers move in tight around my wife, protecting her like she's the queen herself.

A queen that carries a gun, and is hot as fuck, I might add.

The pandemic security guards we were expecting to be manning the entrance lay dead in pools of their own blood just inside the door, and a woman behind the information counter is sprawled in a lifeless heap on the floor.

Bloody boot prints leave a trail up the passage, so we silently follow them, each one of us alert as we move as a pack.

At the end of the first hall, we reach the bank of lifts, one with the doors held open by a dead man dressed in scrubs, his body half in and half out of the carriage.

"Stairs," Smitty barks quietly, so we move to the stairwell, and silently make our way up to the maternity floor.

I take in everything as we move, checking for threats, but also, keeping an eagle eye on my wife, checking that she's doing okay.

It's hard to tell with her helmet covering her face, but her hold on the gun is steady, so I have to assume she's just as locked in on the situation as me.

Reaching the maternity floor, we move with stealth to the ward doors, Vender and JD peering in through the windows before pushing the doors open, only to find more blood.

Fuck.

Two nurses at the nurses' station are still in their seats, their eyes lifeless, red bloody holes in their foreheads, and their brain matter painting the wall behind them.

"Who the fuck are we dealing with?" Smitty whispers, and fuck, I have the same thought.

This looks like a professional fucking hit. Still bloody but not chaotic the way Satan's Rebels would leave it.

The sound of a baby crying has Abbey pushing through my men, and she hurries up the passage towards the shrieking.

"Shit. Angel!" I whisper-snap, charging after her and nearly running into her back when she skids to a stop outside a closet door.

Tugging off her helmet, Abbey's eyes dart to me, and she taps her ear.

I force my fucking ears to work past the pounding of my pulse, and that's when I hear it. Not just the crying baby, but whimpering women.

Turning to my club brothers, I send a few silent signals, directing Vender and Murf down the hall to the fire exit where a smear of blood coats the handle, and order Stocky and Trunk to watch our backs.

"Let me go first, Angel," I whisper close to her ear, and I half expect her to disagree, but she nods, taking a step back.

Fuck. I'll have to reward her for that obedience later.

Pulling my helmet off, I place it to the side on the floor before raising my gun and gripping the handle. Slowly, as I ease the handle down, gasps erupt behind the door like they can see someone trying to get it.

I fucking brace myself.

Quickly shoving the door open, I'm met with wide, terrified eyes of seven women, the screeching baby in the arms of one woman at the back, frantically trying to soothe it as it cries.

"Ringo?"

My eyes widen at the sound of my name coming from inside the room, and I flick the light on so I can see the faces better.

There, at the front of the women, holding a bedpan out like it's a shield, is Andrea Mitchell. Ayden's mum.

"Oh my God. Andrea!" Abbey pushes past me, hurrying in to throw her arms around a dumbfounded Andrea.

"What are you doing here?" Andrea asks, tears filling her eyes.

"What happened?" I ask as the women inside start to relax, although all are still sobbing.

Shit, at least three of them are holding newborn babies.

"We were just finishing up in the nursery with the mums and bubs when we heard yelling. We hurried in here," Andrea starts, needing to take in a steadying breath as Abbey steps back from her, and she gestures to another door behind them, and I realise this closet has two entrances. "I went to go and see... then I heard a scream. I peeked out the door and saw two cops... they shot Tania and Bernice and dragged Dr Madden out the fire exit."

"You didn't hear them shooting downstairs?" JD asks, and Andrea shakes her head. "No... but they had those silencer things on their guns. Like you see in the movies."

I meet JD's eyes, and I know he's thinking the same thing as me.

This definitely wasn't an MC. Probably corrupt cops, although I don't think they'd be dumb enough to wear their uniforms on a hit like this. So maybe not real cops.

"You said they took Dr Madden? How long ago?" Abbey asks, and Andrea nods.

"Yes. She fought them, though. Tried to get away, but they were too strong for her." Andrea shrugs. "It all happened maybe five minutes ago."

Abbey's caramel eyes flick up to mine, swimming with concern.

"Why would anyone but me come looking for Dr Madden?" she asks. "Daniel said no one knows."

"He did. I guess he was lying."

Abbey's jaw ticks as she clenches her teeth.

"Why are you here to see Dr Madden?" Andrea asks, gaining my wife's attention again, and when Abbey smiles, it's strained.

"Just a follow up from when…" Abbey trails off, and Andrea nods, sympathy in her eyes over Abbey losing her child even though I'm pretty sure she doesn't believe what Abbey just said.

"We should follow the trail," JD mutters behind me, and I grunt in agreement.

"Have you called the police yet?" I ask Andrea, and she shakes her head.

"Our phones are in our lockers, and the closest landline is out there…" Andrea frowns in confusion. "But those men were the police."

"No, they weren't," I grunt, wishing I had more time to explain. "All of you remain in here. We'll contact Officer Zimora. He'll bring the right men to deal with this."

Andrea nods. She knows Officer Zimora. He helped Lexi when she was being hunted by her dad and brother.

With another quick hug between Abbey and Andrea, we leave the small space and reconvene out in the hallway where Abbey and I refit our helmets.

"Let's follow the yellow brick road." Smitty smirks, and I don't miss the way my wife rolls her eyes at him through the open visor. "What? It has a better ring to it than *'blood smeared stairwell'*."

JD, Murf and Trunk chuckle as we head for the fire exit.

Carefully checking to see if the coast is clear, we enter the fire escape stairwell and follow the drops of blood down until we hit the basement level.

The morgue.

Abbey's feet falter as she goes to step into the morgue foyer, and my mind goes back to the day I pushed her through here in the wheelchair, and the way her frail body coiled tight at the sight of Dr Madden standing outside the door, waiting.

I try to remember what the doctor's expression looked like. If there was any sign I missed that could have hinted at her being a part of stealing Abbey's baby, but I come up blank.

I guess I wasn't focusing on the fucking doctor. I was focused on my broken wife.

But fuck, there are so many questions now… Like how the fuck this could have even happened? That day when Abbey and her baby were rushed in, they were separated. I stayed with my Angel. I held her hand and fucking wept, thinking she was going to fucking die.

Why the fuck didn't I watch what was happening with the baby? Why didn't I send my men to follow the nurses and doctors that took the baby away to 'work' on her? How was Bobbi taken out of the hospital without any other staff noticing?

And the funeral service we used to prepare the body and lay Bobbi to rest in the sealed casket? What the fuck happened there?

There's so much more at play here that we don't even fucking understand, but I'll get to the bottom of it, if it's the last fucking thing I do.

My hand falls to the small of Abbey's back as I try to pull back on my building anger, and her helmeted head turns up until her eyes meet mine.

"We can wait here if you like?" I tell her, and she shakes her head.

"No. I need to do this."

I wanna argue that she doesn't, but I hold my tongue, pushing back my protective nature, knowing she needs to be the one to decide.

Smitty, JD and Vender quickly move in front, their guns raised at the door as we approach.

"Gun, Angel," I remind her, and she stiffens like she didn't realise she had it pointed to the floor at her feet.

"Shit," she mutters, lifting her arm and aiming ahead.

Standing outside the room Abbey thought she'd said goodbye to her daughter in, JD peers over his shoulder checking that we are all ready, and then on his nod, Vender kicks the door open. It bangs back against the wall as he leaps in, followed by JD and Smitty.

We only make it in a few steps when Vender and JD lower their guns, their perplexed expressions darting to us.

"No one's here," Vender mutters, his eyes darting to the trail of blood, which stops in front of the wall of metal doors.

The mortuary fridge.

I glance at Abbey again to find her shoulders drooping, her eyes hyper-fixated on the fridge. Hyper-fixated on a certain door.

The door that was opened to reveal a baby. The baby she was told was hers.

"Angel?"

Her tear-filled eyes dart up to mine. "That poor little baby. Who did she belong to?"

"I don't know, but she wasn't your Bobbi," I remind her, and Abbey shakes her head.

"Apparently not."

Pulling my wife to my side, I give her a squeeze, hating that she has to deal with such a betrayal.

It's then that I see it. Blood oozing from one of the closed silver doors.

"How fresh is that?" I ask, gesturing my gun to the doors, and JD hurries over to examine the blood.

Bending, he takes a look before shooting wide eyes our way.

"It's fresh."

Everyone's guns are raised and ready again in an instant.

"Let's open it up." Smitty strides over, not the least bit fazed with being in the morgue, gripping the silver handle and tugging the door open.

It swings wide, and he reaches in, pulling on the drawer, which makes a scraping sound as it slides out, and there, on the steel table, is Dr Madden. Her throat cut, her eyes wide yet completely black.

"Well, fuck," JD mutters. "I guess we're not getting any answers from the doc then."

Abbey's shoulders drop as she stares at the woman who had answers for her.

Fuck. I was hoping this would be easy so she didn't have to deal with any more disappointment.

"Hey." I wrap my arm around her waist from behind, and tug her backwards out of the room before spinning her to face me. "This is nothing but a bump in the road. I'll get Andrea to find the records of the nurse who was working that day with Dr Madden."

Abbey's cheeks flare hot with frustration, but still she nods, not ready to give up.

JD calls Zimora, telling him about our find and the scene here at the hospital, and I send Murf and Trunk back up to the maternity floor to ask for Andrea's help with the records for the other nurse.

"Either someone knew we were coming and wanted to make sure we didn't get the information we wanted…" Smitty grunts as he comes to stand with me and my wife. "Or, and I hate to say this out loud, Abbey, but other people know your daughter is alive."

She nods quickly, her sweet eyes hard with anger.

"Either scenario isn't good," she snaps as the tension starts to coil tight in her body again.

"Let's find the security room." Smitty claps his hands together overdramatically. "It's time to watch some reality TV."

That makes Abbey laugh, and she shakes her head.

"Has anyone told you that you're crazy?"

Smitty shrugs. "You're the first for today. It's a common daily occurrence."

I grin, because he's fucking right.

I have to say though, I'm a little fucking surprised he showed up today. I told him I was going hunting, but didn't fucking invite him to come along since this isn't actually club business, something he's been very fucking vocal to me about.

He's given me so much fucking grief over everything I've done for Abbey, even fucking insisting I marry her so it would be more acceptable for the club to be helping.

And while that part is something I didn't mind, it hasn't really stopped Smitty's fucking digs about club resources being used for personal situations.

But there's one thing a guy like Nate Smith can't ignore, and that's when a child is in danger.

I guess it doesn't matter *why* he's here. It just matters that he is, and I'm fucking thankful for it, even if he is a fucking loose cannon.

We go in search of the security room, finding it on the first floor, but whoever came here took care of this room probably soon after entering the building. Blood sprays the walls, a dead guy slumped in the chair in front of a wall of shot up monitors, and all hard drives have been removed.

"Fuck," JD hisses, shaking his head. "You think this was Allen's men?"

I shake my head. "Not cops, but maybe someone he's paying. Either that or Banes has ties to black market hitmen."

"So, not only am I not safe, but now my baby isn't either... again."

Abbey's snarky tone has Smitty taking a step back, and not for the first time I clock that he's fucking terrified of my wife when she's angry.

Probably because she doesn't obey him like a puppet.

I grin at that, because the old her would have.

"We need to give her something to take her anger out on." Smitty leans close but speaks loud enough for Abbey to hear.

"I could take it out on you, Nate."

"You could, yes. But that wouldn't be a fair fight... For you. I am a man."

Abbey scoffs. "You are a—"

"Anyone feel like going on a rampage?" Murf chuckles as he strides towards us holding some papers.

"Yes!" Smitty barks, quickly putting space between him and Abbey. "Where? And who?"

Murf grins at our Prez. "First stop, Redfield to visit Nurse Thatcher."

"Nurse Thatcher?" I ask, and Abbey's eyes go wide.

"Is she the nurse who helped Elizabeth Stone steal my baby?"

"Looks like it. Or at least, she's the nurse who worked with Dr Madden that day. She also took leave after that shift and hasn't been back."

Abbey's wide eyes dart to me.

"It's her. It has to be."

"It's the best lead we've got." I smile at my wife before addressing my club brothers. "Let's find Nurse Thatcher and give her a true Southern Sadist's introduction."

6

ABBEY

The old Californian bungalow belonging to Caroline Thatcher looks deserted, as if the owner fled in a hurry. Ringo's men scour the house from top to bottom for any leads, all while with every passing second, the rage inside me grows.

I'm back to where I was before Bobbi was born. Terrified for her safety, only this time she isn't hidden safely inside my womb. She isn't even remotely close to me.

She's with strangers. Strangers who may or may not be caring for her the way she deserves.

"Angel, you're going to wear a hole in the carpet," Ringo says from the entryway of the shitty little living room, and I shoot him a glare, annoyed when he doesn't even flinch.

"You're really going to give me shit now?" I snap, and he holds up his hands in surrender.

Shit, I'm practically vibrating with anger, ready to explode.

"Why don't you sit down? The guys are nearly done."

That does it. I see red, his calm tone scraping against my last nerves, making it feel like he's telling me to calm down, even though he never actually says it. A strangled scream tears out of me as I grab the first thing within reach and hurl it across the room.

"I don't want to sit down!"

The TV suddenly blares to life, triggered by the crash of what must have been the remote I threw, and a news reporter's voice fills the room.

> *"The spate of gang-related crimes in the area has increased, and locals are starting to fear for their safety. Everything from local boys being taken and killed, to a supermarket and an airfield turned into war zones, and now, a massacre at the local hospital."*

The camera pans out, showing Fox Pines Hospital in the background, with a solid wall of police and emergency vehicles lining the front. Behind them, coroners move in and out, carrying black body bags and loading them into a waiting van.

> *"Sources say we are amidst a bikie gang war that has somehow become entangled with a questionable church, and the drama surrounding the young girl who went missing weeks ago. Abbey Delany."*

I stiffen.

"I'm Abbey Musgrove now, bitch," I mutter, right as Ringo's big hands land on my upper arms, pulling me back against his chest.

"You tell her," he chuckles, kissing the top of my head.

"Locals are putting pressure on law enforcement to forget about the pandemic and focus on the safety of citizens, especially after learning a motorcycle club has acquired a property on the fringes of Fox Pines."

"Fuck," Ringo mutters under his breath, just as Smitty's voice cuts in.

"It's begun. They know we're here now. Guess I'll have to start wearing my best smile for the cameras."

Glancing over my shoulder, I see Smitty grinning, completely unfazed by the news.

"You're not concerned?" I ask as Ringo releases me and moves to the remote, flicking the TV off.

"Nah. This shit happens every time we relocate. Locals get their panties in a twist until they realise we're not here to cause trouble."

I scoff, jutting my thumb towards the now black screen.

"Pretty sure that news report contradicts that."

Smitty shrugs. "They'll all know the truth in the end, and then, they'll bow when I ride into town."

I snort a laugh, and Smitty shoots me a wink.

The man is truly delusional.

"We can't find anything of importance." JD's voice has me turning to the entry as he tries to school his grim expression. "No laptop. No devices. She did leave an old driver's licence behind. But that's about it."

Stepping forward, Ringo holds out his hand, and JD passes him the ID card.

"It's a start," Ringo mutters, glancing at it. "Send a picture of it to Lewy. Ask him to pull up every record he can find on Caroline Thatcher and her family. Maybe she's hiding away with someone, or owns a property somewhere else."

JD nods, accepting it back. "Will do."

"Uh, fuck," Smitty mutters, and we all turn to see him peering out the front window. "Pigs are here. Looks like the nosy neighbour next door ignored Vender when he told her to mind her own business."

My eyes widen as I glance out the window too, spotting three police cars blocking us in, and six cops striding up the gravel driveway, hands on their holsters, ready to draw their guns.

"Fuck, call Zimora," Ringo snaps to JD, who I notice is already doing that as he presses his phone to his ear, while Smitty hurries out of the room calling to the other men in the house, "Pigs incoming!"

I spin in a panic as Ringo moves to me. "We're breaking and entering, aren't we? Am I about to get arrested? Are they Allen's men?"

"Shhh," Ringo murmurs, his big hands coming to my arms, rubbing soothingly as his whisky eyes lock with mine. "We'll tell them we came to visit a friend and found the place empty. That we're concerned for her welfare. There's no need to panic, Angel."

Two of the officers walk past the front window, trying to peer in through the white sheers, and my heart kicks into overdrive, flipping in an uneven rhythm inside my chest.

"No... shit. They will take me away from you," I whisper, my gaze darting towards the back of the house.

"Uh-uh, Angel. Running will get you shot. Let's just see how this goes."

Thump. Thump. Thump.

I jolt at the sound of a fist pounding on the door, and I expect Ringo to step forward and answer it, but instead, Smitty strolls casually down the hall like he owns the damn place and opens the front door.

"Ladies. Good to see you."

Ladies? Did he just call two male officers, *ladies*?

"We've had a report of a burglary in progress. Are you the owner of this property?"

"What?" Smitty gasps overdramatically, and when I flick my panicked gaze to Ringo, I find a smirk tugging at his lips.

Why aren't they worried?

"Shit, Ringo, is someone stealing stuff?" Smitty asks, shock lacing his tone, and Ringo scoffs, shaking his head at his President's dramatics before stepping into the hall where the cops can see him.

I try to stop him, but he's too strong, and he frowns, pointing at the floor by my feet. "Don't move."

I want to yell at him for bossing me around, but also... he used *that* tone. The one that has me obeying without question.

I'll be a brat later just to annoy him for using his sex Dom voice on me while we're fully clothed and clearly not playing.

"Hello, Officers," Ringo sighs, stepping up behind Smitty. "Let me guess, the old bat next door called to say we were breaking in?"

I know Ringo told me to stay put, but I can't help edging closer to the window, squinting through the sheers at the two officers glaring at my husband through the open door.

"Who called us is not your concern," the older officer snaps. "Answer the question. Are you, or anyone with you, the owner of this property?"

"No, Officer," Ringo answers just as Smitty cuts in.

"Define owner."

I roll my eyes on Ringo's behalf.

Why is the President of an outlaw MC basically like a child?

"Excuse me?" the officer barks, and I stiffen at the sharp edge in his tone, my gaze scanning the front yard for the other officers.

I instantly spot two standing in the driveway, but I can't see the other two.

"The truth is, we came to visit a friend," Ringo explains. "When she didn't answer, we broke in through the back door because we were worried. We haven't heard from her in a while, and well..." Ringo stalls, and even though I can't see him from where I'm standing, I can still picture him gesturing over his shoulder. "She's gone. Looks like she packed in a hurry. We were about to contact Caroline's family to see if they've heard from her."

"No need," the older officer barks, waving one of the other officers over. "We'll handle that."

"Fabulous," Smitty claps loudly, making me jump.

Jesus, this man. Why is he like this?

While the older officer speaks quietly to the one he waved over, the younger cop bellows in through the open door. "Everyone outside! Line up on the front lawn!"

My heart thrashes harder as I hear the heavy boots of the other club brothers echo through the house, making their way to the front.

"Hey, it'll be okay." JD's voice startles me, and a mousy squeak flies from my lips before I can stop it.

My eyes go wide as I slap my hand over my mouth, while JD's gaze snaps to the front door.

"Did they hear that?" I whisper, and even though he slowly shakes his head, I know he's lying.

He can't be sure, so I glance back through the white sheers to see the two officers, frowning as they peer in.

"Everyone out now! Or this won't go well for you!"

Shit. Shit. Shit.

I've never been in trouble with the police before. The only time I've dealt with them was when I went to them for help, only to learn they wouldn't.

They are all in on it.

As the men start filing out, Ringo steps back into view, holding his hand out to me.

"With me, Angel. Follow my lead."

I glance from my husband to JD, who gives me a reassuring nod, so I step forward, taking Ringo's hand. I feel a little steadier the moment he touches me, and he slowly leads me out of the house behind his club brothers.

The second we step outside, I feel every officer's gaze lock onto me, tracking my movements as Ringo guides me onto the lawn, keeping me at his side.

The only thing that slightly calms me is how casual the other guys are. They're not scared of the police, even though they carry guns... oh shit. The guns! Our guns!

Ringo's hand tightens in mine, clearly sensing my tension, and I lean closer, whispering under my breath.

"The guns."

Peering down at me, Ringo simply winks. "What guns?"

I'm about to snap at him when I remember how smoothly he slid mine from my grip earlier, setting it on the kitchen counter when we discovered the house was empty.

"Everyone step an arm's width apart," one officer yells, as the other two I couldn't see earlier emerge from the back gate, nodding to the oldest officer.

The Sadists start sidestepping to spread out, but Ringo keeps me close, refusing to budge when I go to drop his hand. I cast a worried glance around, noticing a small group of bystanders across the road, phones raised, recording everything.

Are they allowed to do that?

"You hard of hearing?" the oldest officer snarls, and I stiffen at his abrupt tone, dragging my attention back to the cops, all staring at my husband.

"I heard you perfectly," Ringo snaps back.

"Then why are you two still standing together?" The younger officer steps forward, puffing out his chest like he's someone to be feared.

He's barely a man given his scrawny physique.

"This is my wife," Ringo says calmly. "Before I step away from her, I want assurances that you'll be respectful when you search her."

Every officer in front of us raises his brow at the request, but it's the white blond officer, who looks like he uses a tub of gel in his hair every day, who responds.

"Not surprising that you know what comes next. So, you should also know what happens if you refuse."

A low rumble vibrates in the back of Ringo's throat as he glares at the cocky officer, so I tug on his arm.

"It's okay," I tell him, prying my hand from his and stepping sideways. "It'll be fine."

Reluctantly, he lets me move away, and I lift my chin and meet the cocky blond officer's gaze.

"Since there's no female officer present, I know any search of me will be professional and respectful since I'm sure you don't want the news catching wind of anything less."

I nod my head towards the bystanders across the street, and a couple of the officers glance that way, while the Southern Sadists chuckle quietly along the line.

The officer's jaw ticks, and when he moves to step towards me, the older officer presses a hand to his chest and redirects him to the far end of the line.

Relief washes through me when a different officer steps forward to frisk me. I hold my arms out willingly, allowing him to search me for weapons, but the only thing he finds is my phone, which he places on the grass a few metres away.

Thank goodness I didn't bring my knife with me inside the house. It's actually tucked into the pocket of my leather jacket, draped over the seat of Ringo's motorbike, so unless they insist on searching the bikes too, I should be okay.

I watch Ringo from the corner of my eye, sure he's doing the same with me, and once the weapons search is done, the officers move on to names and identification.

Mine is tucked into my phone case, but I don't want them to see it. I don't want them to know who I am, because the name they'll find is Abbey Delany, and I'm not her anymore.

"Got any ID on you?" the oldest officer asks me, and I shake my head, even as my eyes betray me and flick to my phone lying on the grass.

His eyes narrow, following my movement, and land on my phone.

Shit, Abbey! You just gave yourself away!

Bloody hell. I'll never survive the underworld Ringo lives in if I can so easily give myself away like that.

With another narrowed look in my direction, the officer moves to my phone, bending to pick it up, and pops the phone case free, finding exactly what I was desperate to keep hidden.

"Shit," I whisper.

"It's okay, Angel," Ringo rasps quietly, and I hold his gaze for a beat as the officer studies my identification.

He can see the worry in my eyes, but there isn't a trace of it in his. He's cool and unbothered, his lips kicking up beneath his beard.

God. This man really does have a way of making me feel better... Until his expression shifts, a faint frown tugging his brows as his gaze flicks down the line.

I snap my attention in the same direction and spot the officer holding my identification, showing it to a couple of the other officers, and then, one by one, their gazes shift to me.

My heart sinks to the pit of my gut as they step back a little, murmuring to each other as they pass my licence between them.

Shit. Shit. Shit. I already know where this is going.

The police have been looking for Abbey Delany. A minor. Said to have been in trouble.

Six weary glances sweep over each one of the Southern Sadists before landing back on me, and the oldest officer approaches, sweeping his hand towards himself.

"It's okay, Abbey. Just step over here. You're safe now."

Panic snaps my attention to Ringo for support to find him glaring.

"She's perfectly fucking safe with me."

"You! Shut the fuck up!" the officer barks, pointing sternly at my husband, before glancing back at me. "Abbey. Your family has been concerned."

I scoff, his comment doing nothing but lighting a raging inferno under my skin.

"You should take another look at my licence," I snap. "I'm not a child, Officer. I'm nineteen, and married to Cameron Musgrove." I jerk my thumb in Ringo's direction.

"We know this must be a fake licence," he counters. "You're only seventeen, Miss Delany. There was an Amber Alert."

I roll my eyes. "I *am* nineteen, and that Amber Alert was a false report made by an abusive mother. So unless you have a reason to arrest me, Officer, I'll take that back and be on my way."

The group of officers fall silent, frowns tugging at their brows, while further up the line where JD and Murf stand, I catch flashes of teeth behind beards and barely contained grins.

The screech of another car skidding to a stop draws everyone's attention, and a familiar face steps out of the patrol car.

"Sorry, we got held up at the hospital," Officer Zimora says to his fellow cops, as another officer unfolds himself from the vehicle and joins him. "We've got this. It's okay."

The officers all frown again, but the way they respond to Jason makes it clear he outranks them, and after a brief exchange they move further away to have a quiet discussion.

"You know," Smitty mutters from a few men up the line, leaning forward so I can see him. "I was a little worried for the pig's life for a second there. Doesn't he know what you can do with a helmet?"

I jerk back like he just slapped me, just as Ringo curses.

"Fuck's sake, Nate. Not the fucking time for jokes."

"Who the fuck is joking?" Smitty fires back. "Didn't you see that guy's skull she caved in with her—"

I'm about to fly off the handle at Smitty when Jason Zimora steps up to us, saving his life.

"Sorry about that," Jason apologises, which is when I notice the six officers leaving. "I'm spread thin today."

My brows shoot up.

I knew he was on their payroll or something. Maybe more on the Marx payroll, but is he *really* saving us? A known outlaw bikie club?

"How's your first week on the job?" JD asks, and when I glance his way, I see he's addressing the other officer that arrived with Jason.

"Interesting," the man replies. "Who knew Timber Valley had this much crime?"

JD chuckles. "And who knew you'd be working with us? Hope you've got the balls to do what's expected."

"Dallas is new but loyal to what we are working towards," Jason interjects, his gaze flicking to the other patrol cars as they begin to back away. "He knows who his real boss is."

As the patrol cars drive off, the line of Southern Sadists breaks apart, dispersing as if they've been given silent permission to leave.

"Anything from the hospital?" Ringo asks, his big hand sliding over the back of my hip, drawing me into his side, and just like that, my panic ebbs, and I melt into him.

"Unfortunately, no," Jason sighs, resting his hands on his hips. "But we did find a nearby house that caught the gunmen on their security cameras when they cut through his property."

Jason nods to the other officer, Dallas, who pulls out his phone and holds it up showing two guys frozen on the screen.

"They ditched their masks while cutting through the property, but their faces haven't come up in our facial recognition yet."

I lean in as Dallas angles the screen towards us, and even though it clearly shows their faces, I don't recognise them.

"Merc's," Ringo mutters, and Smitty nods in agreement.

"Looks like it," Smitty says with a shrug. "Seems like someone is willing to do whatever it takes to get the same information we're after."

I stiffen at his words, the image of Bobbi cradled in Elizabeth's arms flashing through my mind.

Why do they want her? This can't still be about the cult... can it?

"How does anyone else know?" I squeak, my emotions getting the better of me. "I know it sounds crazy, after everything he's done, but I believed Daniel when he said no one else knew."

Ringo and JD share a look before Ringo's gaze finds mine.

"I don't know, Angel, but it seems like someone does."

My heart slams into my ribs, and I stagger back a step, that familiar dread wrapping tight around my chest with the same fear that haunted me while I carried Bobbi inside me.

They're never going to stop.

It feels like they are always one step ahead of us, which means they might get to Bobbi before we do... and that thought alone is unbearable.

If those vile monsters get their hands on my little girl, I won't survive it.

I just won't.

"Angel." The deep gravel of Ringo's voice drags me out of my spiralling, and I glance up to find him holding up his phone to me.

Frowning, it takes me a moment to realise what I'm seeing on the screen.

"Is that?"

"Yep," Ringo gruffs. "Apparently she turned up ten minutes ago, stabbed two Marx men when they tried to stop her, and promised worse if anyone interrupts her."

My eyes widen as my gaze flicks from the screen, up to Ringo.

"She stabbed her own men?"

"She did. And apparently, not even her boyfriend can get close to her."

My mouth falls open in shock.

"Is she going to kill Daniel?"

"I don't know, Angel. But we need to get back there right fucking now."

7

RINGO

The moment I pull up my hog, Abbey shoves me out of her way, scurrying off my bike, her fingers frantically trying to get her helmet unfastened and off as she runs towards the barn.

"Angel! Stop!" I call, needing her to slow the fuck down before she gets herself stabbed too.

Of course, she doesn't fucking listen. She's got tunnel vision right now, and her goal is to get to Hush before she kills Daniel.

"Where are they?!" I hear her yell the moment she bursts into the barn, so I fucking toss my helmet carelessly aside and hurry in after her.

The picture Riggs sent me was of his men getting patched up, and in the background, that feisty little mute assassin was wielding that massive fucking knife of hers, coated in blood and pointed right at her pissy boyfriend, who looked like he was trying to stop her.

Her attack wasn't lethal. Nothing but flesh wounds, so I know Hush wasn't aiming to kill. Just ward off.

But, fuck, what's she up to?

The moment I breach the threshold of the barn, I catch Riggs' eye, and he points towards the back of the barn, where the passage leads to bunk rooms, and a fucking cell.

My boots pound loudly on the polished concrete floor, echoing up the hallway before I come skidding to a stop when Jared, Dee's boyfriend, steps out of a room, aiming a fucking gun at me.

"The fuck, man," I snarl, and he shakes his head, his menacing glare as hard as mine.

"I'll put this down only if you promise not to fucking touch, hurt or kill my girl."

I growl, trying to see over his shoulder into the room where Abbey must be.

"As long as she doesn't touch, hurt or kill *my* girl, then you won't have a fucking problem with me. Now get that thing out of my fucking face."

Jared's blue eyes flick between mine like he's trying to figure out if I'm lying, before giving me a single nod and lowering the gun.

Then I swing my fucking fist.

The smack against Jared's jaw is loud, the force knocking him on his arse, and I leap over him, charging into the room. I'm only a few steps in when I have to pull up fucking short as a knife sails past my head, nicking my fucking ear, before lodging into the plaster wall behind me.

"The fuck!" Abbey screeches, and before I can stop her, she leaps on her friend, Dee, sending them both to the floor. "You just threw a knife at my husband!"

"Oh, fuck." Jared hisses as he drags himself up off the floor, and we watch Abbey straddling her friend, throwing fists, and Dee blocking each blow with some sort of ninja fucking mojo.

Jared and I turn wide eyes on each other, both of us a little thrown off by Abbey's big fucking balls right now, and I can't help but feel a little satisfaction as my gaze tracks the red indent of my fist blooming on Jared's jawline.

"Stop being a smug fucking prick and help me separate those two," he snaps, and I chuckle as he shoulder bumps me on the way past, before following him into the fray.

Together, we risk flying fists and ninja skills to stop the catfight.

"Angel! Enough!" I snarl, hooking my hands around her middle and hauling her backwards, even as her arms and legs flail, trying to get back to her victim. "I'm okay," I reassure her. "If she wanted me dead, I would be."

"Fuck you, Dee! How dare you hurt him!" she screams, and as Dee shoves Jared off her, she simply grins our way and flips us both off.

"Would you stop it?" Jared snaps at her. "You're going to make things worse."

She rolls her eyes at him.

"Calm the fuck down now, Angel," I rasp roughly against her ear as she struggles. "Or I'll take you inside and lock you in my room."

She stills, stiffening in my hold.

"You wouldn't."

I chuckle, but there's zero fucking humour in it.

"I fucking would, and you know it."

She huffs, slumping into dead weight, so I place her feet on the ground and turn her to face me, engulfing either side of her face with my hands.

"I'm fine. I'm alive. It's barely a scratch."

Her eyes shift to my ear, more anger contorting her face when she sees the trickle of blood.

"Angel," I warn. "It's fine."

With another huff, she rolls her eyes, throwing her hands up in defeat, so I take the risk and release her, hoping like fuck she doesn't try to attack her friend again.

"Are you both done?" Jared snaps, glancing between the two girls.

"For now," Abbey responds, causing Dee's lips to kick up in a grin, and then, both girls start fucking laughing.

"Fucking hell," Jared mutters. "I need a drink."

He's fucking right about that. For a guy who doesn't drink much, I really want one myself.

Raking my hand through my hair, I turn to see Daniel, cowering in the corner, still alive and shackled, but covered in blood as he watches on through the eye that isn't completely swollen shut.

For a moment, it takes me a bit to figure out where most of the blood is coming from, and then I realise it's from the crotch of his pants.

I turn back to Dee. "Did you cut off his pin dick?"

She stops her silent laughing and smirks before mouthing, *'not yet.'*

"K-keep h-her a-away f-from m-me," Daniel stutters, his whole body trembling.

"She made it bleed though," Jared grunts, clearly not happy about his girl messing around with her victim's dick.

All of a sudden, Dee's hands start flying around, and then Jared's do too, and I realise they are arguing via sign language.

I don't know why she doesn't just talk. She obviously can, and knowing that pisses me off.

But perhaps that's the point.

"Righto, you two. Cut that shit out and fill me the fuck in. I don't have the patience for this bullshit."

Dee finishes her signing argument by flipping Jared off, which makes him fucking growl, and she smiles, approaching him and rising up on her toes to kiss his jaw. He growls again, under his breath this time, glaring down at her as she struts away and pulls her knife out of the wall.

"You two are weird," Abbey muses, which finally makes Jared fucking smirk.

"Shut up, Yeb." Jared addresses my wife. "Takes one to know one."

"God, stop. My nickname was the worst," Abbey sighs, rolling her eyes, and Jared snorts.

"I think Marcus will disagree with you, since his was Suc."

They both start laughing, and I recall Abbey telling me that as kids, she, Lexi, Jared and Marcus made up coded nicknames or some shit. They used the last three letters of their first names and turned them around, which is how Abbey got Yeb.

"So are you going to tell him, or am I?" Jared asks his batshit crazy girl, and she shrugs before pointing to him.

I'm kinda fucking relieved, since it will take less fucking effort if he tells us.

"Lexi filled us in on what this prick told you." He gestures to Daniel, who doesn't even bother looking up at us.

I bet he wishes he was dead... wait...

"How the fuck did Lexi know?" I snap, which is when I notice Abbey cringe.

"I may have updated her in a text message."

My brows shoot up. "I thought we agreed to keep this contained."

Her shoulders drop, even as her cheeks heat, and a look I'm becoming all too familiar with flashes across her face.

Anger.

"So what? I'm not allowed to tell my best friend?"

"Angel, I didn't say that. But maybe we should have discussed it first. I would have asked you to tell Lexi not to tell anyone."

"I did tell her not to tell anyone!" she screeches, which is when Dee steps in between us, holding a calming hand up, before flashing Abbey her phone screen, and once she's done reading, Dee flashes it to me."

'Technically, Lexi didn't tell me. I may have snatched her phone and read the messages.'

"The fuck, Dee!" Jared barks, and she simply shrugs, like it's no big deal.

"Why did you do that?" Abbey asks, and Dee taps out her response on her phone before showing us.

'I could tell by Lexi's expression that she was concerned. I won't apologise for snooping. Your baby girl is alive, and I'll do everything I can to help you find her. Even if that means chopping off Daniel's puny dick.'

"Look, she didn't find out any new information anyway," Jared interjects. "Usually the threat of dismemberment makes guys talk, but Daniel really believes no one else knows where Bobbi is."

'Which is why he still has his little prick.' Dee holds up her phone, and Abbey nods, sighing.

"Someone else knows, and I don't know how." She spins to face me. "Do you think someone has accessed my messages or something?"

I shrug. "Maybe."

I don't tell her that I don't actually think that's it at all, because I fucking can't. It's a real possibility. But worse is that I have a fucking strong feeling there's a mole inside my club. Or at least, inside the boundaries of my property.

Neither scenario sits fucking well with me, and now I can't even be sure my barn or house isn't fucking bugged.

We leave Daniel to sit in his bloody mess, which Jared tells Abbey is from Dee etching the word rapist into the thin skin of his cock with her fucking knife.

Don't get me wrong, the prick deserves it, but the fact that Dee can do that so easily has the hairs standing on the back of my neck.

Being okay with doing that sort of thing usually takes years of desensitising. Dee is Abbey's age. How the fuck can she do the things she does so easily like she's been doing it for years. She would have had to have been a young child when she started killing.

Fuck. I actually don't even want to think about what that means.

We rejoin my club brothers and some of the Marx crew that aren't currently on duty, sitting around the bar in my barn.

To my surprise, Alana has taken it upon herself to play bartender, which now fucking explains why there's a large congregation at the bar.

"Your sister is showing them her bar skills." JD chuckles as I approach, and Abbey grins, looking up at me curiously.

"I didn't know your sister works as a bartender."

"She doesn't," I grunt, shaking my head at my fucking sister.

Fuck, I need a holiday. Far, far fucking away from everyone... except my Angel. She'll have to come with me.

"Oh," Abbey giggles, eyeing the chaos my sister is creating by trying to do some sort of fancy cocktail shaking that's spilling everywhere.

I'm about to yell at my sister when I see Abbey's smile fall, her gaze dropping to the floor like she just remembered something bad.

Probably that her daughter is in danger.

Fuck.

Taking out my phone, I shoot Lewy a message asking him to meet me outside the barn, before I usher Abbey away from the brewing madness.

Stepping outside, the chill in the air is crisp as the sun sets, and Lewy hurries towards us, coming from the thick line of trees.

"Where did he come from?" Abbey asks, and I grin, linking my fingers with hers.

"I have him set up in a hidden hut. He's been working with Riggs and his team to improve our security."

"Oh." She nods, her eyes not leaving our tech guru, who rarely shows his face.

He's a skinny fucker. Not necessarily lanky, but just skinny, dark hair, dark eyes, dark beard. Matches his soul really. But, fuck, he's good at what he does, especially when he has the right tools at his disposal.

"Ringo, Abbey." He nods to both of us as he nears.

"Let's go for a walk," I grunt, leading him and Abbey to the path that weaves around my house. We walk silently, before stepping off the path towards the tree where I ate my wife out on our wedding day.

Fuck, that was a good way to celebrate.

"Where are we going?" Abbey asks as she nearly trips on a protruding tree root, but I manage to keep her upright.

"Just here, Angel. Where no one can hear us."

She snorts, and I imagine she's remembering how much noise she made when she came on my face and knew anyone close by would have heard her.

"Give me an update on Caroline Thatcher," I ask Lewy when we stop, and he nods, not even faltering at the odd location I led us to.

"Her parents are dead. No known siblings. She has an aunt who lives in New Zealand. She withdrew all her cash from her bank the same day…" Lewy stalls, his eyes flicking to Abbey before coming back to mine. "The day Bobbi was taken."

Abbey's hand tenses in mine at hearing her daughter's name, but I keep my eyes on my club brother as I speak.

"Unless she has connections like we do, then there's no way two women and a baby would've been able to breach the closed international borders and fly to New Zealand," I muse, kinda fucking thankful for the pandemic in this instance. "State borders have been erratic, but a lot fucking easier to cross. Look into her socials and known friends. It's likely someone else is helping her and Elizabeth to keep Bobbi hidden."

"Already on it." Lewy nods before flicking his gaze to my wife. "We'll find your daughter. I promise."

Lewy smiles then. A rarity, but it's still daylight enough out here for Abbey to see it, and I feel her hand relax in mine as she nods.

"Thank you."

Lewy leaves us then, disappearing into the scrub like he was never here, and I pull Abbey to my chest, looking down into those big dark eyes that still carry so much pain.

"He's right. We will find her." I press a kiss to her hair, and she sighs, locking her arms around me.

"Waiting is a killer."

"I know it is, Angel. Maybe you should find your sister," I rasp against her hair, not wanting to pull back. "I bet she'd love to spend some time with you."

She nods against my chest. "I should. She's probably been worrying about me all day."

"Probably," I agree, pulling back as she does to peer back down into her eyes, wondering if I should tell her the plan I'm weaving in my head.

"I could use a hot shower too." She cringes, grabbing at her ponytail. "I think I have a family of bugs caught in my hair."

I chuckle at that. "They are probably part of the family of bugs splattered against my visor."

"Ew." She screws up her nose, the action making her look all of her nineteen years before her expression turns mischievous. "Wanna come shower with me?"

"Stop trying to get me naked, woman," I growl, tugging her closer and nipping at her lips as she giggles.

When she pushes back from me, she walks backwards, swaying her hips all sexy like, and fuck, my cock is already responding to her sneaky, sassy ways.

"I'll make it worth your while," she coos, right before a squeak flies from her as she trips backwards over the same fucking tree root as before, landing butt first in the dirt.

"Careful." I hurry forward, but skid to a stop as she springs up, dusting her hands over her arse.

"I'm okay."

I laugh, watching her poke a cheeky tongue out as she spins and runs for the house.

Fuck, she should know better than to run. I will always chase her.

8

ABBEY

"**A**ngel."

The rumbled rasp of Ringo's voice drags me out of a deep sleep with a groan, but I can't find it in me to open my eyes.

"What?" I murmur sleepily.

"I need you to wake up, Angel." He gives me a little shake, and I groan again, too exhausted to obey.

My body still feels relaxed after he followed me up to our room late in the evening. He used his fingers on me... down there, while sucking on my boobs, and well... drinking. I was going to stop him, but it felt so good, and it was a relief to empty them. He reminded me afterwards that I need to keep up my milk production for Bobbi, and even though it's highly unconventional, I can't help but wonder if the universe hasn't been keeping me prepared for her return this whole time.

"Angel, come on. I need you to get up. We have to go."

My eyes spring open at his words, immediately locking with his as panic rushes through me.

"What's wrong? Are we being attacked?"

In the faint glow coming from the bathroom, I see a small smile kick up his lips.

"No, Angel. We aren't under attack." He reaches down, brushing some of my hair back off my face. "We're going for a little drive."

I frown. "A drive? Where?"

"Less talk and more getting out of bed, woman," he chuckles quietly, standing from the bed and moving across to his closet.

I sit up, rubbing my eyes as I try to piece together why the hell he's waking me in the dead of night to go for a drive.

Shit, what time *is* it?

Reaching over to the bedside table, I snatch up my phone to see that it's 3:18 AM.

"Why are we going for a drive at three in the morning?" I groan as Ringo comes out of the wardrobe, tossing a pair of jeans and hoodie on the bed.

"You'll find out soon enough," he offers vaguely, before retrieving my chucks.

I look over the clothes, slipping out of bed, even more confused.

These aren't the type of clothes I would wear on the back of his motorcycle, which means we must be going in a car.

I want to keep pestering him to tell me where we are going, but I know him well enough to know he would have told me already if he was going to. So, I do what he asked, and get changed.

Once I'm dressed, he leads me quietly through the house, our footsteps light so we don't wake anyone. I half expect to find JD and Jols waiting for us, but we don't come across them at all. Instead, we slip out the back door and follow the path in silence, the dark closing around us until the shadowed silhouette of someone up ahead has me tensing.

"It's okay, Angel. It's just Riggs," Ringo whispers, urging me to continue up the path with him, and for a moment, I wonder if the house is in danger. But no... he'd never leave his mum behind. Or his sisters. And I know he'd never leave Tahli behind, either.

As confused as I am, I stay quiet as we approach Riggs, who simply gives us a nod and leads us deeper into the bushland surrounding Ringo's house.

The longer we are out here in the dark, the easier it is to see, my eyes adjusting to the moonlit night well enough that I can make out the path we are walking on.

We follow it up the large hill, onto the ridge, and my heart aches as memories take me back to when I walked this same path with my shadow tailing me while I missed Ringo desperately.

Mule. Even though we didn't say much to each other, it was the unspoken communication that we connected with.

I really knew nothing about him other than he took his job seriously, but I could tell he had a kind heart. He didn't deserve to die protecting me. I feel the weight of that every day. I feel the weight of all the deaths that have happened because of me.

I'm hardly worth it, but I won't let their deaths be for nothing.

One day, when this is all over, I'll tell Bobbi all about the brave men that fought to protect her. They will live on in stories. I'll make sure of it.

The idea that I'll get that chance to share that with my daughter has my heart flipping in my chest. I want that so bad… but also, I'm terrified of it as well.

The demons in my head keep reminding me that maybe this has all happened for a reason. Maybe I was never meant to be Bobbi's mum. Maybe, I'm not good enough to be the one to raise her.

"Nearly there." Ringo's whisper drags me out of my thoughts, and I blink up at him as we step through the trees into another clearing, encased in tall wire fencing.

I simply nod, spotting the shadow of a car up ahead on the other side of the fence.

This all seems very… secretive.

Riggs leads us through a gate in the fence I didn't even know was there, and we slip into the car quickly. Me and Ringo in the back, and Riggs up front in the driver's seat.

Usually there are more of his men, but right now, it's just the three of us, and that alone has a thousand questions wanting to escape my lips.

"What's going on?" I can't help but ask after clipping my seatbelt in place.

"We are going to meet someone, Angel. But it's top secret." Ringo smirks down at me, and I frown, because not one part of what he said sounded playful.

Something is wrong.

It appears that Riggs already has his instructions, remaining silent as he drives. To where, I have no idea at first. That is until I begin to recognise the familiar path.

We're heading back towards Timber Valley.

I should be tired given the time of day... or night... or morning... whatever it is. But I'm too wired, curious, and concerned.

Every time I glance up at Ringo, he simply smiles down at me, sometimes pressing his lips to my hair, sometimes shooting me a wink.

I'm completely at a loss for what's happening, so I sit patiently and wait, only perking up again when we turn off towards Redfield, not Fox Pines.

We were only here just hours ago, at Caroline Thatcher's house, and before that, the last time I was at Redfield, we caused absolute carnage at the grocery store, saving Tahli from my mum and sister.

I've been to Redfield more times lately than I have my entire life growing up in Timber Valley, and I don't carry one fond memory of this place.

We drive through the quiet streets, passing through the housing estates before reaching the town centre, which is like a ghost town this time of night.

When the car slows, I glance out the window to see red flashing lights illuminating a sign that says, The Red Room.

My brows hitch as I turn back to Ringo.

"You're taking me to a strip club? Is this your idea of a date?"

His lips twitch, even as a low chuckle rumbles from the front seat as Riggs flicks the indicator on, turning us into the parking lot.

"Not a date, Angel. But I'll be sure to avoid bringing you here when I do take you on one."

My cheeks heat with embarrassment, but also a little excitement, because I've never been on a proper date before. And Ringo and I... well, we skipped everything and just jumped into marriage. A marriage of convenience, but still, now I can't imagine *not* being married to this man.

Once the car is parked, we all get out, the night air chilly as Ringo weaves his arm around my waist, tugging me into his side as we approach the only strip club in the Timber Valley region.

When we step inside, the music and the atmosphere immediately take me back to Leather and Lace. My sanctuary for a short time.

I miss the girls there. Ariel. Shadi. Martini and Daffney. They were so beautiful and so caring. They didn't have to take me in like they did, but that's just the type of women they are. I was so lucky to stumble across them. It's like the universe knew I needed them at that time.

"You know, nothing good happens after midnight."

The familiar voice comes from behind the bar, and I look over to see Griffin Marx stepping out from behind it.

"Especially in a place like this." Ringo chuckles, and Griffin's lips spread wide as he approaches.

"I have private rooms if you and your girl want some alone time. Plenty of tools and toys to explore."

My cheeks flush hot, and I dart my eyes to the floor as both men chuckle.

God, did Riggs hear that too?

"As tempting as that is, we have more pressing matters." Ringo's voice turns serious, cutting straight through the chitchat to get down to business. "Is everyone here?"

"They are. Follow me." Griffin nods, his smile dropping and shit... what is happening?

I think I preferred him being playful and suggestive.

"Ringo." I hiss quietly as we follow Griffin through the pretty much deserted showroom and past a black curtain, leading us to a passage. "What's going on?"

Ringo glances down at me, and just winks again, and I want to stomp my foot and demand someone tell me what the hell is happening, but again, I remind myself that Ringo is doing this for a reason.

I just don't know what that reason is.

We pass a series of rooms, all with the doors open, and my heart races at the things I see.

Whips. Chains. Paddles. Benches. Dildos. Other contraptions that I have no idea about.

Would Ringo really take me into one of those rooms? He said it was tempting. Is he into that stuff? Would he really want to chain me up? Whip me?

Panic rises quickly in my chest, and I stumble over my own feet, nearly tripping both of us.

"Shit, Angel. You okay?" Ringo rights us quickly before I feel his analysing eyes roaming my face. "Angel."

I shake my head, not wanting to have this conversation here, in this hallway, with these people around us, so I blow out a breath and shake him off.

"I'm fine."

He frowns, knowing I'm talking shit, but doesn't question me further as I keep moving forward, following Griffin to wherever it is he's leading us.

I ignore my surroundings for the rest of the short walk, my gaze zeroed in on the back of Griffin's dark head of hair until we step into a room with a large conference table in the middle, and I stop in my tracks.

Sitting around the table are Dee, Jared, Devon Marx, and the two sisters, Bec and Amanda Angel.

"We're clear," Riggs says from behind me after closing the door, and all eyes shift to me from the table.

"Will someone tell me what the hell is going on?" I snap, throwing my hands up in frustration.

"You didn't tell her?" Bec glares over my shoulder at Ringo, who quickly moves to my side and re-links our fingers.

"No. It was too risky. Couldn't be sure we weren't being watched or listened to."

What?

Watched?

Listened to?

"Even inside the Marx car?" Amanda asks from where she's sitting across the other side of the table, a warm mug of coffee in her hands.

"I can't be sure the vehicles haven't been compromised."

Amanda and Bec frown at that, and I huff, snatching my hand from Ringo's grip.

"Still don't know what's happening," I remind him, and his face softens.

"We're here to figure out a way to find Bobbi."

I blink. And then blink again.

"I thought we were already doing that."

What the hell am I missing?

"Technically yes." Ringo gestures to a chair at the table, and I absentmindedly move to it and sit my arse down. "But you and I are on the same page about Daniel. I believe he didn't tell anyone about his mum and Bobbi. He would never risk his mum's life. So it begs the question... how did someone obtain that information and beat us to the hospital?"

"Someone must have overheard Daniel at the airstrip." I frown, trying to think back to everything that happened that day. All the chaos. Who was around?

"Possibly." Ringo takes the seat next to mine. "But where was the other place he said the words out loud?"

I feel like I'm being quizzed, but as I think over the answer, I realise he's helping me to put the pieces together.

"At your place... the barn."

"Exactly." Ringo nods, not looking happy about that at all.

"But your men were there," I point out, and he nods.

"Yes, they were."

"And the Marx guys." I gesture my head towards Griffin and Devon, and Ringo nods.

"Yep."

"So what... are you saying one of them is a mole?"

I watch as Ringo's lips thin, something that's hard to see past his beard, but from my position, I see it.

"Possibly," is all he says, and I rest back in the chair, stunned, my eyes flicking to the timber top of the table as I search my brain for another reason.

"In that case, it could be Riggs," I point out, my eyes quickly finding the head of Marx security also sitting at the table with us.

"It could be," Ringo admits.

I balk at that, wondering why Riggs is sitting at the table with us if that's the case.

"So what you're saying is, we can't trust *anyone*?"

My tone is snarkier than Ringo deserves, but I'm feeling too fed up to rein in my anger right now.

When is this ever going to end?

A small whiteboard slides across the table in front of me, and I read the words Dee has written.

You can trust us, and my aunties. Angel Org does this stuff all the time. Find women and children that are being abused or wronged, and save them.

"So you save people?" I snap, glaring up at the two women Dee wants me to trust. "You take them from their bad situations, but then what happens to them?"

"That depends on the circumstances," Bec answers. "Some go into the Archer Network and are placed in new homes. Some we help right down to the finest details of eliminating the threats against them."

"And some come to me." Devon speaks then, gaining my attention, and I glare at the man that tried to kidnap me in the alley outside Leather and Lace.

"So you kidnap people to save them?" I hiss, and a slow, sinister smirk tugs at his lips.

"Sometimes."

My brows shoot up because I wasn't being serious, but everything in the way he responded tells me he *is* being serious.

When my gaze flicks to Ringo, I see him smirking too, reminding me that kidnapping me to save me was exactly what he did.

God... these men.

"Why do you want to help me?" I ask, dragging my gaze back to Devon as a shiver ripples up my spine.

I swear, if the Devil could take human form, it would be in that man.

"Unfortunately, we weren't in a position to help when you first went into Ringo's care." Amanda speaks this time, placing her cup of coffee on the table. "Hush has made sure we are aware daily that we fucked up. And she's right. We should have thrown more money at the politicians or border cops and whisked you across the other side of the country. Our resources were stretched thin during the lockdowns, but we want to help, and this has gone on for too long already. It's time to reunite you and your little girl, so you both can start living your lives together."

A lump forms in the back of my throat, because I want that, but also, I'm terrified of it as well.

What if I'm a bad mother?

"If there *is* a mole in the Marx crew or the Southern Sadists," Bec continues for her sister. "Then we are your best bet. We can make things happen in the background that the others won't know about."

When I glance next to me where Dee is sitting, she offers me a slight smile and nods in reassurance. I trust her, I really do, but I don't trust *everyone* in this room.

My gaze shifts up the table to Riggs. He has done nothing to make me question his trust. Hell, he's been watching over my sister and I've trusted him completely. But now... I'm questioning everything. Everyone.

Like, could the mole be one of Ringo's sisters? Millie tolerates me, but that's about it. Or what about Ringo's team? JD. Murf. Trunk. Stocky.

What about Mex and Vender? There are so many possibilities.

"So what do we do? Elizabeth isn't meant to call for two more days, but by then, it might be too late." I all but panic, and Ringo's warm hand slides onto my thigh, giving my leg a gentle squeeze of support.

"We'll get our hackers and cyber wiz to work day and night until they locate Elizabeth Stone," Griffin declares. "We already have them working on accessing the data for the last call between Daniel and his mum. We will find them, Abbey. We promise."

"I need you to promise me something else," I add, and Griffin nods, like he's willing to do whatever it takes. "If one of your men is the mole," my eyes flick to Riggs before returning to Griffin, "you *will* kill them yourself, in front of me, so I know they have been dealt with."

Devon chuckles next to his cousin. "I like her."

"Consider it done, Abbey. We don't tolerate snakes in our ranks." Griffin nods.

"Would you feel more comfortable if I'm reassigned?" Riggs speaks up, and I glance at Ringo for assistance, but he just shrugs.

"It's up to you, Angel."

Licking my lips, I stand from my chair, slowly moving to the end of the table where Riggs is sitting.

He shifts in his chair, watching me, and I study his face for any sign of betrayal. I don't see anything amiss, but that doesn't mean he's not hiding something. I've been gullible before, and people lie. Some too well.

I don't quite know what to do here. Do I just take everyone's word for it? Do I risk the safety of Bobbi by accepting that Riggs isn't considered a threat by anyone else?

I've trusted him with Tahli. Trusted that he would keep her safe. And he has. But Tahli isn't the target. Bobbi is.

I'm getting paranoid. I know that. But shit. I have to do everything I can to protect my little girl, so if I step over the line, it's only because there's this wildness inside me that would do just about anything to protect her.

My gaze drops down the front of Riggs' black vest. It's some sort of combat vest, with pockets and whatnot. It's padded, so it's hard to tell if he's hiding anything underneath.

There could be more weapons or... a camera or tracker...

"Strip," I rush out without another thought, and a moment later, Ringo's chair scrapes against the floor as he stands abruptly.

I'm about to throw my wife over my fucking shoulder when she spins on me, holding up a stern fucking finger.

"Don't."

"The fuck are you doing, woman?" I snap, and a slow smirk tugs at her pink lips.

"I didn't think you would be so insecure." She nods her head back towards Riggs, and I ignore Griffin's and Devon's fucking cackles at my fucking expense.

"You want to see cock, darlin'? You only have to ask," I growl, and her brows shoot up as her cheeks flush pink.

"I'm trying to see if he's hiding anything under his vest." She grits between clenched teeth, her eyes turning to murderous slits as she glares at me.

"Do as she asked," Griffin orders, still trying to stop fucking laughing at me. "Show us all what you're packing."

"Not a problem." Riggs stands from his chair, and as my wife turns to watch the fucking strip show, I drag her back against me, wrapping my arm across her chest protectively.

Okay, so probably more possessively, but fuck, I'm only fucking human.

Bec and Amanda giggle quietly together as they watch on, and Hush doesn't even bother watching the show, too busy spinning her fucking massive knife in her hand like it's a fucking fidget spinner.

Like me, Jared looks annoyed, his eyes trained on his girl, rather than the strip show happening right in front of my wife.

"I don't have anything to hide," Riggs declares as his heavily padded tactical vest hits the floor, leaving him standing in a black long sleeve Henley. "I am loyal to the Marx family, and I would *never* put a child in danger."

Reaching behind his neck, he pulls off his shirt, revealing his fucking eight pack and the coiled brawn of his arms.

Abbey stiffens against me, while two slow whistles come from the Angel sisters, who seem to be enjoying this show the fucking most.

Holding his arms out, Riggs does a slow turn, showing the room his entire fucking physique. It's hard to believe this man is in his forties.

"As you can see, I'm not wearing a wire." When he faces us again, his hands shift to the buckle of his belt. "You need to see more?"

"No," Abbey rushes out, right as the Angel sisters declare, "Yes," in unison.

The corner of his lips kick up at the playful sisters' eagerness, but he's a smart man. He doesn't take his eyes off Abbey, nodding at her and bending to pick up his shirt off the floor.

"My name is Seth Riggs," he starts talking casually as he re-dresses, "I grew up with Conrad Marx, the second eldest of Ewan's children. Ewan made me one of his soldiers when I was fourteen, and by the time I was twenty-nine, I became Captain."

As soon as his shirt is back on, covering all that fucking skin, I relax a little, and so does Abbey.

Did she like what she saw?

Fuck that. I'll remind her with my tongue and cock exactly what she's got, so she doesn't fucking think about him shirtless again.

"While I understand that you don't truly know me, or even the Marx family," Riggs continues, slipping his vest back on. "I hope you will allow me the opportunity to prove that my men and I will do what it takes to get your little girl back safely."

In my arms, Abbey slowly nods, her dainty fingers coming up to grip my arm wrapped across her chest for support.

"I'm sorry. I'm just... paranoid, I guess."

"Fuck that," Jared hisses from his chair. "You have a right to be concerned, Abbey. Someone is snitching."

Everyone in the room nods at that, and Abbey turns in my arms, those big caramel eyes locking with mine.

"Who could it be?" she asks, her voice laced with concern.

"I don't know, Angel. But from here on out, everyone is a suspect."

Her brows shoot up. "Even JD? Jols?"

I nod. "Yep."

"Your ma? Your sisters?"

I shake my head. "I highly doubt it's them. In fact, I'd be willing to bet my life on that."

"Are you prepared for the fact it could be one of your club brothers?" Devon asks from his lazy slouch in his chair, and I turn my attention to the dark-haired man that most know as the Devil.

Devon Marx is one man you don't want coming for you in the dead of night.

"I'm prepared that it could be anyone." I nod, and Griffin bobs his head beside his cousin.

"I'm prepared it could be one of my men too," he states, his jaw ticking. "Even if we go right back to the day the warehouses were messed with. The common denominator here is Marx men and Southern Sadists. Too much has happened for it to just be a coincidence."

Griff is fucking right, and it sits like a lead fucking weight in my gut that one or more of my men may have had a hand in it. Which is exactly why we are here. Why I'm not involving my club and going outside it once again to figure out what the fuck is going on.

Abbey and I return to our seats, and for the next couple of hours we discuss possible moles and scenarios, and how the fuck we can weed out the snitch.

By the time we are done, Abbey is yawning, exhausted from only getting a couple of hours sleep before I woke her, so we finish up, and I lead her back out to the car, where she says a quick goodbye to her friends, and slides sleepily inside.

"Do you want me to return with you?" Riggs asks once I close Abbey in, and I take in the guy who has done nothing but protect us because that's what he's been ordered to do.

"Yes. I trust you. And she does, too." I gesture to the back seat, and Riggs nods.

"I'll do what was discussed tonight. Everyone is a suspect from now on. Even my closest men."

Sighing, I clap my hand on his shoulder. "Me too. It guts me to think my brothers might have been in on this shit from the beginning. Whoever it is will wish they were never fucking born by the end of this."

Riggs grunts in agreement, and I step back, rounding the car as Riggs slips into the driver's seat.

Abbey nuzzles into my neck as we drive through the quiet streets of Redfield, and as soon as Riggs puts the radio on, the cabin filling with the soft hum of music, my Angel shifts to press her lips to my ear.

"The things that were in those private rooms," Abbey whispers against my ear, "have you used things like that before?"

I smirk into the darkness, my gaze flicking to Riggs in the front, his concentration focused on the road.

"Some of them," I respond in a low, quiet voice.

"The cuffs and chains, or whatever they were?" Her breath warms my ear as she whispers against it.

"Yes, Angel."

"Do you... like that?" she breathes, and I wish I could shift back and see her face properly. I bet there's an embarrassed blush tinting her cheeks.

"I enjoyed it at the time," I admit honestly, and she stiffens a little.

I don't know if it's because my admission involved the use of BDSM instruments, or if she's remembering times similar things were used against her.

"Do you… want to do that to me?"

There's a slight squeak in her quiet whisper that has my lips lifting at the reminder of her inexperience. She doesn't sound mortified at the idea of it, so I have to assume she's just innocently curious.

Shifting closer, I press my lips to her ear this time.

"Maybe one day, when all of this is over, we can explore some of the instruments used in BDSM. Once you've had time to heal, Angel. You've endured so much. We have plenty of time to try things. See what you like and don't like, together."

She brushes her cheek against mine like a cat bunting, showing affection, and I realise that perhaps the idea of BDSM with me is more of a turn on for her than even *she* was expecting.

"I don't want you to go without," she murmurs against my ear before giving it a nip, confirming that, yeah, she fucking likes the idea of exploring more with me.

Just the thought has my cock rising in my pants.

"Angel," I growl quietly, nipping her ear too. "Your trust is the biggest turn on I've ever experienced," I admit, running my hand up her thigh, gripping the denim as I fight for control. "All I need is *you*. Doesn't matter how. I don't need a BDSM scene with you. I just need your trust. To know you are giving yourself to me. That gets me harder than any bondage session will."

A quiet whimper escapes her, and as my hand travels higher, she parts her legs for me.

"You like me submissive though, right?" she breathes, and it catches the moment I brush my thumb over the seam of her jeans, right over her sweet cunt.

"I do love your submissive side, Angel," I rasp, my eyes flicking to see if Riggs is watching, but his eyes are still cast forward as he drives. "But it doesn't always have to be like that. I also really fucking like it when you're a brat."

She giggles quietly, spreading her legs a little wider again.

"If I said I wanted to tie *you* up," she whispers, rubbing her face against mine again like she enjoys the roughness of my beard. "Would you let me?"

My cock jerks at the thought, yet I still shift uncomfortably, not entirely sure I'd be into it, but also knowing I'd let her if that's what would make her happy.

"If that's what you want, Angel. Then yes."

She draws back in surprise at my response, her eyes trying to study my face in the dark without much success.

"Really?" she asks, and I nod, brushing my thumb over that teasing seam again.

"Really."

Her breath hitches, and those plump lips part before she leans in again to speak quietly into my ear.

"It does sound kind of hot having you tied up, unable to move, and at my mercy." She moans faintly as she nips my ear again, and, fuuuuck me, my cock grows uncomfortably hard. Like a stone fucking rod.

"Angel," I hiss into her hair, pressing my thumb harder against the seam of her jeans. "Don't do that or I'll fuck you right here."

She moans, a little too loudly, and my eyes flick to the rearview mirror in time to see Riggs looking away.

Fuck.

I'm about to pull back, but then he turns the music up louder, so loud I know he won't be able to hear.

I'll probably owe him for this, but fuck, when my wife is needy, I *need* to make her feel good.

"Cam," she whimpers as I flatten my palm against her mound, and I trail kisses across her cheek until my lips seal over hers.

I feel the vibration of her next moan as we kiss, our tongues clashing in a level of desperation that we can't give in to right now, because stripping her bare and fucking her raw isn't something I intend on doing in the back seat of a moving car with a fucking audience.

Abbey grinds against my hand in desperation, so I make quick work of flicking open the button and tugging the zipper down, before sliding my hand into the tight space between the denim and her wet cunt, teasing her clit for a few long beats before I give her exactly what she wants.

My fingers.

I know her body enough now to know what works quickly, and aside from sucking on her heavy tits and drawing the warm milk out, the other thing that gets her over the line fast and hard, is some good old-fashioned g-spot stimulation.

Sliding my fingers through her wet folds, I find her entrance as she parts her legs further, and I slip my digits in.

Her moan is loud, and it's possible Riggs might have heard it, but she's too far gone to care, and fuck, so am I.

My one goal in life, in *this* very fucking moment, is to make my woman soak my fingers and come around them, so I focus on that, hooking them inside her and massaging the sensitive spot as she grinds against me, chasing her release.

When she stops kissing me, I know she's close, too lost in her need to come, so I trail kisses back to her ear, nipping on it as I give her the other thing that seems to work like a charm.

Dirty talk.

"Fuck, Angel. Your cunt is so wet for me. Do my fingers feel good?"

"Yes," she pants, again too loudly, but I'm not willing to draw attention to that and risk her stopping right now.

"Imagine if we were in one of those playrooms right now," I rasp. "Would you let me tie you up and spread you wide?"

"Yes," she breathes, grinding faster.

"Would you let me do whatever I wanted with this sexy little body?"

"Yes!" she yells this time, her inner walls starting to tense.

"Would you let people watch the way I pleasure you? Watch how your needy cunt can't get enough of me? Of my fingers?" I curl them faster. "Of my tongue." I flick my thumb over her clit. "Of my cock stretching this tight little hole?"

She spasms then, her climax slamming into her as ripple after ripple tears through her, the muscles of her cunt kneading my fingers like they would my cock, desperate for my cum.

I barely notice the hard ridge of my cock straining against my jeans, my focus purely on my wife, as her cries die down, and her body goes from tense to relaxed as her orgasm recedes.

"Cam," she breathes, and this time, I only just hear it over the music.

"Angel." I smile as she blinks her eyes open.

"There's no way Riggs didn't just hear that, hey?"

I chuckle at the resounding tone in her question, like she's already come to terms with that fact.

"Probably," I admit, and I can just see the lazy cringe that flickers across her face.

"Whoops."

Grinning, I ease my fingers out of her, bringing them up between us, and just as I'm about to draw them into my mouth, she leans in too, stealing one for herself.

I groan at the feel of her tongue gliding up my finger, and I instantly picture my cock instead of my finger, causing the fucker to jerk with yearning in my pants.

Since I can't fucking do anything about it right now, I slide my other finger into my mouth, tasting her sweetness as I suck it off, and my Angel does the same with my other finger.

It's fucking hot, both of us sucking on my digits, practically kissing each other at the same time, and I almost regret starting this here in the back of the fucking car while we have eyes and ears nearby.

Pulling my fingers free, I roughly grip her chin, holding her in place as I catch my fucking breath.

"I think you liked the idea of Riggs hearing us, Angel."

Panting too, she jerks her head out of my grasp and flops back against the seat.

"It's what you do to me," she admits. "God, you'll have me fucking you at those club orgies before I know it."

I throw my head back laughing and watch as she zips up her fly.

"Angel, if you fuck me in the throes of an orgy, it will be all your doing, not mine."

She tuts, although I see it more than hear it from the glow of the dashboard filtering in from the front seat.

I'm about to lean in for another kiss when she stills, a frown tugging at her brows, and she reaches behind her, pulling out her phone.

The moment her eyes scan the screen, they widen, and flick back to me.

"I just got a message," she says loudly, over the music, and before I can ask who from, she turns the screen for me to see a number I don't recognise, but the first line of the text tells me all I need to know.

Abigail, this is your mother...

10

ABBEY

Reading over the message my mum sent has me reeling.

> **Abigail, this is your mother. You really shouldn't leave your sister alone to go traipsing all over the countryside with your kidnapper. Are you sure you can trust those animals to keep their hands off her?**

What the hell... She knows we aren't at Ringo's?

But how?

It's just past six in the morning, and we are approaching the location we snuck off from hours earlier, so I wait until we stop, and fly out of the car, hitting call on the number.

"Abbey, wait!" Ringo barks, but I ignore him, hurrying across the grass to the gate in the fence we went through earlier, only to find it locked, but the moment the call connects, I stop walking anyway.

"I was expecting an abusive text, but a phone call is much better," my mother snaps through the phone, and I grit my teeth, clenching them so hard I fear they will shatter.

"Tahli is none of your concern!" I snarl, and my mother scoffs.

"On the contrary. She is. You are. And so is little Bobbi."

I stiffen, my feet suddenly feeling like lead.

"Bobbi is dead," I snap, and my mother laughs, although there's very little humour in it.

"Nice try, Abigail, but I know she's alive. A little birdy told me so."

My knees practically give way at those words, and as I start to tumble, Ringo catches me, once again always there when I need him.

"I don't know what you're talking about," I practically whisper as Ringo carries me in his arms, cradled to his chest.

"Of course you do. Cut the BS," she snaps, her tone impatient. "We know Bobbi is alive and well, and soon enough, I will have my granddaughter in my arms, and there's nothing you can do about it."

"Stay the fuck away from her!" I yell into the phone, only for her to start laughing at me.

"Unlikely, but I suppose we could come to an agreement." She sighs, and I want to reach through the phone and gouge her eyeballs from her head. "Like, give Tahli back to me and I'll consider walking away from your bastard child."

"What?! No way! Why would you think I'd ever let either of them go to you? You're fucking crazy!"

"It's Tahli *or* Bobbi. One or the other," she snaps, and I get a little satisfaction knowing I'm annoying her.

"Or what?" I snap back as Ringo walks over the top of the ridge, carrying me down the path into the thick bushland.

"Or there will be consequences. Just be thankful I'm giving you a choice, but bear in mind, this offer won't be on the table for long. After that, you can say goodbye to both your sister and your daughter."

I open my mouth to speak, but I'm too shocked to string two bloody words together.

"You see, I know you're finally understanding me now," she says smugly. "I'm giving you options. Now, the obvious choice would be to hand over Tahli so you can keep your daughter, but the thing is, do you really think you're fit to be a mother? You've killed people, Abigail."

I stiffen, and flashes of faces rush through my mind. Some I knew. Some I didn't. But all are covered in blood.

"You're a monster," I choke out, saying it to my mother but feeling like it's really meant for me.

"Me?" she scoffs. "I'm not the one who killed your father, Abigail. *You* did that, didn't you? So who's the real monster here?"

My dad's face jolts into the forefront of my mind then. The tears that flowed from his eyes as he revealed the ugly truth about our family. How I wanted him dead for letting awful things happen to me. And how I left a gun so he could do it himself.

I may not have pulled the trigger, but I was definitely the one who killed my dad.

Monster!

"Shut up!" I scream, although I don't know if it's to my mum or myself.

Ringo reaches for the phone, so I flail in his hold, stumbling from his grip to dart away so he can't take it from me.

"I HATE YOU!" I scream into the phone, and my mother simply laughs.

"So dramatic, Abigail," she tuts. "Your daughter, or your sister. You decide. The clock is ticking."

The call ends then, the line beeping a couple of times before going dead, and I stare at it in my grip, blurred by the tears I didn't realise were falling.

"Ringo! There you are!" JD's panicked voice cuts through my growing meltdown, and I glance up to see JD, Vender and Mex rushing up the path.

"What is it?" Ringo barks, and JD skids to a stop before us, his eyes darting from Ringo to me.

"It's Tahli. She's gone."

I'm running the next second, my heart thrashing wildly in my chest as I navigate the path in the dark, my phone still clutched tightly in my grip.

Was my mother teasing me? Does she already have Tahli? Have I been set up tonight? Whisked away for a secret meeting while really the mole was kidnapping my little sister?

"Tahli!" I scream as the house comes into view, the lights already on inside, like the whole house has been awake and searching for her. "Tahli!"

"Abbey!" Jols comes crashing through the back door. "I've looked everywhere. I can't find her."

I barely look at Jols, too scared all I'll see is a traitor, so I bolt past her, bursting inside and charging for Tahli's room.

My name gets called by multiple people, but I ignore all of them, needing to see for myself that my sister is really gone.

She'd chosen a room downstairs, right near Alana's, and my feet slide on the floor as I reach it, gripping the doorjamb, and swinging myself inside to see... nothing.

Just her empty bed. Her sheets crumpled and slept in. Her clothes still hanging messily from the drawers. A half-drunk glass of water on the white bedside table.

"Tahli!" I call again, diving to the floor to look under the bed, only there's nothing there either.

Fisting my fingers in my hair, I stand and spin on the spot, my mind racing at where she could be, because she has to be here, right? She's not actually gone... right?

"Angel."

The deep rasp of Ringo's voice doesn't calm me the way it normally does. Instead, I see the man who woke me at three in the morning and convinced me to go somewhere with him, taking the one man with us who was charged to watch over my sister.

"No." I shake my head, backing up. "She's here. She has to be."

"They've looked everywhere. Lewy is checking the security feed now."

I still shake my head.

"No, she's here. It couldn't have been that easy for my mum to get to her." I stab an accusing finger at my husband. "You were the one who took me away."

"You know why I took you," he growls, his face turning red with anger, and it hurts, right in the centre of my chest, because part of me wants to accuse him of having something to do with this, but the other part of me will literally die if the one person I thought I could trust has betrayed me.

I can't speak. Tears fall, and a war wages in my mind. I don't know what's right or wrong. Real or fake. I don't know if I can trust my own thoughts right now.

"Abs, you know me. Better than anyone. I know you know I would never ever do anything to hurt you, your sister, or Bobbi. You know I love you. You know I love your sister. And you know I already love Bobbi like she is my own. Tell me you know that."

There's pain in his voice. Lashing pain that I know has the ability to break him completely, and that's the very thing that breaks through my panic, reminding me of my reality.

A loud sob escapes me, and I slap my hand over my mouth, shaking my head.

"I'm sorry."

His shoulders drop in relief, and in two long strides he reaches me and pulls me into his arms.

"It's okay, Angel. We both don't know who to trust right now." He pulls back, hooking his finger under my chin and lifting my head until our eyes meet. "But we have to trust each other. We'll never get through this if we don't have that."

I nod, fisting his shirt. "I love you. I'm sorry," I mutter.

"You don't need to be sorry." He presses his lips to my forehead. "Come on. Let's search for your sister while Lewy does his thing."

I nod, giving him a long squeeze before we emerge from Tahli's room and go in search of my little sister.

We spend ten minutes searching the lower floors, and then make our way upstairs.

In Ringo's room, the lights are on, obviously left that way from others searching, and I notice through the windows that the sun is slowly rising, lighting the sky beyond.

There aren't many places to hide up here, so I check under the bed while Ringo checks the bathroom, and then I step into the wardrobe, the light already on.

"Tahli?"

"Abbey!"

The screech of my name fills the small space, and a moment later, my little sister bursts through the hanging dresses and coats, throwing herself into my arms.

"Oh my God!" I cry with an umph as we collide, and I hold on to her so tightly as Ringo stares in at us from the open doorway.

"We found her!" he calls, and I can hear excited and relieved yelling beyond, but keep my focus on my little sister.

"Chook, what the hell?" I snap, shoving back from her to take her in.

Her blonde hair is a mess, and she's still in her PJs, clutching something in her hand.

"Don't what the hell me!" she yells right back. "I woke up, and my lamp was on, and I don't remember leaving it on, but then there was this note, and I read it, and I panicked, and I came up here but you were gone." She shoves me. Hard. And I stumble backwards, nearly tripping over Ringo's riding boots. "You were GONE!"

"Chook, I..."

"Riggs wasn't here either! I went over to the barn looking for him, and he wasn't there. No one was around. No one even saw me. I could have walked right down the road and I don't think they would have even noticed."

My eyes flick to Ringo. "Where was everyone?"

"I don't know, but perimeter security is still tight."

"Except for where we left," I point out, and Ringo nods.

"There were a couple of Marx men that knew we had left. That's why we got off the property without a hitch."

"Where did you go?" Tahli cries, still distraught, and then I remember what she said.

She woke up. Her lamp was on. And there was a note.

My eyes flick down to her hand. "Is that the note?"

Tahli nods, holding it out to me.

Taking it, I unravel it from its crumpled ball form, smoothing it out as I start reading, and I swear, the blood in my veins turns to ice.

Tahli.

Those bad people have kidnapped you.

Don't let them get in your head.

Mummy will have you back safe and sound soon.

Your grandfather is really looking forward to spending more time with you.

He said he really liked the flower you wore in your hair yesterday.

See you soon.

Love Mum

11

RINGO

"Everyone off my property! NOW!"

My club brothers frown, their gazes shooting to the Marx crew as if I'm only speaking to them, and not everyone.

"Ringo." Abbey comes rushing down the steps, Alana on her heels. "What are you doing?"

"Someone here went into Tahli's room and put that note next to her," I snap, my eyes remaining on the gathering crowd of men. "Lewy has confirmed that the cameras were covered in some sort of foam spray, and since no one was picked up sneaking onto the property, it means whoever went into her room was already here amongst us."

My gaze flashes to my Angel to see her pale, but she quickly shakes it off as she glances around.

"But we need them," she whisper-snaps. "Who will watch the property? Who will protect us? Your mum and sisters?"

"Uhhh, yeah, big guy. Who the hell is making sure I don't get slaughtered in my sleep?" Alana asks, actually sounding concerned instead of annoyingly playful for once.

"What's going on, man?" JD asks as Smitty approaches, and, fuck me, everyone I glance at looks fucking suspicious. Like all of a sudden they've sprouted devil horns and are revealing their true evil fucking nature.

But they aren't. They look just the same as they always do. It's just my fucking paranoia.

I know exactly why Abbey reacted the way she did when we were in Tahli's room earlier, because fuck. We have no fucking idea who is fucking us over. No fucking idea who we can and can't trust.

"Who are we tossing?" Smitty sing-songs as he casually strolls to my side, looking back over the Marx men and Southern Sadists watching on.

"Everyone," I snap, glaring at him.

It takes him a moment to notice that I also mean him, and when it clicks, he flinches back, slapping a hand to his chest.

"Moi?"

I roll my eyes at his dramatics.

"You, and you." I turn to JD before shifting my gaze to Jols, who is standing behind him. "And you. Fucking everyone."

Jols and JD frown, but I ignore them and turn back to the growing crowd.

"All Marx crew are no longer required," I announce loudly so everyone can fucking hear. If I have to repeat myself, I'm gonna spill fucking blood. "All Southern Sadists return to the Fox Pines compound. I'll be returning there later."

The Marx crew glance at Riggs, who nods, and they turn and start packing up their stuff, while the Sadists scratch their heads dumbly for a moment, so I face Smitty.

"Get our guys back to the compound. I'll return as soon as I can."

"You the boss now?" Smitty snaps, looking pissed at me.

"When we are on my land, yes," I hiss back, not in the fucking mood for his bullshit.

If he has a problem with it, he can have it out with me later.

Spinning on my heel, I point sternly to JD as I pass him on my way back to the house. "Pack your shit. I'll meet you back at the compound."

"The fuck."

I keep walking, knowing he will follow, along with Jols, Abbey and my sister, and as soon as we are back inside, I close the door and press my finger to my lips.

Everyone falls quiet, and Abbey's frown looks like it's going to permanently stick with how deep the lines in her forehead are, but I need to explain, without *actually* fucking speaking.

Taking a page out of Dee's book, I snatch up the notepad and pen off the buffet and start writing. Once I'm done, I slap the pad down on the table, pointing to it.

"That's all I can give you for now. Please do as I've asked."

Abbey is the first to read it, as JD, Jols and Alana close in, and my ma and Millie move across the room with Tahli.

One by one, they read my note, and once they are done, I take the entire notebook, light the gas stove, and set the notepad on fire.

Ma doesn't even scold me as I drop the burning paper into the empty sink, and turn on the exhaust fan to help reduce the smoke.

"You all know what to do," I bark before pointing to Abbey. "Help Tahli with her stuff, then meet me upstairs."

She nods, an almost numb expression on her face, but she does as I ask, moving to her little sister and taking her hand to lead her down the hall.

"Ma," I sigh, facing the one woman who has always stood by my decisions, and fuck, I hope that hasn't changed.

"When you say everyone," she croaks, sounding tired, "you mean me too, don't you?"

I nod, moving up to her and gently gripping her shoulders.

"I'm sorry, Ma. You know I'd never ask you to do this if it wasn't absolutely necessary."

Her smile is soft and warm as she stares up at me, her hand lifting to cup my cheek.

"I know, Cameron. I trust you, but I worry…" Her eyes well with tears. "Promise you'll come back to me."

I nod. "Always, Ma."

She pats my cheek, nodding as she steps back. "Should I pack my bikini?"

Millie and Alana laugh, and I smirk at my ma's humour, turning to see that JD and Jols have left the living room as well, doing as I asked of them.

"I have questions," Alana speaks up, and Millie scoffs.

"How did you pass high school? You can't even follow simple instructions."

Alana rolls her eyes. "I just want to know if I can take some of those sexy Marx men with me."

"Jesus Christ, Lans. No, you fucking can't." I glare at my sister. "They are returning to the city, and you are going somewhere else. Just do as I've fucking asked."

"Fine, Jesus," she scoffs, her face turning red as she shoulders past me, and Millie offers me a shrug, following our sister.

Fucking hell.

Outside, the Marx men load SUVs with their things while the Sadists mull around their bikes, smoking and chatting, and even though they don't seem to be in a hurry, they are still packing their shit onto their bikes.

Satisfied that everyone is doing exactly what I've asked, I go upstairs, taking two at a time, and pulling out my phone as soon as I step into my room, making the call to the only person I feel like I can trust to keep my ma, my sisters, and Tahli safe.

I tap my foot impatiently, watching from the bay of windows in my room as my club brothers start to hustle when our Prez barks something I can't hear. I huff as the call tone rings, my phone pressed tightly to my ear, and I'm about to hang up when it finally connects.

"Speak," he barks, and I hope like fuck that making a deal with the Devil is the right thing to do.

Taking in a deep breath, I respond. "I need your help."

12

ABBEY

I should be used to the chaos that has become my life. I don't know why leaving Ringo's property has affected me so much. Probably because despite the constant threats and danger there, with him and his family, I felt safe.

It was the first place that felt like home, and I'm pretty sure Tahli felt the same way given how devastated she was when she was ushered into the cars that finally arrived to pick up her, Doreen, Alana and Millie late last night. My little Chook clawed at my arms as Alana peeled her off me, trying to separate us, and the moment she was dragged free, my heart sank.

It feels like it's happening all over again. I feel like I've lost something.

I know I haven't though. I trust Ringo. I trust his decision and know he would never put them in danger.

Ringo's big hand squeezes my thigh as he rides, the rumble of the engine rather soothing as I tighten my hold around his waist a little more.

"Nearly there, Angel." His voice comes through the speaker at my ear as he slides his hand up and down my thigh, soothingly.

He knows I've been crying. It was pretty hard to hide, and not just because of the mic embedded in my helmet picking up my sniffling.

The shuddering was pretty obvious.

God, I'm going to look frightful when I pull off this helmet. Maybe I can just wear it everywhere until I stop sobbing.

The unremarkable cars that collected the people most precious to me and Ringo had followed us most of the way after leaving Ringo's property, but when we turned off the freeway to head into Fox Pines, they kept going east.

There are so many possibilities of where they could be taken. Will they be turning off and heading north towards the high country? Perhaps they are driving towards the Gippsland Lakes, or maybe they are driving right through and heading across the border to New South Wales?

Shit. Not knowing is going to eat at me, but the deal was no one would know where they are being taken, which is why I feel sick to my stomach with worry.

Releasing my thigh, Ringo steers us off the main road and onto the gravel driveway of the new Southern Sadists Fox Pines compound.

Reluctantly, I peel my head from Ringo's back and watch over his shoulder as we weave up the driveway, the old barn and the series of shipping containers coming into view past the tall pine trees.

As we pull into the main area, my eyes instantly dart to the light pole in the centre of the large yard, and flashes of Wendy's face fill my mind.

The way she still glared at me with hate past the blood and swelling in her face. The way there was still fear in her eyes despite that.

You did that, Abbey. You're a monster!

"Abbey!" Nessy calls as Ringo shuts off the engine, and I shift my gaze to the fire drums, and where Nessy is sitting on Vender's knee, his large hand resting possessively over her thigh.

I wave to her, glad she can't see my face hidden under the helmet, because I don't have a smile for her or anyone right now.

I feel drained.

I'm so ready for this shit to be over, but how many times have I thought that?

How much more can I possibly handle?

You can handle as much as you need to, for your daughter.

Shit. My head's not in a good place right now.

Ringo helps me off his bike, and when he tries to assist me with my helmet, I bat his hands away, only for him to bat at mine.

"Not happening, Angel. Let me do it."

My shoulders drop as I sigh, and he takes that cue to help slide off the helmet, my head immediately dropping, my eyes focusing on his boots.

"Eyes up," he demands, and I want to deny him. I want to be a brat and tell him to piss right off.

But I also don't want to do that. He hasn't done anything wrong. All he's done is support me. Turned his life upside down for me. Put his family in danger for me. All because he loves me.

And I love him.

So, even as moody as I am, I give in to the part of me that wants to be ordered around. That's used to being ordered around, and I glance up at my husband.

His eyes soften when he takes me in, his big hands coming up to engulf each side of my face, those big, calloused thumbs grazing under each eye to wipe away my tears.

"She'll be safe. This will all be over soon."

I nod, because I don't think I can talk without sobbing, and he leans in, pressing a bearded kiss to my forehead.

And just like that, I sink into him once again.

He's my place to fall. I'll never not need him.

"Now you're on *my* fucking land." Smitty's grating voice has me stiffening, the sound of his boots pounding across the gravel behind me stopping as he speaks again. "Tell me why the fuck you kicked us off your property."

"It's complicated, and something I'm not willing to discuss until I know more." Ringo sighs, clearly not wanting to deal with his President.

Easing from Ringo's grip, I turn to face Smitty, my eyes narrowing to slits as I lock onto someone I *can* take my anger out on.

"*Your* land?" I scoff, crossing my arms over my chest. "I thought this land belonged to the Southern Sadists, not Nate Smith."

"Angel," Ringo warns under his breath, but I ignore him, quirking a brow at Smitty.

"Same fucking thing," Smitty snaps, glaring back at me, and jabbing a finger my way. "You're getting a little too big for those size six girly shoes, Charity."

My face falls at the name.

I should turn and slap Ringo since he was the one who started that shit. But instead, I keep my focus on the loopy leader of the club.

"They are still smaller than that head of yours," I point out, and Smitty's jaw clicks as he stares at me.

"Stop glaring at my wife." Ringo's hands come down on my shoulders, steering me away. "She has a fucking point."

"It's a big, but beautiful head, don't you think?" Smitty smirks, and I roll my eyes.

"I think not."

He scoffs as Celina sidles up to him, flashing me a smile as her hand presses to his chest with affection. "It's a very *handsome* Presidential head."

I can't help but snort, and Smitty growls a *'thanks'* to her, groping her arse and lifting her by her globes as she wraps her legs around him.

I don't know what she sees in that man. He's unpredictable. Irritating. And far too full of himself for my liking.

Then again, perhaps I'm just in too much of a pissy mood.

"Church in five!" Smitty calls before practically eating Celina's face as he strides towards the barn, still carrying her.

"I feel ill." I cringe, and Ringo chuckles, spinning me to face him.

"You gotta watch that sassy mouth around him, Angel. I worry one day he's gonna lose his patience with you."

"I can handle him," I scoff, and his beard kicks up at the corner.

"I have no doubt, but you see the thing is, if he steps over the line, I'll have to kill him. And that will bring us a whole heap of other issues we're not ready for."

"Listen to your husband." JD laughs from behind me. "He's sometimes right."

Grinning, I glance over my shoulder to see JD and Jols, hand in hand like they are so often these days.

"Let's go have some girl time." Jols smiles, bobbing her head towards the fire and gathering Doxies. "Leave these brutes to their worshipping and shit."

I snicker at that, taking Jols' hand as she reaches out, but before I can get far, Ringo hooks his arms around my waist and tugs me back.

"Don't go far," he rasps against my lips before claiming them, and I don't even care that there are people watching. This guy... the way he makes me feel like it's just him and me... I'll never get enough of it. Of him.

"Alright, you two." JD laughs. "Cut it out before you make the guys horny."

That pulls me up, and I break the kiss, cringing at JD. "Don't be gross."

"Just stating facts." He laughs, holding his hands up in surrender, and Jols tugs me to her side.

"We all know the horny one is you, Jimmy," Jols snickers, and his smile is from ear to ear as he grips his crotch and does a little thrust towards her.

We all laugh, and I start to relax, feeling a little lighter for the first time today.

As Jols leads me away from the guys, they make their way over to the barn, and I try not to feel Ringo's loss too much. Because that's weird, right? Being so clingy.

"So what happened?" Jols whispers as we walk. "Where's Tahli?"

Frowning, I glance at Jols.

Didn't Ringo tell them not to ask questions?

Is Jols... the traitor?

She was in the house. Sleeping just a few doors down from Tahli's room. She could have snuck out of bed and planted that note on Tahli's bedside table.

Shit... No... Surely not. I'm just overthinking... right?

"She's somewhere safe," I say quietly, and Jols frowns, her blue gaze darting to me as she stops walking.

She opens her mouth to speak, but then snaps it shut, glancing over her shoulder to where the guys just disappeared inside the barn.

I stiffen, waiting for the backlash. If she is the traitor, she'll surely ask more questions... or maybe not. That would be too revealing, right?

Oh Jesus. I'm not good at this.

"Okay." Jols nods, turning back to me and offering me a soft smile that doesn't meet her eyes. "Well, welcome to no privacy. Just so you know, I'm not giving up the bungalow, so the four of us are about to become even more acquainted."

Her smile is wide, and a laugh bubbles from me as I realise she's right.

JD and Ringo share a bungalow. Their beds are so close to each other that I can reach out and touch the other one, so yeah, there will be absolutely zero privacy.

I'm not entirely sure how I feel about that, but I guess it is what it is at this stage. Hopefully we can find Bobbi soon and then things can go back to normal... whatever that is.

Just thinking of Bobbi brings my mood back down. I'm so scared for her. I hate that we are here, not doing anything when we should be out looking for her. But where do we look? Our best bet is waiting for Elizabeth to call Daniel.

Shit... I forgot about him.

"Where's Daniel?" I ask as we take a seat by the fire.

"In the dungeon." Jols gestures her head towards the shipping container that I know sits over the old Vixen's Lodge Estate dungeon. The same dungeon I beat Wendy to a pulp in.

Flashes of my fist, encased in a metal knuckle duster, rush through my mind, and the feeling of it cracking against her cheek, tearing her skin open, sends a shudder through me.

Monster.

I can't run from what I did. Who I became... *who* I've *become.*

"I want to see him," I say quietly, watching Jols stiffen in my peripheral.

"Daniel?" she asks, like she's hoping I'll say no.

"I *need* to see him." I shift my gaze to hers, catching the concern washing over her expression.

"Is this going to be a Wendy repeat?" she deadpans, and I shake my head, knowing deep in my bones that it won't be... I think.

No... no, it won't.

Monster.

"I need Daniel alive for now," I remind her, and she shrugs.

"He's not alone down there. Brody's on watch, and Lewy is set up ready for when Daniel's mum calls."

"Oh..." My brows shoot up.

I hadn't realised everything they were doing. I kind of thought he'd be locked in the dark, much like Wendy was.

Standing, I shoot Jols a reassuring smile that I don't think works, and make my way across the yard, tugging my jacket closer to my neck as I walk, trying to keep myself warm.

When I reach the shipping container, I ignore the sign that says, *Southern Sadists Only*, and pull open the door, stepping inside.

Lewy is sitting behind a wall of monitors at the other end of the container, his gaze shooting to me as I close the door.

"Uhhh, you shouldn't be in here."

I smile, like I didn't just hear him speak, and hurry to the ladder staircase that goes down under the earth.

"Ringo's in church," I say as I go, not really giving him an answer, and he curses, his chair scraping across the old timber floor.

"I can't let you go down there." His voice is loud now, and I glance up to see him at the top, glaring down at me, so I shrug.

"I just have a few questions for him. Which is *my* prerogative, since he's *my* prisoner. Not yours."

Lewy's dark brows hitch, and he gives me a nod. "Best not kill him then."

I roll my eyes and continue down. "Wasn't planning on it."

When I reach the bottom and glance back up, I see Lewy run his hand anxiously through his hair, but he doesn't try to stop me, so I spin and face the door, which is ajar.

Tugging on the heavy metal, it creaks open, and Brody steps into view, his brows high, his eyes questioning.

"Don't you start with me too," I snap, and he holds his hands up in surrender, never looking more like his brother than in this moment.

"Hey, we're all good. Just no killing yet. Ringo will literally cut my nuts from my body if I let that happen before you get your daughter back."

I grin, stepping inside and pulling the door closed, and Brody shifts back to sit in a chair in the corner by the door.

I take in the space where I unleashed my monster on Wendy.

The only colours I see in my head when I think back over that time are black, white, and red. Lots of red.

Daniel is laying curled in a ball on the concrete floor along the back wall. He's not asleep, though. His eyes, although swollen, are open, watching me as I approach, lowering to sit in the middle of the room.

For a long moment, we just stare at each other, and I hate that I feel bad for him. How could I after what he did to me with his friends? After the way he treated me at school. After the way he chased me through the forest, and pushed me, wanting to kill my baby. A baby that is potentially his.

My cousin's.

My stomach rolls at the reminder that it was my cousin who took my virginity. My cousin, who wooed me, made me feel special, and wanted.

God, that seems like so long ago now.

But here he is, the guy that destroyed my life. He may not have known he was my cousin at the time, but he knew what he was doing when he agreed to have sex with me to help his family rise through the ranks of the church... the cult.

He knew what he was doing when he raped me. Shared me with his friends to rape me too. When he hit me. Choked me. Forced so much vileness onto me, so much that I can't even bear to think of it.

"When did you know that your mum took off?" I ask, and he blinks painfully a couple of times before slowly pushing himself to sit up.

Clearing his throat, he rests his back against the wall, and answers.

"When we got back home from the Chapel... it was later that night," he explains. "At first, my dad and I thought she just wasn't home yet, but then my dad came running out of their room, saying her clothes were gone, and we knew. It wasn't until she sent me that photo of her and Bobbi that I thought about the stuff we were hiding in our shed, and I found it gone."

Stuff?

Sitting taller, I ask. "What stuff?"

"Medical supplies."

I stiffen, but it's Brody that responds from behind me.

"Medical supplies? What sort of medical supplies?"

"Uh..." Daniel clears his throat again. "At first I thought it was just a heap of PPE and stuff, for the pandemic, but then I noticed some other stuff too."

"What other stuff?" I snap, gaining his attention off Brody.

"Baby stuff. Nappies. Formula. And a humidicrib."

"A humidicrib?" I squeak, glancing up to see Brody now standing next to me.

"You mean your old man was the one that stole from us?" Brody hisses, and Daniel frowns, shaking his head as his confused eyes dart from Brody to me.

"I-I don't know. I have no idea where it all came from. It arrived in some trucks, and Dad had them put it in our shed. That's all I know. I didn't know there was baby stuff until I went snooping ages afterwards."

"You get that, Lewy?" Brody asks, and I stand, frowning at him to see him talking into a radio.

"Yep, got it." Lewy's voice comes through the radio speaker, and I frown.

Glancing around, I see there have been some modifications done in the dungeon since the last time I was here.

There are cameras set up, their lights blinking, and I realise Lewy is recording everything.

"So you really don't know how your dad got that stuff, other than some trucks dropping the supplies off?" I ask, and Daniel shakes his head.

"He just told me it was nothing for me to worry about, so I didn't." He shrugs, looking innocent and reminding me of the version of him I thought I loved.

Ew... I feel ill.

"What did your old man do when he discovered it and your mum gone?" Brody asks. "Did he call anyone?"

"Not that I know of." He shakes his head. "I know he was worried about her. Muttered something about not wanting to dob her in, and as fucked up as he is, he loved her. He wanted to protect her. I know he was messed up with all the incest stuff, but he was a good man."

I scoff. "He wasn't a good man, Daniel. He was evil, and I killed him."

I watch his reaction, but he simply nods. "I know."

"You don't care?" I ask, and he shakes his head.

"Nothing I can do about it now." He shrugs, and the fact that he doesn't seem to care pisses me off.

Why isn't he crying? Screaming abuse at me for taking away his dad forever?

This won't do at all.

"I can still hear his screams," I snarl, curling my lip as I glare at Daniel, finally seeing a flicker of pain in his eyes. "Reliving them helps me fall asleep at night."

"What's wrong with you?" he cries loudly as a sob lurches from his throat.

"Nothing is wrong with me, Daniel. My eyes are wide open now. I'm finally who I'm meant to be."

"This isn't you," Daniel seethes. "You're a sweet girl. A mother. You have a baby to worry about now. Mothers don't act like this!"

"And fathers don't push the mother of their child in the hopes they will both die!" I scream, lurching forward, and loving how he flinches back.

My hand cracks across his face, and the sound echoes in the small space.

"She might not be mine!" Daniel cries.

"But what if she is? How will you walk away from that?" I fist the front of his grotty shirt, snarling in his face.

"I-I-I don't know!" he yells. "Maybe I can be a good dad to her."

I shove back from him, needing the space because the urge to kill him is so close to the surface that I know I won't be able to talk myself down off that ledge if I get much closer.

"You? Be a good dad to her?" I laugh manically. "Let's think about that for a moment, shall we?"

I start pacing in front of him, feeling Brody close by, but not looking to see exactly where he is, because my attention needs to be honed in on my cousin right now.

"Imagine Bobbi *is* yours," I say. "Imagine she brings home a boyfriend when she's seventeen. Imagine he coaxes her in and then betrays her by RAPING HER!" I scream, and his flinch is so satisfying, I almost start laughing again.

"Imagine he invites his friends to rape her too... while *he* watches," I hiss, balling my fists, and fighting every instinct in me from finding a weapon and ending him right now.

"Imagine them tying her to a table, spreading her legs so wide she's practically doing the splits, even though she's not a FUCKING BALLERINA!" I have no control as my mind goes back to that place. The feeling of the ropes burning into my wrists and ankles. The agonising burn of my muscles as they protested against the unnatural stretch. The feeling of wishing I would just die, right then and there, so it would all just stop.

I can feel my fists hitting his face. I watch as he takes each hit, not cowering away, like he deserves the pain of each blow.

"Imagine her young, inexperienced body, open and exposed to them, while one fucks her painfully deep and hard, and another shoves his fingers inside her arse so brutally, she can feel his nails SCRATCHING INSIDE HER!"

I fist his hair, slamming his head back against the concrete wall, and still, he doesn't fight me.

"Abbey!" I hear someone yell, but it's distant. Not really here because I'm somewhere else.

I'm back there. On that day.

Just let me die.

"Imagine another with their dick so far down her throat that she fears her jaw is going to break, while she chokes on her own puke, fighting not to drown in it as her lungs protest, starting to SUFFOCATE!"

Strong hands wrap around me from behind, dragging me backwards, and I kick my legs out, landing a couple of blows into Daniel's gut as I keep reliving that day.

"Imagine all of that happening to her, Daniel! Imagine it! And imagine while that's happening, the other guys jack off all over her like she's nothing but a piece of WORTHLESS TRASH!"

"STOP!" he finally screams back, and I shove at the hands keeping me at bay.

"Why, Daniel? Does that make you uncomfortable? It shouldn't," I snarl, my spittle flying from my lips. "You did that, Daniel. TO ME!"

"I-I—"

"Don't you dare apologise!" I snap, kicking my legs out again, desperate to get my hands on him again. "You never cared about me, and I'm fucking fine with that. But *imagine* all of that being done to your DAUGHTER!"

"STOP! NO!" he screams.

The hands holding me suddenly disappear, and the cold metal of the knuckle dusters are pressed into my palm.

I don't second guess it. I don't even look to see who placed them there. I just slip them on like they were made for me, and the monster in me takes over, just the way it did with Wendy, although this time, the monster is in for a long, slow torture.

Taking my time, I feel the crack of Daniel's rib cage, and with every hit, a slither of the horrible memories from that day is vanquished from my mind.

I could do this all day. Each blow a therapeutic release, but it's the distant crack of a gun that snaps me out of my daze, and I turn to see Brody running for the stairs.

13

RINGO

"So what you're saying is you don't trust us?" Smitty barks from the head of the table, and I'm about ready for this fucking meeting to be done.

"What I'm saying is, from now on, information will be limited and shared strictly on a need to know basis," I snap, and he glares down the table at me.

"Oh sure. You used *my* men and *my* fucking stepdaughter to kidnap a pregnant teenager. Sneak her into the fucking compound. Hide her in your room, then declare her yours when she's discovered. She ate our food. Used our hot water. And then was the reason for the pigs sniffing around while we were out dealing with a breach at the warehouses." He leans forward in his chair, the old fucking thing squeaking. "Shall I go fucking on? Because you've done a whole fucking lot that isn't very fucking clubman-like, and now you want to sit here and tell us you don't trust us?"

"I did what you fucking wanted." I grit my teeth. "I paid for the lie with the club beating. I married her when you demanded it. What the fuck do you want from me?!"

"Your fucking loyalty!" Smitty booms, surging to his feet, his gun already in his hand and aimed straight at me.

Chairs scrape the floor as my club brothers lurch back from the table, but I stay seated, glaring at my President.

"My loyalty?" I scoff. "What are you really pissed about here, Nate? That I finally woke up from my fucking zombie coma after Hope died and I'm no longer your puppet? Or that I found someone who makes me happy while you're stuck in a marriage to a woman you don't love, while forcing Celina to kneel just so she can earn privileges the other Doxies don't get?"

The crack of the gun is deafening, splinters of wood exploding overhead where Smitty's gun is now pointed.

"I should fucking kill you!" Smitty roars, and I slowly stand, seeing JD, Vender, Mex, and well... a lot of guys with their hands on their guns, ready to draw.

But not at me.

"If you wanted me dead, I would be," I snap. "If you want me and my wife to leave, we will. Just say the fucking word and I'll walk away right fucking now."

Lowering his gun, Smitty breathes heavily like he's fighting for control, but the gun gets placed on the table as he jabs a finger towards me.

"You would choose her over us?" he asks, but it's more of an accusation.

"No," I answer honestly. "I would choose *her* over *you*."

Smitty's face turns red. "Isn't that what I just said?"

"No." I shake my head, glancing at my club brothers packed into the small room we use as church at the back of the barn. "I'm not choosing my wife over the club, because they would never fucking ask me to. You are the one doing that. Last time I checked our bylaws, the role of President wasn't a fucking dictatorship."

Smitty slams his fist on the table again. "You're walking a thin fucking line!"

Suddenly, the doors burst open, and Brody flies into the room, gun raised.

"What happened? Who am I shooting?"

All eyes are now on our prospect, whose eyes are wild as they dance around, ready to fight for any one of us, and the tension that was engulfing the room slips away as Smitty grins.

"Well, fuck. It's about time we patched in this son of a bitch."

The room remains quiet for a moment, the only sound is Brody as he starts laughing.

"Really? Do you mean that?"

One look at Smitty, and I can tell he's going to say no. I can tell he was only fucking with him.

Well, fuck. I'm already on the outs with Nate. I may as well go out with a fucking bang.

"Damn straight!" I slap my hand on the table. "Call the vote, Prez."

Smitty's jaw ticks as he glares at me, but turns back to our club brothers.

"Alright, listen up!" Smitty calls, even though everyone is fucking quiet. "Next order of business is Brody Dean. He's been kicking around here for a while now. Fucking our Doxies. Eating our grub. Sending us all batshit crazy over the way he makes up his own fucking lyrics for songs. But he's also stepped up of late. So let me hear your thoughts."

"His taste in music is questionable." Spud speaks up first. "Fucking teenybopper shit does my head in. But, fuck, he's had our backs."

Fists pounding over hearts fill the room in agreement, and Brody fucking beams.

"Jesus Christ. He's gonna get such a big fucking head over this," JD mutters, "but as Road Captain, and the ugly fucker's brother... I couldn't be prouder of the way he's stepped up to protect Abbey."

Pounding fists over hearts sound again, no one but Smitty flinching at the fact my wife's name was brought up.

"Little shit needs to learn how to fucking bargain shop instead of getting the big brands when he goes with the Doxies to the shops," Tups, our Secretary grumbles, "but he's not afraid to go in guns blazing when he's ordered to."

Again, more fists.

"How about you?" Smitty hisses. "Sergeant-at-Arms. What do you think?"

He already knows what I think, but this isn't about my spat with Smitty. This is about our prospect becoming a fully patched member, so I drag my gaze from my bitter President, and lock eyes with Brody.

"You've bled for me. For my wife. You jumped through the window of a moving fucking van for me. For my wife. You've clawed at the dirt of the grave of my wife's baby. You've helped protect my ma and my sisters." I jab a finger in his direction. "As far as I'm concerned, you've been my club brother for a fucking while now. I'm stoked to make it official."

Brody's eyes turn glassy as his smile grows impossibly wide, and he thumps his fist over his heart, his eyes on me.

"Anyone else got anything to add or dispute?" Smitty snaps, and Vender steps forward, clearing his throat.

"Despite me and Mex trying to fucking claim Nessy for ourselves, you, a little fucking shit of a bloke, have been the voice of fucking reason." Vender continues as Mex chuckles next to him. "You can be selfless when you need to be, so in my eyes, you make the type of club brother I want to ride alongside."

More fists pound, and Brody grins like a fucking idiot, puffing out his chest.

"Alright. Enough of the lovey-dovey shit," Smitty whines. "All those in favour of patching in Brody Dean, show us your hands."

Every fucker in the room raises their hand, and Smitty doesn't even bother asking if anyone is against it.

"Then it's fucking done. This ugly fucker, Brody Dean, is one of us." He points to Brody. "Get the fuck over here."

Cheers ring out through the room, my club brothers slapping Brody's back as he rounds the table, walking with his head held high.

This part of the patching in is shared by the President and Sergeant-at-Arms, so I move around the table, coming to Nate's side, even though I want to punch him, and together, we present Brody with the full cut as Spud wrestles the prospect one off his back.

"You earned this," Smitty says, holding up the cut. "Don't forget what it took to become part of the brotherhood."

Brody turns, slipping it on, and tugging at the front, spinning to face us, fucking proud as punch.

"From this day on," I tell him, "You wear our colours. You represent every man in this room, and every man in this room will ride for you, and die for you."

Brody nods, his eyes turning glassy again as Smitty speaks up.

"Southern Sadists, we chant."

And as one, with Brody joining us this time, we chant.

> *"May the road rise up to meet us.*
> *May the wind be always at our backs.*
> *May the sunshine be warm upon our faces.*
> *May the rain clouds never be black.*
> *We are the Southern Sadists MC.*
> *Ride 'em high.*
> *Ride or die."*

"Yeah!" JD yells, barging through the guys to get to his little brother, sweeping him up in his arms for a brotherly hug before Brody is lifted onto the shoulders of Vender and Mex, and they start cheering as they carry him from the room.

"You and I gonna have a problem?" Smitty asks from behind me as the room clears out, and I sigh, turning to face my President.

I've pretty much undermined him here today, so yeah, I'm pretty sure we are gonna have a problem.

"If you want me to leave, Nate, just say the word."

For a long moment, he just stares at me, his eyes dancing between mine like he's trying to get a read on whether my words hold the truth.

"Who the fuck else is going to do your shitty job?" he snaps, before the tip of his fucking finger pokes my chest. "But secrets don't fucking sit well with me. Right now, you're on thin fucking ice. I can't have this disloyal shit floating around my club. The men are unsettled enough."

I hold up my hands. "Not being disloyal. But my family and their safety is my prerogative, and unless I'm using club resources to help them, then it's none of your concern."

His eyes narrow. "So you're not using club resources? Outside help then." He comes to his own conclusion. "The Marx family? Fuck, man. Don't you fuck up the deals I have going with Griffin so we can work this fucking zone. He's taking the heat from his psychotic old man for us."

"It's nothing that will blow back on the club. And no, it's not the Marx family. End of fucking conversation."

Brody's voice cuts through Smitty's disapproving grunt, and I turn towards the open doors leading to the main floor of the barn, which looks more like a fucking hoedown bar than a clubhouse.

"Ringo!" Brody calls again, still perched on my club brothers' shoulders, and when he spots me, worry flashes across his face.

"What the fuck now?" I snap, and Brody visibly cringes.

"It's, uh... Abbey. She's uh..." He hesitates, but the moment I start storming towards him, the rest spills out. "She's in the dungeon... unleashing her anger."

"The fuck?!" I seethe, already veering off for the doors to stop my wife from killing someone... again.

14

ABBEY

Something that sounds a lot like celebrating drifts across the yard from the barn, and nothing about it makes me want to join in. Not even the gunshot had fully pulled me out of my misery, and I'm beginning to wonder if this is just who I am now.

Miserable. Mournful. A real downer.

My gaze sweeps over the names etched into the metal plates of the memorial wall. I wandered here after Brody rushed off. I'd lost the urge to hit Daniel in that moment, but my mind refuses to snap out of this dark haze wrapped around me like a bubble.

Reaching out, I hover my fingers over the name, Jamie Halley - Mule, but stop the moment I spot red coating my hands.

Blood.

Daniel's blood.

And I'm still wearing the knuckle duster.

Oh… should I wash it? How does one take care of a knuckle duster? And does it even need taking care of?

"Abbey!" I hear a yell. Ringo's yell.

Turning to glance over my shoulder, I see him bounding from the dungeon shipping container, his eyes frantic as he searches for me.

I guess he's seen what I've done. How I left Daniel beaten and bloody.

How can he even love me?

Jesus… I'm so sick of feeling like this.

Glancing back at the memorial wall, my glassy eyes lock onto Mule's name.

"Am I redeemable?" I whisper. "If I get Bobbi back, and she grows up to find out what I've done. Who I've killed. The monster I can be… Will she hate me?"

"Abbey!" Ringo's voice is less frantic now, coming closer with the sounds of his pounding boots approaching. "Fuck, Angel. Are you alright?"

I don't turn back, shame washing over me as I prepare to be caught red-handed. Literally.

I don't deserve him.

The feel of his strong hands on my shoulders makes me jolt, like his touch finally breaks through the bubble, and a sob lurches from my lips.

"I'm a monster," I murmur as he gently spins me to face him, those whisky eyes roaming over me to make sure I'm okay.

"You're not a monster, Angel." He tries to soothe me, but I shake my head, holding up my blood coated hands.

"These are the hands of a monster, Cam. That's what I've become."

His shoulders drop, like he's finally accepting that, so I steel myself for his disappointment.

"You've become what you've needed to become to get through this. To survive this."

I frown at his words. "I've become a monster. I don't deserve you. I don't deserve to be a mother. My mum was right."

"No way." His fingers dig into my upper arms as he gives me a single shake. "No fucking way am I letting that woman's toxic words settle in your head. You *do* deserve to be a mother, and any woman or mother that says they could never harm someone else is a lying bitch, or living in a fucking dreamland full of unicorns and fairies, because let me tell you, the moment someone hurts their kid, they'll turn into the fucking she-devil herself."

"Not every mother," I whisper, my eyes burning with tears I hate since they are related to the woman who birthed me.

"I guess not *every* mother," he agrees, "but those mothers are the ones who don't deserve that fucking title, Angel. Because if they aren't willing to burn the whole fucking world down for their own child, then they don't deserve to be called a parent."

For a long moment, I just stare up at this big brute of a man wondering how I got so lucky to have him fighting in my corner.

"I don't know if I can be the mother Bobbi deserves," I admit quietly, and those big hands shift from my arms to my face, framing it as he leans in closer.

"Every good mother thinks that, Angel. I know the idea of being a mother is scary, especially after grieving for so long and thinking that your little girl was gone... was in the afterlife with my Hope..." His voice cracks, and big fat tears burst from my eyes as my heart aches for *him.* "But Bobbi's alive, waiting for her mum to find her. Waiting for her mum to hold her and never let her go."

A loud sob escapes me as I nod, trying to smile through my tears, and Ringo crashes me to his chest, holding my head to him like I'm precious, while I hold my arms out to each side, trying my best not to get blood on him.

"Thank you." I sob into his chest, and he squeezes me tighter.

"Come on. Let's get you showered and into some fresh clothes."

I nod against his cut, and when he pulls back, he takes my blood-soaked hand in his, not caring about the mess, and leads me across the yard.

"Is Daniel..." I trail off, wondering if I killed him. I can't really remember.

"He's alive, Angel. You did a number on him though."

I cringe, and Ringo chuckles.

"Nothing he didn't deserve. Don't even think about him. We have a celebration to go to."

My brows hitch. "What are we celebrating?"

When Ringo glances down at me, his eyes are light as he answers.

"Brody got patched in."

That news has me smiling too, so we hurry to the path that leads to the bungalows and take a quick shower.

Together.

That may or may not have involved some suckling... Jesus, my cheeks still flush at the fact we do that, yet it still doesn't feel wrong.

Nothing I do with Ringo feels wrong.

We join the celebrations a short time later, and even though my smile is forced, I start to relax with Ringo remaining by my side the entire time.

There's a big barbeque cook up, the Doxies filling a table with various salads and side dishes, and for a while, I stay in the moment. Not thinking about Bobbi. Not thinking about Tahli. Not thinking about Daniel. Yet thoughts of my mother linger at the edges.

She knows Bobbi is alive. Someone told her. A little birdy, she'd said.

She'd also known I was gone from Ringo's house. That Tahli had been left there. And whoever is working with her, had left a note for my sister. They were in her room. Right by her bed.

The thought makes it hard for me to eat much, but I manage one drink, hoping the alcohol will calm my nerves, but that doesn't work either. I just spend the time pretending that I'm okay. Pretending that I'm present.

"Hey, Abbey. How about a kiss for the new club brother?" Brody snickers, ignoring the growl that rumbles from Ringo, whose knee I'm perched on.

Brody is loving all of the attention, returning to the level of cockiness I first witnessed in him at the previous compound. He was such a dick then. A sex-crazed dick. But he has changed since then. Since shit got real, I suppose.

"I'll pass, thanks. I've seen where that mouth has been."

He throws his head back laughing, proud as punch about that fact, and I can't help but giggle at the guy.

His cackling stops as he grins down at me, his eyes roaming over my face as his expression turns more serious.

"What?" I ask, and his gaze flicks to my husband, who's watching him like a hawk.

Stepping closer, Brody lowers to one knee, bringing us eye to eye.

"Are you okay?" he asks, and I frown, shifting uncomfortably on Ringo's lap.

"I'm fine."

His eyes narrow at my lie, but he doesn't call me out on it.

"Did I do the right thing, or the wrong thing?"

I frown at his question. "I don't know what you're talking about."

"The knuckle duster," he whisper-hisses, and I feel Ringo straighten. "I tried to hold you back, but it was like you were in agony not being able to beat on Daniel, so... I let you go, and well... the things you said..." His eyes turn glassy and his lip curls in disgust. "Did he really do all of those things to you?"

I swallow thickly, not able to speak, so I nod, just once.

"I wanted to kill him for you, Abbey. And I would in an instant if you asked me to, but then, in that moment, I knew you had to be the one to hurt him, so I gave you something to help. Did I do the wrong thing?"

I consider that, letting myself go back to what I can remember of that moment. To the minutes that followed. I'd been ashamed of behaving like that, but Brody is right. I was in agony. I *did* need to unleash it on someone who deserved it.

"You didn't do the wrong thing." I smile softly at him, but it's a weak attempt at best. "Thank you for being there for me. And congratulations on becoming a fully patched Southern Sadist."

He beams, and I flick my gaze to Ringo.

"Did I say it right? Fully patched? Is that the right lingo?"

Ringo's lip kicks up at the corner. "You nailed it, Angel."

"Yeah, you fucking nailed it." Brody beams, standing and turning to the crowd. "Who wants to suck my cock?!"

A squeal flies from me as drinks get thrown at Brody, spilling over me and Ringo, and I duck and hide into his chest as the music gets turned up louder.

Things quickly turn indecent after that, and as Ringo chats to Vender and Murf, I pretend not to notice Helina pulling off her top and kneeling in front of a group of Southern Sadists as they take their dicks out and start stroking them.

A red hot blush heats my cheeks, and I squirm on Ringo's lap, ducking my head yet still watching through the fan of my lashes as Helina sucks on one dick, using her hands to jerk off two of the others, while the remaining guys do the work themselves.

Shit. I can't look away.

"We call that live porn." Ringo breathes against my ear, making me stiffen, and his deep chuckle rumbles against my back. "Want a closer look?"

"No." I shake my head, and Ringo grunts.

"Liar."

"Hey, Darla." Vender calls from next to me and Ringo, and the Doxy magically appears like she's been waiting for this all night. "Murf's cock needs attention."

She beams, her eyes flicking to me and Ringo before settling on Murf, who is sitting on our other side.

"You want some of what they are getting?" she asks Murf, and I squirm on Ringo's lap again as Murf quickly takes his dick out, which is already hard.

Oh my God, are all these men hard?

Is Ringo hard?

I shift my arse a little, wanting to know, and his fingers dig into my hips. "Unless you want to ride my cock here, Angel, I'd suggest you stop doing that."

Heat washes over me from the inside out. I really have no idea why those words have me reacting this way. The last thing I want to do is that, here, with people around watching… right?

I don't respond to Ringo, too caught up in the sight of Darla kneeling and taking Murf's dick in her hand, pumping it up and down his shaft as he runs his fingers through her blonde hair.

"You know how I like it, honey," Murf drawls, guiding her head closer to his lap. "Nice and deep. Let me hear you gag."

I stiffen, my mind going back to a time I want to forget. To the day those five guys used my body as a playground, torturing me with vile acts and depravities I don't think I'll ever get past. But then I remember the time I woke up Ringo by sucking his dick. I gagged then, and even though I was scared, I enjoyed how much he liked it.

"Relax, Angel." Ringo's hands come around to my front, not in a sensual way, but in a calming way, and he presses his lips to my ear. "You're here with me. You're safe. Everything that happens here is consensual."

I nod quickly, annoyed that I'm so easy to read, but I melt back against him, not able to take my eyes off Darla as she glides her tongue up Murf's shaft before circling the rim.

"Darla, are you consenting?" Ringo asks, as if he knows I need the confirmation, and she nods, pumping Murf's dick as her eyes shift to me like she knows I'm the pathetic one.

"I've been in a non-consenting situation a couple of times before I joined the Doxies here," Darla tells me, her tone nothing but serious. "I haven't been mistreated here. These men. This place has helped me to heal. And now, the things I do," she leans closer to me, like she's telling me a secret. "Things I never thought I'd do, let alone like, are all things I consent to. The guys know my limits. And I know theirs, and girl, let me tell you. There's something powerful about making these big brutes go all shaky in the knees as I make them feel good. It might look like I'm serving them, but really, I'm the one with all the power."

"Oh..." I breathe, taking in her bright expression and remembering how I felt the same way with Ringo.

"You want to know why Murf likes it when I gag?" she asks, and even though I shudder, I nod, wondering how it could be anything but him wanting to humiliate her since he doesn't have feelings for her. She's just someone for him to get off with... right?

"When I gag," she starts to explain, "the muscles in my throat go tighter, and he loves that squeeze." She turns back to Murf, whose pupils are nearly blown. "Don't you, big guy?"

"Fuck yes." His hips rise like he's desperate to feel it, and she beams up at him. "You want to come down my throat or on my tongue?"

"Bit of both, Darla," he rasps, pressing forward so the tip of his dick brushes her lips.

"Okay. But make sure you make me gag real good," she purrs, before taking him into her mouth.

My breathing is shallow. Quick. Panting. I'm more affected by this than I thought I would be, and not in a bad way.

Wetness pools between my legs, and the letdown feeling tingles my nipples as Ringo readjusts me on his lap, his erection now a prominent bulge resting against my arse.

I watch, unable to look away as Darla sucks on Murf's dick like it's a lollipop, before she opens her mouth impossibly wide, and he sinks in so far that her eyes start to water.

It looks uncomfortable, which is why I don't understand how she likes it.

"Remember what she said." Ringo breathes quietly next to my ear. "She feels powerful doing this. Just like the way you enjoy making me feel good, she's enjoying making Murf feel good." Ringo squeezes me closer, making me feel safe as he continues. "Look at her other hand, Angel. Can you see it?"

I look from the one around Murf's shaft, searching for her other one, and find it between her legs, moving.

"Is she..."

"Yes, Angel. She's turned on by what she's doing."

I feel so inexperienced right now, despite how many new things I've done with Ringo. But I know my reaction is more about my trauma than anything. I wonder what I would have been like if I never experienced what I did.

Would I join Darla on the floor, kneeling between Ringo's legs and suck on his dick for everyone to watch?

I mean, I do like the sound of it, but I still don't think I'd do it. I think I'd prefer keeping that stuff just between us, but I have to admit, even if it's just to myself, that I really do like watching other people.

When Darla gags, I stiffen, but Murf groans, and Darla's eyes roll back in her head like she's enjoying it.

I'm embarrassed that I'm turned on right now, watching live porn, as Ringo calls it. I know this is a normal thing in the confines of the compound, especially since one glance around the room shows me more Doxies in various states of undress, pleasuring the club brothers, but it's still so wild to me that this sort of thing happens.

"Colour?" Ringo asks me quietly, snapping my attention back to him, and I frown.

Are we doing a sex thing right now?

Given how turned on I am despite my initial hesitation, and the way his dick pokes against my butt, I'd say yes.

Shit.

I don't want to do… orgy stuff.

Is that what he wants? For me to be like a Doxy?

"Orange," I rush out, my throat tight as tears threaten to fall, and in an instant, Ringo stands, sweeping me up in his arms.

He carries me quickly through the writhing bodies, keeping me tucked against his chest as he moves us to the side of the room, away from the chaos.

"I'm sorry, Angel," he murmurs as he sits with his back to the room, bringing my face up to his with the hook of his finger under my chin. "I should have asked you if you wanted to leave when it began. Not insisting on showing you how it can be."

I shake my head. "You didn't insist, and I'm a big girl, Cam. I can speak up." My shoulders drop as I sigh, lifting my hand and poking my temple. "My head isn't right. When I was with Daniel earlier, it brought up some stuff. Some specific stuff that was done to me, and… I want to be able to watch live porn with you. Today is just not a good day."

His lips thin. "I don't need to watch live porn, Angel. You're more than enough to turn me on."

"But you are turned on by it." I glance over his shoulder, seeing Helina is now completely naked with a guy at each end, thrusting into her. "You like watching. You've told me so before."

"I like watching cocks getting pleasured by mouths, cunts or arse, Angel. The people they are attached to don't really do it for me. But you..." He leans in, nipping at my lip. "*Everything* about you does it for me."

I relax, warming from the inside at his words, knowing I feel the same.

"I mean. Watching is kind of hot," I admit, and he grins.

"Are you wet?"

I nod. "I am, but... I can't do this today."

"You don't ever have to do anything you don't want to do, Angel."

"In that case. I think I'm going to turn in early. Today's been a lot since someone woke me at three in the morning to go gallivanting across the country..." I let that hang between us as his smirk grows.

"Let's get out of here then."

"Oh... I mean, you can stay if you—"

"Fuck that," he snaps, his eyes turning dark with anger. "New rule. Any sexual activity that happens outside of our own privacy must be done with both of us there, both of us consenting, and neither of us ever touching anyone but each other. Got it?"

I suck in my lower lip, biting it as my smile blooms.

"Got it."

Shit.

The relief I feel from his 'new rule' is huge. I guess I've been a little worried that if I don't learn how to tolerate these orgies, then Ringo will stop inviting me and just go himself.

"Come on, Mrs Musgrove. Let's get you to bed."

Quickly leaving the growing orgy, Ringo links his fingers with mine and we take the path back down to the bungalows. Even though it's dark out here, the path is well lit, the new changes being made to the compound making it more livable like this is a little town.

It's kind of nice.

Reaching the bungalow, I take the steps first as Ringo stops at the bottom to unlace his boots, and I'm too cold to wait for him, so I hurry to the door, throwing it open, only to gasp as I get an eyeful of JD's arse and balls swaying as he pounds into Jols from behind.

15

RINGO

"Oh shit. Sorry," Abbey blurts as I come up behind her, and she spins in the doorway, crashing into my chest.

"Careful, Angel." I steady her.

"You two coming in?" JD pants, and my eyes lift from the top of Abbey's head to find his fucking pale arse thrusting as he looks over his shoulder at us. "Close the fucking door, it's freezing."

"For fuck's sake," I sigh as Abbey shakes her head, but because she doesn't say anything, I have no idea if she's saying no to going in, or shaking it to clear the image of my best mate's balls swaying with each thrust.

"We'll be done soon if you want privacy," JD grunts, slowing his thrusts, "but if you want to watch, I can draw this out."

"Don't you dare!" Jols yells from her bent over position, and I can't help but fucking smirk.

"Oh, come on, Babydoll. I'll make it feel good," JD tells her, leaning over Jols and doing something that has her moaning.

"Look at them, Angel." I breathe over the top of her hair, and my little submissive shakes her head even as she slowly turns to face them.

"This is weird," she mutters, and I laugh as Jols' hand appears from where JD's body hides hers, her middle finger sticking up.

"It's only weird if you make it weird," she pants, her voice a little unsteady from the pounding she's getting.

"You could always join in." JD grins over his shoulder, wagging his brows. Not at me, but at my wife. "I'll share Jols with you, Abbey."

A possessive growl rips from my lips, and I don't even try to fucking hide it.

"No one touches my wife but me!"

JD and Jols snicker, and Abbey turns to me, her big caramel eyes locking with mine.

"Can we wait outside for them to finish?"

I nod, brushing my thumb over her flushed cheek. "Sure, Angel."

I tug my wife out of the doorway, leaning in to scoop up my throw blanket off my bed, and close the door before leading her to the seat under the window on the porch. I know she said she's not really in the mood to do anything, but she did admit she's wet, so the idea of just snuggling with her on my lap is turning into something more inside my head.

She was turned on back in the barn, despite the moment of trauma that has obviously resurfaced today. I want to remind her that when we come together, nothing else has to exist, but I need to be careful. She's very on edge tonight, and the last thing I want to do is send her into a flashback.

But still... her flushed cheeks are obvious under the porch light, and making her come might actually help her relax.

Lowering to sit in the chair, I decide to push her a little and see how she reacts, so I point to her jeans.

"Take them off."

Her brows shoot up. "Excuse me?"

"You heard me, Angel."

For a long moment, she just stares at me before she speaks.

"I'm not in the mood."

I shrug. "You'll be comfier under this blanket with those tight jeans off." I start to spread the blanket out over my lap. "Now, off with them and get under here."

She chews on her lip like she sometimes does, and I know she's weighing up all the scenarios.

"Don't make me ask again," I tell her, and she smirks.

"And if I say red instead of doing what you asked?"

"Then your pants stay on, and you can be uncomfortable as you cuddle me."

A snicker escapes her, and she shakes her head as she starts undoing her jeans.

"You drive a hard bargain." She glances over her shoulders, checking to see if anyone is around before toeing off her shoes and tugging down her jeans, stepping out of them and draping them over the back of my chair. "What about these?" She points to her panties, and I shrug.

"Leave them on." I want to say I can work around them, but I keep it to myself, almost wanting her to think nothing untoward is going to happen.

I want her to want more. To feel the tension and anticipation. To let the wonder tease her. To have her craving me as much as I crave her.

Lifting up the large blanket, I welcome her onto my lap, and she quickly dives in, the cold night air making her move with a sense of urgency. She straddles my lap, weaving her arms around me, and I wrap the blanket around us, making a little cocoon.

"Shit, it's cold." She shivers as she snuggles into my chest, so I tug her closer, running my hands up and down her back until our body heat starts to make an oven under the blanket.

The grunts, moans and skin slapping coming from inside make us both snicker for a moment, keeping the mood light, and all I can think about is how fucking perfectly she moulds against my body. How I can feel the press of her mound against the hardening shaft of my cock.

Fuck. I don't think I'll ever get enough of my wife.

"You know, I was thinking," I start, and she scoffs on a giggle.

"Now I'm worried."

I snort. "Maybe you should be, because I've decided I want to watch you fuck that glittery dildo you taunted me with last week."

She straightens, pulling back quickly to look at me, her blonde brows high.

"I thought you said nothing fucks me but you."

"I did," I growl, leaning in to nip at her ear, and just like I'd hoped, she cranes her neck to the side, giving me better access. "But maybe if I'm the one sliding it inside you, then it still counts as me..." I grip her hips tightly, and grind up against her. "Fucking you."

Abbey moans, and I nibble a path down her neck as I feel the grind of her hot little mound over the hard bulge of my shaft.

"You like the thought of that," I point out, sliding my hand up to cup her full, heavy tit, and she drops her head back, panting.

"I like the thought of you doing just about anything to me," she admits, and I can't fucking help the growl that escapes.

With the way she's grinding on me, I know she wants more, so I use my free hand to slide between us, finding the damp crotch of her panties, and hook them aside, giving me access to her slick, wet, cunt.

"How about if I slide the dildo inside you?" I breathe, running two thick fingers through her folds, and teasing the entrance of her cunt. "While *I'm* fucking you."

And, fuck me, that visual has my cock straining like a balloon that's about to burst.

"Ohhhh," she moans, grinding down like she's trying to get my fingers to sink inside her. "Do you mean your dick and the dildo... one in the front and one in the... you know. Back door?"

My smile is wide at her innocence. It's something I love about her. I love how she trusts me, even when she's not sure if she's going to like something. She still trusts me to make sure she's okay.

As I tease her soaked entrance, I release her tit and run my hand over the globe of her arse, finding the tempting valley that leads to another form of heaven.

"That's one way of doing it," I rasp, nipping at her ear as she moans, probably not even realising that she just shifted to spread her cheeks wider, so I slip my hand down the back of her panties and between her cheeks to find the puckered little hole in question.

"What I'm talking about though..." I continue as I press my middle finger to her back passage, teasing the entrance there too. "Is sliding the dildo in alongside my cock, deep in your pussy. Both my cock and the dildo stretching you impossibly wide."

She moans loudly, a gush of heat rushing over my fingers from her cunt, so I slip a finger inside her there, and ease the other into her arse as she gasps.

"Maybe I'll put a plug in the back here." I curl my finger inside her tight arse before I continue. "Filling you up completely."

"Cam," she whimpers, completely at my mercy now.

"Would you like that, Angel? Be honest."

"I... I don't know," she pants, easing back to look at me even as she rolls her hips, trying to take my finger in the front deeper. "I think so, but I don't know."

"Colour?" I ask, and she answers quickly.

"Green."

"Good girl," I praise, pressing my forehead to hers, and we lock eyes, staring at each other as I slowly fuck a finger in her cunt and arse. "When we try it, Angel. You will tell me when you are orange or red, won't you?"

"Yes," she breathes, grinding on me.

"And you trust me, knowing I'll stop if and when you need me to. Right?"

"Yes." She moans.

"Attagirl."

"Cam," Abbey whimpers. "I want your dick... inside me. Please."

"Fuck, Angel. I do love the way you beg."

Easing my fingers from inside her arse and cunt as quickly and as gently as I can, I reach between us, undoing my jeans and shuffling them down a little so I don't get my cock caught in the fucking zipper.

When I finally free my stiff cock, I give it a squeezing pump, milking some precum up to the tip.

In her desperation, Abbey's hand wraps around mine, hungrily guiding my cock to her entrance as she rises up.

"I want it in," she groans, and I fucking grin from ear to ear.

My little Angel is starving.

In unison, we release my cock, and she lowers down over me, her wet slick heat wrapping around me as we both moan.

"Fuuuck, Abs. Sinking into you feels like home."

She whimpers in response, nodding frantically as our eyes lock under the dim porch light.

"Yes, that's exactly what having you inside me feels like."

Fuck. I want to beat my chest like a fucking gorilla, eager to let the jungle know who my mate is.

As I slowly thrust up into her, she grinds down on me, rolling her hips as she goes, sexy little moans falling from her lips.

"Angel?" I groan. "You wanna come?

"Yes," she pants, "but not yet. You feel so good. I don't want it to end."

"Then let's ride it out together," I growl, gripping her globes to spread her nice and wide, using them to control her thrusts, forcing her to roll and grind harder.

Laughter floats down the path, and I squint to see who the shadows are headed our way. Abbey hasn't noticed them yet, so I keep fucking her, nice and slow, knowing it's not too obvious what we are doing.

Well... not *yet* anyway. Give us another few minutes and that might be a different story, but right now, it just looks like we are cuddling.

Clenching my teeth, I try to hold back the groan of pleasure that wants to escape as the five shadows start to morph into the familiar builds of Vender, Murf, Trunk, Stocky, and Trigger.

Fuck.

"Hey, there you are!" Murf calls out, and Abbey stiffens on my lap.

"You two look cosy." Vender is the first to step up onto the porch, followed by the others.

For fuck's sake.

Abbey's eyes go wide, locking with mine. She's scared we've just got caught, and I roll my tongue in my mouth to keep from laughing.

"JD and Jols kick you out?" Stocky asks, taking a seat right fucking next to us.

"Yep," I mutter, even as the sound of the mattress squeaking inside meets our ears.

Everyone laughs. Everyone but Abbey, who hides her head in my neck, the pounding of her racing heart beating against my chest.

"Fuck. You think Jols would mind if I watched?" Murf snickers.

"I think JD should be the one to worry about," I say, trying to sound casual, but it's a little fucking hard with my cock buried inside the tight hot heat of my wife's silky cunt.

The guys start talking shit about JD and Jols, probably hoping they can hear, and Abbey shifts on my lap, lifting her hips to try and slip me out.

In an instant, my fingers dig into her hips as I press my lips close to her ear.

"Don't even think about it."

She stiffens again, whispering back. "But they will know."

"Fuck 'em," I growl louder, not even caring if my club brothers hear.

Abbey relaxes into me, my cock sinking all the way in again, and fuck, I have to hold my breath not to make a fucking sound that will give us away.

"Don't you fuckers have somewhere better to be?" I snap, and Vender scoffs.

"Helina and Darla have trains running on them, making it a fucking competition to see how fast each guy can come and in the end, they are going to measure how much cum they can push out of them."

Something about what Vender just said must turn my Angel on, because she grinds her clit against me as she rolls her hips, her breathing picking up.

"And that's not something you fuckers want a piece of?"

"It's Smitty..." Stocky mutters. "He's turned it into a competition where he tries to come inside Celina each time someone else does, and I'm fucked if I want to watch him make it about himself again."

My brows hitch at Stocky's words and the way the others all nod.

Shit. Smitty is losing too much respect. What the fuck is wrong with him lately?

Not wanting my Angel to dry up to discussions about Smitty, I change the subject.

"Did Darla gag enough for you, Murf?"

And there it is, a gush of heat over my cock and leaking out the sides. I'm so fucking stiff inside her that it's impossible not to feel every little movement she makes, including the way her panting breaths are getting faster.

Is my wife going to come? While other people are around?

Fuck if I don't love the idea of that.

I don't necessarily want them to see her, and they can't see anything of her right now, other than her head, but fuck, would it turn her on if they knew what she was doing right now? I'm pretty sure knowing Riggs knew what we were doing added to her pleasure yesterday.

"She's one of the best gaggers I've had," Murf admits, moving his hand to his crotch. "Fuck, now I'm getting hard again."

The guys laugh, and Abbey shifts a little like she needs more friction, so I slide my hand around to her arse again, using the wetness coating her folds and the base of my shaft to lube up my digit, and slip it back inside her tight puckered rose.

She moans into my neck, loud enough that Stocky hears, but I don't look at him, pretending like I don't have a fucking clue what that noise was. It's suddenly a fucking inferno under this blanket, and sweat starts to coat our skin as she subtly rolls her hip and presses back against my finger as I ease it in and out of her arse.

"Fuck, you filled her mouth with cum," Trigger snickers. "How much did you shoot down her throat?"

Abbey's little thrusts get faster, and fuck me, I'm about ready to explode as she moans again, so I go to draw my finger out of her arse, because we need to stop before this becomes a fucking show.

"Don't stop," Abbey whimpers quietly near my ear, and I freeze, keeping my finger exactly where it is.

"Fuuuuck, Angel," I mutter, tipping my head back as my cock swells inside her even fucking more.

"Ahhh... have we walked in on something?" Stocky asks, since he's the closest, getting a better insight into what's going on under the blanket than the others.

"Ringo," Abbey whimpers, her need completely consuming her, and fuck it, those arseholes can wait.

"Fuck, Angel. Hold on," I murmur before barking to the guys. "Fuck off, will ya."

I don't wait to see if they do or not, my lips finding Abbey's as the tension snaps between us, and we forget about our surroundings, focusing on each other.

Abbey moans into my mouth as she writhes on my lap, no longer fucking me in soft little thrusts, but rising up and slamming back down on me, desperate to chase this high.

"Fuck, who knew all the action was happening here," I hear Vender chuckle right as the bungalow door opens.

"Oh shit. Party is out here." JD laughs, but fuck them all, I drag the blanket up as high as I can to hide our faces in a blanket cocoon, making sure Abbey's body is still covered, and then I slip my fingers down to her clit, stimulating her from all directions as I fight to hold it together.

With my tongue in her mouth, my finger in her arse, my cock in her cunt, and my digits rolling over her sensitive clit, her body starts to lock up, tensing from head to toe before she breaks our kiss, throwing her head back and screaming as she starts pulsing around my shaft.

With two more grinding thrusts, I explode too, my nuts drawing tight as cum shoots deep inside her, and I groan into her hair, fucking panting and spent as she goes limp on my lap.

"Well, shit," Jols mutters from the doorway, and Abbey stiffens as if she's just realised what happened.

"Back inside, woman, and get on the bed." JD laughs, and I glance up in time to see him spinning Jols and slapping her arse. "I'm horny again."

"You're always horny," Jols protests right as the door slams shut.

"Oh my God," Abbey murmurs, mortified as Stocky bangs on the door.

"You want company?"

"No! Fuck off!" JD yells back, while Jols giggles inside.

Glancing up, I eye my men, not feeling the least bit embarrassed because, well, this is an MC and this sort of thing happens all the time. But these fuckers know Abbey isn't like the rest of us. They know she's going to be embarrassed.

"Well... looks like it's back to the barn to join the Doxy train," Murf mutters, and Trigger shakes his head, slapping Murf's arm.

"Fuck the Doxies. Come around the side of the bungalow. I'll have you blowing in a matter of seconds."

My fucking eyes widen. Not at Trigger's offer, because that's normal for him, but it's the look of consideration that washes over Murf's face that has me surprised.

"Seconds, you reckon?" Murf asks, and Trigger nods.

"I'll bet you one hundred bucks."

"Huh," Murf nods. "Fuck it. Let's go."

Everyone but Abbey laughs, and I have to wonder if she even overheard that since I'm pretty sure she's in her head right now. Freaking out.

As Murf and Trigger disappear around the corner, Stocky, Vender and Trunk move down the steps, pointing up the path, back towards the barn.

"We'll head back up that way." Stocky chuckles, and I grin, giving them a nod.

When they are out of earshot, and the groans from inside and around the side of the bungalow meet our ears, I grip Abbey's shoulders and shift her back so I can see her face.

"It's okay, Abs."

Her cheeks are bright red, but the devastation I'm expecting to find isn't there.

"I think your dick is like cocaine or something," she scoffs, and I throw my head back laughing.

"Cocaine?"

"Yes." She slaps my shoulder. "I was so ravenous. I think I would have done anything to come on your dick."

"You mean the dick that's now a semi, drowning inside you in all of my cum?"

She giggles and nods.

"Ringo!" a voice calls, and I stiffen.

"For fuck's sake," I grumble. "Will my men never leave me alone?"

I'm about to tell whoever it is to piss off, but then I notice it's Lewy, running down the path towards us.

"What is it?" I ask, sitting taller and bringing Abbey with me as my cum leaks out around the base of my shaft.

"We just got a lead on Elizabeth Stone's location." He pants, rushing to the bottom of the steps.

"How?" Abbey squeaks, turning to look at Lewy over her shoulder.

"She just called," Lewy puffs. "She spoke to Daniel."

16

ABBEY

R ingo's hand comes down on my jigging knee, trying to settle my nerves, but it's no use. I'm far too anxious to relax.

"Angel, we have hours until we stop for the night. Why don't you try and get some sleep?"

I glance over at my husband as he drives the Landy, not a lick of worry etching his features.

But mine?

Well, shit. Maybe someone can just knock me out and wake me up when we're there.

"I don't know if I can sleep," I admit, and his expression is soft and thoughtful as he glances away from the road to me.

Ever since Daniel spoke to his mum last night, I've been a wreck. Lewy managed to track the location and confirmed that Daniel didn't even hint to his mother that he was in trouble, or that we were listening.

I wanted to ask Daniel why he didn't rat us out, but I also didn't have it in me to talk to him at the time.

"Wanna play a game or something then?"

A laugh bubbles out of me. "A game? Like car games? You?"

He narrows his eyes at me, darting between me and the road. "I haven't always been an old guy, Angel. I know about car games."

I scrunch my nose. "What car games did you play back in your day?"

His deep rumbling laugh does wonders for my nerves, and I finally start to relax.

"You're a real brat when you're on edge," he chuckles.

"Maybe you should pull the car over and punish me," I tease, feeling a little bold after what we did last night.

Shit. Even thinking about that has my cheeks heating.

I know we were completely covered by the blanket, but in the end, the guys knew what was happening, and I... ohhh... I like, had an orgasm, loudly, right in front of them.

"I don't need to pull the car over for that, Angel. Just loosen your jeans, and I'll slide my hand in."

My cheeks flush hot, and my lips part as I stare at him.

"You're driving."

"And?" he asks. "You don't think I can multitask, Angel?"

My gaze darts out the windows, at the hordes of motorcycles in front, behind, and next to us on the road.

"They will see," I point out, and he chuckles.

"My club brothers won't mind."

I roll my eyes, and reach over, slapping his shoulder.

"Stop it." I scold him as I sit back in my seat, my jigging knee starting back up as I chew on my nail.

"Talk to me then, Angel. What's going through your head right now?"

My eyes flick to him, worried he can read my thoughts, before I glance over my shoulder into the back seat.

There's camp gear packed for an overnight stay, but amongst it is a baby car seat, the product tags still attached.

Millie bought it online back when I was... pregnant. When Bobbi died... shit, no... when we *thought* Bobbi had died, Millie packed it away in her room so I wouldn't have to see it.

It's like she knew, just like I think I did, that my little girl was never really gone.

"Abs?" Ringo's voice drags my attention back to him, and I sigh, dropping my hand to the seat and shoving it under my thigh to stop me from biting my nails.

"What if I'm bad at this?" I practically whisper as I admit it out loud. "What if she's better off without me?"

I can feel Ringo's eyes on me as I stare forward, straight out the windscreen.

"Your worry is just another one of those mum things that all the good mums worry about, Angel."

"But for real?" I turn and look at him this time. "I don't know the first thing about being a mum. I've never cared for a baby before. I've never looked after *anyone*. I've been controlled by people my whole life. How am I supposed to raise a child? I—"

"Angel, stop."

"No, Ringo." I shake my head, refusing to let him try to comfort me with words meant to appease. "I'm not a good person. I've killed people. I keep seeing their…"

I trail off, clenching my jaw as I fight the threatening tears.

"You see their faces?" Ringo asks, and I nod.

"What if Bobbi finds out what a monster I really am?" My eyes plead with him for brutal honesty.

"I think she'll just see a woman that was fighting for her little girl."

"But I thought Bobbi was dead then. I didn't do those things to protect her. I did them out of hate. Anger."

"Revenge. Justice," Ringo corrects. "Don't forget, those people meant you harm. Some meant Bobbi harm too. They needed to pay for what they did."

I consider that, wondering if I would have killed them if Bobbi had been alive.

If those Rebels had come to the hospital intending to take her, then yes, I still would have killed them. Maybe my mind wouldn't have been ruled by so much hate and anger, but I still would've picked up a gun. I still would've pulled the trigger to protect Bobbi.

The same with Wendy. Maybe I wouldn't have been so… violent. But she willingly put Bobbi in danger. That alone would have been enough.

Some of the people I've killed were fuelled by rage. I know that now. But I also realise something else. I still would have killed every single one of them. The only difference would've been the reason. Rage versus the wild, desperate need to protect.

"I still would have killed them," I admit out loud, and Ringo nods, his expression soft with sympathy.

"And since you can't change the past, you need to focus on the future and what sort of mum you want to be."

"I know what sort of mum I *don't* want to be," I rush out, cringing as I shake my head. "I can't get her voice out of my head, telling me I'm not fit to be a mother."

"Force it out," Ringo growls. "That bitch is the one not fit to be a mother. You're already more of a mother than she ever was. Look how you've fought to protect Bobbi. Look what you've done for Tahli."

His hand squeezes my thigh again, and I turn in the seat, resting on my side as I stare at the man I married.

"I just want all of this to be over. I just want us to be happy. I swear I don't normally cry so much. Or *kill* so much."

Ringo chuckles, his lips kicking up in a crooked smile as he glances at me.

"I've seen your playful side, Abs. Happiness is just around the corner. I'm sure of it."

Reaching out, I run my hand up his arm, feeling the thick corded muscles, and wonder how I got so lucky to have found him.

I stare at him for a long time until my eyes grow heavy, then wake hours later as the car slows, turning off the main road.

Blinking past my sleepy haze, I realise we have made it to the other side of the state since the sign on the side of the road says the Victorian and South Australian border is only twenty-five kilometres away.

"Welcome back." Ringo's voice is light, and I take in his smirk.

"I was snoring, wasn't I?"

He shrugs. "There was more drool and fly catching than snoring, but you did have a go at one stage. Thought a truck was coming for me."

I gape at him as he chuckles, my cheeks heating with a dash of embarrassment.

"Next time you snore, I'm recording it on my phone so you can hear yourself," I rush out, and he simply shrugs.

"That's fine, Angel. I'll just record your come cry and play it back to you."

My eyes narrow. "That will mean war."

"War with you sounds fun." He smirks, wagging his brows as he flicks on the indicator and the car slows again. "We can't get across the state border until the morning, when the cops the Angel sisters have on their payroll are working, so we're staying here for the night."

I want to protest. Scream that we need to keep driving to get my little girl back, but also, I'm kind of terrified to see her.

What if she doesn't like me?

What if she sees the monster I really am?

I get jostled as we turn onto the pothole ridden driveway of a dingy old caravan park, the rumble of the motorcycles idling around us as they roll in too.

I'm not sure what business owner would be happy about a horde of bikers wanting to stay and use their facilities, but whatever charm JD and Spud wield seems to work. Within minutes, we're waved through to the back section of the park to set up camp for the night, and I'm a little amazed at how everyone seems to know their role to get the job done.

Some set up swags and tents, while a group of club brothers assemble what I quickly realise is an outdoor kitchen. Someone gets music going, and another guy starts handing out beers, and it all just flows, like they've done this a hundred times before.

The only odd one out is me, since I'm the only female.

The Doxies were ordered to stay behind, along with a group of club brothers, to watch over the compound and keep up with the construction of their little village. No one but me, Ringo and Lewy knows where we are headed exactly. Ringo wanted to keep it quiet, which of course, pissed off Smitty, but he still insisted the club join the hunt.

Ringo has parked the Landy off to the side, and moves the baby seat to the front before showing me how the seats lay down, and how the self-inflating mattress works.

I've never slept in the back of a car before, and if it weren't for my need to pee and eat, then I'd happily slip inside and hide for the rest of the night.

Once we're set up, Ringo acts as my bodyguard, leading me to the women's facilities, slipping inside to make sure it's all clear.

We are the only people staying in the park so I knew it would be, but I enjoy this protective side of him. It makes me feel cherished and special.

Once I'm done, Ringo leads me back to the camp, and I spot Daniel tied to a tree behind the van, eating a bread roll as two club brothers watch over him.

We needed to bring him along with us. That was quickly decided last night. He's our leverage, should we need it when we arrive in the little seaside town Elizabeth is hiding in with Bobbi.

A barbeque dinner is cooked up, and Ringo fetches us a couple of plates filled with food, and just like he did months ago, he feeds me, clearly enjoying having me on his knee and ordering me to open my *pretty lips*.

It's not long before the men get a little rowdy and bored, and some start to have a competition to see who can piss the furthest.

"Hey Abbey." JD leans in from the seat next to me and Ringo. "You want me to put that piece of shit in front of them so he gets covered in piss?"

Cringing, I shake my head as he refers to Daniel. "No, but thanks."

"You want us to give him a taste of his own medicine?" Smitty's voice makes me stiffen as he steps out from the bushes off to the side. I didn't even know he was there.

Such a creepy fucker.

"We got a few men here that don't mind cock and arse. We could show him what it's like to be raped."

Air gets trapped in my throat at Smitty's words, and a growl rumbles in Ringo's chest, clearly not happy with his President.

Those two have been off over the last few days. Ringo hasn't said anything, but I can feel the tension radiating between them like it's a living thing.

"Our club doesn't rape," Ringo barks, and Smitty shrugs.

"It's just another form of torture. Wouldn't hurt the fucker to know what it feels like."

"No!" I burst up from Ringo's lap, glaring at Smitty. "Absolutely not!"

His brows hitch, and his jaw ticks as he regards me. "Maybe you don't have a say in it, *Charity*."

Balling my fists, I take the three steps to close the distance between us, standing on my tiptoes to get up in his face.

"He's *my* prisoner!" I snap, feeling like the blood in my veins is near boiling.

"No one touches him," Ringo snaps, standing behind me, and Smitty grins like the Cheshire cat himself, holding up his hands and walking backwards casually.

"Fine. No one touches him." He rolls his eyes, spinning on his heel and strutting off in a walk that reminds me of Captain Jack Sparrow.

"Is it just me, or is he getting more and more unhinged?" JD asks from beside us, and I shoot him a glare.

"You started it by suggesting they pee on Daniel."

"Shit," JD cringes. "Sorry, Abs. My bad."

"I guess you're next on Daniel watch then," Ringo grumbles, jabbing a finger at his best mate. "I don't fucking trust Smitty when he's like this. We should've brought Celina along to keep him busy."

"Fine. I'll watch the rapist, but I'm not holding his dick if he needs to take a leak. That's the prospect's job."

We all glance over at the newest prospect as he runs around picking up scraps of food the club brothers throw him to eat.

I shake my head, not interested in being around that stuff tonight.

"I'm going to bed." I turn, hearing the guys call goodnight to me, and I make my way over to the Landy.

Ringo is only a few steps behind me, and I turn to him as I open up the back of the car.

"You don't have to come to bed yet, Cam. You can stay and hang out with your club brothers."

He shakes his head before I even finish talking.

"It's cold. And the only thing I'm interested in is right here." He grins, reaching out to pinch my arse.

I squeak as I scurry up into the back of the car where our made up bed is.

Turning, I watch as Ringo starts to undress outside, so I kick off my shoes and put them aside, before shuffling out of my jeans.

Ringo smirks watching me as I watch him, both of us shedding layers like we do every night when we go to bed.

Although most nights sex is involved. I guess tonight will be different since we are in the back of his car, and there are no curtains on the windows.

Ringo climbs up and closes us in a few minutes later, both of us bumping into each other as we manoeuvre in the small space to slip under the blankets to get warm.

"It's gonna be a cold night, Angel. Make sure you cuddle up to me nice and close."

I giggle as I settle against his side, his arm sliding under me as he draws me even closer.

"It is cold. Maybe I should put my hoodie back on." I shiver, and Ringo reaches over with his other hand, running it up and down my bare back to help warm me.

"You won't need clothes on," he rasps into my hair, his lips pressing there a moment later.

"But it's cold," I whine, and he gives me a squeeze.

"You won't be cold soon, Angel."

I giggle at the little thrust of his hips, letting me know he's already hard.

"We can't have sex in here," I point out, and he scoffs.

"Why the fuck not?"

"There's not enough room." I giggle, already starting to feel warmer from his body heat.

"It's the perfect amount of room," he says, gripping my thigh, and hitching it over his hip, opening me up. "Close quarters, Angel. No way to avoid brushing against each other."

He does another one of his thrusts, and the head of his dick presses to my clit, sending a jolt of pleasure through me.

"But someone might see in," I weakly protest, melting against him as my body heats from the inside out.

"Let them. I don't give a shit about anyone else but you right now," he groans, before finding my lips with his.

His tongue is searing against mine in a kiss that goes on and on. So often we move straight onto other stuff, but this time, Ringo kisses me thoroughly, and who knew just that alone would have me whimpering with need.

"Fuck, Angel. I could kiss you all day," he rasps, his facial hair tickling my neck as he nibbles down to my breasts.

Then, just like he does so often now, he licks and then sucks on my nipple, drawing it deep as my milk starts flowing into his mouth.

His magical hand slides down my body, finding my clit and circling it, quickly building the pleasure inside me to fever pitch.

When he's done with one breast, he shifts to the other, grinding his hard shaft against my thigh as he drinks from me.

In a matter of minutes, I'm writhing against him, the sounds of the men outside slipping away as my focus shifts to everywhere he's touching and kissing me.

Desperate to feel him too, I reach down between us, finding his erection and wrapping my hand around it.

He hisses in a sharp breath, the vibration of it teasing my nipple, and his fingers work faster over my sensitive bundle of nerves as I let myself go.

I cry out as the first spasm hits, his fingers speeding up in a relentless assault, dragging my climax out as wave after wave ripples through me.

When my hearing starts to return to normal, I realise how loud my panting is, and snap my eyes open in shock.

"Hey, beautiful." Ringo grins, and embarrassment rushes over me at how well I can see him from the glow of lights coming in through the windows.

If I can see him, then he can see me.

"Making you come is better than me coming myself."

My brows shoot up. "Really?"

"Fuck, yes." He chuckles, brushing some of my hair back off my forehead. "I love how far you've come, Angel. How relaxed you are with me."

Blushing, I bite my lip and nod. "I love that too. I've never felt safer."

Smiling, Ringo brings his fingers up out of the blankets, licking them clean, his eyes locked on mine the entire time.

Holy moly. This guy could get me pregnant without even having sex if stares had that power. Thankfully, Dee slipped me a package the other day, and I'm now taking birth control, although I know I have to give it some time to be considered in the safe zone.

"Remember that first night you used my fingers?" Ringo asks, wiggling his fingers before my eyes, and I nod, remembering how he'd let me use them on myself. Let me be in control.

It had worked. God, just remembering the feel of his digits sliding through my...

"That was fucking hot." Ringo grins, moving his hand to my breast, and cupping it.

"It was," I agree. "I wanted more. I just..." Frowning, I shake my head at how frustrating it was that I couldn't get past my trauma.

"I know, Angel. You don't have to explain."

"I want you now." I smirk, giving his hard dick a squeeze, finally remembering that I've been holding on to it this entire time.

"You have me, Abs. Back then. Now. And always."

He nips at my lips, and for another few moments, we get lost in a slow, sensual kiss of tongues and nips, and swallowing each other's moans.

"Angel, I want to fuck you now, but it's a tight squeeze in here with the mattress set up. You're not going to be able to ride me, so do I have permission to go on top?"

"You don't have to ask for permission anymore," I tell him honestly, knowing the trigger of missionary no longer happens when it comes to him.

He nods. "I know, but I'm going to be right on top, Angel. Crushing your body into the mattress. Nose to nose. There's no room for me to hold myself off you to give you space to breathe."

I get what he's saying, and I appreciate his concern for me. It may potentially feel smothering. A few months ago, I don't think I would have coped. But now, with him, I'm totally fine with the idea of it.

"Just don't hit your head." I grin, and he shoots me a wink, quickly shuffling beneath the blanket so he can settle over me.

There's something so intimate about being so close. Just the two of us in this cramped space, not able to fully move, but desperate to feel each other.

We both laugh when he hits his head, curses flying from his lips as he gets his foot tangled in the blanket, but eventually he gets comfy, his hard shaft pressed against my seam, teasing me, and I moan.

"You hungry for my cock, Angel?"

"Always," I breathe, spreading my legs wider in the hope it slips in all on its own.

"You want to feel it stretch you open? Hit you deep?"

"Ringo," I groan. "Put it in."

He chuckles, deep and raspy, lifting his hips a fraction, causing his tip to glide through my folds, finding my entrance.

"Here you go," he breathes, his dark eyes locked on mine. "Open wide, Angel."

I relax as his tip presses just inside, and when he shifts closer, his dick sinks in, giving me that stretch he was talking about.

He moves agonisingly slow, thrusting in, rolling his hips, pushing me further into the mattress before retreating. Over and over, my entire body ignites from the tease, already wired to come again.

Travelling my hands down over his shoulders and back, I dig my nails into his arse cheeks, loving the hiss of breath that leaves him, and the way his thrusts grow more urgent.

When he rears up, trying to get deeper, he hits his head, and we both pant out a laugh before the frustration of it settles in.

"We're gonna need a little extra, Angel," he grunts, still grinding into me.

"Extra?" I pant, wondering if he packed the pink dildo he was talking about yesterday, but then his hand slips between us, and I figure he's about to give my clit some attention.

"I'm gonna stretch you extra wide tonight," he tells me as his fingers bypass my clit and go straight for where he's thrusting in and out of me.

"Ohhh," I moan as he squeezes a couple of his fingers in past his dick, curling them up inside me.

"I want to hit all your spots," he pants, thrusting harder as his thumb presses to my clit.

"Cam," I half cry, half moan as his fingers quickly spike my pleasure.

"Fuck, Angel. You need to feel this," he pants as my nails dig harder into the globes of his arse.

"Yes," I whimper, not really sure what I'm saying yes to.

"Give me your hand... down here." He thrusts fast. "Quickly, Angel."

I do as he demands, slipping my hand between my legs, feeling his shaft sliding in and out as he withdraws his fingers.

"Slip yours inside," he orders. "Three or four."

I don't even get a chance to hesitate, his hand guiding mine until I feel the hot wetness of myself as three of my fingers squeeze inside me, past Ringo's dick.

"Fuck yes," Ringo hisses, his whisky eyes nearly blown. "You're such a dirty girl. Can you feel how well you're taking us both?"

"Yes," I moan, grinding the heel of my palm against my clit, and I curl my fingers inside.

"You can take more. Add a fourth finger for me." He pants, thrusting faster, his eyes trained on mine, and I do exactly as he asks, feeling my pleasure build. "Fuuuck, yes. Are you stretched nice and wide?"

I nod against the pillow, and his hand slips out from under the blankets, pressing his fingers to my lips.

"Open up, Angel. Clean yourself off as we both fuck you."

A strangled moan falls from me as he slides his thick fingers into my mouth, and the combination of both of us filling me while he draws his fingers in and out between my lips at the same rhythm of his thrusts has me catapulting into an entirely different universe.

The moment Ringo starts coming, I feel his dick pulsing against my fingers as he spills inside me, the slick heat of both of us washing over my fingers.

I don't know how this man does it. How he keeps showing me new ways to enjoy each other. I always thought sex was pretty basic, but with Cameron Musgrove, even the simplest of positions, like missionary, turns into something sinful, and utterly intoxicating.

It's a pity our euphoric moment doesn't last long, when the car door flies open, and JD's panicked voice barks.

"Smitty has taken Daniel."

17

RINGO

M y cock isn't even dry as I stumble out of the car, trying to do my fucking jeans up as I lock eyes with Abbey.

"Stay here. That's a fucking order."

Her glare tells me I'll be in trouble later, but fuck, I don't know what Smitty is up to, and when I find him, it may be something I never want her to see.

"Mex, Stocky, you watch her. Vender, JD, you're with me."

We storm away, although I'm fucking barefoot as JD fills me in.

"He's not thinking straight. Said Daniel is a Southern Sadist prisoner, not Abbey's, and if he wanted to give him a taste of his own medicine, then he would."

"Fuck." I grind my fucking teeth, looking over the crowd of club brothers still talking shit and drinking nearby to see who's missing.

"Spud's gone. Tups too. The prospect, and a couple of the newer guys."

"His lackeys," Vender mutters, and JD and I nod in unison, glancing around the park.

Their motorcycles are still here, so they haven't gone far, which is when my eyes land on the toilet block.

Fuck. I hope we're not too late.

I have hope in the fact that Trigger and some of the other guys who don't mind fucking dudes are still over with the others. So hopefully that means Smitty isn't making good on his threat to have Daniel raped. But our leader is an unhinged motherfucker, so I have a feeling that whatever we walk in on won't be good.

We hurry over to the well lit toilet block, and I can hear Abbey yelling at Mex and Stocky to let her pass, but the agonising screams coming from the toilet block keep me moving forward, because if Smitty kills Daniel, then we won't have leverage with his mum to hand over Bobbi safely.

The moment I reach the door of the men's bathroom, I kick it open, the fucking thing bouncing off the wall and nearly hitting me on the rebound, but fuck, that's not what has my breath seizing in my lungs.

Shit.

No.

"The fuck are you doing!?" I bellow, launching myself inside, only to pull up short when the barrel of a gun jams against my temple.

"Stand the fuck down," Spud snaps. "Remember who your fucking President is."

"H-help!" Daniel cries, and fuck, I want to look away, but I can't. Fuck. "P-please. I-I'm s-sorry."

"Smitty, man. That's enough." JD pleads from next to me, as our fearless President stands across the room, leaning casually against the wall, as Tups, our club Secretary, rapes Daniel's arse with the pole of a mop, while our new prospect and another club brother hold Daniel down.

"NO!"

The piercing scream has everyone cringing, as Abbey comes rushing in behind us, and this time, Tups stops his assault on Daniel, glancing up at Smitty for direction.

"Angel!" I reach out, trying to grab her on her way past, but Spud jams the gun harder against my temple, and I have no choice but to stay put until I can figure out a way to calm this fucking situation down.

"Oh my God!" she cries, her hands fisting into her hair as she takes in what's happening to Daniel.

Her cousin.

Her rapist.

"Stop it!" she screams. "Stop it NOW!"

I hear the pounding of more feet as club brothers start to swarm the toilet block, but Smitty just chuckles, pushing off the wall and lowering to his haunches by Daniel's head.

I'm expecting him to say something taunting, but Smitty speaks quietly, so no one can hear but him and Daniel.

"What the fuck, Nate!?" I yell, needing him to snap the fuck out of this, but he keeps talking quietly, ignoring me, and listening as Daniel mutters something I can't hear in response.

"Get away from him!" Abbey yells at Tups, who still holds the mop head, keeping the other end buried inside Daniel's arse.

Ah shit. I'm pretty sure there's blood on the pole. What the fuck do we do if they've perforated his bowel?

"This is not how we do things!" I yell, hoping my other brothers will agree and help Nate to see reason. "Shit like this is done on a vote. No one fucking voted for this punishment. This kid isn't even *your* fucking prisoner!"

"So you and your little bitch keep telling me."

Abbey flinches at Smitty's words, her pained eyes darting to each man around the room, and I see the moment when she realises she's in a very fucking dangerous situation, that she's hugely outnumbered in.

"But you see," Smitty continues. "You keep using club resources," Nate points out, and my eyes narrow.

"I was using Marx resources up until we brought this fucker to the compound a couple of days ago," I remind him. "Which you fucking cleared. So don't act like we are using the club unfairly. You came to my place. You insisted on helping."

"True." Smitty stands. "But you and your wife keep acting like it's the Ringo and Charity Show. Not the Nate Smith Show."

A round of grumbles floats through the gathered crowd of men, and Nate doesn't even realise it's because they are reeling at what he just said.

The Nate Smith Show.

I open my mouth to speak, but Abbey beats me to it, saying exactly what I was going to.

"Don't you mean the Southern Sadist Show?" she asks, and Nate's jaw ticks as he shoots her a glare, and then turns back to Tups and nods.

Tups only hesitates for a moment before resuming his task, jamming the pole in and out as Daniel starts screaming in agony again.

"STOP!" Abbey screams, making a run for Tups, but the moment Spud redirects his gun from my head towards Abbey, she skids to a stop.

But fuck that! No one points a fucking gun at my wife!

I don't second guess myself. I just act, lunging at him.

We go crashing to the floor, and I roar as I pummel his face, his gun clattering across the tiles, but the fucker plays dirty, kneeing me in the nuts.

Blinding pain surges through me as my nuts draw up into my body, and I wheeze out a breath, falling to the side and Spud wrestles me off him.

The loud crack of a gun echoes through the space, the sound ricocheting off the walls, and everyone falls still.

I blink, choking through the pain as I look up to see the gun, Spud's gun, in Abbey's hands, pointed directly at Smitty.

"Tell him to stop!" she screams, and Nate fucking grins.

"There she is. Our little Sadist monster."

"Tell. Him. To. Stop," she says again, curling her lip in disgust.

"Fine," Smitty sighs, rolling his eyes. "Stop showing the rapist a good time, Tups."

I sit up, coughing and wheezing as Tups pulls out the pole and drops the shit and blood coated thing to the floor with a loud clatter.

"All of you get away from him!" Abbey's voice cracks as she sees the end of the pole, and never in my life have I been more ashamed to call myself a Southern Sadist.

"This isn't right!" I growl as I stagger up, still bent over as one nut starts to descend. "This is not what our club does."

JD moves over to me, helping me straighten, and Abbey redirects the gun towards the men still holding Daniel down.

"I said, get away from him!"

They both look to Smitty, who nods, before they release Daniel, and shift away, moving to stand by their President.

Abbey shudders out a sob, her eyes darting around frantically like she doesn't know who to trust. And fuck. I hate that. She should feel safe with us now, but I know, after this, she never will again.

"How dare you," she cries. "How dare you be so vile?" She curls her lip at Smitty. "Has that ever been done to you? Have you ever been violated like that? Had to take someone or something inside your body that you don't want there?" She shakes her head. "I should just shoot you."

Tension ripples through the air as all the club brothers crammed into the space shift uncomfortably, and I wish I knew what they would do if she did pull the trigger.

Would they accept his fate, or would they punish my wife?

"Angel." I pant as my pain subsides. "Let's just go."

I glance at JD, and he gives me a nod before eyeing the guys I consider my closest club brothers, to see them all nod too.

With trembling hands, Abbey keeps the gun pointed at Nate, and I know she's fighting with that monster she refers to herself as. She wants to pull the trigger, but she also doesn't.

"Get Daniel," I mutter to Vender and Mex, and they move across to where Daniel is sobbing, curled in a ball.

"This shouldn't have happened," I call, for everyone to hear, turning in the middle of the room as I speak. "The Southern Sadists are about honour. About helping people while living by our own rules." I eye every club brother I can, knowing there are still a lot of men outside. "This." I point to Daniel as Vender and Mex get his pants up, giving him a fraction of his dignity back. "This is the very thing we fight against! It fucking says so in our bylaws!"

I turn, glaring at Smitty, Spud and Tups, three of the longest serving members who know damn well what the bylaws say.

Even so, every man needs to be reminded.

"We will not raise a hand, harm or violate women, children, the elderly, or the defenceless!" I bellow. "This piece of shit deserves to be punished, and he will meet his end when the time is right, but we don't VIOLATE ANYONE! No matter what!"

Abbey's tear-filled caramel eyes meet mine then, and I can see her love for me, even as she still holds the gun pointed at my President.

"I am not the one who has broken our code!" I hiss, jabbing a finger towards Nate. "You are!"

"Are you challenging me for my role?" Smitty snarls through gritted teeth, and I shake my head.

"No fucking way if this is what our club stands for." I point to the mop pole.

Low murmurs travel through the crowd, floating to those gathered outside. I can't tell if they are for or against what I just said, but right now, all that matters is getting my wife out of here before things escalate.

"Put him in the back of my car and load him up on painkillers," I tell Vender and Mex, who lift Daniel by each arm, and help him stumble out on shaky legs.

Abbey's chest is rising and falling rapidly as her gaze darts from Daniel, to me, and back to Smitty.

"You gonna shoot me, Charity?" Smitty asks with a shit-eating smirk.

"Maybe." Abbey shrugs. "You definitely deserve a bullet."

He throws his head back, laughing. "I can't fucking tell if you're serious."

"She's dead fucking serious," I snap, and Nate's smirk falls into another glare directed at me.

"You'd better fucking leave before I decide to gut you like a fish."

"Don't worry. I'm leaving here. But *not* the club. Anyone who comes with me is still a club brother," I say, making sure the other men know we are still loyal to the club, despite what's just happened. "We'll be back, and then we can settle this dispute the Southern Sadist way. In fucking church like civilised club brothers."

Nate's nostrils flare as he growls, looking like he's about ready to leap across this shitty men's room and strangle me. I've defied him. Belittled him. Made him look weak.

I have no idea how I'll be received when we return, but that's a fucking problem for another day.

"Angel," I rasp to my wife while keeping my eyes trained on Smitty.

Glancing over her shoulder at me, she walks backwards, keeping the gun trained on Smitty and his men. The moment she's close enough, I take the gun from her grip and urge her towards JD.

My best mate takes her hand and quickly hustles her through the crowd, the men parting easily for her, making me wonder if they might be on her side after what just happened.

The moment I follow, Smitty starts forward, trailing us, and I keep him in my peripheral as I hurry back to the Landy where JD is removing the car seat so Abbey can get in the front.

"Put it in the van," I bark, and he nods, rushing to the van where Murf and Stocky are already getting ready to leave with us.

Moving to the back of my car, I find Daniel curled in a ball, crying silently on the bed Abbey and I just fucked in not even ten minutes ago.

Shit. How can things change so fucking quickly?

"You take the drugs they gave you?" I ask him, and he nods, clutching onto a bottle of water. "That shouldn't have happened," I snap, hating that it sounds like an apology when part of me has always wanted him to have a taste of his own medicine.

It's one thing to think it. It's another thing entirely to do it.

Daniel sobs, curling up tighter, and my eyes meet Abbey's where she's peering over from the front seat.

As chatter from the club brothers draws closer, I close the back door and get into the driver's seat, starting up the Landy.

The van with Stocky and Murf pulls out when I do, along with JD, Vender, Mex, and Trunk, following on their hogs.

"I've ruined everything for you," Abbey whispers, looking out the back window even as I watch Smitty in the rearview mirror, still glaring our way as we drive off.

"This wasn't you, Angel. This is Smitty not liking when people don't give in to his every order. That fucker thinks he's a king, not a leader that is meant to represent his men, and make sure morals are upheld."

As I turn out onto the road, I can feel her eyes on me, and I glance her way to see those big eyes glassy in the glow of the dash as she speaks.

"I should have just killed Daniel."

My lips thin, and I shake my head. "His death will come after we get Bobbi back."

As she glances back to where her rapist cousin shivers in a ball, I pick up my phone and hit the Angels' number, speaking as soon as the call connects.

"We can't wait until the morning to get over the border. We are twenty minutes away and need clearance now."

18

ABBEY

My fingers dig into the seat at my sides as I watch Ringo through the windscreen, talking to the border cops. The headlights of the Landy are shining on them like they are on stage under a spotlight.

There's a lot of hand gestures from Ringo and one of the cops, like they are arguing, before the other cop takes out his phone and makes a call.

"W-what's happening?" Daniel croaks from the back of the car, and I jerk at the sound of his voice, having forgotten he was even there.

"Don't talk to me," I snap, feeling way too emotional right now, because fuck him, I hate that I felt bad for him.

Bloody *had.*

Bad because he was being raped. Because someone was showing him exactly what it's like to be brutally used like that.

I should be revelling in his misery, but instead, I feel *bad*.

And queasy.

Just thinking about it makes me want to puke.

"I-I'm s-sorry, A-Abbey." He coughs. "F-for what I d-did."

I clench my teeth so tightly that I fear they are about to crumble any second, because fuck him. Fuck him for *only* feeling bad after it's happened to him.

He should have felt bad back when it was happening. Or, better yet, not even considered doing it.

But he did.

And he did it so easily.

But Ringo is right. We can't change the past. It's happened, and we need to focus on what's coming.

"Your apology is too late. I don't need it anymore. I just need this to be over."

My voice is lifeless as I speak, the part of me tied to the trauma he caused already shutting down.

She's done. She's checking out. She's ready to move on.

It's a little hard though when the instigator of your gang rape is bleeding from his butt in the back of the car.

Shit... why did Smitty do that?

My lids fall closed as I fight for control over the tears that want to fall again.

So much pain. So much loss. So much blood.

When is enough, enough?

All of this is because of me. Because of the cult life my mum locked us in. Ringo is at odds with Smitty. I don't even know if what happened means he's no longer a Southern Sadist, but since he's still wearing his cut, the eerie skull on the back looking at me lit by the headlights of the car, I'm going to assume he is.

It's then that Ringo spins and storms back towards the Landy, a savage glare consuming his expression.

He can be an intimidating man when he wants to be. Well, he's like that most of the time, but he softens for me... mostly.

A gush of cold air sweeps in when he gets back into the driver's seat, his eyes darting into the back to check on Daniel before coming to me.

"I don't know what the Angel sisters had to do to make this happen, but we finally have the all clear to pass."

I nod, tugging on my seatbelt again. "Do you need me to drive?" I ask, and his surprised expression meets mine.

"Angel, no offense, but did you see how the van fared after you stole it from the airfield?"

My lips twitch. "That wasn't because of my lack of driving skills. That was because I was out of my mind after Daniel told me Bobbi didn't die."

"Even so," he smirks back, "I'm not prepared to risk my Landy."

I snicker at that, relaxing a little at the brief lightness to our conversation, and Ringo drives the car forward slowly, passing through the pandemic state border security checkpoint.

The van and motorcycles follow behind, and the moment we are safely on South Australian soil, we speed up and drive off into the night.

We don't talk much, Ringo playing Metallica through the radio as the late night turns into the very early morning of Wednesday, just eight weeks since Bobbi was born.

At some point I fall asleep, even though I didn't think I'd be able to with Ringo's music on, but something about it started to soothe the race of my heart, and I ended up thinking about Lexi, and how much she'd like this music.

I miss her.

I miss the times we used to share when we were oblivious to the depraved things our parents were involved in. I miss that lighthearted feeling of wonder about our futures, and what adventures awaited us. I miss our days in the sun, going to parties with our friends, and movie days at Simon's, which usually ended up with someone in the pool, even in the dead of winter.

I miss the time when I was just a girl, flirting with guys and wondering what it would be like to kiss them, the idea of sex so far from my thoughts.

Now, everything has changed, and it's hard for me to wish away the bad things that happened, because if they hadn't, I may never have met Ringo.

The next time I wake, the car is still running, but it's pulled over on the side of the road, and I peer out the window to see Ringo standing in the dark on a scrubby sidewalk, talking with JD and the others.

Stretching, I glance back at Daniel, and as far as I can see he's sleeping, so I slip my shoes on, and quietly get out of the car.

Ringo turns at the sound of the car door clicking closed, reaching his hand out in my direction.

Moving to their little pack, I take his hand and let him pull me against his side, loving how he presses his lips to my head as he listens to JD talk.

"Brody got a couple of calls from some of the guys," he explains, and I can just make out the worry etched over his features from the glow of the car headlights. "They are all panicking. Don't know what's happening and who they should be following."

"I'm not vying for the President's cut. I was just doing what's fucking right," Ringo grumbles, and JD nods. "That's what I told Brody."

"What did Jols say?" Ringo asks, and JD's face turns to stone.

"Don't worry about that."

"Dude, as if we're not going to worry about that." Vender bumps his shoulder against JD's. "Has she heard anything?"

I glance around the group of men, who all remain silent, their focus on JD, and feel a sense of something... is it? Belonging?

"Smitty called her." JD's jaw ticks, and I feel Ringo stiffen. "Said her boy toy is a traitorous sack of shit and won't be returning to the club."

"Fuck that prick!" Murf snarls. "He's off his fucking rocker. And what's with Spud and Tups doing shit like that? I thought that stuff was stamped out ten fucking years ago."

"It was," Ringo snaps. "Smitty's always been a fucking wildcard, but this... this is not the President we voted in."

"Right, well, let's get that piece of shit sorted," Mex bobs his head towards the Landy, "get our little Bobbi girl back to her mumma," he winks at me, "and then worry about the fucking club business after that."

Our little Bobbi girl?

My chest warms. They haven't even met her yet, and they are calling her theirs? Like she's already a part of the family.

I squeeze closer to Ringo as one of the thousands of lacerations in my heart stitches itself closed.

Is this what a real family is like? Caring about someone just because they mean a lot to someone else? Fighting for them, even if it goes against others' wishes?

Shit. Maybe I *can* do this. Be a mum, I mean.

With guys like this around, especially Ringo, I feel like I'd have the courage to face anything.

Pulling his phone out, Ringo checks the time. "We have a couple of hours before the sun rises. Let's scope the place out and aim to go in before daylight hits."

My brows hitch as his words sink in, and I glance around, past the guys, at the scrubby bushland surrounding us.

"Uhhh, are we there? Is Bobbi here somewhere?"

"That way, Angel." Ringo points down the road. "It's a small seaside town. Nothing fancy. Dirt roads and little beach cabins. We'll pile into the van once the guys check out the house. Leave the hogs and Landy here hidden in the bushes."

My heart starts racing, part of me wanting to start running down the road to find my baby. But shit. I don't know how many houses there are or where she is exactly, so I nod eagerly, listening to them make a game plan.

When JD, Vender, Mex and Stocky leave on foot to scope out the house, I pace beside the car, chewing on my nail as my emotions start to climb.

I'm impatient and anxious, and I can feel Ringo's eyes on me, but he doesn't tell me to calm down. He knows how massive this is. How today is going to change my life forever.

Not just mine, I suppose. His too. At least, for as long as he wants to keep me around.

Twenty minutes later, the guys return, a little breathless from jogging, and JD bends, placing his hands on his knees as he starts relaying what they saw.

"House is the second one in on the waterfront. There is dirt road access, plus beach access. A house on either side. One looks to be occupied, and the other looks vacant. A holiday rental, maybe." JD coughs, clearing his throat as he straightens. "We, uhhh, heard a baby crying in the target house. Must have woken as we approached. A light came on inside, the back corner, roadside."

My heart flips, and I suck my lips in, trying to fight back tears.

"Any visual inside?" Ringo asks, pulling me against his chest and running his hand up and down my back.

"Yeah, only from the beach side. I could see a woman walking around," Vender adds.

"Just one woman?" Ringo asks, and Vender nods. "Either the second woman is in bed, or isn't there. Either way, we go in assuming there are two adults in the house. Maybe more."

The men go over a few more details, but I zone out, only picking up words like, the baby must be protected at all costs, and try not to kill the women, but if they threaten the baby, take them out.

After they have a plan of attack, the motorcycles are hidden in the bushes, and Daniel is escorted from the Landy into the back of the van, his body curled over like he's in pain as he walks.

Ringo ushers me to the front of the van, getting me to slide into the narrow middle seat as he gets in next to me, and JD slips into the driver's seat, starting up the van.

The others are in the back with Daniel, while Stocky stays behind with the Landy and bikes, acting as a lookout on the one road in.

My knee won't stop jigging again, my heart thundering in my chest, and I want to chew on my nails, but Ringo has hold of both of my hands like he knows exactly what I want to do.

JD drives the van down the road, and when we round the bend, a dingy little streetlight illuminates a row of tiny houses on the right, and one single street, which is a dirt road.

At the end of the road we are on, there is a sign warning that there's no vehicle access to the beach, and as the car slows, a couple of the guys jump out the side door and run, guns in hand, towards the sandy path between the dunes.

Shit. Shit. Shit.

This is really happening.

"When we pull up, you stay in this car until I tell you," Ringo demands. "Got it?"

I nod, even though I don't spare him a glance, my eyes focused ahead as JD slowly idles the van onto the dirt road, stopping in front of the first house.

"Let's go," JD barks, and again, some of the guys slip out the side door, while JD cuts off the engine and gets out too, following behind.

It's eerily quiet inside the van. I can hear Ringo breathing next to me, and glance over my shoulder into the back to see Murf sitting with Daniel, who has been bound and gagged.

Squinting back through the windscreen, I see the dark silhouettes of the Sadists disappear into the front yard of the second house in, and Ringo releases my hands to take his gun out.

"You doing okay?" he whispers, and I glance at him, trying not to cry.

I bob my head, but then shake it, and end up shrugging, because clearly, I'm not doing so well.

His warm hand reaches up, cupping the side of my face as he presses his forehead to mine in that way he loves to do, and his spicy scent, the one that has me feeling like home, envelops me.

"I'm scared," I whisper.

"I know."

"I don't know how to be a mum."

"I don't know how to be a dad," he rasps. "But we'll figure it out. Together."

A fat tear bursts from my eye, and his thumb catches it, like he knew it was coming.

"You really want to do this with me?"

"Fuck, yes. Not even an ounce of doubt, Abs."

Shit, I love it when he calls me Abs.

"I love you," I whisper past my trembling lips.

"I fucking love you too." He growls in that raspy way of his, and leans closer, pressing his lips to mine.

I sob into his mouth, hating that, yes, once again, I'm crying, but right now, these are happy tears. Any maybe a few scared tears too, but mostly, happy.

The vibration of Ringo's phone breaks us apart a moment later, and his bright screen lights up our faces as he opens the text from JD.

Get in here. Now!

RINGO

My gun is raised as I step through the door, my free hand reaching back to my wife, making sure she doesn't barge past and get herself shot. She clings to the back of my cut, her breathing rapid, desperation clawing at her with the need to see if her daughter really is alive.

"Down there, Sarg." JD uses my title as he steps out from the hallway that leads to two bedrooms, as Vender keeps his gun pointed at a woman who is trembling with her arms wrapped around her waist, perched on a rickety bar stool by the kitchen bench.

"This the nurse?" I ask, and Vender nods as I feel Abbey shift behind me, before she finally shoves past.

"Where's my daughter?!"

The woman flinches as Abbey comes charging for her, but my wife doesn't touch her. She holds herself back, getting in the woman's face.

"Y-you're A-Abbey?" the woman trembles, and I can't hold back the growl that rumbles in my chest.

How could this woman kidnap my wife's baby?! I want to fucking kill her!

"Where the fuck is she?!" Abbey yells, which is when we hear the faint cries of a baby down the hallway where JD came from before.

Darting her head over her shoulder, Abbey's eyes move to the mouth of the passage, and JD fills us in.

"Elizabeth Stone has locked herself in the end room with the baby. We don't have eyes in there. The blind on the window is closed, but Trunk is outside it, in case she tries to escape."

Turning back to Caroline Thatcher, Abbey snarls, and the nurse pales at seeing my wife's monster slip free.

"She make any threats?" I turn to JD as Abbey heads back towards us.

"Just said we can't have the baby."

"That's *my* baby." Abbey shoves through us, stomping up the hallway to where Mex is standing guard outside the room.

Grabbing the handle, Abbey tries to open it, but it's locked, and a heavy sigh escapes her.

"Elizabeth?" she calls through the door, and a moment later, Daniel's mum responds.

"Abbey?"

"Unlock the door. I want Bobbi."

"Bobbi?" Elizabeth asks. "I've been calling her Jane."

I nearly fucking laugh when Abbey's unimpressed gaze locks with mine and she rolls her eyes.

"Really? Jane Doe?" she scoffs, and Elizabeth tries to explain.

"We didn't know what to call her."

"That's because she's not your kid!" Abbey yells, losing patience. "Unlock the door!"

A small cry comes from the room again, and Abbey frantically tries to open the door, knowing it's her little girl.

"Open the door!" Abbey yells, frantic as she looks at me, her eyes pleading for me to do something.

Gritting my teeth, I storm forward, about to kick the door down, when the sound of the latch clicks.

Abbey gasps, lurching for the handle, but I whip my arm out in front of her, stopping her from putting herself in the line of fire.

"Let me go first, Angel. Just to be safe," I grunt, gripping the handle, not even waiting for her response.

I don't remember the last time I was this fucking nervous. My heart is jack hammering, and I raise my gun as I turn the knob and slowly push the door open.

The gentle cry of the baby gets louder, and my eyes track the room quickly, ignoring the furniture, and landing on a woman with tears in her eyes, her features reminding me of her son, Daniel.

"P-please, don't shoot." She holds out her hands. "The baby is fine. She's just hungry."

"Step aside!" I demand, and Elizabeth hesitates, so I lift the gun higher, making sure she can see right down the fucking barrel. "Do I have to shoot you to get you out of the fucking way?!"

"No," she sobs, a shudder rippling through her as she trembles and finally does what I ask, taking three steps to the side, letting me see the humidicrib against the wall.

Keeping my gun trained on the woman, I glance over my shoulder, expecting Abbey to be right behind me, but instead, she's pressed against the wall out in the hallway, her eyes squeezed tight, like she's too scared to open them to find it was just a dream.

"Angel," I say gently, and JD steps up to her, placing his hand on her shoulder.

"It's time, Abbey," he rasps, and her eyes snap open, wide and full of fear as they lock with his. "It's time to reunite with your daughter."

20

ABBEY

I've come to learn that there are defining moments in your life. For me, a lot of mine have been horrific, but a few have been filled with happiness and love.

This, right here though, will be a moment that will be ingrained in my soul for eternity.

A beautifully momentous moment.

On shaky legs, I step into the room, not paying a lick of attention to Elizabeth. Not really even noticing Ringo. Because right now, in this moment, my eyes are trained on the little arms waving, and little feet kicking, as the sound of a small cry connects with my soul like it's a piece of me.

I can't see her face yet. But I don't need to. I already know. I already feel it.

This is my daughter, Bobbi.

Slowly I approach the clear Perspex box-like crib, each step bringing me closer, each step showing me more and more of the little baby within it.

"I just dressed her so she can come out for her bottle," Elizabeth explains, her voice grating on my nerves, but I don't look at her. I don't for a second take my eyes off the little baby with a dusting of white blonde hair and long dark lashes, much like mine.

"Oh my—" I sob, pressing my hand to my lips to stifle any more sobs that want to escape.

Rushing closer, I stare in at the little baby, who stops crying when she sees me, her dark grey eyes blinking as she starts to stare.

Everything comes rushing back.

That day in the forest. Feeling her leave the safety of my body to be placed on my chest. The cute little button nose. Her tiny head, covered in mucus and blood. The way she felt on my chest.

My little Bobbi.

My knees go weak, nearly giving out, but Ringo's strong hands come out of nowhere, holding me up as I try to open the crib to get to my daughter.

"I don't know how..." I sob, trying to figure out how to use the latch, and Elizabeth rushes in, her smile gentle despite the fact JD now has a gun trained on her, and she opens the crib for me.

"Caroline was warming her bottle in the kitchen," Elizabeth rushes out, but I shake my head.

"No. I will feed her."

"Of course," she steps back. "I can get Caroline to bring in the bottle."

Again, I shake my head, glaring at Daniel's mum. "No. I will *breastfeed* her."

Elizabeth's brows shoot high, her mouth opening and closing, dumbfounded, and now, I give her my full attention as I stab a finger towards her.

"You may have stolen her, but I knew…" I punch the centre of my chest. "I knew deep in my heart that she was alive. I've kept up my milk supply for her, and *I* will be the one to feed her."

Tears flow from Elizabeth's eyes as she nods, stepping back, her hands raised as if she's surrendering.

Later, she'll learn that her surrender means nothing. But for now, I need to learn how the hell to breastfeed my daughter.

"Get her out of here," Ringo barks to JD, who steps forward, pressing his gun to Elizabeth's head, and she whimpers as she's escorted out, leaving me and Ringo alone with Bobbi.

Suddenly, I feel out of my depth. How do I even do this?

"I don't…" I trail off, looking to Ringo for guidance, even though he never had a moment to be a father to Hope.

His eyes are warm as he smiles softly down at me, his touch soothing, giving my arm a gentle squeeze in reassurance.

"I'll lift her out. You take a seat."

I nod quickly, not able to talk as I move to the armchair in the corner of the small room, and watch as my big, hulking husband gently lifts my fragile daughter from the crib.

My breath catches as I watch him with her. The hard stare he usually wears melts away, his face lighting up as he smiles down at the little baby, so tiny in his big strong hands.

"Hey there, little one," he coos. "You want cuddles from your mummy?"

As he steps closer with her, I can't help but stare at him and wonder if he's actually a guardian angel, sent to protect me and my little girl.

"Here she is." He smiles down at Bobbi. "Here's your mummy."

He shifts close, handing her to me, and I snap out of my awe and fall into a whole new daze as my hands finally hold on to my daughter for the first time since she was born eight weeks ago.

There are so many tears. I give up trying to stop them. There's really no point. I'm completely overwhelmed, filled with joy that mixes with the heartache of knowing we've been kept apart for so long.

I didn't come prepared for feeding, so Ringo helps me lift my hoodie and shirt, peeling down the cup of my bra to free my breast, and I spend a few anxious moments trying to get her to latch on, knowing she might struggle if she's been bottle fed all this time.

Ringo helps me as much as he can, and after a few attempts at sucking, Bobbi finally latches and starts drinking from me.

I thought this would be more awkward. That I'd feel creeped out or something, given what Ringo and I have been doing since my milk came in, but it just feels so natural. Like I was always meant to do this. Like she was always meant to be mine.

"Shit." Ringo chuckles, and I glance up to see his amused expression through the haze of my tears. "So that's how it's done."

A laugh bubbles from me, and he grins, shooting me a wink and lowering to his haunches to sidle up close.

"Stop it." I giggle. "Don't make it weird."

"Oh, this isn't weird. Just you wait until I want my feed."

I snort at his playful teasing tone, shaking my head as he looks at me and Bobbi with so much love.

He presses a kiss to my arm before reaching up and stroking his fingers down the side of Bobbi's cheek.

I grin at how his fingers look ginormous compared to Bobbi's. Everything about him now seems so huge and manly, because everything about her is so tiny and dainty.

We spend some time, just the three of us, feeding, and learning how to burp her. She gives me the gift of a dirty nappy, and I don't even hesitate to change her.

Ringo spends some time holding her cradled in his huge arms, and I think I fall in love with him even more, for treating her just like a father should.

I don't know who her real father is, and I don't think I ever want to know. None of those predators matter. The only thing that does, is Bobbi, and the man holding her, willing to step up and be her dad.

When she gets sleepy, I'm not really sure what to do with her since she's still technically, not full term, so Ringo helps me put her back into the humidicrib, and even though it's hard to leave her, I need to let her sleep while I find out what the hell Elizabeth Stone intended for my daughter.

Out in the living area, we find Daniel huddled on the floor in the corner, and JD gestures to the other bedroom.

"The women are being watched in there," he explains. "There's been no mother and son reunion yet."

"Good," I snap, feeling the softness fall away as I gear up to deal with my daughter's kidnappers.

Taking my hand, Ringo leads me into the room, and we find the two women bound by their wrists and ankles, sitting against the headboard of the double bed, with tape covering their mouths.

Shit. These guys don't mess around.

"I need you to explain to me what the hell you were thinking by kidnapping my daughter?" I snap, and while Caroline rolls her eyes, Elizabeth starts trying to talk behind the tape.

Vender reaches over and tears the tape off, making Elizabeth gasp.

"I was only trying to protect her, Abbey," she pleads. "From the cult. From the danger that follows you because of it. She was too fragile to move around too much, but we needed to get her somewhere safe, and as you can see, she's been doing great. Growing fast."

Elizabeth takes a deep breath, smiling around at everyone in the room like she's some sort of saint.

"She's due to come out of the crib this week. She's a strong little girl." Elizabeth's lip wobbles as she starts to cry. "I just wanted to keep her safe… when I found out about what that church really was… what my husband had forced Daniel to do."

"I get that you think you've done a good thing here," I snap, feeling my anger bubble to the surface as I stare her down. "And I appreciate you keeping Bobbi safe and looking after her. But the fact of the matter is, you kidnapped her. Made everyone, made *me* think she'd died. Do you even know what that's like, Elizabeth? To lose a child? To feel your heart shatter?"

She shakes her head, sobbing. "No… I…"

I feel different as I stand here staring at Daniel's mum. Different from the girl who stepped into this house not that long ago. My monster is here with me. Not hiding. Not lingering in case it's needed.

It's just here. A part of me. Mingling with the sweet version and creating something new.

I'm a mum now.

I have been for eight weeks, but the lioness in me has been dormant, lying in wait until this very moment.

She's here now. And she'll never leave again. Not while there is breath in my body will I ever let someone harm, hurt, or steal my child again.

"You will know that feeling, Elizabeth," I deadpan, barely blinking. "You will know what it feels like to lose your child. To know they will never breathe again. Never laugh. Never hug you. Ever. Again."

"Wait… no, please. I was just trying to keep her safe."

"Were you even going to return her to me?"

She frowns, hesitating before she nods.

"Lie. That was a lie, Elizabeth."

"No. No, I swear," she pleads. "Once the bad people stopped chasing you, I was going to give her back."

"No, you weren't. STOP LYING!" I yell, and she flinches back, sobbing as she nods.

"Okay. Okay. I was going to raise her myself. Give her a good home and education. She'd be safe with me. I'd never let that cult get their hands on her. And Daniel—"

"Daniel, what?!" I yell. "You think he has a right to my child? He's probably not even her father! And any father that would do what he did doesn't deserve one second of that child's life!"

"Daniel didn't know what he was doing."

I launch forward onto the bed, fisting the front of her nightgown and snarling in her face.

"HE KNEW EXACTLY WHAT HE WAS DOING!"

"No, he didn't! He just thought he was sharing you!"

I rear back and slap her face, the clap loud as my hand connects with her cheek, and she nearly tumbles off the bed.

"It's called rape, Elizabeth! RAPE! SAY IT!"

"Noooo. He would never!"

Flying back off the bed, I ball my fists. "Bring him in!"

I don't know who leaves to get Daniel, but he's dragged in a few moments later by his hair, his whimpers muffled by the gag secured over his mouth.

"Please don't hurt him." Elizabeth sobs as mother and son lay eyes on each other.

"You know, Elizabeth, I sounded the same as you when I begged him not to hurt me." I dart my gaze between the two. "And do you know what he did?"

She shakes her head frantically, not taking her eyes off her son, and I swear, she already knows, but just doesn't want to admit that her precious child could do something so heinous.

"Take off his gag," I demand to whoever will listen, and I watch as Mex roughly pulls the gag off Daniel, his sobs louder as they fill the room.

"Mum, I'm sorry," he cries, and I snap my fingers between them to get his attention.

"Tell your mum what you said when I begged for you not to hurt me."

Sobbing, Daniel shakes his head, and I roll my eyes.

"It's not hard, Daniel. I begged probably hundreds of times, and each time you said the same thing. Tell your mum what it was."

"Noooo," he sobs. "Please."

Gritting my teeth, my nostrils flare as I hold my hand out, and a second later a gun is placed in my palm before I jam the barrel to Daniel's temple.

"No!" Elizabeth screams, and Daniel whimpers.

"Please, Abbey. No."

"Tell her! NOW!" I scream, jamming it harder, and he rushes out the exact words he used to say to me.

"Shut up, you fucking ugly whore. No one cares about you."

"Noooo!" Elizabeth howls, and Daniel's head snaps to the side as Ringo's fist slams into it, releasing his pent up rage over what was done to me.

"Please stooopppp!" Elizabeth cries. "He was manipulated by his father. He's the real monster!" she chokes, coughing past her tears. "Daniel was so distraught after learning that you were his... cousin. He didn't know what to do and knew he didn't want to marry his cousin, but he was worried about the baby's safety. That has to count for something!"

"It just means he was creeped out about finding out he raped his cousin. And as for Bobbi's safety," I scoff. "He already admitted that he pushed me in the hopes that my baby and I would die."

"No. No. No." Elizabeth cries as Daniel groans on the floor. "He wanted to save the baby. When he found out that Minister Banes was going to cut your baby from your body at the ceremony, Daniel knew he had to put a stop to it."

I freeze at her words, running them through my head a few times to make sure I heard them right.

"Did you just say Banes was going to cut Bobbi from me? At the ceremony to marry me to my own cousin?"

"Yes. Yes. That's exactly what was going to happen."

"Are you making shit up?" I ask, not wanting to believe her, but deep down, everything is screaming that this is the truth.

"No, I'm not making it up," she sobs. "That's what the ceremony was for. Why my husband had been so obsessed with the two of you. Daniel was to be anointed with the blood of your womb, taking the gift of your life and handing over a new life to Banes where he would raise her in the church. The cult. Karl told Daniel that your baby was the next pure vessel for the prophet, which Banes promised Karl would be Daniel."

"The fuck!" Ringo snaps. "Are you fucking saying that they were going to make Daniel the next leader of the cult?"

"Yes, Banes was going to make Daniel his apprentice."

For a moment I can't speak, her words weaving together to create a picture of pure vulgar evilness that's too unthinkable to consider.

Yet, I need to know.

"Bobbi was to be the next pure vessel?" I ask, and when Elizabeth nods, I feel bile burning the back of my throat. "The pure vessel for the prophet, which was meant to be Daniel... right?"

She nods again, shame washing over her expression, and I glance down at Daniel, who's lying on his side, crying silently, staring at nothing.

"Does that mean..." JD's question trails off as I nod, and as vulgar as it is to say, I need the words confirmed.

"Bobbi was to be Daniel's pure vessel, for what?"

Elizabeth sobs, shaking her head, and when I glance down at Daniel, I find his soul crushed eyes on me as he answers.

"To procreate pure children, the vessel must be the prophet's daughter."

I fight the urge to gag as the Sadists in the room start yelling, completely disgusted, and as crude as Daniel's words are, they don't actually surprise me.

The things I've learned about my mother and her cult family are the sickest form of depravity there is, and just remembering how Banes, my grandfather, had been with my mother, trying to get her pregnant to have his pure children… that shit is pure evil, and there's no place for it in our world.

"Put him on his knees," I order, and Mex and Murf move to do as I've asked as I lock eyes with Ringo.

"I can do this for you, Angel. You don't need to."

Sucking in a deep, shuddering breath, I shake my head, offering my husband a small smile.

"I *need* to be the one to do this."

"Do what?" Elizabeth screeches, but we ignore her, keeping our eyes on each other, and Ringo holds up a silencer attachment for the gun.

"No! No!" Elizabeth shrieks as I take it and screw it on, while Nurse Thatcher falls off the bed in an attempt to try to get away.

"Thank you for keeping Bobbi alive," I say to Elizabeth, and she howls in agonising pain. They are cries I remember well. Cries I felt rip from me not so long ago, and now that pain is something she *needs* to feel, so I continue. "But the pain of losing her was real. For weeks, I mourned her. I killed in revenge for her. My entire being was rewired because you stole her from me."

Stepping up to Daniel's side, I fist his hair, reefing his head back, his fear-filled eyes locking with mine as he sobs.

He doesn't beg for his life, though.

Not anymore.

He knows his time is over, and so does his mum.

"I'll see you in Hell, Daniel," I snap before releasing his hair, ignoring his mother's screams, and pull the trigger.

21

RINGO

The heart wrenching sobs from Elizabeth Stone stopped about ten minutes ago and Abbey hasn't taken her eyes off the mouth of the passage since. There's so much regret visible on her face, and I just know there's pain warring inside her head, but everyone here knows Daniel needed to die.

Abbey isn't reacting to his death, but she knows the type of heartbreak Daniel's mum is suffering.

Was suffering.

Mex, who has been guarding the bedroom door we left Elizabeth in with her dead son, pops his head out from the hallway and asks, "Want me to check?"

Glancing over at my wife, her cheeks pale even more, and she starts chewing on her damn thumbnail again.

I wish she had let me shoot Daniel and take that burden off her. My wife's heart is too good for this shit.

I know she's strong, but fuck, I just want her pure soul to remain intact. My concern about that hasn't changed. But I know I need to let her do what she feels she needs to do.

"Yeah. Check it out," I grunt to Mex, dragging my eyes away from my Angel. "And make sure the nurse understands how things are going to work," I mutter, and Mex nods, disappearing back into the hallway.

Caroline is huddled at the end of the hallway in the corner, Vender watching over her to make sure she doesn't try something stupid. Like run, or try to attack one of us.

I start slowly pacing, needing to keep moving as we wait, but not even half a minute later, Mex reappears and gives me a nod.

When my eyes connect with Abbey's, there's a moment of vulnerability in them before it disappears, and she nods, as if she's silently telling herself it's okay, before she stands.

"She used the knife we left?" she asks Mex, who nods.

"On her wrists. She uhhhh... died holding on to her son."

My wife's caramel eyes dart to mine as they fill with tears, and I reach out, dragging her to my chest and wrapping my arms around her.

"It's okay, Angel. It's what she wanted."

"I know," Abbey sobs quietly. "And I get it, but Elizabeth was nothing but a pawn in a nightmare she didn't know she was a part of."

Giving Abbey a squeeze, I press my lips to the top of her hair, breathing in the fruity scent of the shampoo she's been using.

"She didn't want to live in a world without her child. It was her decision," I remind her, even though we were the ones that gave her the knife to use.

She could have tried to use it on us and escape, but her mind was set the moment her son died.

This moment was always going to be difficult for my Angel. Especially knowing what we do now about the cult and Daniel being her cousin. They were both puppets being controlled by their parents, but ultimately, evil doesn't win in this story.

While Bobbi sleeps, we spend the next few hours talking with the nurse. She's smart and decided her life was worth living, so she's been educating Abbey and me on Bobbi's needs. Given Bobbi has grown and developed quickly, basically the same as a regular newborn now, things shouldn't be too complicated moving forward.

That's fucking good news, but dread still sits heavily in my gut as questions remain unanswered.

We didn't get a chance to ask Elizabeth, but Caroline was there that day when they all worked together to kidnap Bobbi, so she knows what really fucking happened.

"Was Bobbi dead when she arrived at the hospital?" I ask, and two sets of wide eyes dart to me.

One set hardens quickly, shooting straight back to Caroline.

"Was she?" Abbey snaps, and Caroline gulps, shaking her head.

"No... she was struggling, but alive. Dr Madden moved her into the NICU, and because most of the nurses and doctors were working on the COVID ward, there really weren't many witnesses," Caroline explains.

"There must have been some though," I snap, gritting my fucking teeth. "You can't exactly transport a premature baby in a fucking car."

Caroline nods, her fear-filled eyes darting between me and my wife. "Dr Madden arranged for private patient transport. Someone that owed her or something. They never got out of the ambulance though. The doctor, Elizabeth and I did all the work, and the driver never once spoke to us. He or she just drove us here and then left again. Dr Madden assured us that the driver wouldn't snitch."

Tears fill Abbey's eyes as she stares at the nurse, disbelief washing over her expression.

"The doctor took me to the morgue. Showed me a dead baby."

Caroline nods. "There had been a stillborn delivery the morning before."

In a flash, Abbey's hand whips out and slaps across Caroline's cheek, the sound loud as the nurse sobs.

"I'm sorry. I really am."

"You know anything about the sandbag in the coffin?" I snap, and Caroline shrugs.

"The doc said she would take care of that part. She has all the contacts to pull it off, I guess." Caroline sobs, her focus remaining on my wife. "I was just trying to help my friend."

"Look how well that turned out." Abbey sneers, curling her lip before turning her back on the nurse and focusing on her daughter.

The rest of the day is gloomy, not just from the sombre mood in the house, but from the rain that starts to pelt the cabin windows about mid-morning. Hunkering down, my men get some well-needed sleep as they take turns keeping watch outside and on the road we came in on, and we continue to spend time getting to know little Bobbi.

Caroline takes us through the process of bathing Bobbi, and Abbey feeds her again, something I didn't know if I'd feel okay with since those ripe tits have been mine for so long.

But fuck, the sight of my Angel learning how to be a mum, something which is clear to us all is far more natural to her than even she was expecting. Right before my eyes, I watch the two of them bond, and it's as if they haven't been separated for eight fucking weeks.

It's fucking beautiful.

"You doing okay, man?" JD shoulder bumps me, his hair damp from the shower he had a few minutes ago.

"Yeah," I sigh. "Just admiring my wife and baby."

When I glance at JD, he's grinning from ear to fucking ear.

"You're a good man. You know that, right?"

I frown at his words, and he chuckles.

"Not every guy could look at a kid that isn't biologically his the way you are, like you just won the lottery."

I scoff out a laugh, shifting my gaze back to Abbey as she cradles Bobbi to her chest while running her delicate fingers across her daughter's forehead, speaking softly.

"I have won the lottery." I shrug. "That's what it feels like. I have a beautiful wife, and her little baby needs me to step up and be her daddy. There's nothing that will get in my way of doing that."

"Shit, man. You're gonna make me cry," JD murmurs, and when I glance back at him, I actually see that his eyes are damp.

Shit. I thought he was just taking the piss.

"I'm not hugging you if you start crying," I snap, and his grin turns playful as he leaps on me, throwing his arms around me.

"Give me a hug, dammit," he snickers, and I laugh, trying to push the persistent fucker off me.

"Piss off. If you want a hug, you'll have to wait until Jols can give it to you."

Abbey's soft giggles float across the room, and when I finally manage to get my best mate off me, she has Bobbi on her lap, holding her head up by cupping her chin, while gently patting Bobbi's back, trying to burp her.

"Sometimes, you two act like you're my age." She giggles. "Not like men in their thirties."

"Why, thank you." JD grins stupidly at my wife, and it occurs to me that perhaps finding Bobbi has put everyone in a good mood.

The rainy day turns to night without us coming across any of the neighbours. Thank fuck.

The last thing we need is them calling the local cops.

There's enough food in the house that we can stay here for a few days and not have to go anywhere, so Mex and Murf cook up some dinner, and we settle in for a quiet night by the sea.

The guys do their shift change before Abbey and I turn in to sleep in the single bed in the same room as Bobbi.

It doesn't matter that we have to squeeze onto the mattress together. She fits perfectly against me, tight in my arms, like we were made to fit together.

We talk for a while in the dark, the low light in the humidicrib drawing our attention, and the sleeping angel within. Abbey is exhausted, but she's too wired to fall asleep straight away. Both of us are.

Yesterday, it was just the two of us, and now, we are three.

Okay, so maybe four, because as far as I'm concerned, Tahli is our responsibility too.

Sleep eventually wins out, and I dream of Abbey and Bobbi, just the way they were earlier in the chair as they both stared at each other. But this time, there's a faint glow behind them, and when I blink, a delicate face is smiling down over Abbey's shoulder, pretty blonde curls framing the face of a little girl.

I try to lean closer, needing to see, my heart already telling me exactly who's watching over my wife and her baby.

"Hope," I call, reaching out, but all of a sudden I'm being sucked out of the dream, a dark figure looming over me as someone nudges my shoulder.

"Wake the fuck up," JD whisper-yells as I jerk, instantly going on alert.

"What is it?" I sit up, bringing a groggy Abbey with me.

"Trunk and Stocky didn't check in, and we can't get a hold of them by phone or radio."

Ice freezes every drop of blood trying to rush through my veins as the reality of what he's telling me sinks in.

"Guns!" I snarl, lifting Abbey in my arms and depositing her bare feet on the cold floor a moment later.

"What's going on?" she squeaks, snatching up her jeans and stepping into them.

"We have company. Stay in here with Bobbi, but grab her go bag," I snap, not even bothering to put my jeans on.

That can fucking wait. Right now, I need to protect my family.

22

ABBEY

Caroline rushes into the room, nodding frantically as Vender barks orders at her to protect me and Bobbi at all costs.

I don't know what the hell this kidnapping nurse knows about fighting off bad guys, but I'm thankful to not be alone.

"What's happening?" She asks the same thing I did a minute ago before Ringo went charging out of the room.

"There's still people who want this baby for the wrong reasons," Vender explains quickly. "It must be them. I'll be right outside the door, and Trigger is right outside the window. Just stay in here. We'll have this resolved soon."

Caroline nods as Vender closes us in, and my heart races as I hear the guys yelling to each other, their heavy pounding feet moving around the cabin with urgency. Lifting Bobbi out of the crib, I lay her on the bed, still sleeping, and swaddle her tightly in a thick blanket in case we have to leave in a hurry.

"This is what Elizabeth was trying to protect your baby from," Caroline whispers, her voice trembling as she passes me a tiny beanie hat to slip onto Bobbi's head. "She wasn't a bad person."

"And you?" I snap, lifting Bobbi back into my arms, swaying from side to side in case she starts to wake. "What was in it for you when you worked with the doctor to steal her?"

Caroline's furious glare falls as she ducks her head. "Money. At first." She looks back up at me. "But then I realised I was doing a good thing."

"Is that what you tell yourself so you can sleep at night?" I snap, but our conversation gets cut off by the shattering spray of bullets tearing through the windows, and a scream gets stuck in the back of my throat as I drop to the floor with Bobbi huddled in my arms.

"Oh my God, we're going to die!" Caroline cries out from somewhere behind me, and I hope like hell she's not right. I will gladly die for Bobbi. There's no doubt about it, but I don't want to.

I want time with her.

Why the hell won't this world give me time with her!

I want to see her smiles, and hear her coo. I want to feel her fall asleep on me. Watch her eyes light up when she sees me. Help her explore what foods she likes. What music gets her head bopping. What colour dresses she feels like a princess in.

I'm supposed to take her to kinder on her first day, and watch her join in with the other kids while I reluctantly leave her in the care of someone else so she can socialise and learn. I'm supposed to walk away from the kinder crying, because what mother wouldn't after leaving a piece of their heart alone in the world for a short time.

There are so many moments I need to be there for. To share with my daughter, and I'll do whatever it takes to have them with her, or I'll die trying. Without a doubt.

As glass shatters and wood splinters, Bobbi starts to squirm under me as I try not to crush her with my body. I try to shield her with every part of me, desperate to save her from getting hurt. Or worse.

No.

NO!

I can't think of that.

I will NOT think of that.

Suddenly, the door flies open, and Vender charges in, tearing away the shredded blind and starts shooting through the shattered glass, the silencers they are all using changing what would be loud cracks, to soft whistles.

Caroline grabs the back of my hoodie roughly, quickly dragging me across the floor towards the wardrobe.

"Get in here," she cries, helping me shuffle inside, staying low, and we both huddle in the corner of the closet, shielding Bobbi as best we can in case more bullets come our way.

"Are they okay?!" Ringo bellows from somewhere in the cabin, and the door slides open a second later revealing a savage-looking Vender, his eyes raking over us as I rock Bobbi and press a dummy to her lips as she starts to rouse more.

"Yeah!" Vender calls over his shoulder. "They're okay!"

"Fuck!" JD yells from somewhere outside the room. "Incoming!"

The sound of more glass shattering deeper in the house has us jolting in terror, and Vender closes us in before his retreating heavy boots pound out of the bedroom and down the hallway.

"We're going to die." Caroline sobs next to me, her arms around both me and Bobbi as she tries to protect us.

Shit. She could try to run, but she's not. She's still here, doing everything she can to protect my daughter.

Household items crash to the floor somewhere in the cabin, and grunts and yells are accompanied by what sounds like a scuffle, like the fight has turned to fists.

Shit. Ringo. Please be safe.

I want to check on him, but I can't leave my daughter. I feel so torn right now.

But Ringo is trained for this. He's built for this. To fight physically. To protect.

And Bobbi is nothing but a helpless, innocent little baby that needs me to do everything I can to protect her while her daddy fights the bad guys.

Yes, I know he's not her birth father, but he is hers, and she is his. They don't need the same blood running through their veins for me to know that is undeniably true.

Heavy feet pounding back down the hallway has me stiffening, Caroline's arms squeeze tighter around me like that will somehow protect us if a bad guy finds us.

The bedroom door slams against the wall as someone bounds in, and a whimper of terror escapes me, probably giving away our hiding spot.

"Angel!" Ringo snarls, and I almost start crying at the sound of his voice.

"In here," I rush out, reaching to open the closet door, but it opens before I can do it.

Looming above us, my husband stands in only his boxers and tee, his hair down and wild, blood smearing his cheek, arm and thigh.

"Take this and get Bobbi the hell out of here." He holds out a gun to me, and I take it with a shaky hand, trying not to disturb Bobbi too much since she seems settled with the dummy. "Go up the beach. Find a house and get help. Do whatever you have to in order to get away safely."

"But... what about you?" I rush out as Caroline and I stand quickly stepping out into the destroyed room.

Shit, even the humidicrib has been shot to smithereens... Bobbi could have been in that.

Ringo's big hands cup my cheeks, dragging my attention away from the carnage and back to him.

"I'll be right behind you. Just get the both of you to safety. Please."

There's a desperate plea in his tone, so I nod, my eyes pricking with tears I force back.

Quickly leaning down, Ringo presses a chaste kiss to my lips, as Vender's bellow sends a shiver up my spine.

"More incoming!"

"I'll hold them off, Angel." Ringo drops his hands and glances down at Bobbi, gently grazing the backs of his knuckles over her chubby little cheek before glancing back at me. "Now go."

There's pain in his eyes as he looks at me. It's almost like he's saying goodbye without saying the words, and it splinters my heart in two.

Right now, one side belongs to him. The other to my daughter.

I want to argue, but I don't. I can't because he steps away, spinning on his heel and storming from the room like a man ready to walk into Hell, leaving me standing with my baby, still asleep in my arms.

23

RINGO

I don't know who these fuckers are, but whoever hired them will fucking pay for this.

Two more men burst through the entrance where the front door used to be. They're dressed in all black, their faces covered, and the fuckers have night vision goggles on.

Talk about an unfair fucking advantage.

By now, one of the neighbours would have heard the war raging in this tiny, shitty little seaside cottage. Normally I don't want the pigs to get involved, but if getting cops here means keeping my wife and Bobbi safe, then fuck, I hope someone has called for help already.

"Come on, motherfucker. Come and get me!" I snarl, as fuckwad number one strolls in so fucking casually, that I'm kind of impressed.

Why they aren't shooting anymore is anyone's guess, but the moment he unsheathes a knife Hush would be proud of, I grin.

I don't mind me a little bit of hand to knife combat. Especially since we are all out of bullets. The only gun loaded is the one I gave Abbey.

We came here with seven men, plus me and Abbey. We've lost communication with Stocky and Trunk, and I try not to think about what that means, because I need my head right here, right now, doing everything I can to make sure these fuckers die.

I saw Trigger's body just before when I ducked my head out to check on him. There are so many bullet holes in him that I know it's going to be hard to identify who he is.

We know who he is... was. He died trying to protect my wife and baby, and for that, I will make sure his name is never forgotten in our club.

So with three men down, I'm left with four, all of us with zero ammo, and right now, JD and Murf are hiding, ready to attack from behind, while Vender and I lure the fuckers to us. Meanwhile, Mex has already snuck out on the beach side, and should be closing in from behind any minute.

"Where's the baby?" the fuckwad asks as he approaches, but I just shake my head.

"No baby here, arsehole. You picked the wrong fucking house."

The cunt laughs. "Nice try, but we know the kid is here. Just hand her over and we'll let you live."

Vender scoffs. "Un-fucking-likely."

"Have it your way," the other tosser snaps, his shoulders tensing as they step into the tiny living room, and I shift backwards, luring them in further.

In the blink of an eye, they attack, lunging for me and Vender.

With my focus on the guy attacking me, I manage to dodge the swipe of his blade, swinging my fist in an uppercut which rattles him enough to stagger, and then I reach for his night vision goggles, tearing the fuckers from his head.

He snarls something incredulous at me, his sharp blade slicing across my arm, and I manage to grab his wrist, holding the knife back as we wrestle, falling to the floor.

His knife clatters away, and the melee becomes a rampage of fists and elbows as we pummel each other.

The crack of a gun doesn't stop this fucker from throwing fists, and I have to hope everyone is okay as my men yell, and there's more chaos close by.

In my worry for my team, my momentum gets thrown off, and I find myself under this crazy fucker, giving him the advantage.

I take a brutal hit to my temple, making me see stars, but I keep my focus on the blade just near my hand on the floor.

"There's more!" Mex calls from somewhere, and bullets start spraying the fucking cabin again.

Fucking hell. I thought these were the last two.

Just as my fingers find the knife, the guy above me, gearing up to swing another punch, flies forward with the crack of another shot, blood spraying from his head, showering down over me.

Trying not to get this fucker's blood in my mouth, I shove him off me and sit up to see Mex holding a gun.

"I thought we were out of bullets," I snap, lurching to my feet to see Vender doing the same, the guy he was fighting now dead too.

"I found... Trunk."

I freeze, already knowing what's happened, yet still not fucking prepared for it.

It also explains why there's no fucking silencer.

"Is he…" JD trails off, and Mex nods.

"Throat slit. They didn't disarm him though, so…" He holds up the gun. Stocky's gun.

Suddenly, I feel fucking dizzy. The world spins, and I buckle in half, gripping my knees as I fight to hold it together.

"There's more, man." Mex sounds fucking worried. And that's not a good fucking sign, because not much scares him. "I can't tell how many, but they are hiding in the treeline in the yards across the street."

Movement from the corner of my eye catches my attention, and I see another couple of black-clad men slowly crossing the gravelly street, through the non-existent front door.

Fuck.

FUCK!

Straightening, I hurry to the hallway and call to Abbey.

"Angel. It's time to leave," I bark, and she pops her head out of the bedroom. "Quick, there are more men coming, I need you to go now. Take Bobbi up the beach and find a house to get help."

She nods, worrying her lip, before ducking back into the bedroom, and a moment later, she comes rushing out, Bobbi bundled up in thick blankets, cradled to her chest, her caramel eyes wild with fear.

"You're coming, right?" she asks, and I nod.

"Right behind you."

"There's the baby!" someone from outside yells, and I grab Abbey's arm, urging her through the living area to the opening where glass doors used to be.

"Go. Now!" I yell, and the moment more shots crack through the air, Abbey finally does what I've asked, and runs out onto the deck, down the steps, and up the sandy path that cuts through the low dunes that lead to the beach.

When her shadow gets engulfed by the darkness, I go to spin back to the men charging the house, but another flash of movement at the top of the sand dune has my heart lurching in my fucking throat.

No.

"Gun!" I scream, spinning back to where the dead attackers are lying in a pool of their own blood. "Give me a gun!"

JD, seeing what's got me freaking the fuck out, searches the dead guys and finds a gun, tossing it to me, and the moment I catch it, I turn and sprint out after my wife.

"Abbey!" I bellow, rain and wind pelting my face as soon as my feet hit the sand, and I fucking charge up that path, my legs burning with every step that sinks into the cold sand.

Out here, all I can hear is the howl of the wind and the crash of the waves, while getting attacked by the icy cold rain like flicks of hail that melt as soon as they hit my searing skin.

As I reach the mouth of the path that opens up onto the beach, a scream from my left has me jerking, and the flash of a gun firing feels like it's ripping my heart from my chest.

FUCK! NO!

"Abbey!" I scream, charging in that direction, the burn of my legs barely a fucking afterthought as I spot three shadowed silhouettes up ahead, running up the beach.

One is my wife. And the other two are men dressed in all black.

The faint glow of sunrise lines the horizon, giving me the slightest visual as I get closer.

"Don't shoot the baby!" one man yells to the other as he raises his gun again, directly at my wife.

With my heart just about fucking stopping, I raise the gun in my hand, skidding in the sand, stopping for just enough time to aim and shoot. The crack is loud, and the moment I see the fucker that was going to shoot at my wife fall to the sand, I start fucking running again.

"Just hand over the baby and this will all be over!" the other man yells to my wife, gaining on her.

I hear her scream, and charge forward, running faster than I ever think I've fucking run before.

The man seems determined not to shoot at her, but he's fucking fast, and I can hear Abbey's cries of desperation as she tries to get away.

"Stay away from her!" I yell, gaining his attention, his gaze darting over his shoulder, spotting me on his tail.

He doesn't fucking stop though, charging closer to Abbey, reaching out to grab her. Even though I'm close, I fucking fear I'm not close enough as the flash of a knife appears a moment before he lunges for my wife.

She screams, spinning to face him as he crashes towards her, and time fucking slows as the bundle of blankets containing Bobbi goes flying from Abbey's arms, slamming into the wet sand before waves rush over it.

"No!" I bellow right as a loud piercing crack meets my ears, and I glance back to see the man and my wife sprawled on the sand, and a dark pool of what has to be blood seeping from between them.

24

ABBEY

"**N**o!"

Ringo's bellow is gut wrenching, and I blink my eyes open to see his bare legs shuffling from one direction to another like he's torn between which way to go.

Me or my baby.

The moment he charges for the bundle of blankets getting dragged into the ocean by the waves, I grin, even though I can hardly breathe.

My lungs don't want to work, but my eyes still track his movements as he falls to his knees in the water, scooping up the drenched blankets, bringing them to his chest.

"The fuck!" he snaps, and I open my mouth to speak, but still can't get any air in, the heavy weight on top of me, crushing. "Where the fuck is Bobbi?!"

I inwardly cringe, feeling like I'm about to get told off for the ruse.

In desperation, Ringo abandons the blankets, crawling over to me through the wet sand, and a moment later, the crushing weight disappears and air rushes into my lungs.

"Fuck, Angel." He scoops my head up off the sand, his freezing wet fingers swiping the hair off my face as his frantic eyes dance between mine.

I blink up at him a few times, trying to breathe, before I finally get some air in and start coughing.

"Ringo," I scratch out, my voice husky from coughing.

"Angel, where the fuck is Bobbi?"

"She's okay," I rasp, my body finally relaxing as oxygen seeps into my blood again. "I left her with Caroline."

"The nurse?" he barks, disbelief in his tone, and I nod.

"They wanted my baby, so I led them away the only way I knew how."

"By making everyone think you had Bobbi?" He chokes out like he's struggling with his emotions.

"Yes, sorry for scaring you."

He laughs. It's a weird, unsure laugh, and despite his shaking head, there's a smile tugging at his lips.

"You could have told me, Angel. I just watched you toss your baby to the ground and get swept into the fucking ocean."

"There was no time." I sigh, trying to sit up, which is when Ringo's sharp gaze darts between me and the dead man.

"That's his blood, right?" he asks.

"Yes. I managed to pull the trigger when he jumped on me."

Ringo's big hands engulf my face again, his forehead pressing to mine as he chokes out. "I thought..."

"I'm okay," I remind him, pressing my lips to his for a quick kiss.

When I pull back, I glance over his shoulder at the bundle of blankets that were made to look like I was carrying a swaddled baby.

"You went to save her first."

"I was coming for you next," he growls, and I grin.

"I know, but the fact that you chose her first means more to me than you'll ever know."

"Shit, Angel. I'd give my own life to save both of you. In a fucking heartbeat."

He brushes my hair back, his wild eyes roaming my face, reminding me of not just how precious he makes me feel, but how precious I am to him.

To his heart.

"I love you for that, Cam. Always," I tell him, and words have never felt more true falling from my lips.

I will love this man for eternity. There's no two ways about it.

We might come from different walks of life, and there may be a huge gap between our ages, but I'm convinced he was put on this Earth for me. To save me. To show me how to live.

We share another kiss and hug quickly, before standing and running back to the cabin, hand in hand, the heavy rain that was pelting down earlier now a fine misty drizzle.

We approach with caution, noting that things seem quiet compared to a minute ago, and as we move up the sandy path, we see JD, Mex, Murf and Vender step out onto the back porch, looking bloody, but okay.

"We get them all?" Ringo barks as we approach, and the moment JD lays eyes on his best mate, his shoulders visibly relax.

"As far as we can tell," Vender answers. "Used their night vision goggles to check for anyone else. Outside is all clear, but there are people in the houses peeking out their windows. I doubt it will be long before the cops arrive."

Raking his hand through his hair, Ringo assesses the scene before turning to me.

"Go check on Bobbi." Then his eyes shift to Murf and Mex. "There are a couple of bodies on the beach. Go get them and bring them back here. We need to leave ASAP."

Leaving them to do what they need to do, I rush down the hallway and burst into the room, nearly slipping on some broken glass as I get to the wardrobe.

"Caroline!" I call, tugging it open to find her sitting curled against the back corner. "Oh shit. Thank God," I say, shifting to stand over her and finding Bobbi still asleep, her little mouth sucking on the dummy like she's trying to get milk from it. "It's over. But we have to leave before the police get here," I say, leaning down to scoop up Bobbi from Caroline's arms.

I'm so focused on my relief and how good it feels to hold Bobbi that it takes me a moment to realise Caroline hasn't said anything.

"Caroline?" I ask, leaning to the side to get a look at her face.

Then I stiffen, a gasp flying from my lips as I stagger backwards. "Ringo!"

Heavy pounding feet head my way in an instant, and hot tears burst from my eyes as I try to make sense of what I just saw.

Glancing around the room, or what's left of it, I see more bullet holes in the plaster near the wardrobe... and the wardrobe door.

"Angel. What's wrong? Is Bobbi..." Ringo trails off as he skids in the doorway, his eyes darting from me to where I now stare at the blood-soaked hole in Caroline's side.

"Shit... Looks like she caught a stray bullet," Ringo says, stepping closer and lowering to his haunches to examine the situation. "Bobbi's okay?" he asks, darting his head over his shoulder, and I nod, but since I really have no idea, I snap out of my daze and run to the bed.

Pulling back the bedsheets, I find a clean spot and lay Bobbi down, unwrapping the blanket, checking over her tiny little body.

"She's okay," I sigh in relief, my eyes shifting back to the wardrobe. "Caroline really did protect Bobbi with her life."

Leaning down, Ringo runs his big fingers down the side of Bobbi's face before glancing at me.

"I don't want to sound harsh, but we have to go."

I nod, knowing he's right.

"What about all this?" I ask, gesturing to the house around us.

"We'll burn it with the bodies inside." He moves to his pile of clothes that he didn't have time to dress in before, and starts to get dressed. "We'll take our men back to Fox Pines though."

For a moment, I wonder what Ringo means, because of course we are going back to the club. They have to sort out the dispute with Smitty and... and... then it hits me.

"Stocky? Trigger?" I ask, my voice barely a whisper as I watch the pain flash across Ringo's face.

"Yeah, Angel. And Trunk. We have to arrange another funeral."

My shoulders drop as pain lashes inside my chest, and I suck in my lips, trying to hold back what I'm feeling, because we really don't have time for a distraught woman right now.

"Hey," Ringo breathes, his finger hooking under my chin. "Try not to think about it right now. Let's get you and Bobbi out of here and hit the road."

Nodding, I swallow thickly, leaning into the kiss he presses to my forehead, before he leads me from the room.

Ringo and his men work seamlessly together, like they've burnt down houses before. It turns out this little seaside town is so small it doesn't have its own police station or anything. Just a group of houses along the shore, the residents just trying to lead simple, quiet lives.

The Landy made it out without a scratch, but the van is a little worse for wear. I can't stop looking back at it over my shoulder as it follows behind us, knowing the bodies of the dead Sadists are inside.

I feel so sorry for Murf. Stocky was his best mate, and he's the one driving the van.

JD, Vender and Mex are riding three of the motorcycles, while the fourth is also in the back of the van, crammed up close to the dead bodies.

It's all just... such a waste.

I feel the weight of their deaths just like I did the others. These guys in particular, having been some of the first club brothers I met.

I'm sitting quietly in the back seat next to Bobbi's car seat, where she's still sleeping soundly. I couldn't bring myself to sit in the front and be that far away from her, but Ringo didn't mind. He's been busy making calls as he drives, arranging for us to get back over the border, so they don't search the van and find dead bodies.

I cry for some of the trip, my heart aching over more deaths because of me.

I don't know who those men were that attacked the house, but they were clearly trained. I'm actually surprised we aren't all dead.

The drive from the seaside town in South Australia to Fox Pines is nearly an eleven hour trip, but Ringo is determined to get back to the compound today, so we stop when Bobbi needs a feed or nappy change, and then just keep driving.

Even though I try not to, I fall asleep a few times. I'm worried about Ringo and the lack of sleep he's had over the last few days, but the hum of the Harleys riding alongside us is soothing, and it keeps lulling me to sleep.

When we aren't far from Fox Pines, the day having turned into night once again, my phone starts ringing, and I hurry to blindly answer it so it doesn't wake Bobbi.

"Hello?" I say, reaching over to press the dummy back into Bobbi's mouth when she stirs.

"So you have your daughter back. Congratulations."

I stiffen at the sound of my mother's voice, and my eyes meet Ringo's in the rearview mirror.

How does she know?

Pulling the phone away from my ear, I put the call on speaker and turn up the volume.

"What do you want?" I snap, and she scoffs.

"You have your daughter, now I want mine. Give Tahli back to me."

"Never," I scoff back, and she tuts.

"You might as well hand over your daughter while you're at it. Once the police trace all those deaths in that sleepy seaside town back to you, you'll be going to prison." She gives an unamused laugh. "Twelve deaths. That's a long stretch behind bars. Plenty of time for me to raise your daughter myself."

"Twelve?" I ask, keeping my eyes on Ringo's in the mirror. "You're so sure. What do you know about what happened?"

"I was against it at first. But your grandfather was insistent. He has a lot of connections, Abigail. Many worshippers that believe in the Script of Symme just as passionately as we do. A lot of very powerful men in high government authoritative roles."

"So Banes paid men to kill us and tried to kidnap my baby. Again." I scoff, hoping my voice doesn't betray my nerves. "How did you even know where we were?"

"I told you last time. A little birdy told me. You really should be careful who you trust," she snickers. "And that child is *not* yours, Abigail. She belongs to the church."

"Oh, really?" I snicker this time. "But don't I have to marry my cousin first? And then don't I have to be killed, so Bobbi can replace my life, to be the pure vessel?"

My mother is quiet for a long moment before she responds. "You've been doing your research."

"I have," I agree. "What a pity Daniel is dead, so now I can't marry him. And so is every other rapist fuck that could have been the biological father. So, I guess *you* and your *cult bullshit* can piss the hell off."

"You don't know what you've done!" my mum yells, causing the speaker to crackle, and I glance at Bobbi to see if it disturbed her, but she's still sound asleep.

"Oh, you mean ruining your plans to get your daddy to love you again?" I snap. "You're pathetic, Priscilla."

"You act so high and mighty," she snarls, fury lacing her tone. "But you were never going to be anything special in the outside world, Abigail. But in the church you had a chance to make a difference, and you've gone and thrown it all away. But Tahli still has a chance."

"You're right, she does," I snap back with just as much venom. "She has a chance with me. She deserves a chance at a normal life. At not being married off to a relative and used to create fucking incestual babies!"

"You know nothing!" my mother snarls. "There's a higher purpose in the church. The world is crazy and full of tainted people, but the Script of Symme honours God's true path."

A laugh bubbles from my lips at how ludicrous she sounds.

"The Script of Symme is a load of bullshit, Priscilla. It used to be called something else entirely, and the name was changed because the *cult* got busted by the authorities. When are you going to realise you're fighting on the wrong side?"

"I'm doing the Lord's work, Abigail!"

"You're doing your pedo father's work, that's all. You're a joke!"

"GIVE TAHLI BACK!" she screams, completely unhinged, and I smirk, feeling good about ruffling her feathers.

"No," I snap. "I'll never give her back!"

The moment the words leave my lips, I end the call, my breathing rapid as my hand shakes.

"Shit," I pant, glancing at Ringo.

"You okay?" he asks, and I nod, but then shake my head, finishing on a shrug.

"Someone told them where we'd be," I breathe, my mind racing. "The only people who knew were you, me, Daniel and Lewy."

Even though I can't see Ringo's whole face, I can tell by the narrowing of his eyes in the mirror that his jaw is ticking right now.

"There's no way Daniel could have contacted them without us knowing," Ringo grunts, sounding pissed. "And I can't for the life of me consider Lewy. But fuck, the only other explanation is that it was one of the men with us. They must have passed on our location once we arrived."

Shaking my head, I don't want to believe any of those options.

"There has to be another explanation... right?" I ask, and Ringo shrugs.

"I fucking hope so," he hisses, his knuckles turning white on the steering wheel. "Or we won't be arranging a funeral for three. We'll be arranging it for a lot fucking more."

25

RINGO

Our arrival at the compound is met with fist bumps from some, and curious glances from others as Smitty storms from his cabin, fury etched on his face.

"What the fuck are you doing back here?! You ran away like little bitches! Fucking traitors!"

I don't answer him as I slip out of the car and move to the van as Murf pulls it into the centre of the yard.

"I'm fucking talking to you!" Smitty bellows, and I can see him coming at me from the corner of my eye, but I focus on sliding the van door open, my eyes shifting to the three lifeless men resting in the back before I'm grabbed and spun around. "You're not fucking welcome here!"

Smitty's spittle lands on my nose, and I fucking switch, fisting his fucking cut and dragging him nose to nose.

"Stop being a cunt for a fucking second and have some fucking respect!"

The growling bellow that slips from me holds so much rage, it takes everything in me to hold it back and not kill this fucker.

"Respect!" he screams, shoving back and breaking my grip on him. "You should be respecting *me*!"

"Look! You fucking selfish bastard!" I point into the van, and finally the prick's eyes follow.

His breathing is ragged, his eyes roaming over our fallen, and he takes a step back, fury still contorting his face. Swallowing thickly, Smitty clears his throat, dragging his eyes to the men closing in. He looks stricken.

"We're lucky to be alive," I snap. "Someone knew we were there, Nate. Tore the place up with bullets. We had to burn it all to destroy as much evidence as we could, but we had no way of containing it. The neighbours witnessed a fuckton of it through their fucking windows. Not to forget, we weren't in Sadists territory. We were in Raiders territory, and even they wouldn't have attacked the way it happened. What the fuck are they going to say if they find out we were there?" I fucking hiss. "It should never have happened like that."

With a tick of his jaw, Smitty glares at me, jabbing a finger my way.

"No, it shouldn't. You shouldn't have even gone. Once a-fucking-gain, your pussy whipped arse has gotten club brothers killed!"

I flinch at the accusation.

I'm well aware this is more of a personal battle than a club one, and usually I'd fight Nate on this, but I don't have it in me. Stocky and Trunk were two of my closest mates. They ran into whatever battle I directed them to without fucking argument, and this time, it got them killed. Trigger too. None of them deserved that.

"Don't put this shit on him!" JD roars, shoving between us and getting in Smitty's face this time. "You were meant to be with us! The level of destruction could have been minimised if we were all there!"

"That's not my fault!" Smitty shoves JD back. "We were there until you fuckers ran off like little bitches!"

"BECAUSE YOU RAPED DANIEL WITH A FUCKING MOP!"

Abbey's scream breaks through the building rage between us, all eyes turning to her as she stands a few metres away, little Bobbi bundled to her chest. Gasps fall from Doxies, and I can't tell if it's because of what Abbey said, or because they are seeing her baby for the first time.

"You! Raped! Him!" She seethes, her top lip curling as she bares her teeth, and fuck me, she's never looked more savage.

"Do you know what that feels like, Nate?" She steps forward, ignoring the eyes watching on, and takes the smallest step back. "Do you know what it feels like to have something shoved inside you so brutally, without any lubrication?! The pain of it?! The violation of it?!"

"I did it for you, you ungrateful bitch!" Smitty snaps, and a fucking growl rips from me, my muscles coiling ready to fucking launch myself at him, but I'm halted by my wife as she presses Bobbi into my chest, and I have no choice but to take hold of the little bundle.

"I didn't ask you to do that!" she screams, lurching forward and slapping Nate hard across the face.

An eerie silence hangs in the air as what my wife has just done sinks in, but the moment Nate goes to lurch for her, guns come out. Mine. JD's, Vender's and Murf's. Hell, even Mex pulls out his twin knives, one in each hand like he's gearing up to kill.

But probably the most surprising are the guns from some of our other club brothers surrounding us. Brody is a given. Not only would JD kill him if he didn't follow us, but Brody has become close with my Angel, and I know he'd die for her if he had to. But Ace has his Glock pointed directly at Nate. So do Yabbie, Scooter, Lewy, Dane, Cockroach... fuck, so many of them.

There are others that look confused, and of course Tups and Spud have their weapons in hand, but they can't seem to figure out who to point at, since everyone seems to be turning against the man they follow like fucking dogs.

"I often wished the arseholes that raped me could know what it's like, but they were just thoughts, Nate." Abbey shakes her head, shame filling her voice. "In the end, all I wanted was them gone from this world. Gone so they couldn't do what they did to me to anyone else. Gone so I know when I wake from a nightmare that they still haunt me in, that they can't really get me. Not anymore. But rape?" She shakes her head, her shoulders slumping as she points an accusing finger his way. "You did that all on your own. You did the one thing I've been fighting against." Her hand falls, and she shrugs. "I thought the Southern Sadists were honourable. I thought you were better than those bastards."

Nate opens his mouth to say something, but thinks better of it, realising his people have started to turn against him.

"You raped Daniel?" Celina's unsure voice floats over to us, and a moment later, she steps through the crowd, tears blurring her eyes. "Nate?" she asks, a plea in her voice for him to deny it. To tell her it's all bullshit.

But he can't lie. Not in front of so many that witnessed it.

"It was a method of torture. He was a prisoner." He tries to make an excuse for his actions, but the tears filling Celina's eyes show she doesn't care for his excuses.

A lot of our Doxies have come from bad situations. Most, but not all, had their body violated in some way. With us, they sought a home. Sure, they use their bodies to help satisfy the men, but they do alright themselves. We don't rape women in our club. We don't take them against their will, or coerce them... mostly. That line gets blurred sometimes. But if they say the word, the men stop. If they don't stop, they fucking deal with me.

"Fists, knives and guns." Celina scoffs. "That's what you told me you used to torture for information. Not..." She shakes her head, needing to take a moment to clear her throat. "You promised you wouldn't do that again," she whimpers, spinning around and storming back through the crowd with a few Doxies following her.

The fuck... again?

"Fuck's sake," Nate mutters, glaring at me. "This shit is on you. Not me."

"We're a club. We have rules and bylaws for a fucking reason," I snap, trying not to be too loud in case I wake Bobbi, still bundled to my chest. "You demanded I marry Abbey to help with the club's standing. I used Marx men to help protect my family to free up the club so you could get this place in order and have men to do the new runs. The only thing I'm guilty of is following your fucking orders."

Nate scoffs. "Until you pricks walked away a night ago."

"I walked away from a situation that was *not* what our club stands for. I didn't walk away from the club. I walked away from *you*."

Whispers rush through the crowd, and Abbey turns back to me, taking Bobbi before she starts to walk away.

"Where the fuck do you think you're going?" Smitty growls, and the smirk Abbey shoots over her shoulder sends a fucking chill up my spine.

Her monster.

"I'm not a club brother, so I don't have to be around for what comes next."

Frowning, Smitty turns his glare to me when my wife keeps walking, going to Jols before they disappear from sight.

"The fuck is she talking about?"

"Club rules. You break them, you deal with the Sergeant-at-Arms." I raise a brow, and Smitty starts laughing like a fucking hyena.

I discussed this briefly with Abbey in the car. I need to remind my club brothers that I am loyal to them. That I am here. That I will still do my job. It's a little unnerving how much she looked like she was happy about that as she walked away a moment ago. Remind me to never fucking cross my wife.

"You're going to punish me." He points to himself before slapping his thigh as he laughs harder.

No one else laughs. No one joins his unhinged antics this time.

"You broke the fucking rules, so damn right I'm gonna punish you," I snarl.

Technically, something of this nature would call for banishment or death, but all I need to do is knock Smitty off his pedestal for a bit. Fucking remind him that the rules apply to everyone.

Slipping out of my cut, I hand it to JD, who like the others, is putting his gun away, and all Nate can do is stare.

"You can't be serious."

"Have you known me to fucking joke?" I snap, and his face hardens.

"Fine." He reefs off his cut, not even bothering to hand it to Spud, his VP, who is right by his side.

Instead, he tosses the leather to the gravelly ground like it means nothing, and fuck, that makes my jaw tick like crazy.

"I should fucking banish you!" Smitty yells, struggling to contain his anger at being called out and forced to be treated just like anyone else would be.

"I'm not the one who broke the bylaws. You'll need a majority vote to get rid of me simply because we're at fucking odds."

Rolling his shoulders back like this is going to be a fight and not a punishment, Nate looks me dead in the eye when he says, "I could just kill you."

"Huh," I smirk, opening and closing my hands, getting ready to make them iron fucking fists. "Why don't you?"

"I should," he snaps.

"But you won't." I gesture my head to each side, pointing out the club brothers circled around us. "You know you'll lose their respect."

His jaw ticks. He knows I'm fucking right.

I ball my fists and widen my stance.

"Be a good boy and take your punishment like a *real* president," I snap, and a second later, I swing my fist.

26

ABBEY

I'm exhausted. Both emotionally and physically, but I also feel, dare I say… happy.

I know we are still under threat, but now that I have Bobbi, everything just feels brighter. My heart feels fuller. And the dark clouds that have lingered over me for so long have vaporised.

The compound has been different since we got back a few nights ago. Smitty has been hiding away feeling sorry for himself after Ringo beat the absolute crap out of him, and no one, not even Smitty's two worshippers, stopped it from happening.

Celina had packed her things before the punishment was even through, declaring she can't deal with Nate's brand of crazy anymore, and that being head Doxy wasn't worth it.

She moved back into the Doxy den that night, where she's stayed ever since.

The Doxies were over the moon to finally meet Bobbi. Darla gave me an old pram that her sister left behind, so I've been using it as a bed for Bobbi to sleep in. It's not ideal. I'd love a proper bassinet for her, but since the only other option is putting Bobbi in bed between me and Ringo, and I'm terrified one of us will roll on her in our sleep, the pram will have to do for now.

It's certainly close quarters sharing the small bungalow with Jols, JD and a pram, but we've been able to make it work. Having the extra help has been great too, like last night when Jols got up with Bobbi when she woke at four in the morning and fed her a bottle. I was completely out of it and didn't hear my little girl rousing and later woke up to see JD and Jols snuggled close together, smiling down at Bobbi as she drank down the bottle of formula.

Guilt seeps back in as I think about that.

While I have maintained a milk supply, with Ringo's assistance in the background, it's still not enough. Bobbi started to get really restless and hungry, so I've had to add in some formula feeds as well, and I'm thankful now that nurse Caroline insisted we take the bottles and teets with us before… well, before everything happened. Before she died.

"You're quiet." Ringo's voice drags me out of my thoughts, and I blink a few times to bring me back to the present.

"Sorry," I mutter, offering him a small smile. "Today was a lot."

Today… the one thing I'm *trying* not to think about.

Because today, we sent off Trunk, Stocky and Trigger.

Their cuts were laid over their motorcycles. Their drinks of choice shot down. Their favourite songs played in the background. Their names added to the lists inked on each and every Southern Sadist.

God... There is so much honourable beauty in the way they send off their men.

Their fallen.

At the last Southern Sadist funeral, I killed Wendy. That particular memory swarmed through my mind so many times today that it started to piss me off.

That woman doesn't deserve the airtime in my head.

"It was a lot." Ringo's gaze flicks to mine from the driver's seat. "I'm sorry if it brought up... stuff."

My smile is slight as I stare at my husband's profile as he drives us into Redfield. He knows me too well. He knows exactly what my mind was doing to me, running like a reel in my head.

"I'm sure it brought stuff up for you too," I say, watching his lip twitch as he tries to hide his feelings.

Yes, Cam, I know you just as well as you know me.

"Maybe we can arrange another secure video call to Tahli later." His eyes flick from the road to me. "Would that make you feel better?"

My smile is wide as I nod eagerly. I miss my sister and worry about her constantly.

The day after we arrived back at the compound, Ringo had arranged for me to call my little sister, and she got to see her niece for the first time via video. Alana and Millie were there too, and once we were done, Doreen was handed the phone and cried when she saw Ringo holding Bobbi.

I can't wait for them to meet her in person, but for now, we'll have to stick to video calls. My mum has been calling daily, although I never pick up, and we still don't know who gave up our location while we were in South Australia.

"Do you think we can visit her soon?" I ask my husband hopefully, and he shrugs.

"I'm not sure, Angel." Ringo's voice has a moody edge to it. "You know what *he's* like."

My mood sours a little at the mention of him, and as Ringo pulls off the road and into the parking lot of the Red Room, my eyes land on the man in question.

"Speak of the Devil," I snap, my glare locked on the tall, dark, and sinfully handsome yet chillingly lethal, Devon Marx.

He's standing by the door at the back of the Red Room, his aura pitch black as he stares right back at me.

A shiver ripples up my spine, and I contemplate asking Ringo to turn the car around and leave.

The moment Ringo shuts off the engine, my car door swings open, and I stifle a bloody scream just as Dee comes into view.

"Shit. You scared me," I rush out, pressing my hand to my chest, but Dee isn't paying me a lick of attention, her finger pointing into the back seat, her smile wide.

Wow, I don't think I've seen her smile like that before.

"Okay, okay," I giggle, slipping out of the car and opening the back door. "I can see you're eager to meet Bobbi."

Dee rolls her eyes like that's a stupid statement, and Jared appears behind her looking just as keen.

This time when I get Bobbi out of her car seat, she's wide awake, her blue-grey eyes taking everything in as I press my lips to her forehead, and then pass her to Dee.

I never took Dee, the lethal Hush assassin, as someone that would go all mushy over a baby, but seeing her hold my little girl with Jared reaching over her shoulder and stroking my daughter's cheek, makes me realise Dee is just as human as I am.

I wonder if she wants to have kids one day too.

"Is this what all the drama has been about?" Devon's deep gravel has me stiffening, and before I can stop him, he reaches down and scoops my daughter out of Dee's hands, cradling her to his chest. "Why hello little beauty. Do you have a smile for Uncle Devon?"

I scoff, "Really? *Uncle Devon?*"

His soft expression, which is purely for my daughter, hardens as he glares at me. "You have a problem with that, Blondie?"

"You wanna speak to my wife properly, arsehole?" Ringo snarls, coming to my side, and the smirk Devon shoots us isn't just sinister. It's pure evil.

"I'll take her, thanks." I hold out my hands, expecting him to pass my daughter back, but he spins and walks away, carrying my daughter with him.

"Hey!" I snap, ready to throw down, but then I hear him chatting away, his voice taking on a softer, soothing tone as he walks.

"This is *Uncle Griffin's* strip club. *Not* a place for you, little one. And if I *ever* find out you ask to work here when you're older, Uncle Devon is going to be *very* angry."

A giggle escapes me as we follow behind, stepping inside the club with Dee and Jared on our heels.

Like last time, we go into the back room with the conference table, but unlike last time, the Angel sisters aren't here.

"You gonna give anyone else a hold?" Griffin asks Devon as he takes a seat at the table, instantly shaking his head.

"Nope. She's having Uncle Devon time."

Griffin laughs at his cousin while shaking Ringo's hand and gesturing for us to take a seat.

Ringo and I sit in the same seats as last time, and it's then that I also notice Dee and Jared didn't follow us into the room. Turning to glance over my shoulder in search of them, I spot Dee out in the hallway, and Jared pulling the door shut, closing Ringo, Bobbi and I in with Devon and Griffin.

Why isn't he in here too? Isn't he part of the Marx crew? They call him Crow. And Hush is part of it too, right?

Shit. I don't even know.

"So you were ambushed?" Griffin starts, pouring himself a whisky at the head of the table before offering the bottle to Ringo, which he declines with a shake of his head.

"Yep, someone gave up our location. Only Abbey, Daniel, Lewy and I knew where we were headed. The roads were dead. No one was following us, so it had to have been someone close."

"I gotta be honest, I don't see it being Lewy," Griffin states, relaxing back in his seat before taking a sip of his drink. "He's one of the most loyal guys I've met. He's been completely transparent with us while we've been trying to piece together the warehouse raid."

Ringo nods. "I feel the same."

"Could it have been your captive?" Devon asks, looking totally relaxed with Bobbi in his arms, her little hand wrapped around his big finger.

"Daniel?" Ringo asks, and when Devon nods, Ringo continues. "He didn't have access to a phone to tell anyone. He had people watching him the entire time."

"People you trust?" Griffin asks, and Ringo nods.

"My team was watching him."

"Have you considered it could be one of your team?" Griffin asks. "Because the only other possibilities are that you have trackers on your cars and bikes."

"I'm suspicious of fucking everyone," Ringo barks. "So why are we here? I thought you must have had a lead for us given the urgent request to come tonight."

Griffin rolls his eyes. "Devon sent that text from my phone."

"So?" Devon scoffs. "We have business to discuss. No point in waiting since I was already in town visiting."

I glance between the three guys at the table. Ringo. Griffin. And Devon.

Two are related, but I swear all three could be blood brothers. I hadn't noticed it before, but now, with Ringo still neatly groomed from today's funerals, his hair back in a neatish man bun, you could definitely mistake these three as siblings.

Hell, they even act like it sometimes.

"What fucking business?" Ringo snaps. "I thought you were helping us. I thought we were here because you might have a lead."

"No lead," Griffin says casually, not in the least bit bothered about the anger emanating from Ringo.

"Why the fuck are we here then?" Ringo snaps, and I reach under the table, placing my hand on his thigh and giving it a squeeze.

Don't make Devon angry. He's holding my heart in his hands.

"I called you here about the favour," Griffin sighs while Ringo stiffens.

"The fucking favour?" Ringo lurches forward, leaning his forearms on the table like he's holding himself back from launching himself at Griffin. "You're calling it in now? We haven't resolved Abbey's situation yet. There are people still after Bobbi!"

"Calm down," Griffin says casually. "We're just letting you know what needs to be done soon, so you can start preparing."

"Fine. What the fuck is it you want me to do?"

I tense in my seat, Ringo's anger unsettling me, but I don't blame him.

The Marx family has been helping us with my situation, and the payment isn't money. It's a favour. Ringo owes them, and I'm terrified to think of what it could possibly be.

"Not what I want you to do," Griffin scoffs. "This order has come direct from the top."

My eyes dart to Ringo in time to see his jaw tick.

"Your old man?" he asks, and Griffin gives a single nod.

"Yes."

Slowly, Ringo sits back in his chair again, crossing his arms over his chest as he regards Griffin like he doesn't trust him.

That has anxiety clawing at my chest, and my eyes fall back to Devon, still holding Bobbi in his arms.

Suddenly, panic washes over me, and the trust I had for the Marx men vanishes.

"What is *this*?" I ask, my question taking everyone by surprise, their brows lifting as I stand abruptly. "Give my daughter back."

Devon frowns like I just told him he stinks, and shakes his head. "No way. This is Uncle Devon time."

Slapping my palms to the table, I glare across at the man they call the Devil, wondering if the real reason he's holding her is to keep her from me... are they planning to use my daughter against us to get Ringo to comply? Has Bobbi become leverage?

"I swear to God, Devon. If you don't give her back to me right the fuck now, I'm going to—"

The door bangs open, and I hear Jared cursing as Dee storms past me with murder in her eyes.

"Oh fuck no," Devon sneers. "Keep her the fuck away from my nuts!"

Dee isn't Dee right now. She's Hush, and her death stare is laser focused on Devon.

Unsheathing her huge knife, she glares across the table to where he really does look terrified.

Straightening, I smirk and cross my arms over my chest, loving every bit of fear emanating from the Devil.

"Hand over my daughter, and you can keep your nuts," I tell him, and Ringo chuckles from beside me.

"Shit, man," Ringo snickers. "You should know to never mess with a mother."

"Shut the fuck up," Devon hisses Ringo's way, barely taking his eyes off Dee as she rounds the table, twirling that huge knife as she approaches him.

"Fine. Fuck. I just wanted to hold her. I wasn't going to do anything," he snaps, and I swear, it's the first time I've seen this lethal guy look so human.

Glancing back down at Bobbi, he offers her a gentle smile, tugging his finger free of her little hand. "Your mummy is savage, little one," he coos in a soothing voice that doesn't suit the words he's speaking. "Uncle Devon already misses you."

And with that, he leans down and presses a gentle kiss to her forehead before holding her out to Dee.

Jared is the one to take her, Dee's focus still on Devon as she stares him down like she is planning his death.

God, I love that girl.

When all of this is over, I hope I get to hang out with Dee and learn more about her. She's such a small thing, with a gentle face, but she's so unassumingly deadly.

With my daughter in his arms, Jared rounds the table, bringing her to me. He stares at her for a moment, and when his eyes meet mine, they are glassed over.

"She's beautiful, Abs."

"Thank you," I whisper, my voice catching with the emotion clogging my throat, and I take my little girl back into my arms as Jared gently passes her to me.

"I take it you were listening at the door?" Griffin barks, gaining our attention, and I see him glaring at Dee.

All she does is flip him off and leave the room with Jared following behind, and Griffin's face flushes red in anger… or maybe humiliation. I'm not exactly sure.

"That chick is going to turn on you one day, cousin," Devon sighs, flopping back lazily in his chair. "One day you're gonna wake up with that fucking sword of a knife pressed to your throat."

"Been there. Done that." Griffin chuckles, and my brows shoot up as Devon nods.

"That's right. You never even knew she was in your house." Devon chuckles under his breath, but his eyes shift back to me as I lower myself back into my seat.

Wait, no. He's not looking at *me*. He's looking at my daughter.

Is Devon a dad?

The idea of it sounds laughable, but stranger things have happened. He actually seemed comfortable holding Bobbi. Like he's used to handling babies.

As Griffin tells Devon to shut up, I momentarily wonder what they are talking about, and make a mental note to ask Dee. I feel like there's a funny story there I might be able to taunt Griffin with.

Relaxing back in the seat, I take in my little girl, her eyes now sleepy as she sucks on her dummy, trying to soothe herself to sleep.

Reaching up, I graze my fingers over her brow, watching her lids flutter shut, so I keep doing it, loving how easily she responds to my touch.

"So what the fuck is it that Ewan wants me to do?" Ringo snaps, shifting the conversation back to business.

"It's simple," Griffin states, sitting back in his chair and pressing the tips of his fingers together. "Your President needs to be replaced. Ewan wants him out. He's too much of a loose cannon, and Ewan's not happy that we allowed the Southern Sadists into this region with such an unstable guy running the show."

"*We*?" Devon scoffs. "That was *all* you, cousin."

Griffin rolls his eyes, but he just turns his attention back to Ringo as he speaks.

"I thought it was you who controlled this region."

Sighing, Griffin's hands fall to his lap. "I control what Ewan allows me to control. If I don't get this sorted, he'll send someone else in to take over."

"Fuck," Ringo snarls, and Griffin nods.

"Yeah, fuck. We don't like it either. Although Ewan is right about Smitty. He's a crazy motherfucker that's going to do something to get us all in the shit."

"So, you want me to get Smitty to stand down and put someone else in the position?" Ringo asks, his brows tugging in as he frowns. "Or what? The Southern Sadists are out? That wasn't part of the fucking agreement."

"The Sadists are locked in now." Griffin acknowledges with a sigh, like this conversation is the last thing he wants to be doing. "*That* agreement stands, but there was never an agreement made about your President, just the club as a whole. So, in order to fulfil the agreement to Ewan's liking, he wants Smitty out, and he wants his head."

I stiffen at Griffin's words, my eyes flicking to Ringo to see his death glare locked on his Marx friend.

"He doesn't actually mean his head, right?" I ask, and Devon scoffs.

"That's *exactly* what he means."

My gaze flicks between each man, and when it falls on my husband, I find his gaze has dropped to the table in front of him.

"He wants someone to challenge him for the position. A death challenge?" Ringo asks for confirmation, his eyes flicking up to Griffin, who nods.

"Yes. He wants him dead, but not just by anyone. Ewan wants it to be done by you."

RINGO

Calm is anything but what I fucking feel, yet calm is what I try to be as Griffin's words sink in.

Ewan wants Smitty gone. Dead. And he wants me to replace him.

Fucking hell. Could this shitshow get any fucking worse?

"Ewan wants me to challenge the President in a fight to the death," I growl, fighting for fucking control. "Which I could potentially lose, but if I'm lucky enough to win, I have to take the role and run the fucking club?"

"Exactly." Griffin nods, and Abbey gasps next to me.

"No!" she cries. "You can't ask him to do that."

"Actually, we can." Griffin's glare is directed at my wife. "We gave our men to you to use. To protect you all. Not only did that leave the rest of my family and our empire vulnerable, but it cost us wages and some of our men's lives." Griffin sits forward, anger starting to contort his expression. "So, yeah. It's a big fucking payment for a big fucking favour."

As his words sink in, so does my reality.

I always knew the payment was going to be big. For some reason I had it in my head that they might not call on it for a number of years. Figured they'd want me to kill some high-level sob that was getting in their way.

But this... this is fucking different.

Sighing, I run my hand down my face, feeling fucking exhausted.

Ewan Marx wants Nate Smith dead. My President. And he wants me to kill him and take over the Southern Sadists.

"Can we pay your family back another way?" Abbey asks. "Money? Shit, I'll strip on that stage if that's what you want!"

"Like fuck!" I snarl, glaring at my wife, but the moment I see the tears in her eyes, I fucking soften. "Angel. This payment isn't for you to pay. It's for me. I asked them for help. Not you. I will be the one to pay back my debt."

"Fine." She throws her free hand up, exasperated. "Then you strip on that stage." She points to the door, in the direction of the rest of the club and the stage beyond. "I assure you, women *and* men will want to see that!" she yells at Griffin, and I chuckle.

"Angel... are you pimping me out?"

"Yes," she sobs. "Just for people to look at, though."

Reaching out, I cup her cheek, catching a fat tear that bursts free. With her eyes locked on mine, I swear I can see right into her soul at this moment. Her only real concern is me, and what might happen if I go through with this.

"Maybe both of you can get on that stage." Devon snickers. "We could make some decent coin off the two of you. I'll look after Bobbi while you're busy working off the debt..." All humour falls from his face as it turns to stone. "For the next one hundred and fifty fucking years."

His hard eyes dart between me and my wife before he points down the table to his cousin.

"Your debt has nothing to do with me, since I don't bow to my uncle. But I can tell you right fucking now, there's only one other way out of it, and it's fucking cold six feet under."

A low growl reverberates in the back of my throat as I glare at Devon, but it's my wife's hand darting out in front of her, flipping the fucker off that keeps me calm.

"Fuck you, Devon," she snarls. "If this doesn't relate to you, then why are you even here?"

A smirk tugs at his lips as he lounges back in his chair. "I like you feisty. Must be where your little sister gets it from."

Abbey stiffens, but it's Griffin who speaks, trying to calm the situation.

"Abbey, your sister is perfectly safe. Devon is just being a prick to get a rise out of you."

"I hope she annoys the hell out of you while she's there," my wife counters, and Devon's grin grows.

"She's nailing that pretty fucking well. She's made friends with a couple of our younger girls. The three of them are going to give me grey hair."

A slow smile spreads across Abbey's beautiful face.

"She's made friends?"

He nods.

"She's having fun?"

He nods again.

"Like the sort of fun kids have?"

"Yep," he confirms.

"And no church stuff?"

"No fucking way," he scoffs. "I don't allow God worship in my town."

"Ha," Abbey laughs, her caramel eyes flicking to mine. "She's being a kid."

"Yeah, Angel. This fucker might be a prick, but he gives women and children a safe space to heal and learn to live happily again."

Even though she's smiling, she hasn't forgotten why we're really here as she turns back to Devon.

"Why are you in this meeting if it doesn't relate to you?"

Devon shrugs. "Kinda wanted to meet the kid." He gestures to Abbey's arms. "And this fucker needs my brand of godliness to get shit done."

When he bobs his head towards Griffin, Abbey scoffs, but relaxes back again, her eyes falling to her daughter.

"So you're here as a scare tactic?" she asks, and Devon shrugs.

"Did it work?"

She flips him off again.

"Getting back on track," Griffin barks, glancing at his watch. "You know what Ewan wants now. So, start planning for it. Figure out a way to challenge Smitty without being fucking obvious. Use him as a scapegoat if you have to. Just get it done soon."

"How fucking soon?" I snap.

"Ewan would say yesterday. I, however, will play interference until the end of the month."

Griffin stands as if that's the end of the fucking conversation, so I stand too, stepping in his path as he tries to pass.

"And once it's done? Once I'm in the role I never wanted to be in, what will he ask of me then?"

"Just that you don't run the club like a crazy fucker and be sure to stick to those morals of yours."

"That's it?" I ask and he nods.

"That's fucking it."

Clapping me on the shoulder, Griffin steps around me and moves to Abbey to get a better look at Bobbi, but my wife is done with these Marx men right now, and she shifts away, not letting him get close.

I try to picture myself as the Southern Sadists President with Abbey by my side, but right now, it's hard to see.

I've never wanted that role in the club. I was hoping to step away from it a bit more once all this shit is over, and focus on my new little family. Maybe make it bigger if Abbey is keen on that idea.

But fuck me. How am I meant to do that and run an outlaw club?

It'll put a bigger target on my back, and in turn, Abbey's too.

"How long will I be expected to remain the President?" I spin, facing Griffin, and it's like he was waiting for me to ask.

"You'll have to ask Ewan. If you're lucky, he'll let you walk away in maybe five years." Griffin shrugs. "Maybe ten. Who knows?"

Five or ten fucking years...

When Abbey's eyes meet mine, I instantly see the uncertainty in them.

She's not going to want an MC life for her or Bobbi. And fuck. I don't blame her.

Maybe this is what the real payment is. I'll have to give up her and everything I love, just to keep protecting her.

Fuck Ewan Marx. The only reason he agreed to give me his men was so that he could take control of yet another fucking thing.

Grinding my teeth, I reach out and take my wife's arm, gently escorting her to the door, her distraught expression nearly fucking breaks me.

When we step out into the passage, Jared's and Dee's glares are directed at the Marx men, and I get a little satisfaction that even though they are both on the Marx payroll, their real loyalty lies with Abbey.

Walking out to the car with us, Dee and Jared dote over Bobbi, and swoop in for a closer look when Abbey puts her into the car seat.

When Jared gives my wife a hug, I don't even get jealous, because, fuck. I know he'd protect her. Maybe even better than I can, given this new fucking turn of events.

I give them a few minutes to say their goodbyes, and not long after, we're back on the road towards Fox Pines, the streetlights of Redfield fading as we drive onto the pitch black country roads.

"Let's just keep driving," Abbey whispers, and I glance her way to find those big doe eyes already looking at me. "Don't go back to the club. Let's just go. Leave this place behind and start over somewhere else."

Reaching out, I cup one side of her face while steering with my other hand, my eyes darting between her and the road.

"I wish it were that easy, Angel. But Tahli needs you. And my ma…" I let that hang in the air the moment guilt flashes over her expression.

"Yes. Of course. You're right." She shakes her head, clearly annoyed at herself, the movement dislodging my hand, so I re-grip the steering wheel. "But Cam… you can't do what they want."

My heart fucking races at the reminder of Ewan's payback request.

Well, I guess it's not really a fucking request, is it?

"I don't have a choice," I rasp, watching a hare dash across the road up ahead and disappear into the long grass.

"There has to be another way," she pleads with me like I can change the situation, and my heart fucking sinks.

"There's not," I state, wishing we didn't have to have this fucking conversation.

Somehow, I need to find a way to throw Smitty under the bus to make challenging him acceptable. If I had known about this a few days ago, I could have used the punishment I gave him for what he did to Daniel as the challenge. I could have declared him not fit to lead us. But that's been dealt with. My knuckles are still fucking scabbed up from it.

"What if you go to Ewan and explain the situation? Surely he'll understand," Abbey whisper-yells, clearly getting angry, and I want to yell back. But I don't.

There's no point in getting angry with each other when it's really someone else we are angry at.

"Angel, stop. You saw how Griffin and Devon are. They are two men you don't want to get on the wrong side of. But Ewan. He's something else entirely." I grip the wheel so tight, I feel the scabs on my knuckles splitting. "I don't want to fucking do what he wants, but I have no choice. It's not just me who will suffer if I don't. It will be you. Bobbi. Your sister and mine. My ma." I shake my head. "I'm fucking sorry, Angel. But this is the life of organised crime. If we're not getting hounded by cops and detectives, then we're making shady business deals and hoping our best mate doesn't stab us in the back."

Her quiet sobs float to me, and one look at her and all I see is the back of her head.

She's hiding herself from me. Probably disgusted with the man she married. Probably trying to figure a way out.

I wanted to change, to be a man worthy of her love. But maybe pieces of shit like me can't be rewired like that. Maybe we're only given fleeting samples of happiness, just enough to keep us chasing it, knowing deep down we'll never win that lottery. We'll never know what it feels like to keep it.

Fuck. I know what I have to do, and doing it will probably kill me. It will ruin me worse than taking Smitty's life ever could. But for my beautiful Angel... My fucking heart and soul... I know the only way to make her and Ewan happy is to obey him... and say goodbye to her.

A million words flicker through my mind as we drive back to the compound, all of them words I should say to my wife, but I don't speak a single one of them.

I can't.

I just fucking can't.

She sobs quietly as I drive, trying to hold in her pain, but every now and then, it escapes in a loud sob, and all I can do is rest my hand on her thigh and give it a gentle squeeze, hoping it's enough.

The moment we turn off the main road onto the compound driveway, she swipes frantically at her eyes, trying to get the tears to stop, but it's really no use. Anyone who sees her is going to know she's been crying from her puffy eyes.

I keep that to myself, though. She might *actually* kill me if I annoy her right now, and I can't protect her if I'm dead.

The floodlights are illuminating the yard up ahead outside the barn, and I frown as we get closer, seeing two SUVs parked off to the side that I don't recognise.

Slowing the Landy, we idle forward as I try to figure out what the fuck might be going on.

"Angel, check my phone," I snap, and she springs into action, taking my phone from the console and opening it. "Any missed calls or messages?"

"No." She shakes her head before taking out her phone too. "None on mine either. But there also isn't any service."

"Something's not right," I hiss, pressing my foot to the brake and quickly flicking off the headlights.

"What is it?" Abbey rushes out, fear lacing her tone.

"We've been gone a few hours, and in that time, no one's called. No one's texted. Now there are two cars I don't recognise. That wouldn't normally mean shit, but since I usually get fucking memes off JD every half hour, and no one has warned me about visitors, I've got a bad fucking feeling."

"What do we do?" she whispers like someone might overhear. "Wait. Who is that?"

I glance in the direction she's pointing, towards the line of trees near her side of the car. I squint, trying to make out what she can see, since there's no fucking moonlight to help tonight, and it takes me a moment to spot two figures, rushing from tree to tree, coming towards us.

"Gun," I bark, taking mine out, and Abbey finds hers a second later before scurrying over the middle console and into the back seat.

"Should you reverse the car up?" Abbey whispers into the dark, and I grunt in response, watching the shadows move closer.

"I don't think they are a threat," I say a moment later, taking in the feminine and male silhouettes. As far as I can make out, they keep darting glances over their shoulders back towards the barn, so to me, it looks like they are running from something. Not running *to* attack.

"Ringo… I'm scared. Bobbi…"

"I know, Angel. Trust me, I won't let them hurt her *or* you."

With one hand on the gun and the other ready to shift the car into reverse, I wait, watching them dash closer.

"Oh, wait," Abbey gasps. "I think it's Nessy."

Holding my breath, I hope like hell she's right because they are getting too fucking close for comfort, but a moment later, they spring from the treeline, darting over to us, Nessy and Brody coming into view.

"Fuck," I sigh, relieved it's them, and I put the window down. "The fuck's going on?"

"You gotta go!" Brody pants, desperation in his voice. "Get Abbey and Bobbi outta here."

"Why?" Abbey cries. "What's happening?"

"Abbey," Nessy pants, "it's your mum and grandfather. They are here!"

28

ABBEY

I try to remain strong as Brody and Nessy speed back down the driveway in the Landy, my heart in the back seat, still sound asleep, unaware that her mum is about to face off with her biggest threat.

"Say it again," I whisper.

"She'll be fine. Brody will call Devon as soon as he gets service, and Bobbi will be with your sister in no time."

I nod, trying to let his reassuring tone ease my mind, but all I feel is gut churning sickness as I watch the car pull onto the road and drive away.

They'll be okay. The threat is here with me, not chasing after her.

I think of the Rebels then, remembering how nearly every time we left to go somewhere, they would appear. I'm thankful most of them were dealt with. We haven't seen any since the airfield, but I know some remain.

Either they are regrouping, or doing what's smart, and keeping their distance to stay alive.

As the headlights fade in the distance, I turn and look towards the barn where light is flowing out from the main doors. It's quiet. There are none of the typical sounds of biker celebrations or Doxy orgies.

It's just quiet.

"Angel, you don't have to go in there. We can jump on my hog and ride the fuck away."

I nod at Ringo's words, but he knows I will. I have to, for me. For Bobbi. I have to face the real monsters once and for all.

"I don't understand why they are here." I glance up at my husband. "And why they are still alive. Wouldn't Smitty try to kill them?"

Ringo shrugs. "He might be waiting for you to come and do it yourself."

"I get the feeling that they aren't exactly prisoners," I mutter, glancing back towards the barn, and Ringo's fingers slip against mine, linking our hands.

"I get the same feeling. But you know Smitty. The crazy fucker always has a surprise up his sleeve. Maybe he's luring them with kindness and getting ready to strike."

"Maybe," I grumble, and we start walking quietly up the driveway towards the barn.

It's cold out here, but the chill I feel in my bones has nothing to do with the temperature outside, and everything to do with the people inside that barn.

As we get closer, we can hear background music playing, but the only voice we can pick up is Smitty's. It's not loud enough to make out what he's saying though, so it's hard to gauge what the atmosphere is like inside.

Glancing around the yard, I notice the fire drum alight, hot embers floating up as the wood inside burns, yet no one stands around it. There are no lights coming from the few tiny houses that line the yard, and the only lights coming from the direction of the bungalows are the faint ones lining the path.

"I have a bad feeling about this," I whisper, and Ringo's hand squeezes mine, dragging my attention to him.

"Keep your hand near your gun, but don't make it obvious you're carrying if you can. Is that knife still in your boot?" he asks, and I nod. "Good. That's your backup."

"Hopefully, I won't need it," I whisper, and his strained smile isn't the least bit reassuring.

"First thing you do when we go in is track my team. Make sure you know exactly where JD, Murf, Vender, Mex and Jols are. They will move into place to get close to you without me asking, and if shit goes bad in there, you do what they say to get you safe. Got it?"

A grin tugs at my lips. "You're so bossy."

He smirks back. "You fucking love it."

The next thing I know, his lips are pressed to mine in a very quick, yet searing kiss, helping somewhat to ease my nerves and reminding me that I'm not alone.

I have him.

I have the others.

We will be okay.

When Ringo reaches for the small side door, I take in a deep breath, preparing myself to see my mother and Banes. My grandfather.

This is it…

Swinging the door open, Ringo steps inside, tugging me in behind him, our hands still locked together. With my free hand, I keep it just behind my back, ready to reach for my gun if I need it.

"Ahhh, finally," Smitty sing-songs, and as Ringo steps aside showing me the space, I forget how to breathe.

There, sitting casually like they are having Sunday sippers at a table with Smitty and Spud, are Banes, my mother, and my sister, Maggie.

Shit.

SHIT.

My heart lurches at the sight of seeing them again. Especially sitting so casually on Southern Sadists soil. I kinda hoped they'd be strung up like pigs.

"Breathe, Angel," Ringo murmurs under his breath, and I give his hand a slight squeeze as I take in more air, focusing on my breathing, and not looking scared.

Last time I saw them, I was living in a world where my daughter was dead. I was ruled by my grief. My heartache. If I were still living in that world, I'm quite certain I would have pulled the gun out and shot all three of them by now.

But that's not my reality anymore. I still want them gone, but the raging violence I felt before isn't there.

"What the fuck is going on?" Ringo snaps, moving us deeper inside, all eyes on us.

Shit. What was it I was meant to do when we stepped inside?

Oh, that's right, find the others. See where they are in the room.

Quickly, I scan the space, finding Jols just to my left with JD close by. Murf is with Lewy over to the right, and Vender and Mex are across the room, behind Smitty.

That's when I see two more people here that don't look like they belong.

The first is Blake Moore. The guy Smitty had sent into the Rebels undercover. We haven't heard from him in ages, and had wondered if he was dead, but maybe he's just been focused on keeping the ruse alive. Or maybe he's switched sides.

The other guy is wearing a leather cut that says Rebels on it. Panda, I think they call him.

I look around, expecting to see Ian Allen somewhere, but he's not here. Hopefully he bled out and died after the airfield attack.

"We have some visitors," Smitty sing-songs again, like the weirdo he is. "They've come to meet *little Bobbi*."

The blood in my veins turns to ice.

"As you can see, Bobbi isn't here," Ringo snaps, and I can tell by his tone that he's likely glaring at Nate right now.

What's Smitty playing at? Is he tricking them?

It's the most likely explanation.

"I can see that." Smitty grits through clenched teeth, and I get a little satisfaction at catching him off guard. "You should go and get her. Don't be rude to our visitors."

Oh, hell no.

"What is this, Nate?" I snap, and his furious glare darts to me.

I called him Nate on purpose, knowing it would piss him off in front of his 'guests.' It's blatant disrespect, but right now, I don't give a shit about his bloody pride.

"You should show more respect to your elders." Banes dares to speak, and my eyes lock with his. "Honestly, Priscilla. Didn't you teach her anything?"

My lips twitch as my mother shrinks back in her chair, embarrassed after getting scolded by her father.

"Oh, she taught me stuff." I grin. "She taught me that I don't want to be anything *like* her."

Soft snickers float around the room, which only seems to annoy those sitting and standing around Nate's table.

"Hmmm." Banes sits back in his chair, crossing his arms over his chest. "She has the devil in her, Priscilla. Lucky you gave life to two more beautiful daughters."

My lip curls in disgust at his words, but he drags his gaze from mine, focusing on Maggie.

"Come here, Maggie." He pats his lap, and my sister stands from her chair.

I practically gape as Maggie rounds the table to go to him, glancing at me with a smug grin, like she just won the popularity vote, and I lost.

As she lowers herself to our grandfather's knee, I stiffen, feeling Ringo's hand squeeze mine in support, watching as Maggie links her hands behind his neck, and lets him place his big old wrinkly hand on her thigh, rubbing it up and down, way too high to be considered innocent.

No.

Shit.

No, she hasn't... he hasn't...

"Where's my granddaughter?" my mum dares to ask, ignoring what her father is doing to her other daughter.

"Not here," I snap, and she rolls her eyes.

"Fiddlesticks, Abigail. Go and get her now."

My brows hitch. "Even if she was here, I wouldn't get her. You aren't going anywhere near her."

"You little bi—"

"Why don't we get down to business." Smitty claps his hands, standing from his chair and rounding the table as everyone watches on.

"What fucking business?" Ringo barks. "We don't do business with paedophiles."

"Business is business," Smitty snarls, clearly having enough of being made to look like he's not in control. "And this is *long* overdue."

"What is?" Ringo snaps, and I swear, you could hear a pin drop as we all wait for Smitty to clue us in on what's happening here.

"A trade."

For a long beat, no one speaks, but I feel Ringo squeeze my hand, and this time I don't think he realises he's doing it a little too tightly. "What sort of trade?"

The Rebel, Panda, steps forward, hoisting a bag onto the table, unzipping it, and pulling out a handful of cash.

"Nine hundred K, as requested," he mutters, smirking at Ringo as he hands the cash to Smitty.

"The fuck!" Ringo growls, dropping my hand and taking a step forward. "What's the money for, Nate? We don't fucking trade with cunts like this."

Smitty waves Ringo off, running his thumb along the stack of one-hundred-dollar bills.

"You know what this money *can* do for us?" He holds it up for everyone to see. "Everything we had went into buying this land to give you a home, but this money can buy us riches to enjoy on the land. More hogs. More housing. More deal buy-ins." He brings the money down and fans himself with it as he rolls his hips. "More women."

"Hell, yeah." Spud thumps the table next to my mother, who jumps in her chair before shuffling closer to her father. "We're overdue for some fresh pussy!"

Some Sadists cheer at that, but most don't, and a quick look at the Doxies shows they aren't happy, either.

"Just imagine what we, as a club, can do with this cash." Smitty beams, looking around the room at his club brothers. "Without it, we're going to be scraping for fucking food. We'll need to work twice as much to bring in money. Hell, the piss might have to be rationed."

Grumbles fill the air, and a chill runs down my spine at what I'm witnessing.

Smitty is trying to convince the club that doing business with my grandfather is in their best interest.

Why would he do that? Is this another ruse of his? Like the day we all thought he was going to kill JD, but he was really testing JD's loyalty to Jols.

What the hell is his angle?

"We don't do business with predators, Smitty. Cut the shit!" Ringo yells, and shit, the venom in his tone sends a ripple up my spine.

Sometimes, I forget how scary he can be.

My monster.

"You need to shut the fuck up!" Smitty bellows at Ringo, silencing everyone. "You need to remember your fucking place! I am the President of this club. Not you!"

"I am the fucking enforcer, and I'm telling you, this goes against our fucking code!"

Slamming the wad of cash down on the table, Smitty stabs his finger in our direction.

"You and your fucking code bullshit! I've had enough of you thinking you can use my club for your own fucking gain."

Ringo scoffs at that. "I'm not going over this with you again, Nate. I haven't used the club, and the only one to gain from this deal is *you*." Ringo points to the cash. "You won't share your spoils with the men. If they're lucky, you'll find them some extra pussy and hope it keeps them distracted while you build yourself a fucking palace and sit yourself on a fucking throne."

"Nonsense." Smitty waves him off, not even bothering to fight harder to deny it. "Now, let's finalise this deal."

Turning his back on Ringo, Smitty faces my grandfather.

"You have yourself a deal. The money for Charity *and* her spawn."

My heart stops at Nate's words, as chaos erupts in the room.

Guns come out from all directions. Ringo's and his team's directed at their President, while Smitty's lackeys jump into action, directing theirs at us, and the other club brothers scattered around, pointing guns in different directions, not sure who they should, or want to, point theirs at.

"The fuck!" Ringo roars. "It was you this whole fucking time! The fucking snitch was you!"

Smitty laughs, turning to face us like there aren't guns pointed right at him.

"I'm running a business here. And you and your cock are fucking it all up."

Ringo yells something else, but all I can hear is the blood rushing through my veins and my thunderous heart.

Smitty? He was the one feeding my mum information? He was the one that gave up the location of the house we were at by the sea?

"How?" I snap, storming forward and ignoring Spud's gun pointed directly at my head, bringing it closer. Inches closer. "How did you know where we were in South Australia? Only four people knew the exact location."

Smitty smirks, pressing his hands together in front of him like he's going to start praying.

"I thought you'd never ask." He laughs like a maniac. "It's amazing the information one will give up while being raped with a mop."

I gape at him, tears pricking the backs of my eyes, while shouts fill the room as others become enraged by his answer.

"Tell me this is just one of your stunts, Nate." I step closer again, and the barrel of Spud's gun is now only an inch from my forehead. "I need you to tell me this is another dramatic hoax before I…"

He scoffs. "Before you what? *Cry?*" He laughs again, pouting, and Ringo's temper snaps.

Lunging for Nate, Ringo releases an animalistic growl, but JD and Murf are right there, holding him back, only making Smitty laugh harder.

"No, sweet Charity, this time, I'm not fucking around. Don't take it personally. It's just *business.*"

My lip wobbles, and I hate that he sees it, his lips spreading wider like the sight pleases him, so I fight off the tears that want to fall and suck in a steadying breath as I nod.

"Okay. This is real. You really have been playing us. Lying to the club. Working with predators," I scoff, flickers of memory coming at me. "It all makes sense now. Insisting on helping us, feeding me that bullshit line about being willing to die for your men. What a load of crap."

He shrugs one shoulder. "Like I said. It's just business."

"Right. Just business. I get it now. I finally understand how *business* is done under your rule." A calmness I wasn't expecting washes over me, and I think about my little girl, hoping she's on her way to safety, glad she isn't anywhere near this. Near me and what I have to become to survive in this world.

"Exactly." Smitty grins, pleased that we're on the same page, and as he turns his grin to the rest of the room, I quickly assess everyone around us too.

Ringo's hand is shaking, his gun aimed right at Smitty, and even though JD and Murf are holding him back, their guns are still aimed. One at Spud, and one at Tups.

Some club brothers are confused, their frowns matching the drop in the angle of their guns, while others have chosen their sides, pointed at Smitty, their own President, and some at my husband.

My mother is clinging to my grandfather's arm, while Maggie is huddled on his lap like the terrified little girl she is. But Banes looks calm. As do Panda and Moore.

I don't know how long Smitty has been working with them and against me, but I know it's been long enough for him to tell them about Bobbi being alive, and honestly, that's all the betrayal I need to learn to know we are *never* coming back from this.

So this is it. I wonder *who* will walk out alive.

"So you do business by double crossing your club," I state, subtly reaching to the back of my pants, my hand wrapping around the gun. "What an admirable President you are."

Smitty beams, clearly not picking up on my sarcasm, and in the time it takes to suck in a single breath, I flick my gaze to Spud and the barrel he has aimed at me, bring my gun up, point it at him, and pull the trigger.

RINGO

The crack of the gun is deafening, trigger fingers all around the room nearly letting loose as Spud's pained cry rips through the air. His gun clatters to the floor, his knees crashing down right after, and for a long moment, it's like the whole fucking room is holding its breath as everyone turns their focus to the source of the shot.

My wife.

Fuck. Her caramel eyes are wild as she stands there with her arms outstretched, gun aimed straight ahead, the dark smoky effect around her eyes making her look fucking lethal. Her leather jacket adds to how fucking tough she looks right now, but the most terrifying part of her is those fucking beautifully savage eyes.

They are laser focused right now, zeroed in on her new target.

My President.

Fuck.

My cock starts to wake at the sight of my wife looking all badass, and I will it the fuck down, because now's not the fucking time.

A choking sound falls from Smitty's lips, snapping me out of my Abbey daze, and I quickly scan the scene.

Spud, the club's VP, who is Smitty's lackey, is groaning on the floor like a little bitch, gripping his upper arm as blood spills over the concrete floor.

"You fucking cunt of a woman! You shot him!" Smitty jabs a finger in Abbey's direction like no one fucking knows it was her, but my Angel doesn't cower. She simply nods.

"You're next, arsehole."

And… there's my cock. Fully fucking hard at the most inconvenient fucking time.

How am I meant to do this shit with a fucking hard-on?

"She shot one of us!" Spittle flies from Smitty's mouth as he keeps stabbing the fucking air in my wife's direction. "She broke our rules!"

"Oh, please." Abbey rolls her eyes before refocusing her death stare on the club President. "I shot *through* him. He was in my way."

We all blink a little fucking dumbly until her words sink in, and then I glance across the space to the table where Panda *was* standing. Only he's not standing anymore.

He's flopped back in a chair, crimson blooming over his chest, soaking his white tee as he coughs up blood.

Fucking hell. Did she… mean to do that?

Who the fuck taught her that trick?

I instantly think of Riggs. That fucker and his closest men taught Abbey and my sisters some tricks of the trade. It wouldn't surprise me if he *did* teach her to shoot through someone else to hit a target behind them.

No one rushes to help Spud or Panda. The Doxies are all huddled together in the back corner, keeping their distance, and the men in the room are clearly fucking torn about who they should follow, given their confused expressions.

Fuck. This couldn't have worked out more perfectly if I'd planned it.

I've been ordered by Ewan Marx to kill Smitty and replace him as President of the Southern Sadists, something I really didn't want to fucking do until now.

Now, I know the fucking truth, and this fucker *needs* to die regardless of Ewan's fucking order.

Slowly, I lower my gun, and Abbey's gaze catches motion as I hand it to JD.

"What are you doing, man?" JD whispers, but I don't answer him, my eyes locked on my wife as she frowns, clearly trying to figure out what I'm doing too.

Neither of us wanted this, but taking control of the club is the only way to ensure she is kept safe. She has Bobbi. Her sister. Her friends. She'll learn to live without me. Fuck, she can live a normal life that doesn't involve Harleys, cuts, and violence.

A happy life.

The life she deserves.

Her eyes glass over as her lids flutter, like she knows exactly what's about to happen, and I wish we had more time to talk about this, but we don't.

"Smitty!" I call, dragging my gaze from my beautiful wife to face the club President, rolling my shoulders back, and making my voice loud so everyone can hear. "I challenge you for the role of President."

Gasps instantly fill the room as I quickly rake my gaze over the gathered crowd, spotting grins spreading across some of my club brothers' faces, while others turn red in anger, and the remaining still look fucking confused.

The men who are grinning seem to be happy I'm doing this, and it makes me wonder if they've hoped for something like this to happen.

Smitty is a crazy motherfucker, and while he can be a wild ride, he can also be so fucking unpredictable that you never really know if he's going to pat you on the back or shoot you.

It's not a good way to live.

"You can't fucking challenge me!" Smitty's bellow gains my attention again to find his face beet red as he glares at me. "I'm the President! I say what goes, and I demand everyone shoot this traitor now!"

He points at me, glancing around the room for support, yet no one budges.

"You know the bylaws, Nate," I remind him. "A president can be challenged for the role in a public fight. Fists or knives. You know the fucking deal."

Scoffing, he throws up his hands like I'm the dramatic one, doing a three-sixty to take in our club brothers, and clearly noticing some aren't on his fucking side.

"This is ludicrous. Shoot him! He's trying to destroy this club!"

"Not trying to destroy it. Only doing what's right," I explain, meeting the hard stares of some of the men. "If we don't stick to our rules and morals, then we are no fucking better than those Rebel pricks." I stab a finger in Panda's direction, who is now deathly pale as he bleeds out. Moore hasn't moved to help him, his own confusion written across his face.

Who does he take orders from? Nate or me?

He's been working undercover for the Southern Sadists, which Smitty arranged, which leads me to believe he hasn't always been working against us. But somewhere along the way, recently, Nate switched sides. For money. So maybe Moore has switched sides too.

"You think you can do better than me?" Nate scoffs. "Who secured this land so we could move out of the fucking burbs? Who has kept every fucker here sheltered and fed? Who has just made this club even richer?"

As guns lower, I start to pace before Nate, knowing my relaxed persona will piss him off.

"Actually, it was me and JD that secured this land for the club," I remind him, making sure my voice is loud again so everyone can hear. "We negotiated with the Marx family to operate out of this area. We ensured the sale price was a fucking steal for only one hundred fucking grand since no one wanted to buy the land the house of horrors burnt down on." Ignoring Nate's scoff, I flick my gaze to Abbey to see Jols at her side, whispering in her ear. "The shipping container deal was secured by Mex and Vender. The containers have, and continue to be converted by the club brothers." I gesture to the room. "Not you."

"Semantics," Smitty scoffs, basically digging his own grave given the glares that harden towards him from the club brothers scattered around the space.

"The money to feed everyone comes from the fucking kitty," I continue. "And it's the Doxies that source the food and cook for every fucker here. Not you." My eyes meet Casey's for a moment, and a flash of pride widens them. "The only thing you have done," I turn back to Smitty, "is go against our fucking rules to secure *yourself*, not the club, a huge chunk of money. There's no fucking way anyone here will get to see much of its spoils but you."

Nate's lip twitches as he glares at me, and I stop pacing to glare right fucking back.

"I challenge you!" I bark.

"Fine! Fists or knives?" he snaps, and this time, I smirk.

"Knives. We fight to the death."

More gasps float through the room. Some, more manly, while others are clearly from the Doxies.

"Cam." Abbey's gentle voice comes from behind me, and I glance over my shoulder to see her wet eyes.

The sight nearly fucking breaks me. She knows what this means. We both do.

A life of service to the club for who knows how long. This sort of life isn't for everyone, and fuck, the person she was just a few weeks back blended right in, but she was never meant to be that person. That killer. That ruthless, hardened shell of a human.

She is soft in the best fucking way, even despite how hard she tries to fight it.

It's not a bad thing.

Fuck, it's part of what drew me to her in the beginning. My pretty blonde Angel. Sweet. Innocent. Kind right down to her soul.

And now, with Bobbi... well, an MC is no place for a kid.

I swallow thickly, clearing my throat before I speak.

"This is how it has to be Angel. I'm sorry."

Her lips part like she wants to say something, but Nate's grating voice cuts through our moment.

"Stop fucking stalling," he snaps, and I turn my glare on him to see him shedding his cut and shirt. "You wanna play king fucking dick, then let's get this over and done with so I can piss on your corpse."

"He'll be pissing on your corpse!" Abbey yells from behind me, and I glance over as I tug off my cut to see Jols and JD holding her back as she snarls at Nate.

The man in question laughs like a fucking hyena at her, which fucking has my jaw ticking with rage.

This prick needs to learn some fucking respect.

Tables and chairs are moved to the sides of the room, forcing Banes and his fucked up little family to stand, while Panda's now dead body gets dragged outside by a couple of the guys.

When Banes, Priscilla and Maggie start for the doors, a wall of Sadists stop them, forcing them back into the corner to watch.

If things go bad for me, they'll think they've won. But if I win, then they are absolutely fucked. Coming here was really fucking dumb. I can hardly believe they trusted Nate. They should have easily seen through his bullshit.

Passing my cut to Abbey, I stand before her, cupping her cheek that's flushed red with anger and fear, and those big doe eyes blink up at me.

"I love you, Abs."

"I love you too," she whispers, the pain flickering in those caramel pools, a sight I'll never forget.

"You know why I have to do this," I murmur, grazing my thumb over the apple of her cheek. "But I'm also doing this for you and Bobbi. And my club brothers. It's the right thing to do."

Even though she hesitates, her nod in understanding is a fucking relief. She's been around long enough now to know how things work in my world. It's far from the world she should be living in, but she's here for now, and soon, she'll get her happily ever after with her daughter.

"I *need* you to win," she breathes, taking a moment to clear her throat. "Because after you win, you and I are in a fight. I have things I want to say."

My lips spread wide at her words and the way her dark eyes flare in anger. "Okay then, Angel. You and I are in a fight. I'll make sure to win so I don't miss the grilling you're going to give me."

She grins, but it's slight. "There will be boxing gloves involved. I definitely need to smack you around."

Throwing my head back, I laugh, and JD and Jols, who are standing on either side of my wife, join in.

"Okay. You have a deal." I chuckle through my words, and her smile falls a second before she reaches out, gripping the end of my beard, and tugging me down to her height.

"I'm gonna make you my bitch," she snaps. "And then…"

She trails off, and I raise a brow, trying not to cringe at the burn of my facial hair getting assaulted.

"And then?" I ask, and she shrugs.

"And then." She leaves it at that, smashing her lips to mine.

I ignore the hoots and wolf whistles around us, wanting everyone to just fucking disappear and leave me alone with my Angel. My fucking heart.

"Come on, you fucking pussy. Stop stalling because you know you're going to lose."

I pull back from my wife at Nate's cutting words, my jaw ticking as I let my anger free to course through my veins.

"Be right back, Angel," I snap, stepping away from her as she releases my beard, and flick my gaze to JD. "The moment this starts to go south, you get her the fuck outta here and go to Devon. Do not fucking deviate from the plan. Knock her the fuck out if she tries to fight you."

"Hey!" Abbey snaps, and I shoot her a wink, ignoring her fucking death glare.

"You got it, but do me a favour and don't let it go south." JD claps me on the shoulder. "You have more support in this room than you think. *We* don't just need you alive. *This club* needs you to lead it."

Fuck. I never wanted this. I've never even spoken of such fucking things to him before, so I know my challenge is a shock to my best mate, yet he's here supporting me, wanting this for our club.

With a nod and one last long stare at my wife, I turn and face Nate Smith.

He saved me once. Gave me an outlet to unleash my rage, but now, things have changed.

He's changed.

I've changed.

So now, the club must change too.

Rolling my head, I stretch it from side to side, holding out my arms as Tups searches me for any hidden weapons, and JD does the same to Nate.

Once that's done, Celina approaches with an old wooden box that she must have fetched, which holds identical blades in it. The challenge knives.

The last time they were used was probably fifteen years ago. That time, the President won, holding his role in the club.

I can't let that happen tonight. Even if I have to die too, Nate Smith is going down with me.

Being the President, Nate gets to choose his knife first, spending way too fucking long deciding which one he wants to use and not even noticing when Celina doesn't meet his eyes.

They've been on the outs since she found out what he did to Daniel, yet he still gives her arse a slap when she turns and steps over to me, like he still fucking owns her.

Moving to me, she holds the open box that now only holds one knife, her eyes flicking up to mine.

"Kill him, Ringo," she whispers. "He's toxic."

My brows hitch at her bold words. I know they aren't an attempt to get on my good side. I can already see how much she despises him, but it's risky for a Doxy to wish death on a club brother without risking punishment.

She's been his old lady for God knows how fucking long. Longer than I've been around. I don't know the story of how they came together, but I always assumed she fucking worshipped him.

Maybe I was wrong.

"I'm intending on it," I rasp, reaching into the box and taking the other knife. "But if it goes bad, take the girls to the Red Room in Redfield. Griffin Marx will protect you."

She gives me a slight nod before stepping away, clearing the space between me and Smitty.

"Let's get this over with. I've got some money to spend," the cocky fucker hisses, and his words flip my switch, rage soaring to the surface, and without a second fucking thought, I lunge for him.

My blade slashes across his bare chest, leaving a bright red line that starts seeping blood, and he fucking gasps like a chick, like he can't believe I actually did that.

And then... it's fucking on.

He lunges and I dodge, slashing his arm as I spin away, but the fucker nicks my hip on the way through. We fucking dance around each other for a bit as the room erupts in support for each of us, getting a slash in here and there, my focus on his wild crazy eyes, and how fucking excited he looks to kill me.

Slashes of blood bloom on both of our torsos as we fight, and when Smitty slices through a few of the names on my inked death list over my ribs, he throws his hands up in the air, cheering like he's fucking won.

Taking the opening, I lunge at him, not slashing this time, but stabbing his fighting arm.

He roars in agony as I plunge the blade in through skin and muscle before hitting bone, and he pants as spittle flies from his lips the moment I reef the fucking thing out.

"You fucking idiot!" he snarls. "You don't know what you're doing to this club. There's more going on than you know!"

"Oh, yeah?" I snap as we dance around each other again. "Enlighten me."

"You think I just randomly picked this land to buy?" He laughs like a fucking hyena again. "This land was owned by Terence and Viktoria Hill. They ran a fucking sex club out of this place."

I dodge his now left-handed swing, which doesn't even come close.

"I know all about the Vixen's Lodge scandal, Nate. Tell me something I don't fucking know."

His eyes darken as a sinister glint flickers in his glare. "Banes isn't just paying for your wife and her bastard kid." He swipes awkwardly at me again, and again I dodge it. "He's paying for the one last hard drive the cops couldn't find hidden on the property."

My dancing feet fucking still, and Nate's smile widens.

"See, you don't fucking know everything."

"What fucking hard drive?" I snap, and the cunt waggles his brows.

"There was one hard drive the cops never found. One that holds probably the most incriminating evidence on it, linked to the dark web and the site, Carnal Unicorn."

Gasps float through the air at his words, and the mention of the online trafficking site that was shut down just after this place burnt to the ground rings a bell.

"Banes is the founder." Smitty points his bloody knife towards Banes and Abbey's mum and sister, and the old fucker doesn't even look bothered.

"Some of my best work," he mutters, and roars of anger erupt across the room, some of the loudest coming from my wife.

I sneak a glance at her to see her fury locked on him, Jols and JD holding her back just like they did before.

Fuck. I knew Carnal Unicorn had been linked to the cult churches, but I didn't consider that Banes was the brains behind it all.

"When I realised the connection between Abbey and Banes, it was too easy." Smitty verbally vomits all his secrets, fuelling the fire in the pit of my gut even more. "It all fell into my lap. I tried to get rid of Charity politely, but *someone* had a hard-on for her straight away."

"It's Abbey! Not Charity!" she screeches from behind me, and Nate rolls his eyes.

"Whatever. You'll always be a charity case to me!"

"Hey!" I lunge for him again, and the fucker dodges my attempt to stab his guts. "Show some fucking respect to my wife!"

Nate scoffs. "Pfft! She's only your wife because of me. I ordered you to marry her thinking you wouldn't, since you were still a broken fucking man over Kylie and your own kid. But you fucking did it. And it was never because you were forced." He fakes a gag. "You wanted that shit. Sweet, innocent, barely legal pussy."

I fucking lunge at him, a roar flying from my lips, and he dodges it at the last second, getting in a stab to my fucking hip.

I stagger, feeling the burn of it radiate up my torso and down my leg as blood rushes from the fresh wound.

"So when that backfired..." He continues to spill his secrets, and I let him. Even if he wins, he's digging his own fucking grave right now. "I went to the Rebels, or at least, I sent Moore to them." All eyes shift to Moore, and the fucker shrinks back, stepping into Big Joey's chest, one of our loyal members who fucking holds him in place. "Our rivals were the perfect fucking plan, but noooo, you fuckers kept fighting them off."

We continue to dance around each other as Smitty spews the information like it's somehow going to save him, so I take it all in, trying not to let it get to me. I can't let my emotions rule me in a fight for my life. I need to stay focused and strategic.

"What about Allen?" I snap. "Was he part of your fucking plan too?"

"Allen was a different story," Smitty scoffs, swiping his knife awkwardly with his left hand and missing me. "He had his own agenda, which was fucking up my plans, but finding out Bobbi was alive is what put a spanner in the works." He cackles. "In a good fucking way."

When his eyes flick to the bag of cash by Tups' feet, I understand what he means.

"Money?" I ask, and he nods proudly.

"The reward to hand your wife and the kid over to Banes went up. But you fucking kicked us off your land, remaining tight-fucking-lipped about what was happening. Even Lewy wouldn't spill." He shrugs, baring his teeth a little as he spits, "So I took matters into my own hands."

He's had it out for my wife for longer than I thought, and fuck if he hasn't hidden it well.

His deceit just adds to the list of reasons why this has to happen.

This has to end now. I might die at the same time, but at least he will be gone too, and I know JD will make sure Banes gets what's coming to him.

Smitty and I stare at each other, waiting for someone to make the next move, and he's the one who finally gives in, swiping at me again.

I lunge forward, my only focus to take him the fuck down, and the moment my knife pierces his skin, his knife plunges into me.

Pain bursts in my gut, but I focus my attack on his neck, driving the blade in over and over, slicing though the veins that course up the column, his blood painting us both as I plunge that fucking knife in so many times that I lose count.

I feel us falling. I hear the yelling and screaming, but all I see is Nate's surprised expression as blood coughs past his lips, and the moment we hit the floor, my head bounces off the fucking concrete, sending me into a pitch-black vortex of nothingness.

30

ABBEY

I nearly trip over my own damn feet as I lurch in the direction of Ringo's lifeless body, but I'm jerked back when roars erupt throughout the room, fists flying in every direction as club brothers turn on each other.

"What's happening?" I cry over the yelling, and Jols' frantic eyes dance over the scene surrounding us.

"They need guidance!" she yells so I can hear her. "That's what's happening."

"Get her out of here!" JD bellows before he disappears into the fray, but I shake my head frantically, jerking free of Jols' grip.

"Hey!" she yells as I take off through the colliding bodies, towards my husband.

I duck just in time to miss a random swinging fist and get down and practically crawl the rest of the way, managing to get through everyone to find JD and Celina on the ground with Nate and Ringo.

Crawling up to them, I brush shoulders with JD as he pats Ringo's cheek, while Celina starts howling as she stares down at Nate's lifeless body.

"Is he alive?" I ask JD, who nods.

"He's out cold, though. Not real fucking convenient when we need him to get control of his fucking men."

I glance around at the chaos. Glasses breaking, chairs shattering, and tables crashing to the floor as they are used as weapons.

Looking over my shoulder, I search for Banes, my mum and Maggie, but I can't see through the lashing bodies.

"You need to do it," I say, grabbing JD's arm and shaking it. "Tell them to stop."

"I can't," he scoffs. "I'm not an authority figure to them. And you shot Spud, our VP."

I roll my eyes. "I shot him in the arm. He's still alive. Why isn't he doing anything?"

"Are you stupid?" Celina sobs, her gaze looking harsher than I've ever seen it. "The balance has shifted. He's not loyal to Ringo. He's probably run off by now."

I glance around, realising I don't remember the last time I saw him. Shit. Shit. Shit.

My eyes track over Ringo. There's blood all over him, but I know a lot of it is Smitty's. He has two gashes on his torso. One on his side and one on his hip.

I have no idea how serious they are, but the fact he isn't waking up is scaring the hell out of me.

"Ringo." I reach for his head, turning it towards me a little. "Please wake up. We have a fight to finish."

Tears burn my eyes, but I try to fight them off. I need to see clearly with all the chaos surrounding us.

Cupping the side of his face, I run my thumb over his cheek like he often does to mine, finding my thoughts drifting to God, or whatever holy being there is that can help us right now.

"Please let him live," I whisper. "Please. I'll do anything."

The screams of Doxies huddled in the back corner meet our ears, and Celina's anger falls away as concern takes over her expression.

"They are going to kill each other if someone doesn't stop this."

I fear she's right. This needs to end.

I know I'm not an authority figure, but someone has to take action, so I let go of Ringo and slowly stand, taking out my gun and weaving through the crowd.

I get shoved, and jostled, and have to duck more swinging fists again, but I make it through to the bar, which is covered in shattered glass, and I swipe my arm across it to clear the way before hoisting myself up.

Standing on the bar top, I use my boot to kick off some more shards before staring around the room.

I can't see my mum, sister, or Banes, and my heart sinks knowing they have gotten away, but I guess they'll keep for a different day.

Forcing myself not to think too much, I lift my arm high, pointing my gun to the ceiling, and pull the trigger.

The crack is loud, halting some, so I pull the trigger again, shooting a second round, which has most men freezing in place, blinking around to see what's happening.

"YOU NEED TO STOP!" I yell as loud as I can, and slowly, eyes upon eyes land on me, and I feel my cheeks heat like I'm under a spotlight.

A loud whistle sounds, and Vender leaps up onto the bar beside me, Mex doing the same on my other side a moment later.

"LISTEN UP!" Vender yells, and the violent shouts dull to a whisper. "There you go, Abs. You tell them how it is."

I blush at Vender's words, wanting to ask him to do it for me, but I need to do this. I need to help put an end to this since it mostly came about because of me.

"You need to stop fighting!" I call, trying to dig deep and remember the tips I got from having to get up in front of the class and talk at school. "Ringo challenged Smitty the right way according to your bylaws. The fight was fair, and Ringo won. He's alive, and when he wakes, do you really want him to find the men he's been fighting to protect at each other's throats?"

A rumble of chatter floats through the crowd of men as they glance at each other, but their eyes still come back to me.

"I understand a lot of you are confused. I know losing Nate will be painful for many of you, but the club has rules for a reason, and according to them, your new President is Ringo. So stop being a bunch of babies, shake hands or hug it out, and then clean up this mess, because when Ringo comes to, he's going to be the best damn President this club has ever had!"

"Damn right!" JD yells from the centre of the room.

"You fucking heard her!" Mex bellows. "Get this shit cleaned up!"

And just like that, the club brothers around the room start bro-hugging and smiling at each other like they weren't just punching the living hell out of each other.

"My God, I don't think I'll ever understand the way you men think."

Mex and Vender chuckle at my words before Vender leaps down, reaching up to help me down too.

As I weave back through the crowd, this time not fearing I'll catch a stray fist, I get small smiles and nods from the men, and it warms my heart a little at how safe I feel despite the fact these are all very dangerous men.

Lewy is already working on patching up Ringo's wounds, and JD and Jols are there on the floor beside him, staring down at my husband, who still isn't moving.

A flutter of panic courses through me...

What if he doesn't wake up? What if he's slowly dying?

I start pacing, chewing on my thumbnail, too scared to move any closer to see if my husband is still alive.

Please don't die. Please don't die.

"He's awake!" JD calls, and a sob escapes me, my knees buckling, but this time, it's Casey and Darla who catch me.

"It's okay, Abs." Jols half laughs, half sobs as she turns to look up at me. "This fucker is hard to kill."

We all giggle at that, and I find my feet again as Ringo's groan meets my ears.

"Did I win?"

"Yes, you fucking crazy bastard!" JD laughs. "You won! Smitty is dead."

I feel like I should be cheering, but the glee just never comes.

Smitty was the crazy one, that's for sure, but his death doesn't make me happy.

I don't know if it's because there's been so much death already, or because I know what this means.

Not that I wanted my husband to die, not ever, but now... now he's the ruler of this club. He's the new President of the Southern Sadists.

It's good for the club. But for me, not so much.

"Cameron Musgrove, otherwise known as Ringo, is our new President!" JD calls, and the sound of fists thumping over hearts fills the space.

Glancing around, I find the men all looking this way. Some wearing smiles. Others frown. A couple glare.

JD and Lewy shift in unison, helping Ringo sit up before lifting him to his feet, and he wavers on the spot for a moment, pressing his hand to his head.

"Fuck, I've got a killer headache."

"A head like that should ache," JD chuckles, and the rumble of Ringo's matching laugh has the corner of my mouth tugging north.

He turns in a half circle, his eyes scanning the space, and I instantly know they are seeking me out. I get the feeling he's checking to see if I've run.

I should. This lifestyle is hard, and I'm still on the fence as to whether I want Bobbi to be a part of that, but shit, I love Ringo. Like heart crushingly so. I don't want to lose him, but to have him, is to be a part of this life... for good.

"Angel," he rasps, and his voice nearly melts me.

The sight of him standing with his shoulders hunched forward, his skin covered in blood and some dodgy bandage work by Lewy, is almost too much to bear.

Shit… I can't leave him. I can't live in this world without him, no matter where I am. Look at everything he's sacrificed for me. For Bobbi. No matter what sort of life I live from this day forward, it has to have him in it. It just has to.

"We're still in a fight," I snap, but there's no venom to it, and his sluggish grin has me mirroring it.

"I fucking love fighting with you, Angel."

A laugh escapes me, and I take a step towards him when a voice stops me.

"A deal is a deal."

We look to the side to see my grandfather, my mother, and my sister, Maggie, being held at gunpoint by Murf.

Shit. They didn't escape.

A swarm of butterflies race through my chest and down into the pit of my belly, and I can't tell if it's fear or elation.

They are still here. They aren't chasing Bobbi. I can still end this.

"It doesn't matter who the leader of this club is," Banes snaps. "The money has been paid, so give us Abbey, Bobbi, and the hard drive, and we'll be on our way."

I flinch at the balls on Banes. Or maybe it's not balls, but delusion?

"Old man, you fucked with the wrong people." Ringo sighs, like he can't be bothered dancing around the situation like Nate often did, and he tries to straighten a little more, using JD as support. "We're an MC. We do business differently, and fucking handshakes and conversations don't always work out. The deal you had with Smitty is now null and fucking void."

"I don't think so." Banes shakes his head, his eyes flicking to me before going back to Ringo. "We agreed to the club's terms."

"Not the club's terms," Ringo snaps. "This was never brought to a vote, so the only deal you made is with the guy dead at my fucking feet."

I have to give it to my grandfather. He does a damn good job at remaining poised. The only sign that Ringo's words have affected him is the slight flare of his eyes.

"You're an idiot for coming here," I snap, gaining his attention, as well as the sneering glares of my mother and sister. "Trusting Smitty was a mistake that was always going to get you killed."

"You little bitch!" my mum screeches. "How dare you speak to your minister like that!"

"Oi!" Jols gets up in my mother's face. "Don't speak to her like that. You forget you're on our turf now. Back the fuck off!"

I bite back my grin as my mum flinches back, Maggie gripping her arm as her eyes go wide.

But Banes remains stoic.

"Do we have empty containers?" Ringo asks, and Vender answers.

"We have heaps. Want them separated?"

Ringo nods. "Throw Spud in one too, as well as this fucker."

Ringo points to Blake Moore, and his club brothers move forward, taking each of our new prisoners away, my family in tow.

The moment they are out of the barn, I rush to Ringo, finally letting go of my hard façade that I needed to keep in place to get through that whole thing.

"We need to get him cleaned up and in bed," I call to whoever will help, and even though his face is pale, drained of any colour, his eyes soften as they lock with mine.

"We can be in that fight later, right?"

I grin. "Yes, later. I want you strong for when I kick your arse."

Rumbles of laughter sound around us, and I stand back watching on as JD and Lewy get Ringo situated on a chair and start to clean him up some more.

Ringo watches me as I watch him, his eyes never wavering, almost like I'm what's helping him remain strong as the guys poke and prod the cuts covering his torso to get them clean.

"Ahhh, Ringo." Celina clears her throat, almost sounding scared. "Me and the girls can start moving Smitty's things out of the President's cottage, and move your things in."

Shaking his head, Ringo's eyes dart to me. "I don't want that place, do you?"

I shake my head too.

"But you're the President now," Darla jumps in. "You have to stay in the President's cottage."

"There is nothing in the bylaws that states the President gets his own damn cottage," Ringo hisses as the pain from the wound cleaning gets to him. "You Doxies can have it. There are two bedrooms and a fucking over dramatic bathroom with a spa. The men can start work tomorrow to expand it, so each woman eventually gets her own room."

A series of feminine gasps fill the air, and I look around at the Doxies and the disbelief washed over their faces.

It's like they've never been shown kindness.

"What about you and Abbey?" Casey asks. "Don't you need a house?"

Ringo's gaze flicks to me, and for a long moment, we just stare at each other.

I can't tell what's going through his head. Does he think I'm going to leave? We haven't had a chance to wrap our heads around any of this yet, but he made it clear in the car that he has to be here for the club, and even though I don't know how that will work with Bobbi, I do know that we will figure it out.

"It can wait," Ringo finally responds, but his eyes never leave mine. "Let's get the women out of the barn and give them a real home to live in. We can worry about the other stuff after that."

A smile tugs at my lips, and his follows.

Cameron Musgrove really is a good man. A selfless man. He may not be able to leave this club behind because of Ewan Marx, but I get the feeling that things would have turned out this way, regardless. This club *is* his family, and the men and women here are some of the most individual, crazy, yet big hearted people I have ever met. They mean a lot to him, and for a moment there, I forgot how much they mean to me.

The vibration of my phone in my pocket breaks my gaze from Ringo's, and I fish it out, seeing the screen flashing with a video call from the letter T.

I can't hit accept fast enough, holding the screen up as it connects, and tears instantly blur my eyes as I see my sister Tahli, holding Bobbi in her arms.

"Oh my God!" I cry. "You got her!"

"Yes," Tahli giggles. "Brody and Nessy brought her to me. She's getting a little restless, so Nessy is just preparing a bottle for her now."

"Angel, come here." Ringo's order has me moving blindly to him, too focused on the sight of Tahli and Bobbi together to take my eyes off the screen.

When I'm near, he pulls me backwards, and I fall into his lap as he looks at the screen too. "Hey there, kiddo."

Tahli rolls her eyes. "I'm not a kid."

"Yes, she is." Devon's head pops up behind my sister. "If the only thing you want for dinner is chicken nuggets, then you're a damn kid."

She rolls her eyes at him, and I smile at the fact my sister doesn't seem the least bit scared of the normally terrifying, Devon Marx.

"Thank you, Devon," I rush out, hoping I really can trust this man and his secret sanctuary to keep my sister and daughter safe. "Thank you for taking them both."

"I will protect them." He says it so matter of factly that I can feel how true his words are.

"Send word to your uncle." Ringo angles the phone his way a little more so he can be seen on the screen too. "Smitty is dead. I am now the President of the Southern Sadists MC."

Devon's brows shoot up, and I'm worried he'll say something that will give away that Ringo was forced to do it, but he doesn't say anything incriminating. "Will do."

Bobbi takes that moment to start crying, clearly hungry, and Devon's hard expression softens as he looks over Tahli's shoulder, down at my daughter.

"Hey, hey, little one. No need for the tears. Uncle Devon is here."

Tahli scoffs. "*Uncle Devon?* You're not her uncle."

Devon's dark glare flicks up to the screen. "Your sister is like a mini you, Abbey."

I giggle, and Tahli rolls her eyes. "You say that like it's a bad thing. My sister is as tough as nails, and I'm the same, so you'd better not hide the chicken nuggets from me."

Ringo and I burst out laughing, and we spend another few minutes chatting and watching as Nessy helps Tahli get settled in an armchair, showing her how to feed her little niece a bottle.

I don't want to end the call. I could honestly sit there all night and watch them, but I can't.

Ringo needs to get cleaned up properly and go to bed, and I... I can rest well tonight knowing Devon is keeping my heart safe.

Unfortunately leaving the barn isn't that easy, and Ringo is engulfed with questions, congratulations, warnings from those who aren't sure he's the right man for the job, as well as a discussion on what has to happen next.

I was waiting for them to discuss some sort of ceremony, but apparently, all that happens is Smitty's President's patch gets removed from his cut and given to Ringo to sew onto his. Which of course, I will do for him.

The Doxies know better than to ask if one of them should do it, like they normally would.

The men discuss the need for church in the morning, plus messages to be sent to the other chapters and their business associates to announce the change in leadership, and finally, JD and Jols help me get my husband back to the bungalow.

We do all the things we need to do to get cleaned up and into bed. Jols and JD settle into the bed next to ours, which feels less weird than it used to, and I snuggle carefully against Ringo's side, mindful not to put too much weight on him and aggravate the nicks and cuts Smitty left behind.

Ringo passes out pretty quickly, and when I hear heavy breathing coming from Jols and JD, I stick my fingers in my ears, not wanting to hear them fornicate right next to us.

Eventually, they finish up and fall asleep too, but me? I just lie there, staring up at the ceiling for hours.

My mum, sister, and grandfather are here on this property. It's unsettling, to say the least. Them showing up here and us locking them away just seems too easy, even though it really wasn't.

Did they really come here willingly expecting to get what they want? I'm kinda waiting for the other shoe to drop. Is it a trick of some sort? I can't make sense of why they would trust the motorcycle club where my husband belongs, to deliver on the deal they made.

I also can't stop thinking about Smitty.

What happened in the barn runs like a reel in my head. The feeling of Smitty's betrayal is really hitting me now, but also... his death.

He was such a lunatic of a man, and we clashed more than we got along, but a part of me is sad he's dead. Sad this is what it has come to.

Yeah, he's obviously played a big hand in everything that happened surrounding me, Bobbi, and Banes. All for some money, but I feel like it was more than that.

Like when he gifted Bobbi a tiny club leather jacket at her funeral. Was all of that a lie? Was he pleased that she was dead? Or pleased that she was alive knowing he could use her as leverage?

Ugh, the entire thing makes me feel sick.

Slipping out of the bed, Ringo doesn't even stir, so I throw on a hoodie and jeans, along with my boots, and creep out of the bungalow.

It's a little after four in the morning. The estate is practically silent this time of morning, and there's a calming peace to it. So calm that I don't even realise until I'm there, that my feet lead me to the row of shipping containers being used as cells to keep my family locked up.

A couple of club brothers I don't know well are guarding them, plus Murf, who spots me straight away, standing from the hay bale he's sitting on.

"Is everything okay?" he asks, and I nod, raking my gaze over the row of containers.

"Can you see inside?" I ask, and he nods.

"We have a peephole."

I grin. "That sounds creepy."

"It does." He chuckles, waving me closer to the first container, and pointing to the door and the small hole.

Standing on my tiptoes, I press my hands to the cold metal door and look in through the small hole, spotting my sister, Maggie, huddled in a ball on the floor in the far corner, sound asleep. Seeing her like this, I'm reminded that she's in her mid-teens with her slight frame and the way she curls in on herself, appearing more innocent. It pains me to see her like this. Locked up. Probably scared. She's a product of her environment. She doesn't know any better, and just like me at her age, pleasing my mother was a top priority.

Maggie has been brutally against me all through this, but she's only doing what she thinks is right because she's been brainwashed into thinking that way.

I hope with time, I can help her to understand what's right and wrong about all of this.

Moving to the next container, I see my mum sitting huddled in the corner, her head resting on the wall, her lips parted as she snores, and nothing about her makes me feel remorse.

All I see is an evil woman. Yes, she is also a product of her environment from when she was a child, but she broke free. She had a chance to turn it all around, and the moment she saw an in, she took it, using me to try to get on her father's good side.

I'll never understand her or the beliefs she's followed through her life, and I'll never forgive her for being a piece of shit human that didn't protect her children.

If her head exploded off her body right now, I wouldn't even shed a tear.

Sighing, I step back from that peephole and move on to the third container, peering in to see Banes. My grandfather.

He's sitting up, leaning against the back wall, his eyes wide awake. Around his wrists are cable ties, and around his waist is a chain that looks like it's secured to the wall, so he can't try to escape.

Stepping back, I turn to face Murf and point to the door. "Can you open it, please?"

His brows shoot up, his hand coming to the back of his neck, clearly uncomfortable.

"Ahhh, I'm not sure Ringo would like that."

I lift a single brow. "Murf, don't make me wrestle the keys off you."

He chuckles. "Fine, but the door stays open so I can get to you if you need help. Just don't get too close. He's chained up, but there's some give in the chains."

"Okay," I say, stepping back as he opens the lock on the door, and pulls the door wide, revealing my grandfather.

As I step inside, Banes lifts his head, stiffening when he sees me.

"Abigail." He stands like his wrists aren't bound and chains don't bind him to the wall. "I've been expecting you."

"Tell me about the hard drive," I say, and a slight frown appears.

"We can discuss that, but perhaps first, you can join me in prayer."

"Nope," I rush out. "No preaching your bullshit here. Tell me about the hard drive."

He sighs, looking disappointed in me like I'd even care.

"The hard drive is not your concern."

"I'll be the judge of that," I snap. "Tell me."

"Fine," he sighs, widening his stance like he would at the altar standing before his congregation. "Carnal Unicorn was a vital part of my legacy. I spent years building the most profitable underground entertainment this country has ever seen."

"Entertainment? Don't you mean a trafficking ring?"

"You might call it trafficking, but I call it a lucrative business. Membership was high. The word was spreading, not just about the online entertainment I provided, but the word of our Lord."

I scoff. "You know the problem with religion and people like you? You use it to justify your actions. The Lord forgives everyone who asks for forgiveness, right?"

"The Lord will guide those who seek to repent their sins." He smiles warmly, and I roll my eyes.

"So, you molest your children, repent to God, get your forgiveness, and do it again. And again. And again."

"I have never molested my children!" he booms, but I don't even flinch. I was expecting it.

"Did you, or did you not, have sex with Priscilla? Your daughter."

"Your mother was training to be a vessel. It was her duty to open for the prophet."

A sick shiver ripples up my spine at his words, and I wish I'd brought my gun.

"The prophet being you?"

He nods.

"Yeah-nah. That's molestation. Incest. Paedophilia, depending on whether she was of legal age, and given some photos I found of her when she was younger, I'm going to guess she wasn't."

"You speak of things you don't understand."

"You're right. I will *never* understand how a father can do that to his children, and shit, probably grandchildren too. Have you raped Maggie?"

His eyes darken, and I kind of like that I'm pissing him off. "It wasn't rape."

My breath hitches, air getting trapped in my lungs and dread slamming into me at his words.

"You had... sex with her?" I can't even help the squeak in my voice.

"I lay the flame within her. She will burn until she bears under the blessing of Symme."

I stagger back, his words a sick confirmation that clogs up my throat with rage, and my back collides with a chest, a gasp escaping me as I spin to see who is towering behind me.

31

My Angel's caramel eyes dart up to mine, terror flickering through them before relief washes over her from head to toe. I didn't mean to scare her, but being woken by one of my club brothers to tell me my wife was in a container with her grandfather kind of lit a fire under my arse, and now I'm tired, grumpy, hurting, and fucking wild with fear that something might have happened to her.

"We'll talk about the fact that you snuck out later," I snap, and her eyes flare as she sucks her lips in between her teeth, biting down.

Does she even know how fucking sexy she is?

"You have tainted my granddaughter," Banes snarls, drawing my attention, and Abbey spins back to face him.

"We've gotten off track," she says, and I know she's struggling with her emotions right now. I heard enough before I stepped inside to know what Banes did with Maggie.

I should just shoot the fucker now.

"The hard drive," Abbey snaps. "What's on it?"

"Evidence." He grins smugly, and I ball my fucking fists, fighting the urge to lurch forward and smash his smug fucking grin right off his face. "There is video footage of high-level government officials doing not so savoury things, as well as a list of names and locations. But again, nothing of your concern, Abigail. But it was a concern to the previous President of this club."

Shit. Smitty.

"Explain," I bark, and Banes remains quiet for a long moment, his eyes tracking over me and my wife. I notice his eyes linger on our hands and the way our fingers intertwine, and at how close we stand to each other.

"You don't see the irony in the man you've chosen to be your husband?" he finally speaks, and fuck, I wish he'd just shut the hell up. "You've only been of legal age for a short time, Abigail. How is that different to me and Maggie?"

A strangled gasp flies from Abbey's lips, and I want to fucking kill this motherfucker right the fuck now, but we need answers first.

"You're kidding, right?" Abbey snarls. "Maggie is still a fucking child! And you're her grandfather! There are so many things wrong with that, and nothing like me and Ringo. Now stop stalling and explain what Smitty had to do with the hard drive!"

"I see you speak just as vulgarly as these thugs," Banes snaps before finally answering her question. "The hard drive is encrypted, so Mr Smith couldn't open the files, but he could read the filenames. I guess seeing one named Nate Smith had him worried. Part of the deal was for me to wipe him off the hard drive. But he was a fool. I never intended to delete his files."

"Are you saying..." Abbey chokes, not able to finish that sentence, and fuck, I don't even want to think of what he means but I can't help it. I fucking know what this means.

"It all makes so much more sense now," I mutter over Abbey's head. "He was trying to cover his own arse."

"Desperate men do desperate things to protect their secrets," Banes preaches, making me want to fucking gut him right the fuck now.

"So he didn't want anyone to find out he... what? Raped a woman?" Abbey asks, and Banes scoffs.

"Not a woman. A child. Two to be exact."

My world tips on its fucking axis and I nearly stagger back, but Abbey's knees go weak, and she nearly collapses, so I hold her up, bracing her shoulders, helping her stay upright.

"Smitty... raped two children?" Abbey squeaks, and Banes shakes his head.

"You call it rape. I do not."

"Oh, my bad," she scoffs. "I should have said he *lay the flame within two children*?"

"Yes," Banes answers so casually, like we aren't talking about one of the worst violations a human can do to another. "I'm sure if you speak with Celina, she will confirm that it was an honour to have Mr Smith's blessing in the name of the church. Look at how she's flourished ever since. Wendy too, although I believe she met her death at your hand, Abigail."

I fucking stiffen, running his words through my head over and over to make sure I fucking heard him right.

Celina? Wendy?

Is he saying Nate found them through that fucking trafficking ring? That he raped them and then fucking kept them?

I think back to the relationship they all had. Celina was his favourite, gaining old lady status, but was she here of her own free will? She never acted like it was any other way. But then, I guess he probably groomed them if they were underage when they first met.

Shit. Fucking Smitty. I wish he was still alive so I could see his face when he realised his secret was no longer a fucking secret.

Then, I'd kill him in the most painful way.

Fire.

"You're all sick!" Abbey yells, pressing her hand to her mouth like she's fighting the urge to hurl. "This is all just so… sick!"

"Your attempted insults do nothing, so let's focus on business, shall we?" Banes sneers, parting his lips to speak again. "That hard drive is worth more money than you can possibly imagine on the dark web. I'm happy to split the sale. Fifty, fifty. Just hand it over and set us free. You'll get your money and never have to see us again."

This fucker is delusional if he thinks we are fuelled by money and I'm about to tell him so when Abbey speaks.

"You know, I kinda hoped you would somehow slightly redeem yourself," she says, shaking her head in disbelief. "Instead, you've done nothing but cement your death."

Spinning, those big doe eyes meet mine, and I can see she's ready to leave, so I take her hand and lead her out of the container, ignoring Banes' attempts to get us to stay.

"Lock it up," I bark to Murf, who nods and does what I asked, as Abbey looks around to the men.

"Okay... who was it?" she asks, cocking her hip and crossing her arms over her chest. "Who dobbed me in?"

Fingers get pointed at Murf and Teddy, one of our young Sadists, and I smirk at how the latter flinches back when Abbey's hands fly to her hips.

"What's the saying? Snitches get stitches?" she snaps, and Teddy's gaze darts to Murf.

"He ordered me to." He points to Murf, who just rolls his eyes.

"No offence, Abbey." Murf holds up calming hands. "But I don't want to fucking die, and the quickest way for that to happen is to keep shit from my President."

"Too fucking right," I mutter, the burn of the cuts flaring now that the adrenaline from being inside that fucking container with the most twisted fucking man I've ever met has worn off.

Trying to appear like I haven't been fucking sliced and diced in the last six hours, I slip my arm around Abbey's shoulders, drawing her closer to me, and gently leading her away from the containers that are now acting as a fucking prison block.

The further away we get from the containers, the more I let go of my façade, and I start to limp, needing to lean on Abbey.

"Shit... I'm sorry." She wraps her arm around my back, trying to help me.

My hip hurts more than the gash in my fucking side. I was worried when the knife went into my gut that it would hit something vital, but as far as the guys could tell, I got fucking lucky.

"We need to get you back to bed," she whispers as we start crossing the yard, but I shake my head, and redirect her towards the container that sits over the dungeon.

"I wanna speak to Lewy first. He told me he has the hard drive Smitty was selling to Banes. Apparently, Nate had asked Lewy to try to access the files."

"Oh... What are you going to do with it?"

"I don't know," I admit, limping up to the door and tugging it open.

Lewy's head pops up from behind a screen in the back end of the container, and I hobble in with Abbey closing the door behind us.

"Sarg... I mean, Prez. Do you need something?"

I chuckle. "Shit, man. I don't think I'll get used to being called Prez. I've been Sarg for so fucking long."

"You'll get used to it." Lewy waves me off.

"The hard drive. Any luck with your tech geeks getting into it?"

"Ringo!" Abbey scolds me as I lower to a seat, and Lewy chuckles.

"It's okay. They *are* geeks."

Abbey smiles, but it doesn't meet her eyes.

She's clearly exhausted. I guess she couldn't sleep earlier, but I need to get her into bed. There are some serious decisions that need to be made tomorrow... or I guess it's really later today given the current time. But either way, she needs to be clearheaded, and the best way to achieve that is sleep.

"One of my guys has been able to get through the encryption on some of the files, including the one Smitty was worried about."

My fucking brows shoot up, watching as Lewy stands, holding out a file for me, so I take it, hesitating to open it.

"I've ahhh... blurred out certain things," Lewy explains, "but you *really* need to see who's in the pictures with him."

I don't tell Lewy I think I already know, my eyes flicking up to Abbey's to silently ask her if she wants to look away, but she just nods towards the folder, so I slowly open it.

"They are screenshots from videos…" Lewy trails off, and even though I was expecting to see younger versions of Nate, Celina and Wendy, I wasn't quite prepared for just how young they were.

"Oh my God," Abbey gasps, her hands flying to her lips as tears gather in her eyes. "They are so young. Are they even teenagers?"

I shake my head. "I don't know, Angel. Fuck…" I hiss. "I should have known. How didn't I fucking know?"

"How could you?" Lewy asks. "As far as I can see from the first video, the girls were purchased at some sort of auction. But Sarg… shit, I mean Prez…" Lewy scolds himself, but I don't even care about that shit.

"What is it?" I ask, knowing whatever it is, won't be good.

"Look at the other pictures." He directs me, and I flip through them until I see what he needs me to see.

"Spud and Tups," I mutter, and Abbey stiffens.

"Spud is locked up, but where is Tups?"

"Video surveillance had him going into his bungalow after Spud was dragged away. I haven't clocked him leaving since," Lewy offers, and I slowly stand.

"Keep an eye on his bungalow. If he exits, call Mex and Vender to grab him and lock him up too. Otherwise, we'll deal with him when the sun rises."

"Copy that," Lewy says, nodding our way.

"Do you ever sleep?" Abbey asks, and Lewy offers her one of his rare smiles.

"Sometimes during the day. Otherwise, me and caffeine are best friends."

She giggles, and we leave, fucking slowly since I can't seem to hide my hobble now.

Jesus Christ, I'm too old for this shit.

We make our way back across the yard and down the path to the bungalow. I'm dog fucking tired, and I can see my Angel is now too, so I'm surprised when she stops at the bottom of the steps to my bungalow, looking like the weight of the world is on her shoulders.

"Angel?" I ask, and she sighs, tipping her head back to look up at the black sky of nothingness since the clouds hide all the stars.

"I don't know how to make this work."

Shit. My fucking heart sinks.

Is this it? Is she going to leave my old arse now?

"You want out?" I ask, hating how my voice cracks.

I told her before we got married that she could end it when all of this was over. I don't want her to, but I'll never force her into something again.

Those doe eyes blink up at me, the faint glow of the porch light showing me her flushed cheeks, and I brace myself for the worst.

"I don't want out, Cam. I love you. I just never pictured having to raise Bobbi and Tahli here on a compound. I kinda thought we'd live with your mum and sisters on your property." She shrugs as disappointment washes over her. "And now that you're the President... if I'm at your property and not here with you, it's only a matter of time until you find yourself an old lady."

Her lower lip wobbles as she says old lady, and I reach out, cupping her cheek.

"Angel, no. Never. You are *it* for me. My wife. My old lady. My missus. My girl. My *Angel*," I remind her, stepping up closer and pressing my forehead to hers. "I don't know how to make this work either, but wherever I am, you are, got it?"

"But Bobbi... Tahli..."

"Angel, let me ease your worries. When I say *you*, I mean them, too. We are a *family*, and I know it's all so new and messed up now that I'm the President, but we will navigate it together." I press my lips to the apple of her cheek before I continue. "I want to be Bobbi's dad and a big brother to Tahli. I feel like Hope brought you all to me to fill the hole she left. I need *you*, Abs. I don't think I can do this without you."

Pulling back, her eyes dance between mine, her hands coming up to fist the front of my cut.

"If even one of the Doxies comes on to you and tries to steal you from me, I'll fuck them up." She stabs a sharp finger to the centre of my chest. "And I'll fuck you up, too. I'll—"

"Shhhh," I chuckle, pressing my finger to her lips to get her to stop spitting venom at me. "The *only* woman I want is you until the day I die. I'm *yours*, Abs. You own *me*, not the other way around."

She pouts, and it's fucking adorable.

"You own me too," she whispers, rising on her toes to press her lips to mine.

For a minute, I forget that I'm covered in cuts, or that I'm sporting two deep fucking gashes. I just feel her, taste her, smell her, and know, without a doubt, that I'll love no one on this Earth more than her. Ever.

When we slip quietly back inside the bungalow, Jols and JD are still sound asleep. I hold my fucking breath, trying not to make a sound every time I twist the wrong fucking way, feeling the burn of my hip and gut. My wife can see the pain I'm in, and helps me back into bed, and once she joins me, I finally relax again.

I'm out like a fucking light in no time, but a loud bang has me gasping awake, who knows how long later as I jerk up in pain and blindly search for my gun.

"Shhh, it's okay." Abbey's soothing voice fans against my ear, and I blink a few times to clear the haze from my eyes. "Someone is banging on the door."

"Who the fuck is disturbing my beauty sleep?!" JD yells, dragging his naked arse out of bed, not even fucking concerned that he's flashing my wife.

The fucker swings the door open, early morning light flowing in around him as one hand scratches his head, and the other scratches his fucking arse cheek.

Jesus fucking Christ. Maybe I should've taken the fucking President's cottage.

"This better be good," JD snaps. "I was having the best dream."

"I can fucking tell." Vender chuckles. "Can you point that thing in another fucking direction?"

JD looks down, obviously spotting his hard-on, and just shrugs, hiding the fucking thing with his hands as both Abbey and Jols giggle.

"What do you need, Vender?!" I call, and JD steps aside so Vender can see in.

"We have a problem," he grumbles.

"We have a lot of fucking problems," I mutter. "Which one brings you to my door at fucking sunrise?"

"Tups is gone, and he's taken Spud and Banes with him."

32

ABBEY

Standing outside the shipping containers, I take in the carnage Tups left behind.

One man dead, one fighting for his life, and two stirring from their concussions.

"How the fuck did this happen, Lewy?" Ringo snaps at his IT guy, who shrugs, his eyes wide with panic.

"The cameras didn't pick him up leaving his cabin."

"He went out the window," Mex calls as he rounds the corner, heading our way. "I just checked it out. The door is locked, but the back bathroom window is wide open."

Ringo's glare shifts back to Lewy. "So how didn't you spot him on any of the cameras?"

"I dunno, Prez. I'll check over them again, but I really didn't notice anything." Lewy takes off his cap, running his hand through his dark hair in distress.

"Check them again," Ringo barks and points to Mex. "Go with him. He needs a second pair of eyes. He's fucking exhausted."

Mex nods, leaving with Lewy, and I move to the container Maggie is in. Looking through the peephole. She's huddled in the back corner crying, her wide eyes trained on the door like she's waiting for someone to come in.

As Ringo checks on Murf and Teddy, who are sporting the concussions, I move to the next container to get a look at my mother.

The light inside the container is flickering on and off, and my mum keeps glaring at it like the light is doing it on purpose.

"I was in and out after he hit me over the head," Murf mutters, drawing my attention, and I turn to see a trail of blood running down the side of his face. "But I heard enough. Tups was going to free the mum and kid too, but Banes told him not to. Said they'd just slow them down."

My brows shoot up.

Huh, does Priscilla know that her daddy dearest ditched her?

"How long ago?" JD snaps right next to Murf's ear, making him groan, his hand coming up to his temple like he has a pounding headache.

"The sun was rising. That's all I know."

"They can't have gotten far. Check to see if any vehicles are gone, and get every fucker out of bed," Ringo orders. "I want them manning the perimeter."

"Got it." JD claps right before barking orders into a handheld radio.

I take a step back, trying not to get in anyone's way, watching my husband so naturally step into his role.

I wonder if he realises that he was made for this. To lead. To govern. I feel like he's been doing this sort of thing for a long time. Making sure things got done when his role was the Sergeant-at-Arms.

Gunfire sounds from the thick treeline across the clearing, and I stiffen, half expecting bullets to spray our way as JD barks into the radio.

"Where is that coming from?!"

"Perimeter bordering the Bossier Estate. They are running across their field," the voice says, and I quickly fumble for my phone.

"The Bossier Estate is Shaun's property," I rush out, opening my phone contacts to find his number and hitting call.

It rings twice before picking up, his voice breathless.

"Abs, are you okay?"

"There are bad men on your property. Three of them," I blurt, my eyes flicking to Ringo to see him watching me. "Make sure your parents are safe."

"I can see them running across the field. Heard the gunshots," Shaun confirms. "There are more running after them."

"Yeah, they are the good ones," I tell him, not wanting to go into detail right now. There's no time for that.

"Gotcha. My brother is getting the dirt bikes ready now. Simon is with me. The three of us will herd them back your way."

"Wait! No!" I yell, but the line is already dead, and I lock eyes with Ringo.

"What is it?" he asks, moving to me.

"Shaun and two others are going to try to herd Tups, Spud and Banes back this way on their dirt bikes. You need to tell your men not to shoot them," I cry, and JD is on his radio relaying that information a second later.

"It's okay, Angel. Your friends will be fine."

I shake my head, scoffing, because he doesn't know that.

Ringo ignores me, turning to the few men nearby.

"Get the mum and kid out, but keep them apart. Let them hear and see what happens when you mess with the Southern Sadists."

A round of wolf howls come from a couple of men, and I shift out of the way as they do what Ringo asked.

Gunfire echoes in the distance, with some yelling, and the sound of dirt bikes.

I should probably call Rhys and let her know two of her boyfriends are risking their lives right now, but then again, what will that help? She's better off being oblivious to it all until after the fact, because knowing her, she'll get here by any means possible, and end up getting hurt herself.

I don't want that.

Jols sidles up next to me as my mum and sister are led out of the containers, Maggie moved up one end, and my mother up the other.

"You hear that?" Ringo asks my mum, who simply curls her lip in disgust at him. "That's the sound of traitors getting what's coming to them. Banes being one of them."

My mum pales then, and Maggie's sobs meet my ears, so I glance over my shoulder to see her hands tied in front of her as her eyes scan the treeline where the sound is coming from.

The radio crackles right before a voice comes through.

"Got 'em. Heading back."

Everyone but my mum and sister visibly relaxes.

Mex and Lewy return while we wait, and JD orders the men lining the perimeter to head back to the clearing.

"You doing okay?" Jols asks, and I flinch a little, realising I was so focused on everything happening around me that I kinda forgot she was there.

"Yeah. I guess. I just want this to be over." I mutter the truth as the dread of it all sinks in.

For this to be over, justice needs to be served. Or perhaps revenge? I'm not sure, but it means more death. More violence. More of what the monster in me craves, but everything that the angel in me fears.

"How does it feel to be married to the President of an MC?" she snickers, urging a grin out of me, although it's only slight, because shit... Smitty was her stepdad.

"Jols... Smitty... You must be—"

"Relieved." She cuts me off. "I know he saved me and my mum, and on the outside, it looked like he'd done a good thing. But we were beholden to him. And not in a good way."

Jols chews on her lips, looking around like she's checking to make sure no one is listening.

"I did care about him, Abbey, but he held saving me and my mum over our heads. They may have been living separate lives mostly, but he had her working for him on the side. Always controlling her money, and reminding her that he had me in his care. She was scared of what he'd do to me."

"Like when he dragged you back here after the raid on the Rebels compound?" I ask, and she nods.

"He's gone now, and learning what he did…" Jols shakes her head, her blue eyes flaring wide with anger. "If Ringo didn't kill him then I would've."

There's so much conviction in her voice that I don't doubt that for a second.

"So, let's not talk about that fucker anymore and stop dodging my question." She wags her brows, and I frown.

"I've already forgotten what it was."

Giggling, Jols reaches out and grips each of my shoulders.

"How does it feel to be married to the President of an MC?"

This time I giggle, remembering what we were talking about.

"Feels the same as always so far." I shrug. "I can't really picture how it will be after this though."

"Well, there will be celebrations once this is all over. And, just FYI, if Ringo says it's a rule that the President fucks his wife in front of everyone at those celebrations," she uses air quotes when she says celebrations, "then he's lying."

A laugh bursts from me, and we both giggle, leaning against each other, receiving some sharp glares off our men.

"Stop it. You're going to get me in trouble," I snicker.

"Don't act like you don't want him to spank you."

"Oh my God, stop!" I squeak, and Jols cackles next to me.

It's in that moment that a horde of men start showing through the trees, stepping out into the clearing and leading three prisoners towards us.

I go rigid at the sight of my grandfather limping, and Jols must notice because she takes my hand in hers, giving me the extra support I need.

"Let him go!" my mum yells, but no one pays her any attention, or my sister, who is sobbing again.

I can't look at her. I feel weak when I do. Like I'll cave and give in and just let her go.

I don't know what to do with her yet. She's just a misled kid. Groomed. She needs some sort of rehabilitation.

Shit. Does that even exist for a situation like this?

"Ringo, you need to take a look at this," Mex grumbles as he passes us with Lewy on his heels.

He hands Ringo some papers, and I watch as Ringo scans them, a frown tugging at his brows before he looks up to Lewy.

"Is this the list from the hard drive?"

"Yes. And the last page has some locations," Lewy answers. "As you can see, some of them were used to store things, some as safe houses, some as ahhh... recording studios."

"And some used as clubs," Ringo mutters, handing the locations page to JD before he scans the other list again.

When his eyes flick up to me, I know he's seen something I probably don't want to know about, but he quickly redirects his gaze to Lewy.

"You find footage of what Tups did to break those fuckers out?"

"Yeah, caught it all from the hidden camera over there." He points to some trees nearby, but I don't see any camera. "Tups came out of the dark with a cricket bat and a knife. Moved faster than I've ever seen the old fucker move."

Ringo scoffs. "Adrenaline will do that."

Chatter washes through the crowd of gathered Sadists and Doxies as they congregate outside the shipping containers. Tups, Spud and

Banes get shoved to their knees before us, a Sadist behind each one, and guns pressed to the back of each of their heads.

I try to ignore the sounds of Maggie's sniffling, but it's hard as I look at the scene the way she must be seeing it.

She's terrified, that's for sure. There are dozens upon dozens of leather clad bearded men, none of whom look savoury. There are guns, knives, cigarettes and tattoos. All the things the church preaches is the work of the devil.

If that's the case then I'm a devil worshipper for sure, but I know better than to listen to that rot.

These men are dangerous, there's no doubt about that. But there's honour amongst them.

Does exposure to this count as rehabilitation for my sister? Probably not.

Moving to me, Ringo hands me the papers, a frown furrowing his brow.

"Take a look at some of the names on that list. You might recognise some."

I'm assuming it's my parents' names, so I nod and take them before he turns and moves out to stand in front of everyone, stepping into his role as President.

"There have been three traitors in our club, working behind our backs, and doing the very thing we fight against," he starts, and my eyes drop to the papers.

I immediately find Delany. Priscilla and Colin. I'm not surprised, but it still stings. As well as Karl Stone with Elizabeth's name in brackets with a question mark.

I then go through the entire list, stiffening as I see more names I recognise.

Some are high-level politicians, and my mind flicks back to when Smitty told me he knew the state was going into another lockdown. He really did have connections in high places, and I bet they are the same ones that are on this list.

I spot a couple of celebrities amongst the hundreds of names, but it's the others I recognise that has my veins turning to ice.

> Hill, Terence & Viktoria.

Not a surprise since they were the previous owners of this land who ran a sex club from their home. The same sex club Rhys and Shaun got tangled up in, but it's the names underneath that gets me.

> Bates. Brian and Julie.

I shake my head, frowning. The surname Bates is familiar to me since it's the maiden name my mum used... but it isn't her real maiden name. She just made it up, because it's really Banes.

It's not just the surname that has me. It's the names, Brian and Julie. I know those names. I recognise them from the news reports after everything came out about Rhys and the sex club and... shit. Brian Bates was Rhys George's biological dad... surely it's just a coincidence.

Glancing up, I see Ringo still talking as he paces, anger contorting his features as he points to Tups, but I can't hear anything he's saying.

All I can hear is the blood rushing past my ears.

When I look at my mum, I find that she's been gagged, and I frown... When did that happen?

I can't even make sense of things right now, because this list... I have to keep reading.

Ryland. Christopher. (Fox Pines Catholic College)

My eyes widen. Ex Principal Ryland? Holy shit!

I don't know why I'm so surprised after what he allowed to happen to Lexi, but now it makes total sense. He was a predator.

All of these people are predators.

When my eyes roam down further, tears instantly burn the backs of my eyes when I see the names at the bottom.

West. Maxwell. (Ruth: out-of-pocket / turnout / drug controlled)

West. Mike. (ex. Con. Category 1 risk)

No.

Shit... Lexi's dad and her half-brother. They were evil men, but knowing my grandfather was a part of who they became makes me feel sick to my stomach.

"What does this mean?" I whisper to Jols, pointing to the words next to Ruth's name, and Jols leans closer to read it.

"Oh, ummm... Out-of-pocket means disobedient or not accepting of the rules," she explains quietly next to my ear. "Turnout means forced into prostitution, and drug controlled means pretty much what it says. She was controlled with drugs. Probably had her so out of it she couldn't fight, and maybe didn't even know what was happening."

My breath hitches, and I feel like throwing up.

Lexi... her mum... she'd told me a bit about stuff that came out, but not that. Does she even know?

"I'll take them, Abs. You don't need to worry about that list right now." Jols eases the papers from my grip, and I nod, fighting back tears as I try to refocus, the sounds of thumping fists over chests gaining my attention.

"The club has voted," Ringo calls. "I hereby strip Spud and Tups of their membership, and punishment will take place in the dungeon at sundown."

I don't know what that means, but Tups starts begging as he gets dragged off in the direction of the dungeon, while Spud remains quiet like he's already accepted his fate.

I'm not entirely sure what just happened, but now that all eyes fall on my grandfather, I focus on my husband, trying to get all thoughts of Lexi's mum out of my head for now.

I have my own mother to deal with. And grandfather. And sister.

"You really are a bunch of barbarians," Banes mutters, and the Sadist standing behind him whips his gun across the side of his head, nearly making him tumble sideways.

My mother cries out to her father, and I realise her gag has been removed, but Ringo speaks again, stealing my attention.

"See that wall over there?" He points to the memorial wall over by the tree. "You are responsible for every man that died."

Banes scoffs, using the back of his wrist to wipe off the blood trickling from above his ear.

"Their deaths were an obvious sacrifice to make room for pure vessels."

"You're so delusional!" I blurt, stepping forward, my gaze flicking to my mother, who curls her lip at me, and then to my sister, who is still crying, even though her glare is cutting.

When I glance back at my grandfather, he is wearing a smirk.

"I am *not* delusional, Abigail. I have faith that all will work in the favour of Symme. Your daughter will be mine, and pure life will flourish."

"She'll never be yours!" I scream, and his smirk gets wider as he stares up at me, before his lids flutter closed, and he starts chanting.

"In fire we trust. In blood we bind.In silence, we serve. In wombs, we rise.Let the vessel yield. Let the line endure.Let Symme look down and find us worthy."

"Shut up!" I yell, recognising the chant I never understood until now. "She's not yours!"

"She is the new vessel," he says with more confidence than he should have, and a chill ripples up my spine.

Is Bobbi safe right now? She has to be. Devon has her hidden away.

"I thought I was the vessel," I snap, needing him to stop talking about my daughter that way. "Isn't that what you wanted me for?"

"I did once, yes." He nods, still so goddamn poised even kneeling in the dirt with a gun to his head. "You're too tainted now. You're only good as a sacrifice to bless the new yield."

"Yield?" I ask, having no clue about the garbage he's spewing.

"Life, Abigail. Life inside the vessel."

"You're deluded!" I snarl, spinning away to try to rein in my building temper, and he starts chanting again, and this time my mum and sister join in.

"Who brought this vessel?" Banes calls, and in unison, my mother and sister call.

"The line."

"Who takes this vessel?" he calls again, and Maggie and my mother follow.

"The flame."

"Who protects the seed?"

"The blood," they chant.

"Who owns the child?" he calls, and my traitorous family chants.

"Symme."

"Shut the hell up!" I scream, charging towards him, ready to swing a punch, but then he holds his hands out to me, like I'm going to run into his waiting arms.

"From sin she bore, in pain she yields," he calls. "The heir to rise, the fire to seal. Not hers, nor his, this child is the flame. Of Symme it grows. Of Symme it came."

"Shut the fuck up!" I yell, wanting to punch him but terrified of getting any closer. "Don't preach your cult shit here!"

"Symme, hear me!" He looks up to the greying clouds hovering low in the sky, blinking as the first drops of rain start to fall. "Flame of the First Blood, do not let this flesh betray its purpose. I am your breath. Your chosen. Your prophet without equal." He holds his hands up to the sky, like he is the one making it rain. "Death is not mine. Death is for the impure, the unshaped."

Shaking my head at his brand of crazy, I stumble backwards, running into Ringo's firm chest, his hands coming up to rest on my shoulders.

"Want me to shoot him now?" he asks, but I shake my head, holding my hand out instead, knowing he'll know what I want.

"Rise in me!" Banes calls. "Stitch bone to bone. Bind my marrow to the flame. Let my blood command the body. Let my will reject the grave."

The heavy weight of a gun gets placed in my palm, and I wrap my hands around it, hearing my mum screaming for me to stop.

"This womb of the world is mine to rule!" Banes calls, eyes open as he stares up at the sky, blinking each time a drop of rain hits his face. "My lifeline will not rot. My seed will not fail. I am Symme's eternal tongue. I speak, and the world kneels! I bleed, and the world obeys! If I die, the world will burn for daring to outlive me!"

I already knew he was delusional, but this God complex is truly disturbing. He actually believes he is a higher being.

I step closer, Ringo's hand falling away from my shoulder, and Banes' eyes snap to me.

"No. No. No!" he panics, flinching as his gaze falls to my gun. "Symme, listen to me! Please! I am not finished. My work is not done! This flesh is not permitted to fail me. This heart beats because *I command it to!*"

Suddenly, my mum starts chanting, and Maggie quickly joins in.

"The line. The blood. The flame. Symme."

"The line. The blood. The flame. Symme."

"The line. The blood. The flame. Symme."

"Do you hear me, flame?!" Banes bellows up to the sky, arms spread out, palms facing the clouds. "I carved your laws into children's bones. I bled your scripture into wombs. I broke my children to build your kingdom. I am your right hand. I am your chosen mouth. I AM THE BLOOD THAT BINDS THIS WORLD!"

"You are the scum that rots this Earth," I snap, having enough of his bullshit, lurching forward as the Sadist behind him steps away.

I shove the barrel of the gun under his chin, and his dark eyes meet mine as he continues to pray.

"I will not die! I will not rot! I do not go into the dark like common men!" he hisses when I jam the gun harder, forcing his head back, yet *still* he prays. "Pull me back, Symme! Stitch my soul tight! Feed on the weak! NOT ME! Don't you dare take me! Don't you—"

The squeeze of the trigger feels so right in that moment, the crack like a whip, echoing across the clearing as blood sprays up like a fountain, before showering down on my grandfather's lifeless body that slumps down onto the gravel.

Hysterical screaming takes a moment to pierce the bubble I'm in, but when I refocus on the here and now, I recognise the grating sounds. My mum and my little sister, Maggie.

Glancing over at my mum, I see her struggling against the hold two Sadists have on her arms, her eyes trained on her father now lying dead.

I feel no remorse for what I just did, nor do I feel the anger of my monster. I just feel right.

That man was toxic. His venom reached so much further than I could have ever imagined. There is no place in this world for people like him. And there's no place in this world for people like my mum, so I lift the gun again, and aim it directly at her.

33

ABBEY

"Who is Brian Bates?!" I scream as I storm forward, my gun raised at my mum, whose face is red in anger, tears wetting her cheeks, sneering at me.

"You wicked bitch!" she cries, not even caring that I press the barrel of my gun to her forehead. "You killed him! You killed our saviour! The world will rot now, all because of you!"

"Mum! Stop!" Maggie screams from the other end of the row of containers, being held back by one of the men, and a Doxy. "Just pray! Symme will protect us!"

I nearly choke on my scoff as I glare over my shoulder at her, but Maggie's tear-filled eyes are determined as she starts to bloody chant again.

"The line. The blood. The flame. Symme."

"The line. The blood. The flame. Symme."

"The line. The blood. The flame. Symme."

Shit… she's so far gone. Rewiring her brain is going to take a lot. I don't know how to do that, but I'll make sure I can find someone who can. She's never even had a chance to learn what's on the other side of this.

Normalcy. Freedom.

Shifting my glare back to my mother, I ask her what I want to know again.

"Who is Brian Bates? He has the same surname you've been using as your maiden name. How are you associated with him?"

She scoffs, her glare locking with mine as her lip curls in disgust.

"You mean who *was* Brian Bates?" she snaps. "Because he's dead."

"So you *do* know him?"

She draws back, and before I know what's happening, she spits in my face, the warm wet droplets slapping my skin, leaving me in momentary shock.

"He's none of your concern!" she screams, and my patience snaps.

I grab her by the front of her blouse and drag her to me until we are nose to nose, my gun shifting to her temple as I bare my teeth.

"Who the fuck was he?!"

"He was your uncle!" she screams back in my face. "We used the same fake last name when we were both banished!" she yells, spittle flying from her lips. "That useless man nearly exposed everything when he got caught!"

I launch back from her, air getting trapped in my lungs for a moment, and I fold in half, trying to breathe.

"Angel." Ringo's hand is on my back in an instant, his warm gentle touch reminding me that I'm not alone. "Let me do this for you."

I shake my head, air finally seeping in, and my glassy eyes meet his.

"Rhys is my cousin." I breathe, a sense of calm washing over me.

What happened to her was horrific. I don't even want to think about it, but all that aside, her biological father was my uncle, and the quirky girl who stepped up to replace me as Lexi's best friend when I failed her is actually my cousin.

I would never have known, and I doubt she knows either.

Ringo's frown is a little amusing, but Jols steps forward with the papers, pointing to the name, which I assume is Brian's, and I can tell by his wide eyes that his brain starts to catch up.

"You…" I trail off, shaking my head in disgust at my mother as I wrap my head around the damage my bloodline has caused. "Your father… your family… are nothing but toxic cultists," I tell my mother, and she instantly tries to spit on me again, but it falls short, hanging off her chin.

"When I get free, I will gather the congregation and take over my father's work so we can rise up and make this world pure."

A laugh slips from me. "When you *get free*?" I scoff. "You think you'll escape this fate?"

"Of course," she sneers, and Maggie's chanting cuts off.

"We have the work of Symme to do!" she cries. "Let us go!"

I roll my eyes at my sister before turning my attention to the Sadists holding my mother in place.

"Cut her ties and let her go."

Their brows shoot up, and gasps fill the air around us.

"Angel?" Ringo asks, and I glance over my shoulder at him.

"She thinks she'll be set free, so it *must* be true. She needs to do the work of *Symme*," I sarcastically deadpan, and then roll my eyes.

A smirk tugs at the corner of his lip, and he crosses his arms over his chest, nodding to the Sadists to do as I've asked.

My mother has the audacity to look smug as they cut through her binds and release her, but the moment she takes a step towards Maggie, I hold up my hand and shake my head.

"Not her. Just you," I snap, bobbing my head in the direction of the clearing. "Off you go."

For a moment, my mother looks a little baffled, her eyes darting between me, Maggie and the clearing.

"If you get past the boundary, I'll let Maggie go too," I tell her, and those evil eyes narrow as she jabs a finger at me.

"If you don't, Symme will rain hell down over you and this cesspool!"

I nod. "I expect nothing less."

She frowns, clearly thrown off by my change in direction, but when I don't budge, she finally takes a wobbly step forward. And then another. And another.

Each step she takes gets faster, and within seconds, she's running, glancing over her shoulder every few metres to see if I'm coming after her.

"You just gonna let her go?" Jols asks, but I shake my head, sighing.

"Who wants to go hunting?" I ask loudly, and when I glance around at the Sadists, smirks start appearing on their faces. "Have at it. Chase her. Scare her. Torment her. Make her piss her pants. Hell, slap her around a little if you like, but *don't* kill her." I turn back to see her halfway across the clearing as the falling rain starts to get heavier. "That's my job."

"Fucking oath!" Vender bellows, and the moment he starts bolting across the clearing, over twenty men follow, war cries bursting from them as they make chase.

I hear my mother scream when she realises they are coming after her, twice as fast as her legs can carry her, and I turn back to face my husband as I blink past the rain.

"I want her to know what it's like to be so terrified that you actually think your heart is going to stop beating."

He nods, reaching for me, and I step into his chest, letting him embrace me as we get drenched by the chilly downpour.

"Why are you doing that?" Maggie sobs. "Just let her go."

"She has to pay for what she's done, Mags. That's just how it is," I mutter, not sparing her a glance.

"I HATE YOU! YOU ARE NOTHING BUT EVIL! A TOOL OF SATAN!"

"You say that like it's an insult," I snap, stepping back from Ringo's chest, and I can tell he's reluctant to let me leave our little bubble. "I don't want to be like you and Mum, Maggie, so if that means I worship the devil, then so be it."

She spews more hate at me, still being held in place, this time with a Doxy on each arm, all of them looking like drowned rats. It's starting to get icy cold out here, and steam billows from our mouths as we breathe, but this has to happen now, despite the weather.

I turn my attention back to the clearing to see Vender chasing my mother into the treeline, her screams echoing across the clearing to us.

"What do you want to do with Maggie?" Ringo asks quietly, and I peer up at him as he steps back to my side, his eyes trained on the chase despite the rain soaking his clothes.

Even his beard is dripping.

"Let's keep her alive. See if we can't find the old version of her in there, somewhere."

He nods in agreement right as a pained scream floats across the clearing to us.

I should feel bad, right? Bad that my own flesh and blood is being traumatised right now?

Maybe this *isn't* right, but it feels right to me.

It feels *just*.

We wait for a while, and Jols brings Ringo a stool to sit on, which reminds me that he's injured. I'd kind of forgotten. He hides it so well around his men, but right now, there are only a few here with us, while the rest are tapping into their primal play, just without the addition of sex.

Those who have radios check in every now and then, letting us know what's happening, but I zone it out. I don't actually want to know what they do to her. I don't care. I just want to know that before she died, she was truly terrified.

Forty minutes later we get a radio call that my mum has no fight left in her, so I order them to bring her back, and one by one, the Sadists appear in the treeline, stepping out like they've just stepped straight out of Hell.

Shit. Sometimes I really do forget how scary these guys are.

When Vender and JD appear, dragging my mother between them, Maggie starts howling.

Maybe I should send her away for this part, but then again, maybe she needs to see this. Maybe she needs to be reminded of what happens when you pick the wrong side.

The rain has eased to a light sprinkle, but the chill is almost painful now, and I try not to let myself think about how cold I am, otherwise my teeth are likely to start chattering.

When the men get closer, Ringo stands, pretending he's not in agony, and he comes back to my side.

"Angel, please let me do this part. I don't want you carrying this weight with you."

Glancing up at him, I find him already looking down at me, our eyes locking instantly.

"I love you for wanting to protect me, but I need to be the one to do this."

His eyes dance between mine like he's trying to read my mind and see if I'm lying.

I'm actually not, which he must see, and his nod comes right before he leans down and presses his lips to my hair.

It's such an innocent gesture, yet makes me feel cherished, and I'm about ready for this bullshit to be over so we can go inside and get warmed up, and he can cherish me some more.

Everyone needs this over. It's taken far too many lives. Caused too much damage. It's time for it to end so we can all move on and start rebuilding.

As the men get near with my mother in tow, I spot scratches over her arms and a few on her cheeks, like the trees and bushes attacked her, but I don't see any swelling like she's been beaten.

"Gave her a good scare." Mex grins at me. "Pants are pissed, just as you requested."

My gaze darts down to spot the dark wetness staining her khaki pants, trailing down her inner thighs. It almost blends into the rain and mud coating her, but knowing what it is, and why, has me quietly satisfied.

"You guys didn't rough her up?" I ask, not bothered by that knowledge, just surprised, and it's Ringo who speaks for them.

"The Sadists don't lay fists on women," he reminds me, his voice strong and clear, like he's making sure to remind everyone here, too. "Unless they are an immediate physical threat, or they are being tortured for information."

Once upon a time, this man scared the hell out of me. I was sure he was going to beat me, rape me, and kill me. How unbelievably wrong I'd been.

I quickly discovered that he's really one of the good guys.

In fact, many here are.

Shifting my gaze back to my mother, I see how exhausted she is. Her whole body is trembling, and she can barely stand on her own. Her cheeks are wet, her eyes are puffy from crying, and she is muddy and completely dishevelled.

It doesn't stop her from sneering at me though, and disappointment washes over me as I realise I'd hoped she would feel *some* remorse before she dies.

"Just there will do." I bob my head towards JD and Vender, who nod and release their hold of her, causing her to tumble into the mud a few feet from the lifeless body of my grandfather.

My mother sobs, but doesn't try to run, and holds her hands out in front of her, palms up, just like Banes did.

Oh, for shit's sake. Not her too.

"In fire we trust. In blood we bind. In silence, we serve…"

Shaking my head, I zone out her praying, which Maggie joins in on, and I check over my gun.

The clip has plenty of rounds in it, but I only need one.

As I step closer, her eyes lock with mine, and I can see the fear in them, despite the steel in her voice.

"It didn't have to be this way," I say, as my mind goes back to a time when I thought she actually loved me.

She held me when I fell and scraped my knees as a child. Smiled when I painted her pictures. Sang Christmas carols with me while we baked. She even danced with me after she'd had a few Shandy's at Christmas lunches.

Somewhere along the way, the woman she'd been hiding couldn't hide anymore.

She popped up every now and then when she got angry, but it wasn't until we moved churches that things really started to change. It was like the kindness in her vanished. She didn't have room for that anymore. Didn't have patience for anything but her dictative ways which now make so much sense.

She wanted back in with her family. She wanted her father's love the only way she knew how. And to get that, she had to sacrifice her own daughters.

I'll never understand how she could do that. How she could use her children as pawns, knowing they would get hurt.

But she did. She knew Daniel was my cousin. She knew what he was doing to me. She knew what was going to happen when she dropped me off to him and his friends with sedatives in my system that would make it hard for me to fight.

She knew, and still she let it happen, and got angry when I asked her for help.

Priscilla Delany might have been a mother to me once, but she hasn't been for a long time, and I can't let her live to see another day.

Not just because of what she did to me, but because of what she planned to do with Bobbi and Tahli, and what she was already letting happen to Maggie.

Tears pop from my eyes as I lift the gun. I can see her mouth moving, but I can't hear anything past the pounding of my heart.

Her face contorts in anger, and I know she's spitting hate at me, but she doesn't try to run. She still thinks Symme will help her despite her father thinking the same.

What a foolish woman!

"You are a shit mum, and a shit human," I snap, and her mouth stops moving as she bares her teeth at me. "You were gifted three daughters to love and cherish, and you threw that all away for a made up religion that worshipped a man who romanticised incest, paedophilia, trafficking and murder." I press the barrel of my gun to her forehead, and her sneer falls away like she's finally realising this is really going to happen. "There's a special place in Hell for people like you, and I hope you're stuck in an eternity of torture and suffering."

Unlike with Banes, my hand trembles this time, my finger squeezing the trigger that almost seems like there's resistance behind it.

Time slows. There is no sound here. There is barely a breath of wind as my heart gives in, and accepts that I have to kill my own mother in order for my little family to be safe. I pull back on the trigger, and I feel the recoil of the shot, but I don't hear it, my mind still trapped in a bubble.

My eyes catch everything, though. The way she jerks back. The crimson spray that bursts from the back of her head. The stunned look on her face, forever frozen in place as she falls awkwardly back into the mud. And the pool of blood that follows, running over the wet and muddy ground, a crimson stream that seeps into the pooled blood of her father.

There you go, Symme. *Now* the Earth is pure.

Strong hands clasp my shoulders, and in an instant my hearing returns, like I've just woken from a deep sleep, the sounds around me crashing in.

Screams meet my ears, and I turn to see Maggie, distraught, her eyes trained on our lifeless mother, her hands reaching for her as Doxies hold her back.

"Talk to me, Angel."

Ringo's deep rasp draws my attention, and I blink through my falling tears to find his concerned expression, those dark eyes roaming over my face.

"I want Bobbi back now." I sob, and his eyes melt with empathy.

"Of course, Angel. It's time for her to come home."

34

RINGO

The problem with killing is that afterwards, you have to get rid of the body. Multiply that by fucking eight, and things get a whole lot fucking harder.

After Abbey executed Banes and her mum, we held church and voted that getting rid of Tups, Spud, and Moore was best practice too, their bodies being added to the pile that included Smitty and Panda. We needed to clean shop and move the fuck on, so that's what we did.

And then there was the man we lost who was guarding the shipping containers. We decided to put him on ice until we can arrange his funeral.

I know Abbey was eager to get Bobbi and Tahli back, but she was patient with me, understanding that we needed those loose ends tied up before I could leave.

In church we also voted on roles, since our leadership had just been wiped out.

JD was voted in as my VP, and Vender voted in to take on my old role as Sergeant-at-Arms, with Mex stepping in to take JD's old role as Road Captain.

The role of Secretary was handed over to Murf, and I couldn't be more fucking stoked about the team at my back. *My* fucking team.

By the time all that got done, and we had a small celebration, night was falling, and my wife's exhaustion matched my own. So we turned in early, ready for this day to be left behind.

Maggie has been giving my men hell. Abbey didn't want her tied up, but we've had to resort to that since the little shit keeps attacking anyone that goes into the container she's being held in.

We've agreed that a container will be made into a bungalow for Maggie as soon as possible. It'll still be a jail cell, but Abbey wants her sister to be comfortable, hoping that over time, as she gets treated with care, that her sister will start to snap out of this rage she's in.

I don't know if it will work, but I'll give my wife whatever the hell she wants.

"What time will they get here?" Abbey asks as we pull onto my property, my barn and home coming into view.

We haven't been away from it for long, but everything feels different now.

Maybe because we aren't in a constant state of flight. That'll take some fucking time to get used to for everyone.

"Should be within the hour," I tell her, glancing over at her and feeling my chest warm at the sight of the way her face lights up.

"Why do I feel so nervous?" she asks, those big caramel eyes going wide, and I smile.

"I don't know, but I kinda feel the same. I guess we haven't had a reprieve like this since we met."

She nods, the tips of her teeth making an appearance as she chews on her lip.

"What's running through that head of yours, Angel?"

She grins, almost mischievously. "How sore are you?"

My lips slowly spread wide at her question, knowing exactly where this is going.

"Not too sore to fuck my wife if that's what you're getting at."

Her smile is stunning as her cheeks flush a pretty shade of pink and her eyes somehow look like they flare brighter, lighting up her whole face.

Fuck, she's beautiful. *So* fucking beautiful.

When I pull up the car and shut off the engine, Abbey quickly gets out, clearly fucking eager, so I sweep up my phone, shoot a message to Devon to drive fucking slow, and follow my wife inside my house.

Our house.

We've decided to stay here for the time being while the compound is being finished. At church, I ordered that everyone else's cabins get built and finished before they start on the new President's cottage. For now, when we need to stay there, we will stay in my shared bungalow with JD and Jols.

I want my club brothers and the Doxies to be settled first. I want them to feel like they have a say. That they belong. That the compound is their home.

Inside my house, I open the shutters and turn on the central heating before following Abbey upstairs.

She's a lot faster than me, given I'm still fucking healing, but my cock is already hard knowing it's going to be soaking in her tight hot heat within minutes.

When I step inside my bedroom, I find Abbey already stripping out of her clothes and pointing to the bed.

"Get naked, Mr President. And get on that bed."

"I thought I was the fucking Dom in this relationship," I snap, and she giggles.

"You are, but you're injured and you need to listen to your nurse."

I can't help but fucking chuckle, quickly shedding my clothes to do as my *nurse* has ordered.

As I get comfy on the bed, I watch her get a towel and place it on the edge of the mattress, before she opens the drawer, bringing out the lube and... shit... my fucking flesh light.

"Angel?" I ask, a warning in my tone, and she waves me off.

"Shoosh. Be a good patient and relax."

I scoff. "I'm anything but a good fucking patient."

"Well, if you're not good, then you don't get this." She points to her panties, still covering her sexy pussy, and I fucking grin.

"You drive a hard bargain."

"I aim to please. You just need to trust me, like I trust you."

That has my brows shooting up, and I can see she's dead serious, so I nod, doing as she asked, and relax.

She climbs on the bed, positioning herself between my legs, lube in one hand, the fleshlight in the other.

"How does this thing work?" she asks, and I chuckle, reaching out to point at the buttons.

"This controls the vibrations, and this changes up the suction."

She bites her fucking lip again, her cheeks turning redder as she nods.

"So lube first, and then this?" She waves the fucking thing around, and I nod, biting back a smirk, my fucking heart pounding in my chest with anticipation.

I haven't even considered using that fucking thing since my cock was introduced to her cunt and what it feels like wrapped around me. But *this*... having her here with me, wanting to use it, is just another level of fun I wasn't expecting.

She's feeling bold, and I fucking love how comfortable she is with me now. To have her trust is like winning the fucking lottery.

I hold my hard, rigid cock up for her while she drizzles lube over it, before placing the tube aside and wrapping her dainty little hand around my girth.

"Ahh, fuck!" I jerk under her touch as she fists my cock, nice and fucking tight, just the way I like it. "Don't really need that thing, Angel. Your hand is enough."

She giggles, her eyes roaming over my cock and balls like she is fucking fascinated by them.

"I know, but the idea of this turns me on," she admits, those doe eyes flicking up to meet mine.

"Fucking have at it then, Angel. Whatever you want and need, I will give you."

Her smirk is almost wicked as she pumps my cock from base to tip, and I worry I've just agreed to something I know nothing about.

Releasing my cock, she starts to feed it into the silicone pussy lips, and perhaps the sexiest thing about this is how she tips her head sideways, getting a good view of my tip disappearing just inside.

Her cheeks are red hot, and I know she's turned on. I fucking hope this is *everything* she needs right now. I want nothing more than to give it all to her.

"Like that?" she asks, her gaze jumping up to see me nod before moving back to watch more of my cock slip inside.

Fuuuck. I fist the sheets beside me, gritting my fucking teeth, my cock more sensitive than it normally is when I do this.

It's her. My sexy as sin wife eagerly sheathing my cock in a male fuck toy.

Lifting my hips a little, I help to feed my cock right in, feeling it hit the end, the fleshy device gripping me, and I grit my teeth as I fight to stay in control as she moves it up and down my shaft a couple of times.

"Now turn it on," I rasp, and her eyes move to the side as she presses a button.

My hips buck as a gentle sucking motion starts up, my back arching as I fuck up into it.

"Fuck, Angel. I'm not going to last long with you doing this to me."

She snickers, pressing the button again to increase the suction.

"I want to make you come," she breathes, and I can tell she really is turned on right now. "I want to make you feel so good, Cam. I want you to know what it's like when you completely consume me."

Fuck. She presses the button again, and I arch back, digging my head into the pillows, thrusting up against her hand and the device, ignoring the burn of my wounds as my wife does exactly what she said she wants to do to me.

"Part your legs wider," she says, and I fucking do, assuming she wants more room, but the next thing I know, her tongue is gliding over my fucking nuts, and a choked sound lodges in my throat.

"Fuuuck!" I yell, and as if that's not enough, she fucking sucks one of my balls into the hot heat of her mouth.

I buck, thrust, fucking into the thing faster, knowing this orgasm is going to come really fucking fast.

My eyes are squeezed tight as my face contorts until I feel something I really wasn't ever expecting.

The press of her finger at the entrance of my arse.

"Whoa!" I hiss, clenching my fucking cheeks together, and she fucking tuts at me.

"Relax. It'll feel good. I promise."

My fucking eyes are bugging out of my head as I look down my body at her, trying to fucking concentrate, but it's a bit hard with that thing still sucking my cock in, the rhythm steady.

"Angel. That's not... I... fuuuck..." I moan as she teases the entrance, running her finger over my perineum, and back to my puckered opening.

"Trust me," she breathes, and fuck, I do trust her. I've just *never* considered doing this.

I want to though, now that she's teasing it. I'm fucking aching to have her... shit, I want her *inside* me.

The fuck.

That's very fucking new, and something I didn't know I ever wanted until now, but the idea of her slender little finger slipping inside a place so fucking forbidden, has me ready to fucking nut.

"Okay," I pant, spreading my legs wider, and trying to relax my fucking clenched cheeks so it's easier for her.

I don't know where she's gotten this confidence from, but I'm fucking here for it. I love that she feels this comfortable with me. I know she's my match in every fucking way.

When her finger starts to press into my arse, I have to fight not to come. I want to feel her finger fuck me there. Feel what it's like for her when I do it to her. Feel her fucking consume me, just the way she said she wants to.

Somehow, my wife manages to change the sucking action again, the pull of the fleshlight harder and faster, and I fucking open like a flower for her, feeling her finger sink in past the ring of muscle, and seat inside.

It's then that I feel it. Intense convulsions of pleasure I've never fucking experienced building and building, and oh fuuuuuuuck!

I fucking yell, thrusting up into the fleshlight as another kind of euphoria slams into me from deep in my arse, and I explode in a whole new way.

Ripple after ripple is wrenched from me as my prostate is massaged from deep inside, a different type of orgasm I've never experienced slamming into me. I'm slightly aware that my cock is still fucking hard and hasn't come from it yet, the entire thing nearly too fucking overwhelming, but Abbey's mouth closes over my balls again, sucking one in, and I... ROAR!

This time, the normal sort of climax I'm used to feeling takes over, piggybacking on the other one. Wave after wave sends cum shooting from my cock, deep inside the fleshlight, as my wife continues to suck on my balls and fuck her finger into my arse until I'm fucking legless.

When she's successfully wrenched every tiny slither of pleasure from me, Abbey pops my nut free, her wild eyes blinking up my body as she grins.

"That was *so* hot."

A laugh bursts from me, and I tip my head back on the pillow, staring up at the ceiling, still trying to catch my fucking breath.

"Do I even want to know how you learned how to do that?"

She giggles, slowly easing her finger from my arse.

"There may or may not have been a discussion with the Doxies you weren't privy to at yesterday's celebrations." She snickers, turning off the fleshlight and easing my softening cock from it too. "I'll have to thank them for the very detailed instructions." She giggles, and I immediately shake my fucking head.

"Fuck, Angel. Don't you *dare* tell them you did that to me," I say, with not a slither of anger in my tone.

When I glance up, she's smiling proudly, and fuck, she should be proud. She set out to blow my mind, and that's exactly what she did.

"Get that pussy up here," I order, and her smile falls even as those flushed cheeks turn redder.

She quickly discards the fleshlight and uses the towel to wipe her hands off before she does what she's told, moving up my body to straddle my torso.

She already knows where I want her slick cunt, and I waste no fucking time, gripping the firm globes of her arse and dragging her forward so I can taste her arousal.

Gliding my tongue up her centre, I dip it between her folds, tasting her gathered wetness, and her sweet moan fills the room.

Her clit is already so swollen, almost as if what she did to me edged her, so I know she won't take long either.

Reaching down to my soft cock, I run my fingers through some of the remaining lube, deciding my Angel is going to get a taste of her own medicine.

As I start sucking on her clit, and she holds on to the headboard for support, I urge her legs wider with my hands, before pressing my lubed fingers to her arse.

She doesn't even flinch.

Fuuuuck, will I get to fuck this tight arse one day? She seems pretty fucking keen to have my fingers there again. Maybe taking my cock isn't such a far stretch.

As I ease my finger into her back passage, she whimpers and writhes over my face, and I flick my tongue over her needy clit quickly, working up a friction.

"Yes! Ringo!" she cries, grinding down on me.

That's my good girl. Take everything I give you.

Moving my tongue from her clit down to her entrance, I dive it in, stretching it as long as I can as she stops grinding, and starts fucking my face.

Inside her arse, I press up towards her pussy, and I shift my free hand under her, diving three thick fingers into her cunt. She cries out, and from my vantage point, I watch her tits bounce as creamy milk starts spraying from her nipples.

That fucking sight alone has my cock rising again, and I latch my lips over her clit to give her that complete consuming feeling.

Incoherent words and sounds are falling from her lips, and the moment I feel her muscles lock up around my fingers, she screams.

My Angel convulses around me in a quivering climax that has her slickness gushing into my mouth and over my bearded chin. She jerks through each ripple until it subsides, leaving her panting breaths to fill the room.

"Shit," she pants, shifting to move off my mouth. "My milk squirted all over the headboard."

My shit-eating-grin is huge, and I take in the droplets of milk dripping down the headboard, a growl reverberating in my chest.

"Bring those tits here. Give me a taste."

The moment I ease my digit from her arse, she does exactly as I've asked, leaning over me and guiding her peaked nipple to my lips, milk already beading on the tip.

I latch on, hearing her gasp and feeling my cock thicken even more, the sweetness of her warm milk hitting my tongue still as much of a turn on as it was the first time I did this.

Her fingers delve into my hair as she arches into me, like she's been just as desperate for this as I have, and the second she slips that nipple free and presses the other to my lips, we both stiffen.

Our eyes meet, going wide as we both hear the same fucking thing.

For fuck's sake.

There are cars approaching.

ABBEY

Ringo tells me to go to Bobbi while he cleans up the mess we made, so I do a quick bathroom cleanup and get dressed, racing downstairs just in time for the front door to open.

I see Alana and Millie step inside first as I hit the bottom step, and the moment Tahli steps in, I bolt to her.

Her eyes go wide as she sees me charging towards her, but she's all smiles, rushing forward to meet me halfway, and we slam together in a tight embrace.

"Oh, you two are going to make me cry," Doreen says as she steps inside too, and I look up to see her carrying my little bundle.

Bobbi.

A sob escapes me, and Tahli eases back so I can go to my daughter, and I don't hesitate, hurrying closer to accept her from Ringo's mother.

The next however many minutes are a whirlwind.

Nessy and Brody come inside, the two we charged to protect my little girl with their lives looking happy hand in hand, and I have to wonder what Vender and Mex will say about that.

I'm not sure what's going on with the four of them, but whatever it is, they'd better do right by Nessy.

Bobbi immediately starts fussing in my arms, and I peel back the blanket to stare at her.

"Hey, little one. What's the matter?"

"She's probably hungry again." Nessy steps up to peek down at Bobbi. "She's due for another feed."

"Okay, uhhh." I look around at all the people, noticing Ringo isn't down here yet, and decide there's no way I'm getting my boob out to feed Bobbi down here in front of everyone.

I could feed her a bottle, I suppose, but my breasts are still pretty full since Ringo didn't get enough time to have his fill. She may as well have that, and I'm desperate to bond with her again. The poor thing has been shuffled around from person to person since I came back into her life, and I want her to have more stability.

I want her to get to know me.

"I'll just go upstairs and feed her," I say, turning to Tahli. "I'll be back down soon. We have some things to talk about."

I have to tell her about Banes and Mum. About how Maggie is locked up at the compound. About how this nightmare is basically over.

There's still a concern with Ian Allen, but no one has heard anything from him since the airfield, so with any luck, he bled out in the bushland surrounding the airfield and we'll never have to see him again.

Tahli nods, stepping forward to press a kiss to Bobbi's head, before I excuse myself and take my daughter upstairs.

"This is your new home," I say to her in a soft voice, carefully taking each step up to the landing. "One day, when you're older, we can go out to the pond and feed the ducks. I bet you'd like that." I coo, smiling at her as she screws up her face, a small cry passing her lips.

"I know you're hungry," I say, stepping into Ringo's room, *our room*, and finding him waiting in the living area.

"Is someone hungry?" he asks, and I smile.

"Someone is. Lucky you didn't have too much before," I say, blushing, and Ringo chuckles.

"Come and feed her in here." He gestures towards the bedroom, and I frown, since the only place to sit and feed her in there is the bed, while out here there's an armchair and a couch.

I mean, that's totally fine, but sitting in a chair would be better.

Following him around to the bedroom, I'm not really paying much attention to anything but the bundle in my arms, so when I look up, seeing a hole in the wall, I freeze.

Wait... No, not a hole. A *doorway* that wasn't there before.

"What..." I trail off, confused about what I'm seeing.

The huge framed mirror that was sitting on the floor leaning against the wall has been moved aside, revealing a door I didn't know was there.

"Open it." He grins, and I frown, so bloody confused.

"Has that always been there?" I ask, and he nods. "The whole time?"

He nods again.

"I should've told you about it sooner. I was going to surprise you with it after you had your baby, but none of that went to plan, and we thought she'd died, so I kept it a secret." He rakes his hand through his hair, almost like he's nervous. "I'm sorry, Angel. I didn't want to upset you."

I'm dumbfounded as I shake my head. "I don't understand. Keep *what* a secret?"

Moving to the door, he turns the handle and pushes it open, revealing a short passage that opens into another room, and instantly, tears well in my eyes.

"Is that?"

He nods. "I had Mills and Lans clean it up and air it out when we went to South Australia to find Bobbi." He gestures for me to step inside, so I do, rocking Bobbi as she starts to get more impatient for her meal.

It's almost too unbelievable. There's a room here. A *nursery*. Completely set up with a bassinet, cot, change table, an armchair and a bookshelf lined with teddies, toys and books.

I spin back to Ringo in disbelief.

"I don't understand. This has really been here the whole time? What was it used for before?" I ask, sitting in the armchair when Ringo gestures for me to take a seat, and I give in, rearranging my top so I can get my breast out, and I start feeding my daughter.

The moment her cries cut off, and she starts drinking, relief washes over me, and I relax back in the chair a little more.

"This was meant to be for Hope," he admits, and now I feel like crying.

Oh. My. Goodness.

This *poor* man.

My *poor* man.

"Shit, Ringo. I'm sorry. I didn't think. I—"

"Abs, stop. It's fine. I've had a long time to get used to this not being for Hope. I closed it off and never wanted to see it again until you came along." He smiles warmly down at me. "Then I knew, without a doubt, that this room was really meant for you to nurse Bobbi in. And maybe even a child of our own one day."

Bending, Ringo brushes the back of his finger over Bobbi's cheek as she feeds, looking down at her with so much love and care that it makes me want to cry.

"The furniture was originally for Hope, but all of the bedding is new. And the toys too. Some of them were from the chest."

I scan the room again, finally recognising some of the things people gifted Bobbi at the funeral.

The books, a cute pink teddy, and a yellow rattle I remember were from Rhys and her guys. Jared and Dee too.

On the bookshelf next to the teddy are tiny pink ballet shoes, and perched behind them is the small white ukulele Lexi and Ayden gifted.

The trinkets and beaded jewellery the Doxies gifted are sitting on top of the chest of drawers, and on a hook next to the wardrobe, the Cinderella dress-up costume hangs.

There's a small basket of toys off to the side, and I know a lot of that came from the Southern Sadists, the game of Twister JD gifted, sitting on top, and on the floor next to the basket, is the little pink motorcycle helmet Jols wanted Bobbi to have.

On the back of the door, I spot black leather hanging on a hook, and I frown, gesturing my head that way.

"Is that…?" I trail off, and Ringo nods, moving to it and taking it off the hook, holding it up for me to see.

It's the black leather jacket Nate gifted Bobbi with the Southern Sadists logo on it, and the patch saying, *'Little Princess Bobbi'* on the front.

"I wasn't sure if you'd want it. I can burn it if you like?"

I shake my head, my burning eyes flicking back to Ringo. "I know it was Nate that gave that to her, but I kinda feel like it really comes from the club. I'd like her to have it."

With a warm, sympathetic smile, Ringo nods before hanging it back on the hook.

My eyes move over everything again… there's so much here to take in, and one shelf on the bookshelf catches my eye.

The framed photo of us on our wedding day is angled in this direction, and the memory of that day we shared comes rushing back.

In the photo, I'm on Ringo's lap, and we're both laughing, looking at each other, my hand resting against the ivory satin stretched over the swell of my stomach, right where Bobbi was.

This was one of the gifts Ringo had for Bobbi. He gave me an identical one that sits right next to our bed.

My gaze drifts to the CD propped up next to the frame. The One Direction CD.

I smile wide as I gesture my head towards it. "Bobbi is going to love listening to that."

Chuckling, Ringo moves across the room to the shelf, picking up the CD and staring at it.

"Maybe I should have burned it."

"Ringo!" I gasp, and he grins, chuckling as he places it back on the shelf.

"I still can't believe you played that teeny bopper shit to walk down the aisle to."

"I found it quite fitting." I giggle, and the way his lip quirks higher at one corner has me melting.

This man.

Reaching out, he picks something else up off the shelf, and I watch as he pops open the small velvet box.

Oh... the bracelet.

"It's a little big for her." He smiles, angling the open box my way so I can see the mostly silver piece of jewellery with gold detailing and the tiny silver and gold butterfly charms dangling at each end.

"She'll grow into it before we know it." I smile, and he nods, staring at it for a moment, his thumb grazing over the inscription of her name.

On the back of it, he had '*Love Dad xx*' engraved on it. I'll make sure she always knows just how special that bracelet is, because it's more than a piece of jewellery.

It's a declaration. One that melts my heart all over again.

"Are you sure about the room?" I ask, needing to make sure he's not going to get triggered every time he steps foot in here. We can figure something else out if we need to.

Ringo's smile is broad as he shifts his gaze between Bobbi and me.

"It's actually cathartic to be in here again." He looks around the room that was originally meant for his daughter. "When Hope died, I just closed it up and covered the access doors with mirrors. That way I could pretend there wasn't even a room here. But I want Bobbi to use this room. At least until she's older, and then maybe she can have the one next to Tahli's new room downstairs."

"You've thought of everything," I whisper, feeling too emotional to speak too loud. "Thank you, Cam. I absolutely love it."

He can't seem to take his warm smile off his face as he moves to the door on the far wall, pulling it open. Behind it is some sort of timber panel, and he turns back to me.

"That's another mirror, out on the landing. I'll remove it later," he states, turning to look back over the room. "But this is all yours now. All Bobbi's. So you do whatever you want with it. I can paint it a different colour if you want or—"

"Cam. Stop. It's perfect just the way it is. Way more than I could have ever given Bobbi by myself."

He shifts nervously, hands in his pockets as his gaze drops to the floor.

"So... you'll stay with me?" he asks, his eyes finally jumping up to mine.

Shit. Is my husband nervous?

"Cam, I—"

"Say you'll let me love the both of you," he stumbles forward, falling to his knees by my feet, his big hands coming up to grip my thighs. "I'll fucking do *anything* to keep you, Angel. If you want to run, I'll run. I'll take my ma and sisters with us and we'll leave this shit behind."

Tears well in my eyes as I stare at him, taking in the desperation in his tone.

He really would do that if I asked him to. He'd leave the Southern Sadists. Go against the Marx family.

All for me.

"Cam, I'd never ask you to do that. I don't want to do that. I want to stay here with you. I know we'll have to live at the compound as well. But we'll make it work. I don't think it matters where we are just as long as we're together."

His shoulders drop, and his relief is written all over his face as he sighs and leans forward over the top of Bobbi, pressing his forehead to mine.

"I'm gonna give you the world, Angel."

"You already have," I whisper, closing the short distance to kiss him.

Everything has happened so fast. We've barely had time to let the events of the last few days sink in, but I never imagined my husband was feeling so concerned. Worried that I'd leave.

As we pull back from the kiss and stare into each other's eyes, I realise I'm not the only one that's changed this year.

He has, too.

I know he's helped my heart heal in so many ways, but I realise now I've helped stitch his up too. He'll never get Hope back, but I'll make sure she's remembered. I'll tell Bobbi about her. That her big sister rests peacefully under the Jacaranda tree, and hopefully one day, I can give him a child of his own... one day.

36

RINGO

I wish I could say the last four weeks have been fucking peaceful, but then I'd just be lying.

We were home for a week and a half before the state went into another fucking lockdown. Thank fuck it didn't last too long, although it was nice being trapped on my property with my wife and our family for twelve days, but the shit I've had to squeeze into a fucking week has been a logistics nightmare.

There's been streaming meetings with other chapters. Calls with the Angel sisters and a personal face to face with Ewan and Leo Marx. Not to fucking forget, having to meet with Officer Zimora in private to hand over the hard drive and make sure all of this shit gets swept under the rug.

We sent a big chunk of the money Banes left behind to the seaside town we brought carnage to in South Australia, managing to strike a deal with the Raiders MC so they don't fucking come gunning for our arses.

We donated some of the money to the Fox Pines Hospital. Anonymously, of course. And some has been sent to the families of our fallen.

Lewy's been working behind the scenes to get records changed into Abbey's name regarding her parents' belongings, while Abbey has been trying to find some extra help for Maggie. Mental help. Something that's fucking hard to find.

Lewy also has his team of hackers working behind the scenes to remove anything that pops up about the havoc that was caused across the state from everything that happened. But unfortunately, we can't control the media, and the local news still mentions the spate of crimes linked to organised crime at least once on the news reports each week.

We managed to spend a day with Lexi and her friends. All of them were besotted over Bobbi, and some tears were shed when Abbey revealed details of the hard drive, and how her grandfather was linked to all of their suffering. The moment Rhys found out she and Abbey were cousins, I thought I'd lost my fucking hearing.

That chick can scream louder than anyone I've ever fucking met.

But shit. It was emotional as fuck, and I'm glad Rhys had her guys with her, so they could give her the support she needed.

On top of that, I've been secretly trying to arrange a little getaway surprise for Abbey's birthday. The first birthday she's had in years that will be filled with happiness instead of trauma. And the first of her birthdays with me.

So... we are going on a fucking date.

I, Ringo, President of the Southern Sadists MC, am going on a date with my wife for the first time, and I'm *fucking nervous*.

I don't want to fuck it up, mainly because this is something I haven't done before, so I'm new at this.

Abbey hugs me from behind as we ride, breezing up the freeway, into the city.

Apparently, she's a big fan of pasta, so I'm taking her to a well-known Italian restaurant that will hopefully have her moaning as I watch her eat.

She was nervous about leaving Bobbi, but my ma, sisters, and Tahli have it all under control, and given Bobbi has been thriving, Abbey doesn't have anything to worry about.

The restaurant is bustling when we step inside sometime later, slipping out of our leathers just inside the doorway, to reveal nicer clothes.

Abbey blushes up at me when she catches my eyes roaming over her, checking her out, her silky legs very fucking tempting in the sexy red dress she's wearing that really doesn't match the cold weather outside.

"Stop," she hisses, past her smile.

"I'm going to be hard right through the meal," I mutter, giving her another once over. "No wonder you got dressed in your leathers before coming downstairs. You knew we wouldn't leave the house, didn't you?"

She giggles at that, her smile relaxing when the hostess approaches us, and we quickly secure the face masks we're required to wear unless we are eating.

The hostess leads us to a table in the back half of the restaurant. With social distancing rules in place, all tables directly next to us are empty, and I can't say I hate that.

It's nice to have a little privacy and not have to worry about anyone hearing our discussions.

Our food comes out quickly, and we eat and chat quietly together, enjoying this somewhat normal day.

Well... the pandemic shit isn't fucking normal, but not being fucking chased is.

"Tell me about your first time." Abbey grins, holding the glass of wine to her lips and taking a sip.

"My first time?" I frown, and she wags her brows, putting her glass down.

"Yeah. Your *first time*." She leans closer, speaking quieter, like she doesn't want anyone to overhear. "When you lost your virginity."

A laugh bursts from me, and she grins wide.

"Angel, you don't want to hear about that shitshow. There's nothing sexy about it."

"I don't care about sexy. I just want to know the younger version of you."

Relaxing back, I rest my elbows on the arms of the chair, debating if this story is something I really want her to know about. It's fucking embarrassing, that's for sure. I don't think I've even told JD, yet here, with her, I can't help but want to tell her every fucking minor detail of my life if she wants to know about it.

"Fine," I rasp, biting back my grin. "But you're not allowed to laugh or use it against me."

Her eyes widen. "Ohhh, do tell."

I snort, taking a sip of my water, before deciding that if there's anyone worthy of knowing this embarrassing fact about me, it's her.

"There's not much to tell, really. Macey was a year above me in school. I was fifteen. We were at her house. Her mum went out for dinner, and we ended up naked on the couch."

"And?" Abbey nudges for more information.

"And I nearly came in my pants when I touched her bare for the first time, and when we finally got around to the deed, I was basically a two pump chump."

Abbey's lips thin.

"Don't you fucking laugh." I stab a finger in her direction, and she shakes her head, even as her smile grows wider.

"I swear to fucking God if you laugh, Angel, not only will I never tell you anything like that again, but I'll take a fucking vow of celibacy for a month."

She gasps, her mouth dropping open. "You wouldn't."

"Try me," I snap, and she stiffens.

I'm fucking lying of course, because as if I can stay away from her, but right now, she doesn't need to know that.

She stares at me for a long moment, but there's still amusement tugging at her lips.

"I guess you got in some more practice after that?" Abbey asks, trying not to laugh, and I grin.

"A bit. But none of it mattered until you."

Her eyes soften. "Same. As far as I'm concerned, it's only ever been you."

Fuck.

For her, everything before me was trauma. Even when things were okay between her and Daniel, after finding out he was actually her cousin, what were the good parts are tainted even more.

"It was always meant to be just you and me, Angel."

"You and me." She smiles, those eyes flashing from under her dark lashes as she rests her arms on the table and leans forward, giving me a spectacular fucking view of her cleavage.

"Angel..." I rasp, licking my lips as my mind goes straight to wanting to peel that red fabric down and latch onto her ripe nipple.

"Yes, husband?" she purrs, knowing all too fucking well what she's doing to me.

"There's this little secluded place we can go to just outside the city..." I grin, my gaze flicking back up to hers to see her lips spread wider.

"There is?" She leans closer, practically squeezing her tits together. "How secluded?"

Fuuuck, her voice is almost sultry, and my cock is hard just thinking about taking her there.

"Very secluded. Only accessible by motorbike. Lots of trees. A high cliff face to block the wind."

"Oh yeah? What are we going to do there?"

She's playing a fucking dangerous game. At this rate, I'm not going to be able to walk outta here without people seeing my fucking hard-on.

"Well, to celebrate your birthday, I'm going to lay you out on my ride, reverse style, get those fucking leathers back off you, push that red dress up your thighs and eat you for fucking dessert."

Her lips part as a breathy little moan slips free, her cheeks flaming with heat I know matches the building inferno between her legs.

"We should go then." She breathes, and I chuckle.

"I'll pay the bill."

She nods, standing quickly. "I'll just use the ladies room first. Meet you at the entrance?"

"I'll be waiting." I wink at her, and she smiles while biting her fucking plump lip, before fitting on her face mask, scooping up her leathers, and hurrying off towards the bathrooms in the back.

Fucking hell, even watching her walk has my cock straining at the sway of her hips.

Maybe I should've booked a hotel, but it would've been too fucking hard to find something. Most aren't running in the city, and those that *are* have been turned into isolation accommodation.

Fuck. This world is fucking crazy.

I ignore the strange looks I get from the other diners as I move through the restaurant, towards the front.

I get it.

I'm a little too rough around the edges to be in a nice place like this, but that's their fucking problem. Not mine.

I pay for our meal before slipping back into my leathers by the door, waiting for my beautiful wife to join me.

I hope she fucking hurries. I'm starving for her, even though I had her early this morning. I swear I can't get enough of my Angel, and the idea of fucking her out in the open on my bike is going to tick off one of the hundreds of fantasies I have about my wife.

I can't fucking wait.

37

ABBEY

After peeing, I hurry to get myself dressed in my leathers, but since this stall is so tiny, I know I'll have to do it out by the basins.

Flushing the toilet, I unlatch the lock on my stall and move to the counter, dumping my leathers on top. I quickly wash my hands, peering up into the mirror and seeing just how flushed my cheeks are.

Ohhh, Ringo would have loved seeing them like that. He would have instantly known how turned on he'd made me.

I smile at myself as I hear the door squeak open, and drop my gaze back down to my hands to finish washing up.

I can't wait to get my birthday present off him.

His mouth on me… eating me.

I bite my lip as heat pools between my legs.

Jesus, I don't know if I can even make it to this place he's going to take me. I'm so… horny.

Shutting the water off, I turn to search for the paper towel dispenser, and gasp as I come face to face with someone I'd hoped I'd never see again.

"You killed my nephew."

Air gets trapped in my lungs as I stagger back, only to bump into the basin, my hands immediately reaching back to steady myself.

"Nothing to say, slut?"

"You need to leave!" I yell, hoping someone will hear, and Ian Allen's face contorts in a sneer.

"I'll fucking leave once I've gotten what I've come for."

Shit. Shit. Shit. My phone is with my leathers on the counter, and my eyes flick to it sitting right on top.

It's at least three metres from where I am, but only a few feet from where Ian is.

"There's nothing for you here!" I yell louder, and he chuckles.

"Bitch, *you* are what I need. I'm gonna take you with me and do everything and more that my nephew and his mates did to you. I'm not even going to kill you. I'm going to keep you until the day I fucking die."

I believe every word he's saying. If he takes me, I'll likely never be found, but Ringo is here in this building. Surely he'll come looking for me soon, right?

Shit. I have to believe that, which means I have to make sure Ian can't take me anywhere.

"I'm not going anywhere with you!" I yell, and his eyes darken, his stare lethal.

"Yes, you fucking are. You have to pay for what you did to Donny. And I'll take that payment with your cunt, your mouth, and your fucking tight arse."

My chest is rising and falling too quickly. I need to calm the hell down. I've been in situations like this before, even with this very man.

He raped me before. At the chapel. I can't bear to go through that again. But I don't want to be the victim here. Last time we saw each other, I was the one hunting him.

But shit, I was different then. A different version of myself who lived in a world that Bobbi didn't exist in. A world that she'd died in. A world far different from the world I live in now.

I'm not the same person.

He takes a step forward, and I immediately notice his limp, and shit, my lips slowly spread wide as I remember slicing the knife across the back of his ankle.

"Why the fuck are you smiling?" he snaps, and I feel the old me that has been hovering in the background as she steps back into my skin.

"Does it still hurt?" I pout, mocking him, and his old ugly face turns beet red.

"You think it's funny? I have to work behind a desk now!"

"Ohh, poor Officer Allen," I tease. "I guess it's better than being dead like Donny."

"You shut up, you fucking whore!"

I shrug, shifting along the bench a little, hoping to subtly move closer to my phone.

"Stop. Please. I'm sorry." I whine in a mocking tone, saying the words Donny said when I caught up with him at the airfield. *"P-please I'll d-do anything."*

I deliberately stutter the same way Donny did, and Ian launches himself at me.

I dodge him, lurching towards my phone, but he grabs me from behind, dragging me backwards, and my fingers skim the dangling leathers as I go down to the tiled floor.

"You fucking slut. You'll pay for what you did to him!" he yells, and I inwardly grin, because if he's yelling, then someone might hear and get help.

I claw at the tiles as I'm dragged across them on my stomach, but I keep talking. Keep poking the bear.

"When I shot his shoulders, he howled like a FUCKING PUSSY!" I scream. *"P-please... s-stop..."* I mock, and Ian shoves me over, onto my back, settling his heavy weight over my pelvis and legs, despite the way I flail.

"You vicious cunt! I know what you did. I was there!"

I grin up at him, ceasing my attempt to get free.

"Oh, that's right. You were. But you stood back and watched, didn't you?" I curl my lip at him. "Did you like the part where I gave him a taste of his own medicine?"

"Shut up, bitch!" He backhands me, the sting across my face just helping me to sink further into my monster.

"He deep throated that gun so well before I blew his brains out," I say sweetly, and he snaps.

Fisting each side of my head, he slams it back to the tiles, and I instantly see stars as pain bursts through my skull.

A strangled scream rips from me right as the wail of my ringtone starts to echo through the room, but Ian ignores it, wrapping his hand around my throat and squeezing.

I claw at the side of his face as I start to panic, but remember the best thing I can do is not panic, so I try really hard to calm the hell down as I choke and feel like I'm going to suffocate.

"My Donny didn't deserve to die like that!" he yells, squeezing tighter, and well... I guess he's decided just to kill me and not take me with him.

Perhaps poking the bear was the wrong thing to do.

Squeezing my hands between us, I clutch them together and shove them up and out, managing to dislodge one of his hands from my neck, and I roll, gasping as he scrambles to get a hold of me again.

Tears stream from my eyes as I try to claw my way across the tiles, only managing to get a little way before he's on my back, his feet shoving between my legs, trying to pry them open.

"No! NO!" I scream, knowing I'd rather die that be raped again. "GET OFF ME!" I scream, reaching for my dangling leathers, needing to get to my phone.

My head gets shoved hard to the tiles, the fucker's hand pressing down, his body weight against it as he holds me in place, and I feel cold air hit my lower back as my dress gets shoved up.

"NO!" I scream before a loud crash rips through the air, and the thud of heavy boots charges in.

With my head turned to that side, I see the boots stop just beside me, and a sob gets stuck in my throat.

"Get. The. Fuck. Off. My. Wife."

My sob releases as the relief of hearing Ringo's voice washes over me, and the weight pressing into my back disappears as my husband steps forward.

I scramble quickly across the tiles to my leathers, and tug them to the floor next to me as I look up to see Ringo's hand around Ian's throat as he pins him to the wall, his brutal fist slamming into his face, over and over.

My hands tremble as I pick up my phone and open it, clicking straight into the app that Lewy insisted the club start using, and I hit the big red button.

An alert sound rings from Ringo's back pocket, and I know the app is doing what it's designed for, sending an alert to the club with my location so they can get the nearest members or associates to me as fast as possible.

It's not just for me, but for every member, every Doxy, and their families.

Stepping back from the wall, Ringo drags Ian with him, blood smearing Ian's face as he chokes and struggles to breathe.

"No one touches what's mine!" Ringo snarls into Ian's face. "The fucking penalty is death, motherfucker!"

My monstrous husband fists Ian's hair, and slams his forehead into the rim of the basin, the cracking sound loud, sending my stomach rolling.

It was the basin cracking, not his skull, I tell myself, shuddering as I watch on as Ringo drops Ian's limp form to the floor.

Oh shit, who am I kidding? That was definitely Ian's skull.

For a moment, I think that's it. Ian's dead, and it's finally over, but a wheeze crackles up from his parted lips, and he rolls his head in my direction, his blood-filled swollen eyes blinking at me.

It's the creepiest thing I've ever seen. Something straight out of a horror movie, and I'm so distracted by it that I don't see Ringo take out his knife until it's plunging right into Ian's ear and straight into his brain.

Trembles wrack my entire body as I stare at the last bit of light flickering out from behind Ian's eyes, before Ringo shifts between us, blocking my view.

"Angel," he rasps, his voice pained as his big hand cups my cheek, tilting my head back to get a better look at me.

"I'm okay," I sob, really not sounding okay.

"I'm so fucking sorry. I thought you were getting changed, which was why you were taking so long. I never imagined…"

I shake my head, peering up into his deep brown eyes. "It's over," I whisper. "There's no one left to hunt me."

"Fuck, Abs," he sighs, his expression pinched like he's kicking himself for not coming to find me sooner.

"I'm okay. Nothing I can't handle," I tell him, hoping it will reassure him, and he sighs, leaning closer to press his lips gently to the top of my head.

The bathroom door bangs open, and we both stiffen as more heavy feet come rushing in.

Shit. Is it the cops? Will Ringo go to jail now?

"Fuck, man." A voice comes from beside me, and I glance at the shoes, not boots, that look a little too classy and shiny to belong to a biker. "She okay?"

"Yeah." Ringo stands, and I see him reach out and shake someone's hand.

When my eyes travel up, I see it's one of the Marx crew. I can only tell because of the cufflinks that have the same M symbol that Griffin wears, so maybe he's one of the brothers.

It's hard to tell, since his hair colour is a little lighter than the other Marx men I've met, but this one seems nice as he smiles, flashing a playful grin down at me.

"Finally, we meet. I'm Liam Marx. The best brother." He beams, and Ringo scoffs.

"Get your eyes off my wife's tits, arsehole."

My lips drop open, and I look down, realising that in the scuffle, my dress has shifted so much that my breasts are nearly spilling out.

"My bad. Didn't mean it." Liam grins, and I giggle quietly as they start talking shop, and a horde of other men walk in, assessing the situation, and shutting down the restaurant.

Riggs eventually turns up, and people are paid off to keep quiet while they clean up, and right now, I'm thankful Ringo has an alliance with the Marx family. They have helped us out so many times through all of this. We truly are indebted to them.

By the time Ringo leads me out of the bathroom, the restaurant is empty, the lights are mostly shut off, and it's like no one has been here all day.

"Angel." Ringo's gentle voice drags my attention from our surroundings to find him scanning my injuries.

"I'll heal. Stop stressing," I try to say playfully, but his concern never wavers.

"Dessert can wait," he mutters. "Let's get you back home so I can take care of you properly."

I can't even argue with that, because home, close to Bobbi and Tahli with Ringo's arms wrapped around me, is the only place I want to be.

Now, and forever.

38

EPILOGUE 1

ABBEY

"*These little things slip out of my mouth...*"

I can't wipe the smile off my face as I step down off the porch, taking the same path I did twenty months ago, watching Ringo's face as he recognises the same song I played when I was being a brat.

One Direction's *Little Things*.

But hey, I didn't like being forced into marriage back then, even if I did secretly like the idea of being his wife.

My eyes drop down to my little angel, her blonde curls bouncing as she skips ahead of me in her lemon coloured princess dress, tossing flower petals up in the air with a *"weeeee,"* each time.

The crowd laughs at Bobbi's playful nature, and I look up to see Tahli hurrying to take her hand, wearing her own lemon princess dress, as my other flower girl.

"I like your style, cuz." Rhys snickers next to me as she links her arm with mine, and I grin at the cousin I never knew I had until the ugly truth came out. "I'm totally going to walk down the aisle to Paramore when I get married."

"And who exactly will you be marrying?" I ask as we start walking towards the deck by the pond, and Rhys shrugs.

"Hopefully, all of them at once. I just have to figure out a way to make that happen." She wags her brows at me. "Can you imagine *that* honeymoon? Talk about a good spit roasting."

I choke out a raspy laugh, and she beams, her lips not painted black or purple today, even though I told her she could wear whatever colour she likes.

She blows a kiss in the direction of her five boyfriends as we pass them, and I turn my focus to the end of the path by the pond where my husband awaits on the same deck we were married on the first time.

That day was a business transaction even though Ringo and I cared for each other, but today, we are doing it again, with all the people I hold dear in attendance too, under circumstances we both agreed on.

I told Ringo we didn't have to do this, but he was insistent that I have the wedding I've always dreamed of.

The funny thing is, the only thing I wanted to change from the first time was who I wanted here to witness it.

We are renewing our vows in the same place, with Ace officiating again. I'm wearing the same dress because when I went gown shopping for a new one, all I could think about was the ivory satin I wore the first time.

And of course, much to Ringo's disgust, I am walking down the aisle to One Direction.

The weather is different this time. It's spring. The Jacaranda tree is in bloom, its beautiful purple flowers rise up so high that you can see them from the house.

Some things haven't changed over the last twelve or so months, but a lot has.

I've learned how to be a mum and fill Bobbi's days with fun activities and learning. I've learned how to prepare meals with love, with Doreen teaching me how to cook so many different dishes so I can keep my husband's stomach full, something I've realised means a lot to me. I've learned that raising a teenager is a nightmare. Tahli has been giving me a run for my money with wanting to ride on the back of motorcycles all the damn time. And I've learned that the Southern Sadists compound is actually a really nice place to be around now that the toxic leadership is gone.

Both Tahli and Bobbi love it there when we go to stay.

When Ringo's gaze meets mine from the deck, I can tell his eyes are tearing up a little, and it instantly makes my own glassy.

Flicking my gaze to the left, I see Lexi sobbing, holding her flowers as my Maid of Honour, standing next to Dee, Jols and Nessy.

Over on the other side, Ringo's Best Man, JD, holds out a tissue, and Ringo bats it away, his lips moving to say, 'fuck off.'

I giggle.

Oh, my beautiful monster. Always such a tough guy.

Murf, Vender and Mex also stand on Ringo's side, their eyes light with happiness as they watch me approach.

The moment I get near, Ringo holds his hand out, and I stop, turning to face my cousin.

"Thank you for being here, Rhys. And for giving me away."

"No thanks needed, Abs. We're family, and just so you know, I considered you that even before I knew the same blood ran through our veins."

I slap her arm playfully, dabbing at the corner of my eyes. "Stop. You're going to make me cry."

"Don't you dare ruin your makeup," she scolds me. "That's Ringo's job to do later."

My cheeks heat, and I bite my lip as my eyes flash to Ringo, who is nodding.

"That's right, Angel. Get your sexy arse up here so we can move this along and get to the fun part."

The crowd laughs, and his ma scolds him, much like she did on our original wedding day.

"Cameron Eugene, behave yourself."

Ringo's lips twitch into a smirk, and I can't help but have a sense of déjà vu.

I take his hand, and he leans forward, his hot breath fanning my ear. "Let's hurry this along so I can eat your sweet pussy under our tree."

Now my cheeks flame to life on a whole new level, and my eyes dart around as I check to see if anyone heard him.

He simply chuckles, and Ace opens the ceremony, as Bobbi dances around, weaving between all of us, before calling out to the ducks as they swim past on the surface of the water.

This time, when we say our vows, we don't need to read the words off the paper. We already know them, looking into each other's eyes, and meaning every single word, we say the first part together.

"Today, we take our vows of marriage before our family and friends.
We will honour one another when we are together or apart, and always respect each other's differences.
We will cherish the good times, and endure the storms.
Hand in hand. Side by side. Riding this life together and always leaning into the curve."

A tear pools in the corner of my eye, and Ringo reaches out, catching it with his thumb as he cups my face, and I speak the next words to him.

"Cameron, when I say *I love you*, what I'm really saying is that I'll hold on tight until our ride on Earth ends," and then I add a little extra, "and then forever in the afterlife."

His brows hitch, and it's *his* eyes that turn glassy this time, obviously not expecting me to add on my own little touch.

His smile is broad, and he clears his throat, ready to say his part.

"Abbey, my Angel." He winks. "I promise to treat you as good as my leather, and ride you as much as my Harley." And then he leans in closer, adding on a little extra too. "And I will love and cherish you always, and forever in the afterlife."

Another tear falls from my eye, and again he catches it, always taking care of me.

Just like last time, the crowd hoots and hollers, and my smile is wide, my heart so full as Tahli starts chasing Bobbi around, trying to get the rings from the hidden pocket in her little dress.

When we finally resolve that, we exchange new rings, and just like with everything else, I wanted the same black carbide rings as last time, which we exchange, each saying the words, "with this ring, I thee wed," as we slip them on each other.

What I wasn't expecting was for every club brother to take a knee again, their eyes on me like they are swearing fealty, thumping their fists to their chests in unison as they chant.

"May the road rise up to meet us.
May the wind be always at our backs.
May the sunshine be warm upon our faces.
May the rain clouds never be black.
We are the Southern Sadists MC.
Ride 'em high.
Ride or die."

I hear sniffing from behind me and turn to see Lexi crying again, waving me off like looking at her will make it worse, and I giggle, reaching out and pulling her in for a hug.

This.

This is what was missing from my wedding last time. My best friends and my sister. And to finally share this with them, with the added bonus of Bobbi prancing around, really makes this just so perfect.

"Love you, Abs," Lex whispers against my ear, pulling back to smile at me with so much love.

I got my friend back. I got my life back. And I finally have a family that is built on unconditional love, trust, and compassion.

"Love you too, Lex." I smile, trying to blink away more tears, and she giggles, turning me back around to face my husband.

I almost expect him to be glaring at Lexi for taking my attention, but he's smiling, happy that I get to share this with her, and I'm reminded once again that Cameron Musgrove was put on this Earth to cherish me.

Taking my hands in his, Ringo tugs me back into place, nodding to Ace, who closes out the ceremony, confirming again that these men really are big softies.

"May your love grow ever stronger as you ride this life together, reflecting the promises you made here today," Ace declares before he speaks words that fill me with happiness. "By the power vested in me by the Victorian Marriage Registry, I now re-pronounce you as husband and wife."

Ringo doesn't need any more guidance, tugging me in, his arms sweeping around my back before dipping me and crashing his lips into mine.

Cheers and clapping surround us, and even Bobbi's little joyful squeal meets my ears, and honestly, this day couldn't be more perfect.

I kiss my husband with a level of confidence I never used to have, and I sweep my tongue against his in a way I know drives him crazy for me.

"Stop it, wife," he grunts, his lips kicking up as he peers down at me, still arched back in the dip. "You want me to walk around with a hard cock all day?"

I shrug, biting my lip playfully. "Sounds good to me."

He growls, claiming my lips again, and more cheers fill the air.

This time, we don't sneak off to our tree, since Bobbi follows us each time we try, so instead, we enjoy the celebrations, which are a lot tamer than they were last time, given there are more civilians in attendance.

Some of the Marx family are here. Riggs too. As well as the Angel sisters.

I even invited Shandi, Ariel, Martini and Daffney from Leather and Lace, who seem to be getting on like a house on fire with the Doxies, Alana and Rhys. Millie, on the other hand, is quite content sticking by her mother's side.

I never did find out why she needed help from the Southern Sadists once upon a time, but maybe one day, when she's ready, she'll tell me.

Celina stepped back into the role of head Doxy, her confidence returning after Smitty was finally removed from her life, and her new companion is Molly, Smitty's dog who walks with a permanent limp after being shot.

The only thing that still isn't right in my life is Maggie.

She's not here today. But with the help of the Angel sisters, she's now getting rehabilitated at a very exclusive centre in New South Wales.

I made it very clear that under no circumstances were they to drug her.

I know she so easily helped my parents do that to me, but I won't be that person. I know what it's like to have control of your body taken away from you, and I will not do the same to her. Not ever.

We had a little trouble with her in the beginning when she kept trying to take her own life. But Tahli and I visited her often, and the Doxies took it upon themselves to try to help her learn the difference between the cultish upbringing she had, and what the real world is like.

It was actually Celina who formed the closest bond with her, but that may have been because of Molly. Maggie has really taken a liking to the old dog.

Still, she needed more help than we could give, so hopefully with time, a different version of her might appear.

I don't expect her to ever forgive me. Or even like me. I just don't want her to live a life of delusion.

There are speeches and dancing at our reception, much like last time. But this time, anxiety twists my stomach as I find the nerve to take the microphone, preparing to talk in front of everyone.

I should have done my little speech earlier when the others were done, but I just couldn't. I completely chickened out and simply shook my head when I was asked if I wanted to say anything.

"You've got this," Lexi encourages me, the only person who knows what I'm about to do.

I place my untouched glass of champagne down on the table and look over to my husband, who is happily chatting with his mates.

"What if he doesn't want this?" I whisper, my ongoing turmoil nearly getting the better of me, which Lexi has been trying to counsel me on, and she takes my hand, giving it a supportive squeeze.

"Abs, you'll be giving him something he's always longed for. Of course he's going to be happy."

I nod, trying to convince myself that she's right. He's mentioned it before, but we haven't discussed it again.

With the mic in hand, I step out into the middle of the room, and Lexi shuts off the music so I can rip off the bandaid.

"Uhhh, can I have everyone's attention, please?" I say, and the chattering crowd falls to a hush as all eyes turn to me.

Even my husband's.

"Mummy!" Bobbi calls from Alana's arms, her little hand waving to me, her smile wide, reminding me, not for the first time, of someone I'd rather not think of.

I don't need a DNA test to know who her biological father is. It's becoming more and more obvious every single day, but we still had testing done late last year.

I was concerned because of the whole Daniel thing. That if she was born from incest, she might have some sort of genetic defects or something.

But no, Daniel wasn't her father.

Tim Beck was.

If I had to choose one of those bastards to be her bio dad, then it's definitely him. He wasn't necessarily a cruel person. Just a follower. Someone that would do what he was told to do just so he could fit in.

It doesn't mean what he did to me is right, but I'm thankful Bobbi's father wasn't Daniel. Or any of the others.

Still, in my heart, the only father that matters is Ringo, a man who is fiercely protective, with a hard exterior, and a big softy on the inside.

The perfect man to be a father.

"If you'll all bear with me, I'm not very good at talking in front of a crowd," I say clearing my throat, and Ringo's smile is warm as he turns fully to face me, a tilt to his head like he's curious as to what I'm doing.

"Early last year, this man stole my heart." I gesture to him, and his smile grows as he shoots me one of his sexy winks. "He protected and fought for me when the odds were against me. He sacrificed for me in so many ways. Too many to count." I clear my throat as it starts to clog with emotion, taking a moment to compose myself, and Lexi shifts to my side, snaking her arm around me to give me the courage I need to continue.

"If it weren't for you, Cameron, I probably would've been dead by now, and little Bobbi may not have been saved. When we thought she was gone, you held me up, accepted me in every version I was, even when I wasn't very nice, and you grieved alongside me, opening up old wounds."

Ringo's face starts to morph, his smile still there, but emotions redden his cheeks, and his eyes turn a little glassy, knowing who I'm about to bring up.

"I think you're right." I smile at him. "That Hope brought us together. I think she's been our little guardian angel, watching over us and Bobbi, making sure we all had a chance to find each other, and experience happiness."

He nods, his lips parting as he rolls his tongue in his mouth, his eyes dropping to the floor for a moment as he fights back tears.

"But she hasn't stopped fighting for us," I say, ignoring the sniffles that fill the room around us, and Ringo's eyes jump back up to meet mine. "She always wanted you to be happy, Cam. She wanted you to be a father, and you are the most amazing father to Bobbi, but she wanted you to have another chance."

The moment I bring my hand to my stomach, the little pot barely showing, gasps fill the room, and Ringo's eyes drop, eyeing it in disbelief.

"Angel…" He glances back up at me, tears pooling in his eyes. "Are you…"

I nod, my tears bursting free. "I'm having your baby, Cam. You're going to be a father again."

Sobs erupt all around us, and Ringo stumbles forward, falling to his knees before me, his big hands engulfing my hips as he buries his head into the satin fabric where our baby grows.

Cheers, whoops, cries erupt everywhere, and I laugh and cry at the same time, knowing I'm completely ruining my makeup now, and not even caring.

When Ringo glances up my body, tears wetting his cheeks, he looks at me like I'm really the angel he calls me.

Standing quickly, his hands cup my face, his lips pressing to mine, and I feel someone slip the microphone from my grip as we both cry through this kiss.

"Angel," he rasps against my lips, right before pulling back, those whisky eyes filled with so much love for me. "You're really having my baby?"

"Yes," I giggle. "I'm really having your baby."

I'm instantly lifted off the ground as he spins us around, the rumble of his laughter so soothing to my soul.

"Mummy! Daddy!" Bobbi calls, and Ringo lowers me to the floor as Alana weaves through the crowd to get to us.

"Someone wants in on the attention." Alana laughs, and my little girl, only eighteen months old, holds her hands out to us.

Ringo claps and holds his hands out for her, and she practically launches herself into his arms, squealing as he gives her a scratchy kiss on her cheek with his beard.

"Guess what, Bobbi?" Ringo laughs with her on his hip. "Mummy's having a baby."

Her little mouth forms an O, and she looks at me, her eyes moving over me and then around me.

"Where's baby, Mummy?"

I snicker. "In here." I pat my tummy, and she frowns.

"Nooo. Baby not there."

"Yes." Ringo chuckles. "Your little baby brother or sister is in Mummy's belly."

Her frown deepens, and she shakes her head. "Mummy, eat baby?"

Everyone around us listening, bursts into laughter, and Bobbi stiffens in shock, right before throwing her head back in an over dramatic laugh to join in on something she doesn't understand.

So this is what happiness feels like.

This is what I fought so hard for. And to finally have it... to share it with Ringo, who has had his own lifetime of heartache, is truly a blessing.

The music starts up again, and the party escalates with celebration, but Ringo's heated gaze tells me he wants something else, and just that look has me ready for what he has in store.

"I'm ready when you are," I whisper, and his grin spreads so damn wide.

"Our first time was on our wedding night, Angel. Are you ready to take it to another level?"

I nod, my heart fluttering with anticipation.

"I'm ready, husband." I grin. "Let's go."

39

EPILOGUE 2

RINGO

My wife stares up at me, completely naked as I take her in, and fuck, how didn't I notice her tits getting bigger? She'd stopped breastfeeding at the start of this year, and although I still suckled on her ripe pink nipples, her milk eventually dried up.

I don't think there's anything sexier than my wife carrying a child. And this time, the miracle growing inside her is also a part of me.

Fuck, I'm blown away.

I'm also hard as hell, fucking drooling to sink inside her, so I drag my shirt over my head and pop the button on my pants as I point to the bed.

"Bend over."

Even though there's an eyebrow raise, she does what she's told, turning her back on me and bending over the mattress, poking her perfect round globes towards me.

"Face on the bed, and use your hands to part your cheeks."

Again, my Angel does as she's told, now very used to me directing her.

Resting her head on the mattress, she reaches back, gripping her arse and pulls her cheeks apart to expose her pretty little puckered rose.

Fuck, my cock jumps at the sight.

"We're using the big one tonight," I tell her, reaching for the black teardrop shaped plug with the jewel in the end.

"The big one? We haven't used that one before." She squeaks, and I grin, loving how she sounds a little scared, yet spreads those cheeks wider.

"It's okay, Angel. You can take it."

Her breathing quickens noticeably as I reach for the lube and start coating the plug.

"Colour?" I ask, and her husky aroused voice answers quickly.

"Green."

"Good girl." I smirk, drizzling more lube between her cheeks, watching it run over the entrance of her back passage, and she moans, squirming her hips like she's hungry for her arse to be filled.

My Angel has come a long way since the first night I met her. She's very much her own sexual being now, and mostly prefers me to take control and be more dominant, letting her fall into her submissive tendencies so she doesn't have to think or make decisions.

She just gets to feel.

"You want this to fill your tight arse?" I ask, holding it in front of her face so she can see just how big it is, and her breathy moan follows as she nods.

"Yes."

I don't hesitate then, pressing the tip to her back entrance and slowly easing it in.

She helps by spreading her cheeks wide, but when the size of it meets the resistance of the tight ring of muscle just inside, I smooth my hand over her globe.

"Relax, Angel. Let me fill you."

Another moan has her relaxing just the way we need, and the plug finally sinks right in, all the fucking way.

"Fuck, you should see how pretty this arse is with the jewel in it, Abs," I say, shoving my pants down and giving my throbbing cock a good, tight pump.

"Stand up and face me," I demand, and she does, although a little awkwardly as she turns to face me while I step out of my pants and boxers. "Lay back on the bed, feet dangling over the side."

She moves quickly, getting into place, another moan falling from her lips as the plug pushes deeper from the new position. My Angel automatically spreads her legs for me, showing off her glistening cunt, and the way her clit is already swollen with need.

I drop to my knees, pushing her thighs further apart and latching onto her clit like it's a nipple I'm desperate to drink from.

She bucks under me, arching off the bed, her fingers delving into my hair as she moans, and I devour her needy little clit for a few minutes, making sure she's nice and slick for what comes next.

"Cam!" she cries, fisting the sheets beside her, and I break off, not wanting her to come yet.

"I'm going to need your help tonight, Angel." I smirk down at her when her brows lift.

"What do you mean?"

"Well, tonight, we are going to be using a couple of extra toys."

Her cheeks flush the way they do when she gets embarrassed, but she still nods, a very fucking willing participant.

"What toys?" She glances over to the bedside table to see what I just placed on top.

"The pink dildo?" she squeaks, and I nod.

"Yeah. You think you can take *me* and *it* at the same time?"

Her eyes widen, locking with mine.

"In the same hole?"

I chuckle and nod. "In the same hole. Just like the times we've used both of our fingers."

And there go her cheeks again. Fucking stunning.

"Oh... I guess we can try."

"Hell yes we are going to try, and this other toy will help."

I hold up the hand-held device meant for self pleasure, watching her brows tug together.

"I have no idea what that is."

I chuckle. "It's a clit sucker, Angel. You'll hold this over your clit, while I fuck you with my cock and the dildo, and we are going to drench this fucking room."

Her lips part, another breathy moan escaping her, and I bet she just got a whole lot wetter.

She loves my fucking filthy mouth. Loves when I whisper dirty everythings into her ear as we fuck. She told me once she's a visual person, so everything I say pops up like a movie reel in her head, and fuck, I wish I could see her thoughts.

I quickly show her how the clit sucker works, and she tries it out, biting her lip as her eyes dart away from me in embarrassment.

Yeah, she still gets timid around me, and it's one of the things I fucking adore about her.

When she presses it to herself properly, that timidness falls away as the toy works its charm, stimulating her needy clit and turning her wanton.

While she's doing that, I glide the pink dildo through her slickness and ease it inside her.

It takes fucking everything in me not to drive myself straight into her tight, hot cunt, wanting to make sure she adjusts around the size of the dildo before I stretch her wider.

She's pretty fucking full right now with the plug in her arse, and the girthy pink cock filling her cunt, so I fuck it in and out of her, watching how each time the pink silicone appears wetter. Slicker.

"You ready to take me too, Angel?" I growl, trying to hold myself back for as long as possible.

"Yes," she moans. "I'm so close."

"That's good. Make sure you come whenever you need to, but just so you know, I'm not going to stop until you've come a few times, and I've filled you with my seed."

She nods desperately, spreading her legs wider like she's hungry for it, and I hold the dildo in place as I press the tip of my cock to her entrance underneath it.

Then, so slowly, I ease in right alongside the dildo.

"Fuuuuck," I rasp, my face contorting to match hers as the pleasured pain of it hits us both.

It's a fucking tight fit squeezing in, the plug in her arse adding to the crammed space, while the vibrations of the clit sucker travel through, gifting me with the most intoxicating sensory overload I never knew I needed until now.

"You're so big," she pants as I start moving inside her, surging in faster as the ripples of the dildo give me extra stimulation.

"You're so fucking tight," I grind out, my fingers bruising as they dig into her upper thighs, and I pump in and out, watching her tits jiggle with each thrust.

"I feel like I'm going to...ahhhh." She half moans, half screams as I move faster.

"Going to what?" I snap.

"Make a mess," she rushes out, and I fucking grin.

"Please make a mess," I practically beg her. "Dirty me up, Angel. Let's get fucking filthy."

"Oh my God... I'm going to—"

Her orgasm slams into her, sending ripples through her cunt, milking my cock and the dildo inside her as she cries out, arching her back off the bed.

I pound harder, faster, knowing she's pliable as fuck right now, her slickness slippery in the best fucking way.

But I'm not done with her yet. There's nowhere near enough mess.

"Angel," I snap as her hand falls slack, and she nearly drops the sucker. "Put it back on."

Her eyes snap open, locking with mine as her chest rises and falls.

"But—"

"No fucking buts. Put it back on now," I snap, thrusting over and over.

She fumbles for it, but manages to get a hold of it again, pressing it to her, and the moment the suction attaches, she bucks and screams.

"Keep it on!" I order, even though she's trembling like she can barely handle the sensitivity.

And perhaps she can't.

"Colour?" I ask, and she trembles, her eyes locked on mine as I fuck her.

"Green."

Fuck yes.

I go harder, feeling her shudder over and over, and I grip the end of the dildo, working that fucking thing in and out of her in opposite rhythm to my cock, making sure the girthy stretch never stops.

Another orgasmic wave hits her, and fuck yes! This time, she squirts, the spray drenching my cock and balls, but also spraying up onto my stomach.

"Good girl," I groan. "Such a good fucking girl."

"Can I stop y-yet?" she stammers, but I shake my head.

"No fucking way. Keep going. I'm not dirty enough yet."

She whimpers, so I ask again.

"Colour."

"G-green," she pants, writhing, and even though I can tell she's nearly reached her limit, she thrusts back against me like she's hungry for more.

I'm nearly fucking done though, the fight to hold myself back is almost impossible, so the moment she starts coming again, milking my cock as she drenches us both, I let go, throwing my head back with a roar as I pump cum deep inside her.

My whole body jerks with each wave that rips from me, and when it finally subsides, my legs are fucking shaking and weak.

As we both come down from another mind blowing high, I ease my cock and the dildo from her, and relieve her of the clit sucker, turning it off and tossing the fucking thing on the bed.

"You okay?" I ask, and she nods, a drunk-like grin spreading across her face.

"I'm more than okay," she breathes, and I place my hand on her stomach.

"How about this?" I ask, feeling how firm it is. "Wait. When are you due?"

"April." She smiles. "Just before Bobbi's second birthday."

"Fuck." I beam down at my wife. "Our little family is getting bigger."

"It is. How big do you want it?"

I chuckle at her question. "Six kids will do."

She practically chokes on her own saliva, coughing. "Tell me you're joking."

"I am," I snicker. "Maybe."

Pushing herself up on her elbows, she reaches for me, and we ignore the mess we've made, focusing on each other.

"Let's compromise." She winks playfully. "Three kids. But we have sex like we are aiming for twenty."

I throw my head back laughing and hold my hand out between us.

With her flushed cheeks and wild hair, she looks completely ravaged as she takes my hand in hers.

And then we shake.

"You have a deal, Mrs Musgrove."

40

EPILOGUE 3

ABBEY

Ringo squeezes my hand as he practically jogs beside the bed, nurses and doctors surrounding us as I'm rushed into the surgical suite. Each time he looks down at me, he smiles, like he's trying to be encouraging, but I can see the strain in his eyes.

He's worried… and so am I.

So much happens as I'm wheeled into the birthing theatre. Things get hooked up to me, and a fabric screen gets put up over my chest, blocking the view of my very big baby bump.

"Ringo," I whimper as the fear of what's happening really hits me.

His whisky eyes peer down at me as a nurse rolls a stool towards him, and he quickly takes it, looking completely different dressed in the hospital scrubs he had to quickly put on over his clothes.

"I'm here, Angel. You're doing great," he rasps, but his voice matches his strained eyes.

Moving up close to my head, he gently strokes his fingers over my cheek, his eyes jumping around to all the activity happening around the room, before coming back to me.

"I'm scared," I whisper, and those gentle eyes soften even more.

"I know, but remember. This isn't the same as last time. You're safe. In the best place for something like this to happen, and our little baby will be in our arms in a matter of minutes."

I nod, feeling my lower body being moved and tugged, yet not really feeling it at the same time, and my eyes fill with tears as my birth plan flies out the window.

"I didn't want it to be like this," I whimper, annoyed at my stupid cervix that apparently won't dilate any further and has become inflamed.

"Remember what you said yesterday?" he asks as his beard brushes my temple before he kisses me there, his warm, minty breath fanning over my ear. "It's impossible to keep plans when you have children."

My lips tug up at the corners, and I nod, staring around at the room.

There's so much bustling in the space, doctors and nurses talking medical lingo that I'd know if I'd gone to nursing school, but I decided to hold off. I need to be around for my kids, and Tahli too. I will study later down the track when I can devote more time to it, but right now, I kinda wish I knew what they were talking about.

"Hey, Angel. Focus on my voice," Ringo says quietly, leaning close and practically hugging my head to him. And then, to my surprise, he starts singing, right by my ear.

"*Why are there so many... songs about rainbows... And what's on the other side?*"

A giggling sob passes my lips, and I close my eyes and focus on the deep gravel of his voice.

He sang this song at Bobbi's funeral. A song he'd been singing at his daughter's grave since her death. But now, he sings it with Bobbi. She loves watching him play the guitar and sings along with him in her sweet little voice, sometimes by Hope's grave, and sometimes up on the porch when the mood strikes.

It doesn't carry the heaviness of grief, but the willingness of hope, and in this moment, as the surgeon cuts me open to extract our baby, this song couldn't be more perfect.

I think of how far we've come, from that desperate girl that painted herself in blood being kept prisoner by her parents, to only last week when we celebrated Easter and Ringo left a trail of carrot crumbs and powdered bunny prints for me and Bobbi to follow to find the chocolate eggs.

The two events seem like worlds apart. Like they are two completely different lives led by two completely different people... and I guess they are, but also, they aren't.

I'm still that girl sometimes. Trapped in my bedroom. My parents dictating every breath of my life.

Some days are easy, but some are hard. The difference between then and now is I have people who love me. Who will fight for me. And who let me dictate my own life... well, as much as a mother can, because let me tell you, when I lay out clothes for my daughter each day, I guarantee, ninety percent of the time, she refuses to wear it and picks the most random things to wear instead.

But, oh wow, I love that side of motherhood. Letting my daughter decide her own path. Letting her choose her clothes, her shoes, her books. Letting her play the songs that speak to her heart. Letting her just be herself.

As Ringo's deep baritone soothes me, the doctors' voices get louder, and my lids flash open the moment I hear it... my baby crying.

My eyes lock with Ringo's, and tears instantly fill his before he looks over the screen.

"Congratulations, Mum and Dad," someone says. "You have a healthy baby boy."

I can't see anything but the screen in front of me, but nothing is more important than watching this moment as my husband sees his baby for the first time.

He never got to see Hope alive. Everything about that situation was brutally devastating, and deep down, I've been determined to give him something he lost, even if it can't be the same thing.

I follow his gaze movements, and can tell he's tracking our son, and the moment he stands, I know this is it.

I'm about to meet our little boy.

"Here he is." A nurse hands a bundle to Ringo, and his hands look gigantic as he takes it, little hands jerking around as our son cries. But then... he stops, and as Ringo sits, lowering our son next to my head so I can see him, I take in his big eyes as he stares up at his daddy, like he's committing his daddy's face to his memory.

"Hey there, little man," Ringo coos, his deep tone soft and soothing. "Welcome to the world."

I'm crying. It's impossible not to in this beautiful moment, knowing I've helped to stitch a part of my monster's heart closed a little more.

"Abs..." Ringo's glazed eyes dart to mine. "He's just beautiful."

"Like his dad," I whisper, and his eyes soften as he shakes his head. "Like his mum."

"What's his name?" one of the nurses asks, and I bite my lip as Ringo and I stare at each other.

He told me he wanted me to name our child. I've thrown name ideas at him over the past few months, but he just keeps telling me it's my decision. So I chose another name that could be used for a boy *or* a girl.

"His name is Lex Cameron Musgrove."

Ringo's eyes widen. "Cameron is Bobbi's middle name."

"I know. I thought we could start a tradition of having all the middle names the same."

He throws his head back, laughing, and shakes his head. "The next one has to have your name as the middle name. It's only fair."

I giggle. "What if it's a boy? I don't think he'll like having Abbey as his middle name."

"He won't know any different." Ringo chuckles, and we both stare down at our son.

"Lex," he mutters, like he's testing the name.

"She means a lot to both of us," I whimper, my emotions getting the better of me. "She never gave up on me. She sent you to me. I think naming him after Lexi is perfect."

"Yeah. It is." Ringo smiles, leaning down to press a kiss to Lex's forehead, and as the surgeons stitch my tummy back up, Ringo and I get to know our little boy.

By the time we get taken to the hospital room, I'm utterly exhausted, and we spend the next few hours catching up on rest and teaching Lex how to drink from me.

We have so many friends and family who have been eagerly awaiting the news, all of them camping out at our home, in true Southern Sadists style.

The pandemic that swept through the world has settled. There are no more lockdowns. No more requirements to wear face masks, but the world hasn't been the same since.

Even now, hospitals are stricter on how many visitors can be in a room at once, so everyone will have to wait, except for the three very special visitors waiting out in the hall, eager to meet our son.

I've tried to make myself look as human as possible, but I feel pretty sluggish from the caesarean earlier today, but with Ringo's help, we tamed my hair and dressed me in an oversized tee, and Ringo passed our son to me.

"You ready?" he asks, and I nod eagerly, staring down at Lex, wrapped in a bundle, sleeping soundly in my arms.

"I'm ready. Bring our little tornado in."

Chuckling, Ringo opens the door, and the tornado I was referring to bursts in.

"Daddy! Where's the baby?"

Dropping down to Bobbi's height, Ringo scoops her up and points to the bed.

"Mummy has him."

"Oh my God! Him! A boy?!" Tahli cries, bursting in after Bobbi, with Lexi on her heels, and suddenly, I'm engulfed.

Tahli bounces on one side of the bed, and Bobbi scrambles out of Ringo's arms, cramming me in on the other, and they start doting over Lex immediately, while I watch my best friend's eyes fill with tears.

"I told myself I wasn't going to cry," Lexi giggles, and I bob my head towards my son in my arms.

"Come and meet him," I say. "His name is Lex."

Her eyes flash up from the bundle to me, her mouth dropping open as she shakes her head.

"It is not."

"It is." I giggle. "Lex Cameron Musgrove."

"Hey! Cameron is my name." Bobbi whines, and Tahli giggles, reaching across me to ruffle Bobbi's blonde curls.

"Cameron is also Daddy's name, kiddo."

Bobbi screws up her face. "No, it's not. It's Daddy."

We all laugh at that, and Bobbi looks confused as hell, and as I lock eyes with my husband, who mouths, 'I love you,' I know that no matter what life throws at us, we will be alright, because we have each other.

Family is everything to me and my husband. We have some that are related to us by blood, and some that are connected to us through friends and community. The foundation is the same, sharing unconditional support and a sense of home.

I've found my home. My family. And I know my children and my found family will carry on this legacy Ringo and I have built, to continue to protect and fight for those who don't have a voice, for those that need help and guidance, and for those that need their soft place to land too.

I was once weary of being associated with an MC, but now, I'm proud to be the wife of a Southern Sadist. I wear leather with my lace, ride on the back of my husband's hog when I'm not in my mum van, and the only prayer I recite is the one the club brothers say with conviction and a fist thumped to their chest.

"May the road rise up to meet us.
May the wind be always at our backs.
May the sunshine be warm upon our faces.
May the rain clouds never be black.
We are the Southern Sadists MC.
Ride 'em high.
Ride or die."

THE END

Abbey & Ringo's story might be over, but there's more alpha male energy to come with the Marx family!! Grab your fix of alpha male energy with the first book in the Marx Empire series:

DIRTY, DEADLY & MINE
https://geni.us/marxempire1

MEET
LILY & ASHER

WELCOME TO THE MARX EMPIRE

Want a little taste of what's to come in book one?

Get your copy of Secrets & Scars Book 4 Bonus Scene below:

https://dl.bookfunnel.com/4oy60773oj

By downloading a copy of this Marx Empire Excerpt, you will be signing up to Sarah JD's Darker Shades of Romance Newsletter.

READ MORE BY SARAH JD

Want to know Lexi & Ayden's story?

What about Rhys and her why choose men?

Or how about Hush, the savage little mute assassin and her moody

man, Jared?

You can find their stories, and more, here:

https://sarahjdauthor.com/books

Want to join the conversation about your fav characters?
Join my Facebook Readers Group
SARAH'S VICIOUS KITTENS

JOIN HERE!
https://www.facebook.com/groups/
sarahjaneduncanreadersgroup

For more information on books & book signing
events please visit:
https://sarahjdauthor.com

STALK SARAH HERE:

https://qrco.de/bcnvfo

sarah JD

Sarah JD, also known as Sarah Jane Duncan, is an Australian dark romance author living her best life with her high school sweetheart, Mr Duncan.

Sarah can be found in her writing room plotting out her next smut filled romance, packed with angst, violence, and themes so dark you should probably question why you love it so much.

Sarah enjoys torturing her characters. There's nothing easy about their stories. They are hard, gritty, and painfully heartbreaking at times. But what doesn't kill us makes us stronger, right? And when you throw in a swoon worthy guy, or an alphahole you just want to slap, but also fall to your knees and obey, it's the recipe for a rollercoaster ride.

So buckle up. Read the warnings. And let yourself get lost in the dark stories Sarah creates.

SOUTHERN SADISTS MC
RIDE EM HIGH, RIDE OR DIE